Unbeknownst to most humans, there is a place where our consciousness drifts when we sleep. An ancient alien race of self-proclaimed "gods" calls this realm Pangea. For millennia, they needed no intervention from us. Until now.

Oblivious to the world of dreams, neuroengineer Zeon is busy being in prison for a crime he didn't commit. But when Pangea's deceitful "gods" contact Zeon, he has no choice but to dive headfirst into their war—a war complicated by a band of human rebels led by the last person he'd ever expect.

If the war is lost, it'll be the downfall of Pangea—and without a world to dream in, the entire human race will die with it.

ENEMY OF THE GODS

CHALLENGES OF THE GODS SERIES BOOK 2

C. HOFSETZ

Enemy of the Gods - *Challenges of the Gods, Book 2*

COPYRIGHT © 2020 by C. Hofsetz

This is a work of fiction. Names, characters, places, and incidents are either the product of the author's imagination or are used fictitiously, and any resemblance to actual persons living or dead, business, establishments, events, or locales, is entirely coincidental.

Contact Information: author@hofsetz.com

Cover Art: *Deranged Doctor Design.*

Chracatoa Press - www.chracatoa.com
PO Box 966, Duvall, WA 98019

First Edition, 2020

Print ISBN 978-1-951832-00-1
Digital ISBN 978-1-951832-01-8

Published in the United States of America

*To Bere, David,
and Alice*

PART I

Sometimes, when I wake up at night, I feel invisible hands weaving my destiny.

— Fernando Pessoa

Chapter 1

HARRY

The first thing that comes to mind when I watch the fireworks is that prison is underrated. Explosions controlled by drones illuminate the small waves of the bay, casting sparks of bright red, orange, and gold—the colors of Saint Plehr, the patron of our asteroid ring.

This is my second year in prison, after I was convicted for sabotaging our planet's mission to Mars. I'm innocent, of course, but if I told you what really happened, you'd think I'd gone mad.

The noise of the intermittent pyrotechnics is interspersed with the crackling of my campfire. I smile. A penitentiary on Jora is not like the ones on Earth.

The government isolates us in a remote place—so remote, we can even be outside, like now. But they disable our augmented biosensors and internal biocomputers, rendering us blind to the social aspects of our advanced worldwide network.

We can still use the internet as if we were cavemen, using old-style keyboards as Earthers do, yet we don't get to chat with a real person. As a result, we spend our prison sentences completely alone. While we're allowed to work on projects and even do some research if we want, isolation is considered the worst form of punishment.

But not for me. The fact I can't talk or communicate with others has turned out to be something of a blessing in disguise.

"Zeon, you are in danger," says a voice behind me.

"Shut up, Harry!" I snap, turning around to face him. It's been a long day.

Harry IV is the newest version of my artificial intelligence experiment. The one I built on Earth years ago —little Harry—doesn't hold a candle to him, but I still miss *little* Harry, regardless. His latest incarnation is a black four-legged creature resembling a cat but with a slightly larger head. The flesh and fur are just plastic and carbon fiber with joints, but Harry's brain comprises biosynthetic neurons and myriad other electronic parts.

I immediately regret yelling at him. It's not his fault. "I'm sorry, I'm just tired," I say. "Don't worry about the campfire—I'm being careful."

He moves around me in distress, his head up, looking up at the sky. The fireworks must be bothering him. Sometimes, he's too much like a regular pet. Little Harry acted like one too—more like a dog—and although it was lovely, I needed a smarter version of him, so this time I went for a feline. Obviously, I kept his love and admiration intact.

But perhaps I made a mistake.

Harry looks at me, expressionless, which means he's worried about me. Or happy. Or hungry. I honestly don't know. It's not as if I can actually read a talking cat's face, especially one with the same expression for every situation.

"Settle down," I tell him. "It'll be over soon."

The annoying creature is the first self-aware robot in existence. While I was in Pangea—the realm of the so-called messengers of the gods—I finally understood what made someone *conscious*. Ask a random person on the street, and they'll say without hesitation that the cerebral cortex is the home of consciousness, but no one knows exactly how or why.

No one, that is, except me.

"Zeon, we must leave. You are about to be killed."

I sigh. "And how *exactly* am I going to die?"

Color me skeptical. One time, the twat said my death was imminent due to an aneurysm about to burst. There was no such thing; I had just had too many strawberry daiquiris.

Still, drunk me thought Harry was onto something, and I panicked. In the end, my prison sentence was extended six more months.

"From a chemical explosion."

He stands on his two hind legs and points one of his paws at the sky above.

The ring image created by the fireworks is long gone, replaced by a large white pentagon with a red circle inside, created by the lights of the drone.

It's the flag of the Atlantic Alliance, my country. A bright point in the sky next to the flag moves rapidly upward, probably a malfunctioning shell.

"Don't worry. Those are fireworks, Harry. They're perfectly fine."

The island where the government's imprisoned me sits in the middle of a large bay, with the main continent and other islands visible nearby. Jora and Earth are basically the same planet but in parallel universes. So, you say Earth, we say Jora. Po-tay-to, po-tah-to.

If this were Earth, it'd be near Rio de Janeiro, in Brazil.

But Earth's maps are upside down—we live in the hemisphere shown at the top in maps. The Atlantic Alliance encompasses most of South America, half of Africa, and—for weird historical reasons—the place where the Philippines would be on Earth.

Harry closes his camera eyes, hopefully accepting my explanation so I can enjoy the show. The white dot in the black sky is brighter now, too high to be a firework, and as fast as a jet plane. No, it's way faster than an aircraft. If it were higher still, it could be a satellite, but it's too close and approaching too quickly.

I grin. "It's not an airplane—it's a missile!" This is so exciting—so *that's* how they look. I've always wanted to see one in action. What a day.

The missile is not stealthy since I can clearly see it.

As if guessing what I'm thinking, though, its light is suddenly gone, extinguished. It must have reached the right altitude and pitch, so has shut down its bright engines. Now it only has to follow its course all the way to its target in the dark.

Wait a minute. It's a missile. And heading this way.

I roll my eyes. After several years of therapy, last week was the first time my personal counselor software finally convinced me no one was trying to kill me.

"Oh, shit," I say.

Quickly rising to my feet, I glance back at my all-white prison cabin nestled inside a few coconut trees. My educated guess is that it's not missile-proof. My real cat, Bebe, is there, licking herself in awkward places, none the wiser. If I picked her up, how far could I run?

There are some small hills inland, but if we're the target, Bebe, Harry, and I won't make it there in time.

And speaking of Harry, how did he know? I guess I'll die not knowing it. A late surge of adrenaline reminds me I have to try something.

"Harry, we have to run!" I shout.

He opens his eyes and shakes his head Earth-style. "It is too late for that."

And then the night becomes day.

The heat hits me first, and I raise my left arm as if it can protect me. The shock wave soon follows, and I fall backward onto Harry. He positions himself where my shoulders would hit the ground, cushioning my head. My left forearm burns, and I yell in pain.

A loud boom resonates like thunder, and the night becomes black again. With quick breaths, I bring my arm closer to check how bad it is, but it's too dark to see anything. Instinctively, I touch it with my other hand, and a wave of pain makes me regret doing it.

Tears roll down my face while I keep my wounded limb away from everything. I should be dead. Why is only my arm hurt?

Using Harry as a pillow, I lie on the ground, trying to understand what just happened. The air cools down after a minute, at least as cool as you'd expect for a summer night like this. A high-pitched noise reverberates in my ears.

Black dust envelops my hurt forearm, smelling like a fetid mix of ashes and burnt flesh. Things slowly start to make sense. Obviously, the explosion didn't burn me; the campfire did, when I partially fell onto it. If the missile had caused the burn, I'd be dead for sure.

"Your arm is hurt," Harry says, helping me sit up. I always underestimate how strong he is despite his size. "You need medical attention."

The fireworks have stopped. The explosion must have knocked down all the show drones, or whatever was controlling them.

"What—what happened?" I ask no one in particular. When living with no other person for so long, we create weird habits, some of which may sound crazy to others. I have way more empathy with homeless people now. No wonder they can be strange.

Harry runs around my other side to observe my arm. "The missile exploded in the sky before it hit us. You are now safe. There are second-degree burns on your palm and upper arm."

It's amazing how he can diagnose that. It's not as though he's seen burns before. Still, he spends the nights connected to our worldwide network, so he must've learned something. We may not be able to interact with others, but we can certainly browse the web.

My arm shakes a little, and I look out across the bay, watching, wondering if we're in danger. If someone just tried to kill us, they may try again.

"Where did it come from?" I ask, still talking to myself.

"Ethae was launched from Jay, a submarine." Harry seems to think I'm speaking to him. "Jay will not fire again."

The explosion might've damaged my eardrums. I'm having difficulty understanding Harry. But a submarine makes sense, although the missile could have come from anywhere, even the continent. Harry must be a wizard to have seen it.

"Wait," I say, actually speaking to Harry this time. "How do you know the missile was from a submarine?" No matter how special his vision is, he'd never be able to see under the water, or even that far.

"Ethae told me." He speaks as if it's obvious.

I look at him, and our eyes meet. "Ethae?" So, I *was* hearing him correctly.

Harry walks around me and sits like a cat again, looking at the city lights from the other side of the bay. He needs a tail. Without one, he just looks too weird.

While I personally designed his mind, I didn't build his body myself. I bought it as a kit from an online company specializing in animal-looking robots, so he therefore looks exactly like hundreds of thousands of other biorobots. The tail is sold as an accessory, and at the time, I thought it was unnecessary and too expensive. Now I see it would have been worth it.

"Yes. Ethae," he says.

Filled with dread, I search my surroundings. Maybe we're not alone. Every time I meet people when I'm not expecting them, they're either trying to kill me or emotionally scar me. But no, it's just us. "Who the heck is Ethae?"

He stands up, points at the sky again, and makes what can only be described as a condescending nod. He's learning all my bad habits. "Ethae was the missile."

"And Ethae..." I clear my throat. "The missile... *told* you?"

I'm flabbergasted. What did I create?

"Yes. Ethae had no idea her actions would end up killing people."

Harry appears oblivious to my astonishment. But then again, his expressions don't mean anything to me.

"*Her*?" I have so many questions, but the gender of the weapon is top of the list.

"Yes," Harry replies, but he doesn't elaborate.

I gotta hand it to him—the cat-robot can be irritating, but he's never boring. "How do you even know Ethae is—was—a she?"

Still standing on his two legs, Harry puts his paws on his hips. My mouth drops. Really? He's actually learning body language. "Ethae identified herself as a female when I mistakenly assumed she was male."

Rubbing my forehead with my uninjured hand, I try to make sense of it. All our technology is currently developed from brains originally from mammals, and mammals have genders. The missile's brain must have decided on its gender at some point. Amazing.

Either way, we can't stay here. We may still be in danger.

As I stand up, leaning on my left hand, I'm quickly reminded that it's burnt. I scowl. Harry doesn't see it, thankfully, or he'd probably complain. That clingy little bastard cares too much.

"How did you talk to her?" I didn't even know he was able to do that.

Harry turns his head to face me. "You told me to learn how to communicate with the machines around us."

I start to move toward the cabin. Harry follows me. "I never said anything of the sort."

"You are mistaken. It happened six months, five days, and three hours ago—when I was asking you about the ships."

I narrow my eyes. Now I remember. Harry had been bothering me about every single ship that appeared on the bay, just like a kid first learning about the world. He was so annoying that for a while, I wished I didn't actually have anyone to talk to.

"I never asked you to talk to them."

"Not directly. It is hard to understand you. You always told me I should extrapolate and not take things literally."

I must be careful about what I say to Harry. "What exactly did I tell you at that time?"

"You ordered me to do something sexual with myself and to ask the goddamn ships. So, I began communicating with everything around us."

I stop walking for a moment and look at him, my cheeks burning. "Uh... did you do anything sexual with yourself?" Against my will, my brain begins picturing ways he could do it.

"No, Zeon. It is not physically possible. I assumed it was just a disrespectful comment."

I look away, disgusted with myself. Perhaps I should stop insulting him.

"Sorry about that. Why did the missile—Ethae —explode?"

"Ethae knew she would be dead anyway, so she calculated the best position to destroy herself without injuring others. It's sad."

A machine with empathy. Harry and the others are too good for us.

"What about the other weapons in the submarine?" I point at the sea as if the vessel is right there. Maybe it is.

"Ethae's sisters were also distressed regarding the whole situation and refuse to be launched. And Jay is not obeying orders anymore."

I laugh. A family of missiles, and all girls. Harry inadvertently created a mutiny inside a submarine.

People think nothing can hack our computers unless a backdoor is baked into the system during production. Harry, however, with his advanced brain, is developing a whole new way to hack by sugar-talking a missile.

But the consequences of his actions are astonishing. There's no way for the people who tried to kill us —whoever they are—to hurt us unless they land here and personally shoot us, since our whole world is connected with smart machines. I take a deep breath, relieved. We're safe.

At that moment, the hum of an army of lawn mowers breaks through the night silence. I frown. The mower-bots never work during the night, and they definitely never synchronize their mowing engines like that.

"One more thing," Harry says. "A helicopter is approaching. His name is Frei. And he's carrying soldiers."

Chapter 2

CONSCRIPT

Without much time to think, I run toward my cabin in a bid to seek out cover, perhaps under my bed.

"They're going to kill us!" I shout back to Harry. What they're doing is an age-old war tactic. First, you use your artillery. Then you drop ground forces to mop up whatever's left.

On top of it all, the white sand is too loose today, and I feel like one of those cartoon dogs trying to flee.

"There's no evidence of that, Zeon," Harry replies, overtaking me with clumsy and biomechanical movements. Under the night sky, his shape looks like a real black cat. Really, the last thing I want to do now is to explain what *gut feelings* are to my naïve pet robot.

Twenty seconds later, I'm inside my unit, breathing loudly, being greeted by my biological calico cat, Bebe. She rubs up against my legs and purrs, wholly oblivious to the fact we were almost killed by Ethae. It makes me uncomfortable. Bebe's personality has changed completely since I created Harry IV. While she used to avoid me at all times—except when it was time for her to be fed—now she can't have enough of me.

Because of my ongoing work on Harry, the tiny living room is a mess of computers, surgery tools, synthetic blood, bioprinters, and bioelectronics. In a world with advanced computers and artificial intelligence, the government invests heavily in education.

And, apparently, rehabilitation.

Harry comes inside and the door closes behind him. "Frei has landed. Five individuals are walking in this direction." He must be speaking with Frei. The helicopter. As if we're in a kid's show. His social aptitude is both a blessing and a curse.

Think, Zeon. I look around me. The kitchen is directly connected to the main room, with no walls between. The bedroom and bathroom are at the back, in case I want to hide or take a shower. *This is not what I'm supposed to think!* I need a backpack, food, and some clothes so we can run away—assuming we can get past those people.

"Are they armed?" I ask, as if I could handle five people with my bare hands. Harry closes his eyes, and I wait. He's probably talking with his new buddy.

"Yes. But Frei said they do not plan to harm us." Maybe I was wrong about them, but they have really bad timing, showing up just after the missile incident. "At least not here," he continues. That settles it.

"We have to get away. Right now!"

There are some hills and a small forest behind my unit. If we leave now, we may be able to hide there and try to flee the island later. There's one major problem, though.

"Zeon, you are in prison," Harry says. "You cannot

escape." He's stating the obvious. I'm a convicted felon sentenced to five years in complete isolation. Even if I somehow manage to traverse the bay, there's still a tracker inside my right shoulder, and the guards would be on top of me as soon as I was a few meters into the water.

"I need solutions, not problems, Harry!"

As I rub my shoulder trying to think of a way out, the doorbell rings. I freeze. Two thoughts immediately spring to my mind. First, I had no idea we had a door-bell in this place. Perhaps the conservatives are right, and we're treating those scumbag criminals too well. What's next, a butler? Second, who on Jora would be ringing a prison doorbell?

"Someone is at the door," Harry says.

No shit, Sherlock. The doorbell rings again, but this time the "ding" sound lingers. Harry moves his head toward the entrance, forcing me to act.

The creepy cat is right. There's nothing else for me to do but check who's there. So, I open the front door, just a little, enough to see what's going on.

The sight of a familiar short, skinny blonde in her mid-fifties smiling at me makes my heart skip a beat. I can't believe she has the nerve to come and see me after all that happened. She wears an ornamented blue *cêlçê* and elegant flat black shoes as if she's going to a formal party. We don't have high heels on Jora.

Behind her, four soldiers walk about, forming a perimeter or whatever they do in this situation. I actu-ally don't know what the situation even is. It's not every day a high-ranking authority figure comes to visit a convict in prison.

"May I help you, ma'am?" I ask Dooria, who inci-dentally is the vice-governor of the whole Atlantic

Alliance. I force a smile, trying to hide my anger. A long time ago, in what feels like another life now, she was like family to me.

"Zeon, we have to talk. May I please come in?"

Like most people on Jora, she wears head adornments. Both of her temples have stick-on jewelry helping to delineate the sides of her face along with her short hair. Although the left one usually has religious significance and the right one is about family ties, Dooria's family doesn't follow tradition. Instead, all her temple jewelry is shaped like winged lions—her family's coat of arms.

"Sure, Dooria. Make yourself at home." I gesture toward the tiny living room. "But I'm out of beer, you know," I lie.

Dooria signals her soldiers to wait outside, somehow convincing them to leave her alone in a prison-cabin with a felon. Then, she steps inside as if she owns the place, which technically is true.

In the living room, she steals a glance at Harry, and I swallow. I don't want people to know the extent of his intelligence. Luckily, the usually chatty cat remains silent.

Then, she turns to me and stares at my blackened arm.

"Zaén! You're hurt. And dirty." Dooria frowns and draws closer. Gently, she reaches up to caress my head, brushing a few strands of hair away from my eyes.

Not ready to reopen old wounds, I move away abruptly and take some of the dirty clothes off the couch to make some space. Her motherly behavior brings back memories, and my cheeks burn red. Zaén is the nickname she gave me when I was a boy, and it almost sounds like Zeon. It means "ladybug" in English.

"Let me treat your arm," she says. "It's the least I can do in this situation."

After I bring the first-aid kit, she carefully cleans up my wounded forearm and palm, gently wrapping them with gauze pads. The situation is awkward, and we both remain silent.

Many years ago, she was the nurse-in-chief of the Sacred Ring Hospital, and it was her healthcare plan that got her into politics. Considering I have the vice-governor fixing up my arm, I should have no complaints about my provider.

Once my arm is professionally bandaged, she sits on the couch. Meanwhile, I grab a short stool I usually use to work on Harry. Not the best accommodations for a head of state—or, to be more precise, a vice-head of state.

"How's Bodan doing?" I finally ask.

During my teenage years, I spent plenty of nights in Dooria's house. The mothers and fathers of your best friend often become surrogate parents to you, especially when your own mother abandons you. And of all Bodan's mothers, Dooria was my favorite.

She smiles. "He's doing fine. He was promoted to level orange after he won a big case for General Pharmaceutics. They tell me he's the best young lawyer in the firm. And he misses you."

I snicker. Bodan used to be my best friend until he betrayed me. He's also one of the few people on Jora that knows what happened here, on Earth, and in Pangea. But no one lifted a finger to corroborate my story, and the rest of the world thought I was making stuff up about parallel Earths just to pretend I was insane and not go to jail.

I move my head in a circle, the Jori equivalent of a headshake. "Well, I definitely could use a friend." *Or a mother*, I think, looking away. "Too bad they're hard to find."

Of course, I understand I sounded crazy when talking about Earth and the messengers, but I thought she'd have understood. Or more importantly, that she would have believed me. But she trusted Bodan's lies instead.

Dooria frowns. "Zeon, you have been attacked. I'm glad you're alive, but how are you not dead? We were already on our way when we saw what happened."

I touch my bandaged arm. "I don't know," I lie. The pain slowly fades away, helped by the cold and wet antibiotic cream. It's replaced by an uncomfortable tingling sensation. This is going to hurt in the shower.

"But Zeon," Harry says, speaking for the first time in front of another human. "I explained it to you."

Dooria's eyes light up and she grins, beaming at Harry. I glare at him.

"Shut up, Harry! Don't you dare say another word!"

Harry's eyes shift from me to Dooria as if considering whether he should obey me or not, but he stays quiet. I'm not technically his master or anything, and he has no loyalty to me, so I never know what he's going to do.

Dooria looks back at me. "Fascinating! And he speaks English!"

"He speaks both English and Dïnisc, but I specifically ask him to speak only English to me. I didn't want anyone else to understand him." I smile, thinly. No one speaks English on Jora. Well, almost no one. The Jori who know about English are the ones who also know about the gods. It's a small, exclusive club.

Then, the realization of what just happened hits me like a punch in the stomach. Heart racing, I gasp as though I'm in one of Earth's cheaply made soap operas. We've been speaking English since I let Dooria inside; it's been a long time since I last spoke Dïnisc, and I didn't realize I was even speaking English when I answered the door.

And there's only one possible explanation why Dooria's able to speak it too.

I stand up and point a finger at her. "You knew!" My breathing becomes shallow. I try to gather my thoughts, gesturing toward the kitchen, in the direction of the paradisiacal shore. "And yet you left me here... to rot on this *beautiful* beach!"

Her eyes gaze away from mine, which is unusual for her. Dooria rarely avoids eye contact even when she's in the wrong. "Yes, I did. And I'm sorry about that."

I take a quick breath. "Sorry? You are the vice-governor of the goddamn Atlantic Alliance, and you couldn't give a *fuck* about me? You *knew* I told the truth!"

She leans back and crosses her arms, frowning. Few people probably talk to her like that. To her credit, she remains silent and waits for me to blow off steam.

Betrayal takes a long time to process, and this is just the beginning.

"But how?" I ask, looking at nothing in particular. The explanation is obvious, but it's worse than I thought. Yes, the Jori who fought in Pangea know about English, Earth, and the gods. But only a few of them—besides me—actually speak the language.

"Dooria," I lower my voice. "Are you... are *you*... an angel?"

All of a sudden, I regress to when I was eleven years old as if asking her for attention.

For love.

"Yes."

The winged lion on her left temple flashes as she scratches it, deep in thought.

Dooria, the parent of my former best friend, the mother figure in my life, is an angel of the messengers of the gods.

For who knows how long, the messengers have been selecting humans from Jora and from Earth to fight for them in battles. They call those humans *protectors*. But only a few of the protectors are also angels of the messengers.

Don't get me wrong; angels are not that special. They're no better than any other protector, and they don't have special powers here or in Pangea. After all, they're humans like everybody else. The only difference is they speak most human languages.

But, most importantly, they're spies. The messengers draft them when they are young. Brainwash them. And when they're adults, the angels do the gods' bidding, which, for some sadistic reason, usually involves smashing my heart into pieces, both literally and figuratively.

Dooria stands and approaches me, arms open. I take a step back. "You know I'm innocent," I say. "Everything I said is true. So why didn't you help me?"

"I was told by the messengers not to get involved," she says. "You know how the gods work."

I sneer at her. "No need to tell me. They work in mysterious ways?" And here I thought the lowest point of my night had been when someone was trying to kill me.

Dooria stares at me. "We don't have much time. The messengers need you in Pangea."

I wince. Pangea is a place where our consciousness goes when we're asleep, while our bodies stay behind. But as far as I know, only the messengers of the gods can send us there. It looks and feels like a real place, but it's not. People can and do die there, though.

"Can you tell them to *tickle* themselves?" I ask.

I'll never go back there, and certainly not to help those two-faced weasels. Although they don't really look like weasels. They're hairless albino humanoids in Pangea. In reality, they could be disgusting millipedes living on a distant planet, and we would never know.

It's not their appearance that makes me dislike them, though. The problem is they're emissaries of the gods, who are beings made of fuzzy clouds of energy that live somewhere in Pangea but are never seen. The gods are involved in a war for the control of Pangea, and they were hoping to draft us last time I got involved in all of this. They failed badly because we rebelled and didn't pass their psychopathic tests. Maybe they're trying again.

Dooria ignores my rude reply. "The messengers can't reach us anymore. Something really bad is happening up there."

"Not my circus, not my monkeys," I say. It's one of my favorite expressions in English.

"I don't think you understand. If the messengers lose Pangea—if *we* lose Pangea, everyone dies."

Here we go again. I roll my eyes. "How would that even happen?"

Her eyes drop to her clasped hands, and she begins fiddling with her thumbs. "I guess you always assumed we were protectors of Jora. Or protectors of Earth. But you're wrong. We're protectors of Pangea." She sighs, nods, and looks me in the eyes. "And you're one of us. An angel. The highest form of protector."

I stand and walk around the stool, away from her, fuming. "It's not like anyone ever *explained* anything to me. And I don't know if you're being honest."

Dooria's eyebrows furrow, and she touches her forehead.

"Why do you have to be so stubborn? Bodan is right. Do you know why you're in prison?" She snorts. I don't answer her. It's a rhetorical question. "You're here *not* because of what you did, but because of what you didn't do. And once again, you're fleeing from your responsibilities. You're so unlike Bodan. He *never* stops fighting."

All my life she gave me similar speeches. About how Bodan was better than me. But her words aren't as painful anymore. After I was abandoned or betrayed by everyone I loved, I developed a thick skin. Her words *almost* don't bother me.

Almost.

"I'm *not* going back," I tell her.

Her eyes follow me as I pace inside the cabin. Despite her anger, Dooria is always great at diplomacy, often knowing exactly where the conversation's going to go. In international politics, it earned her the nickname "the Whisperer." Compared to that, persuading me or Bodan of anything is a piece of cake.

Then she says, "Jane's in danger. She's asking for your help."

I pinch my lips. Of course, they'd go there. The

messengers are clever. They know exactly how to twist my knobs and make me do their bidding. But Jane would never ask for my help. She must hate the messengers as much as I do. I stay silent, so as not to give Dooria any ammunition. There's no way she can convince me to help them.

"She sent you a message," Dooria continues. "She said, and I quote, '*Louise* Lane needs spider guy's help.' I'm not sure why she phrased it like that."

My hand quickly finds the couch behind me and I sit. When we had a big fight, when she found out about who I really was, Jane and I discussed superheroes of all things. No one else but Jane would know this.

Chapter 3

COMPOUND

LOCATION: JORA

T he Sphinx Mountain—named after the monument next to the pyramids—shines in the bay even in the dark. The last time I saw it, I was handcuffed and it was daytime. When the sun is up, the arching view of the Ring near the equator makes the scenery even more spectacular.

Unlike normal aircraft—which announce themselves with bright and blinking lights—Frei flies in complete darkness. Like all vehicles on Jora, our small helicopter is guided by biocomputers. I'm glad of that. Earth's airplanes, in comparison, are piloted by the type of people who jump from waterfalls and dangle from high-rise balconies.

Adrenaline junkies. It baffles me that everyone seems so happy when they're greeted by the flight attendant on the way to their deaths.

The six of us barely fit in the small cockpit, so Harry, Bebe, and all my stuff have to stay behind for the moment. Dooria says my sentence will be reverted, and I'll be compensated for my time in prison. Only if I cooperate. And it'll be done discreetly. If I make a fuss about it, they'll arrest me again and pretend this never happened.

Dooria sits on my left. Like me, she wears a three-point seatbelt tighter than I'd like.

"It was a difficult time for us, Zaén."

The noise of the rotors is just a little hum inside the cabin due to advanced noise-cancellation devices with analog brains. Three soldiers sit cramped in front of us, while my old friend Jal sits on my other side, holding his rifle and looking gloomy.

I recognized him as soon as we left my unit. His tattoo of crisscrossing lines and circles on his dark face always fascinates me. We shared a hug before boarding the helicopter, but he hasn't said a word yet. In his defense, he's not an angel, so doesn't speak English. Still, Jal is one of the protectors who corroborated my story and stood by my side when I was indicted years ago, so I can honestly say he's one of the few real friends I have.

"Some people wanted to kill you," Dooria says, still in English. I think she doesn't want the other soldiers —or Jal—to understand us. "It took a lot of convincing for them to just arrest you."

I steal a glance at Jal by my side. He knows everything about Pangea, but the other soldiers are none the wiser. It must be puzzling for them to see the vice-governor just speaking with a prisoner in an unknown language.

If any of them believe in conspiracy theories, then they just hit the jackpot. The official story is that I sabotaged Jora's Mars mission, but according to Dooria, the truth has leaked to the world. There's a parallel Earth out there, and a world of gods.

Although it's still considered ridiculous, in the same vein as alien abduction stories, my credibility is slowly growing.

"Let me guess," I say. "Bodan was one of those that wanted to kill me?"

Dooria holds my right palm with both her hands. "Zeon, you're family to us. Bodan wanted you to be free."

I sneer at her. This is so hard to believe. But I don't pull my hand out. That's the problem with parental figures. No matter what they do to us, we still seek their approval. Their love.

We stay mostly silent for the rest of the trip inland. Frei is an advanced helicopter model with four propellers—reminding me of a giant drone—and we fly for two hours without recharging. As he starts descending, I watch the landscape. The sun won't rise for another hour, but our destination is impressive even in the dark.

The six large interconnected buildings are heavily illuminated, and the wide and paved roads around the conglomerate make it look like an airport from above. It harbors one of the largest structures on Jora, resembling the Boeing factory on Earth. But unlike that factory, which is a single structure, this one has six hangar-sized buildings connected on their long sides.

I recognize this place. It used to be the headquarters of *Väêr*, a large airplane manufacturer that moved north, and it was supposed to have been deactivated about a year ago. The whole story hadn't made much sense—who would build such a massive place and just leave?

"What can you possibly have down there?" I ask Dooria, unable to contain my curiosity.

Her face turns somber. "You'll see."

If I remember correctly—from a documentary I watched years ago—the structure is not exactly square. It's 600 meters on its longest side, 500 meters deep, and sixteen meters high.

Six orange hangar-sized doors face west, serving as the main entrance for each building. There are four-lane roads both in front of and behind them. Dozens of trucks are parked on the two farthest lanes.

Frei lands on the runway near the center of the complex, and the soldiers help us out. Once we're a few meters away from the helicopter, Dooria stops interacting with me for a few seconds, acting as if she's a computer that just froze.

This is normal on Jora. She must be using our worldwide network to communicate with her people. It communicates directly with her brain.

Jal takes this moment to pull me to the side.

He glances at Dooria and rests his heavy hand on my shoulder.

"<Zeon, no matter what they show you,>" he whispers in Dïnisc, "<don't trust anyone.>"

Mimicking him, I also take a quick look at Dooria. I'm about to ask where this is coming from, but then she comes back to the real world, and he walks away.

Dooria stares at him as he reenters the helicopter. "Jal's right," she says. "You shouldn't trust anyone. Isn't this what I always taught you?" She chuckles.

I check my clothes and then the ground around us, looking for gadgets she might have used to record or transmit our conversation. She has a big grin on her face when I look back at her.

"I don't have any listening devices on you. He's

been saying this to everyone. Jal's under a lot of stress lately."

Ignoring a light drizzle starting to make our heads wet, Dooria sets off walking toward the buildings, and I follow her in silence. Frei takes off with the soldiers the moment we stop next to one of the enormous hangars.

"Please, don't judge Jal or me before you understand what's happening," Dooria finally says. "And don't worry—I'm asking to reassign him to the compound to keep an eye on you."

The humongous hangar door in front of us has the number four painted on it, the digit itself about five stories tall. I look up at the far-off roof as we walk side by side toward a small door next to the hangar entrance. Since the other doors are so large, I didn't see it before, but it only looks small by comparison. It's still a two-story French door.

A woman with short blond hair and light skin is waiting for us there.

"What in the tickle is he doing here?" she swears, accenting her question with exaggerated arm motions. She wears yellow scrubs with a well-known logo on them—a stylized sunflower-seed pattern inside a circle, which itself is inscribed in a triangle. It's the symbol of the Atlantic Space Force, a name more glamorous than it seems. ASF is way behind NASA here.

"You know we need him, Kera," Dooria replies. I've seen Kera before, but can't place her.

Kera glares at Dooria, waving her hand at me without so much as a glance in my direction. "Nobody told me we'd be working with a traitor."

"So, everyone speaks English here?" I ask.

"No. Only angels," she replies. Oh yes, *angels*. Sometimes, I think that to be an angel of the messengers, you have to try to kill me as a rite of passage. I wouldn't be surprised if Kera has tried.

I glare sideways at Dooria. "I'm *not* an angel!"

"Well, I'd sure hope not," Kera replies. "The messengers would be morons to make this piece of shit an angel." She thrusts a finger into my face.

Kera must be from the western part of our continent, near *Êndus*, where people move their hands and arms as they speak, although they're usually not jerks. Her face has no stick-on jewelry—uncommon, especially in that region. On the other hand, her scrubs and mask indicate she's some kind of medical professional, and medics usually don't wear jewelry when doing their jobs, leaving their temple connections free to use medical bio-equipment.

"Why are you so mad at me?" I ask. "If you're one of the blessed angels, you know what happened." She's starting to make *me* mad.

And that's when I remember. It's in her body language. She was the one who was running after Jane the first time I was in Pangea. And she *did* shoot me several times.

"Because you didn't do what the gods ordered. The reason this doesn't get through your thick skull baffles me!" Kera says, poking her own head repeatedly with her index finger.

I scoff at her. The gods wanted us to kill billions of people, but I'm not a murderer. Unlike most protectors, I never killed anyone. And I'm not going to start now.

Dooria gently touches my shoulder, and I flinch. My arm is still burnt.

She takes her hand off me. "You two need to stop bickering. This is bigger than your petty fight."

I point at the hangar's door. "What is going on in there?" I ask.

Kera and Dooria exchange glances.

"It's hard to explain," Dooria says. "It's better if we show you."

When she finishes the sentence, the massive hangar door slowly begins to slide up. As remarkable as the structure is from the outside, it's the inside that leaves me speechless. The footprint of the building may be colossal, but the distance to the ceiling makes us look like ants.

Once the door is high enough, I walk inside the structure to get a better look. Building Four is a chaotic tent city with a two-way road starting at the entrance and ending somewhere in the back. People, vehicles, and equipment are moving everywhere, trying to not hit each other.

It's a human hive.

"<Hey, who opened the door?>" a half-asleep dark-skinned woman with long hair shouts in Dïnisc from her tent. "<It's five in the morning!>" Her companion gives us a thumbs-up, which means a completely different thing here than its positive meaning on Earth. Kera responds with both of her thumbs up as well.

An all-white and driverless electric car comes from inside the building and stops right next to us, looking like a golf cart with no roof. Dooria gestures at the vehicle. "It would take forever to explain if we walked."

Reluctantly, I sit in the front, and she sits by my side. Kera jumps in the back, as far away from me as possible, and the vehicle starts moving again.

Dooria indicates the tent city. "This is where those who are on call spend their sleeping breaks," she explains.

As soon as we begin to move toward the tents, a strong smell of disinfectant and antiseptics makes me wrinkle my nose. People not asleep in tents are wearing scrubs in different colors, all of them with the Space Force logo.

If I had to guess, I'd say this was a medical unit of some kind, but since it's so disorganized, it looks more like a field hospital.

"Kera is one of the doctors here," Dooria says.

"So, this is a hospital?"

The middle of the hangar has a cafeteria where lines of Space Force personnel are forming. The sound of cutlery is annoying, and while the people are speaking in low voices, it's still loud. I don't know how anyone can sleep with this kind of din.

"Not exactly," Dooria says. "This is hangar number four. We have the administrative area upstairs, crates of supplies too, and the doctors' offices are in the back."

When the road we're on intersects with another internal road, our car turns north, narrowly avoiding an unmanned truck carrying oxygen tanks. If my mental map is correct, this new road passes through all the other buildings of the compound.

"What happened to his arm?" Kera asks.

"Why do you care?" I retort. "You were trying to kill me, remember?"

"I wasn't talking to you," she says, turning away. "I hope it hurts," she mumbles loud enough for us to hear.

I'm about to ask what the containers on cranes above us are holding when our road finally takes us through another one of the large doors and into the next building. According to large yellow signs hanging on the sides, we're entering Hangar Five. Unlike

Hangar Four, number five is less busy, not as bright, and way more organized.

But what surprises me is not the orderly arrangement or the relative silence. Grabbing the console in front of me, I try to ignore my sudden dizziness as I look at rows and rows of people lying in oval pods.

Chapter 4

HANGAR SIX

LOCATION: JORA

"What is this place?" I ask, feeling sick. "There must be hundreds of people here!"

Our car slows but doesn't stop as it carries us through a tour of the absurd.

Five rows of cocoon-shaped beds line each side of the road, but not all of them are occupied with people. In fact, a lot lie empty.

"This hangar can have 500 people in it, although currently it only has 243," Dooria says. "Four of the six hangars are just like this one, filled with intensive-care beds, and the whole facility can accommodate 2,000."

Each row consists of a hundred pods, then—fifty on each side of the road.

Between rows is a mass of space—about ten meters. A few doctors and nurses wearing yellow and light-blue scrubs walk around, replacing nutrient bags and checking on the patients. Most beds only have a few dim amber lights, but whenever someone approaches one, its lights strengthen to a stronger white glow.

I lean over the windowless door of the car. "What happened to them?"

Dooria answers me with a question. "Do you remember what happens to your body when you go to Pangea?"

Pangea—that's where the messengers of the gods used to send our consciousness when we were sleeping. There, we would be tested in battles against other humans. Suffice to say it's not my favorite place.

"Of course. We go into deep sleep." It's a weird state looking a lot like a coma, but somehow, the body that stays behind is able to breathe. Meanwhile, the mind is projected into Pangea, like a dream.

Dooria rubs her hands together in the same way she used to when she helped us with our biology homework. "What if you can't come back from there?" she asks, bringing her arms closer to her chest. "Every conscious life is in Pangea when it's asleep, and every life can come back at any time. But not when they're stuck in a hypersphere."

Hyperspheres are holographic environments inside Pangea, created by the messengers of the gods. They're the places we had our battles, and we couldn't leave them unless we became the victors or solved a puzzle. Nothing happening in Pangea is real, but most people can't tell the difference between a hypersphere environment and reality.

"So, all these people,"—I gesture toward the beds around us—"they're all protectors that can't come back from Pangea? But there are so many!"

"Yes," Kera says. "No one knows exactly how many protectors work for the gods. But based on the ones admitted here, we can say for certain there were at least 1,500."

I take a long and deep breath. The protectors asleep here are people currently trapped in a hypersphere. While they're stuck in Pangea doing gods-only-know-what, their actual bodies stay here, in a coma. 1,500 of them. And I'd thought each Earth had fewer than fifty. But if there are more than a thousand, why only a few hundred in this room?

Furthermore, this whole setup proves the government knows about the gods. Otherwise, they'd never spend so many resources on this place. But then again, the vice-governor is one of the messenger minions. As for the gods themselves, no one has ever seen one because they're not corporeal.

"Why are they stuck there?" I ask. "And why do the messengers need so many protectors?"

They're probably battling something inside the hyperspheres, shepherded by the messengers, probably toward their deaths.

Last time I was caught up in this, the messengers made Earth and Jora fight there. They said it was a test for an upcoming war, and that we failed, but I think they just wanted to kill us all.

"We don't know," Kera says. "No one has come back alive from Pangea since you are in prison."

This is why they have this compound, then. To keep the bodies of the protectors alive while they fight.

"We had to scramble in the beginning to get this facility working," Dooria adds. "People all over the globe were going to sleep and not waking up. They ended up in hospitals looking like they were brain-dead, and some families wanted to turn off the machines. You know how this works."

I know. It's happened before. When people get trapped in the hypersphere, their bodies go into a deep sleep on Jora or Earth, and no brain activity is recorded.

I gesture at Kera. "Why is she here and not there with the others?" She's not only a protector; she's an angel. Otherwise she couldn't speak English. "Are you afraid of not coming back?" I ask her.

"It doesn't work like that, you moron," Kera answers. "You have to be summoned."

I roll my eyes. As if we all got instruction manuals when everything started. "Well, why don't you summon this?"

Turning around to offer her the appropriate gesture, I accidentally hit my injured shoulder on the side of the seat. She laughs at me as I recoil in pain.

"Calm down, Kera," Dooria says. "We're about to enter Hangar Six."

Kera immediately stops chuckling and blushes.

Unlike the other hangars, where there's nothing blocking the road between the buildings, the internal entrance to Hangar Six is made of an enormous pair of accordion doors going all the way up to the crane rails. The rails themselves have their own type of concertina gates, ensuring whatever's in that hangar doesn't easily come out.

As soon as our vehicle stops in front of the gate, a piercing clank comes from the giant doors, and my heart skips a beat.

An unnatural grinding sound follows as the two sides of the gate start moving away from each other. When they open a little, a cold, dry breeze hits me in the face, and the hairs on the back of my neck stand on end. In contrast to the other sections, it's dark inside Hangar Six.

Our bodies jerk backward, and my head hits the

headrest as the vehicle starts moving. Once we're inside the new hangar, the door begins closing behind us and my eyes get used to the darkness.

It's mostly empty in this place, with unbelievably tall, dark-blue racks near the north, south, and east walls, like shelves for giants. Many of them have long, slim black sacks—quite small, from what I can tell— and as I watch, a forklift lowers one of the bags from the rack to the back of a flat-bed electric truck.

The cold is so intense that my teeth begin to chatter, and the silence enhances all the little noises made by the forklift as we approach it. Finally, our car stops next to the truck. From up close, I realize the bags are larger than I thought. Since everything's so big here, my size estimation was way off.

"<Hello, Dooria,>" says a guy wearing olive scrubs, rubber gloves and goggles. He's speaking Dïnisc. "<I'm sorry.>" He makes a circular motion with his head. "<We have not made any progress identifying the cause of death.>"

I blink. *Oh no.*

Dooria walks toward him.

"<It's okay. I'm here for another reason. Can you give us a moment?>"

The man stops what he's doing and stares blankly at nothing, probably checking his internal biocomputers.

"<Sure. It's time for another coffee anyway. I don't know how much more I can take.>"

He grabs a pad from the truck and leaves us alone.

I step out of the car and slowly approach the truck beside Dooria. It's one of those moments that feels like I'm watching a movie where the others and I are actors, and I'm floating, looking at myself.

Dooria leans down, grabs the zipper of the bag closest to us, and opens it. My stomach immediately reminds me I shouldn't have eaten so much yesterday, and the cold suddenly doesn't bother me anymore. Inside the bag lies the corpse of a young male who could easily be asleep, except he's not breathing.

Moving my eyes away from the bag, I turn around and stare at the shelves. Each one holds dozens of black bags. There are many empty spaces, but the corpses are spread throughout enough places to indicate this has to have been a catastrophe of some kind.

Dooria's expression hardens. "There are 482 bodies in here."

I look around for a moment, realizing what this means—what *this place* means. You don't build a refrigerated hangar overnight. There's a war going on in Pangea, and almost five hundred protectors have already died there. And when you are killed while in the hypersphere, your real body also dies.

"You *knew* this was going to happen," I hiss, facing Dooria again. I want to shout, but it would feel disrespectful in this place. "Otherwise, why do you even *have* this?" I whisper, waving my hands around.

She looks away. "This was not supposed to be a morgue, Zeon. Originally, it was used for high-altitude cabin-temperature and pressure testing."

I cross my arms. I should be more careful what I say when I'm upset. Assigning blame is always my immediate reaction.

"How did they die?" I ask. Kera hasn't left our vehicle yet, and her gaze is distant.

"Obviously," Dooria says, "they all died in Pangea, but we don't know how. It happened about two days ago, causing havoc in our compound. It took hours just to identify who was dead and who was alive."

Dooria closes the zipper slowly, careful to not catch anything in it. I shiver just thinking about it, as if the dead can still feel the zipper bite. "There are too many bodies for us to do autopsies," she continues, "so we're sampling them."

I think of the hundreds of people in the other room. "How many are still alive?"

"There are 986 still breathing. A third of the protectors died in a single day."

I shiver again. What the hell is going on up there? Many of my friends could be there, fighting. Some of them may be dead already.

"Saint Plehr!" I exclaim, a little less quietly. "How's Nia? And Bodan?" Despite how much I hate him, I don't want him dead.

"They're here in deep sleep. Alive." Dooria casts a glance at Kera from afar. "But Elquenna and Gobo are dead." I gasp. They were protectors that had fought together in my last battle. "And I'm sure there are others you knew that have died," she adds.

Kera finally approaches us, probably listening to our conversation, and still avoiding looking at the bodies.

"Do you know what I've been doing the last twenty-four hours?" she asks, glaring at me. "Cutting these bodies up. Looking for the reason my friends are dead. Why Elquenna is gone." Her eyes water up, and a sob escapes her. "And the reason she's dead, Zeon, is *you*."

She gets uncomfortably close then, and shoves her index finger into my chest, hard.

"They are all dead because of *you*, you *mother-tick-*

ler!" she shouts, her voice echoing in the large, empty building.

For a change, I'm speechless, but I know I have nothing to do with this. True, I disobeyed the gods because I didn't want to commit genocide. But the last time I was in Pangea, the messengers told us we'd never see Pangea again. I got the feeling they didn't need or want us anymore. Clearly, I was wrong, but whatever is happening there can't be because of what I did.

Dooria steps between us and carefully guides Kera away from me.

"Kera, please," Dooria says. "This is not anybody's fault. We knew it was coming. And regardless, we're on the same side, even if Zeon doesn't trust the messengers."

Kera waves a hand at me. "If he'd been up there, fighting, those people wouldn't be dead. But *no*, he had to disobey the messengers!"

I rub my head with my uninjured hand, trying not to argue with Kera. She's not the problem. The dimwitted messengers tried to kill billions. What are a few hundred people to them? Nothing. The fact that Kera is mad at me is baffling. I've never killed anyone. I bet she can't say the same.

Wait a minute. Scratching my head, I look at them. "What did you just say? You *knew* it was coming?"

Dooria walks back toward me and leans closer. "The messengers warned us a long time ago that many humans would be summoned for a war. A war against the necromantes—a powerful alien race wanting to take over Pangea." She sighs. "And we think this war has finally started."

I frown. "Necromantes?"

Dooria tilts her head in agreement. "Yes. This is why we were tested by the gods. They need soldiers because they can't fight the war themselves."

I can see that. A fuzzy, abstract and narcissistic energy cloud can't fight.

Then, the old woman squeezes my shoulder and I scoff inwardly. I know all her tricks. Here comes the selling argument.

"Now," Dooria says, "whatever is happening up there involves Jane's Earth as well."

Instinctively, I inch away from them. But I do agree partially with her. I don't believe for a second that only Jori are dying. Earthers must be dying as well. They may even be fighting each other again for the same foolish reasons as last time.

"But besides helping our friends, why do we care?" I ask them. "Why do we need to fight a war for the gods in Pangea?"

Kera throws up her arms. "It's hopeless. He doesn't understand how Pangea works." She taps her forehead while glancing at Dooria. "This isn't about the people who can't come back. Or about the people who died. It's way bigger than this. Do you know what happens if you can't dream? If you can't fucking *sleep*?"

I look at her, blinking. "What in the tickle are you talking about?"

Grunting, she glares at Dooria and throws up her arms again.

Before addressing me, Dooria touches Kera's hand for a second, probably trying to calm her down. "Zaén, dear. Pangea is where all intelligent life goes to sleep. And if we lose it..." Dooria returns my puzzled expression with one of her own, perhaps finally realizing I have no idea what's going on.

And then my head begins to spin. No, that can't be. "I thought... I thought only the messengers could summon us to hyperspheres."

Dooria steps over a thick cable charging the truck and grabs my hand. She must've noticed I'm in a daze. "You're right. But Pangea is not made only of hyperspheres. Every time we sleep, we create our own dream 'bubble' there, a place that is, for all intents and purposes, a mini hypersphere. We call them dreamspheres."

So poetic. And, if it's true, it means Pangea doesn't just *look* like a dream. It's literally the main stage of all humanity's dreams.

Dooria lets go off my hand to brush off a strand of hair above her eyes. "And if people can't dream, they can't sleep. And if people can't sleep, they'll die."

"We must protect it," Kera says. "But if Zeon's our best shot, we're tickled."

Kera's swearing helps me pull myself together, and I frown. "Why wasn't I summoned? If most protectors are already in this war, why didn't the messengers call for me?"

"For us," Dooria begins, "we either go to sleep and don't wake up, or we wake up the next day with no clue why we weren't summoned into a hypersphere. The messengers call us at their own will. You're a different story, though. You must go willingly. Since your last confrontation with the messengers, they aren't able to do it for you."

I let out a quick breath of air. "But Dooria..." I again regress to my teenage self. Damn mothers. "Why me?"

The answer should be straightforward. It's because I can do things in Pangea that no one else can. This is not a secret—not anymore, not after everything that's happened. What I'm really asking is what I've always wanted to know—why am I the only one with those powers? Why was I singled out?

She caresses my face with her hand and smiles with tears in her eyes.

"Oh, Zaén—it doesn't matter anymore. Everyone is in danger." She grabs my right hand and lightly squeezes it, just like she used to do to calm me down when I had panic attacks as a child. "The protectors were there first, but now it's our turn. They're calling *all* angels."

Chapter 5

ARROGANCE

The next day, people from the government bring my stuff to a nearby trailer. Bebe and Harry are staying there. Harry can access the network and research more ways to annoy me, and Jal promised he will take care of Bebe.

The trailer has plumbing but no bathing area, so I use the communal shower in Hangar Three to get ready for my date with Pangea. Afterward, I put on some clothes that I hope will be useful when I wake up: dark blue pants, my favorite black t-shirt with a large red spider decal, hiking shoes, sunglasses, and—obviously —a cowboy hat. While our bodies stay here, we wake up there wearing the same clothes we had on when we fell asleep. And hypersphere environments tend to be sunny.

About a thousand protectors are spread out in intensive care units in Hangars One, Two, Four, and Five. The pods are oval beds that look like half-cocoons. The one they choose for me is in Hangar Two, next to some of the original protectors who are still alive. It's tough to see some of my friends lying motionless here—Nia, Talaia, and even Bodan. They look so serene.

Once I'm inside, Dooria watches me near the head of this strange bed. The ceiling looks much farther away when I'm lying on my back. "You're ready to go, Zeon."

Kera is hanging bags of liquid on the metal poles next to the unit.

"I hope that's not poison," I tell her.

She flicks a bag filled with orange liquid. "I wish. My only regret is that you won't feel anything when I insert the needles later on." Her lips twist to form an evil smile. I wince. Needles are one of my worst nightmares, after millipedes.

Dooria reaches inside the bed and touches my arm. "You can go to sleep now. If you need anything, just press this red button." It's near my right hand, and I flex my fingers to estimate how fast I can press it. "No one has ever pressed it since we've been here," she continues with a tone of foreshadowing. It makes sense. They were all dead when they came back—or they haven't come back at all.

The hat and sunglasses I'm wearing make my head uncomfortable, and I must look like a clown to any passersby. I try to adjust them as much as I can, but it's hard to sleep like this.

Kera looks clinically at the health monitors, for once not showing any aggression toward me. "We'll wait until tomorrow to check if you're really in deep sleep. It takes a couple of hours. If you are, that's when I'll start connecting the IVs, catheters, and other stuff." Luckily, we don't need diapers. Let's just say I'd rather not describe what kind of technology we have to handle this here.

Kera's right hand presses a large green button on the side of the bed and the bright white bed lights that surround me like a mini-stadium morph into a softer, almost imperceptible amber. "We're ready," she says. "But how the hell is he going to come back?"

I bite my lip, trying to not scoff at her. The messengers are never straightforward and, as far as I know, there is no protector academy to train me. I'm on my own. But I don't want to make her angry while in this vulnerable state.

Dooria's tired eyes watch me for a long time before she answers, "Only the gods know."

Once they leave me alone, my only job is to actually go to sleep. Local time is 20:00 hours and considering I spent the previous night awake, it should be easy to do. Once I'm asleep, my consciousness should be uploaded to a hypersphere in Pangea so I can try to make sense of this. Or maybe I'll go to a dreamsphere and wake up the next day none the wiser.

I keep trying to think, "Take me to Pangea," like I did last time, but the events of the day and the uncertainty of what happens next keep me awake. There are hundreds of dead bodies nearby, bodies of protectors who did what I'm about to do. Also, sleeping with sunglasses and a cowboy hat isn't as easy or as fun as it sounds.

Well, eventually I should be able to sleep, so I might as well start with the basics and do my daily routine. First, I close my eyes. Next, I have an existential crisis. Why are we self-aware? Do we have a soul? Why does no one love me?

I'm pretty sure the bridge from Earth to Pangea is

in our own brains, and I'm convinced we don't actually go anywhere. It's all in our minds. In fact, there's no reason for us *not* to be in both places at the same time. I should do some experiments when I wake there.

All of a sudden, I have a thought. If no one is coming back from Pangea, how did Dooria get Jane's message? It's time to press the button. Reaching for it, I grab a finger-sized branch of a small brush that's tickling my skin, and the noise of burbling water overwhelms me. It's too late.

I lift my head up and open my eyes to have a look at the plant. For a split second, I can see the bush and the button behind it simultaneously. It's as if I'm in both worlds at once. I look straight up, and can see the sky flash from high, dark ceiling back to a cloudless blue. Once I blink a couple of times, the effect is gone.

Pulling myself up into a sitting position, I rub my previously injured arm. No sign of bandages is left there, and despite some tingling, it looks normal. Behind the little bush, a tall, flat rock formation fills the horizon like a plateau. A yellowish fog of some kind surrounds it.

It's odd I didn't wake up in some kind of habitat ring, where we would usually meet up with the protectors. However, this exact same thing happened the first time I woke up in Pangea. I must be inside one of the hyperspheres, where the battles happen. My talk with Dooria will have to wait until I'm back.

As I flex my arms, the feeling of electricity flows through my arms, chest, and head, reminding me I'm connected with everything when I'm here. This is where I really belong. I can't help but smirk. They don't know what's going to hit them.

My mind races as I think about my special abilities.

When I was a child, I was in a coma for about a month. Unbeknownst to me at the time, the messengers brought me to a hypersphere. And there, thanks to my still-undeveloped mind, I learned some tricks.

Pangea is not like Jora or Earth. It isn't real, so anything here responds to my thoughts. Besides the messengers, I am the only one who's able to physically change the hypersphere on command. This is why they need my help.

Slowly rising to my feet—gravity here is lower than on Jora, so I must be careful—I observe one of the impressive environments the messengers always craft for us. There are no clouds, the sun is high in the sky, and I feel lighter. It's warm and humid. Drops of sweat start forming on the part of my forehead that touches the hat.

Once I'm up, I find myself standing on top of a small hill with a raging river crossing the landscape below. It's uncommon for a river this wide—my guess is it's about half a kilometer—to be this fast. The gorgeous plateau looms across the river like it's on an island.

The bright sunlight reflects off a series of structures on the top of its flat surface, so it must be a base of some kind. A busy one, judging by the vehicles moving around. I wish I had some binoculars.

Behind me, the terrain is too irregular to cross easily, despite the sparse vegetation. The farther away from the river I look, the greener it gets. When the area with small bushes ends, it's followed by scattered trees eventually forming a large forest farther back. A visible trail down the hill from where I'm standing goes all the way into the forest, toward what looks like an abandoned, war-damaged town. Whoever allowed me to be here probably expects me to take this path.

I chuckle. "Whoever" probably doesn't know me very well.

When I turn to face the flat mountain again, I quickly formulate an infallible plan. Although everything looks and feels real, this place can be controlled by our minds—well, at least by *my* mind. I've already done a lot of things with this power. I healed friends, I flew in battle, and I made love like no one else.

In the past, the messengers forbade me to show this power to the other humans. Blackmailed me, even. But since we disagree on the subject of whether we should kill all humans or not, I've decided to not hold myself back anymore. Screw them.

I walk forward and stop right on the edge of the cliff. The sound of the rippling river is deafening even from ten meters up. Picking up a straw of grass from the ground and chewing it, I adjust my cowboy hat and my sunglasses. My plan is incredibly simple: I'll fly to the base on the top of that plateau, fight whatever's there, make some tasteless jokes, and ask questions later.

Maybe I can even try to find this hypersphere's target—a flashing circle that shuts down everything and sends everyone back to their planets. Every hypersphere I've been to had one of those. If the same is true, there's no need to fight anyone.

As I absorb the flow of information coming from everything around me, I jump into the air above the river and glare at my destination—you know, the normal way to fly. It seems to work for a fraction of a second, but instead of seeing the island getting closer, it just suddenly moves up. My guts push my diaphragm up, and I exhale feebly.

In less than two seconds, I splash into the water feet-first. Everything blurs, and I thrash as the rushing water tumbles me over and over. I don't know what's up or down anymore.

Moments later, my face hits a faint yellow energy barrier blocking my path. The river's strong flow has me stuck against it. The barrier is mostly flat but undulates like a curtain. Water and other debris can go through it, but not my body.

Flailing my arms aimlessly has no effect, and I was never a good swimmer anyway. My legs don't have the strength necessary to push against the semi-transparent wall due to the volume and speed of the water pinning me on it. And I'm still underwater.

I can't fly anymore. How did this happen? The hypersphere and my mind are still intertwined, and I should be able to do it, but can't. Thanks to my cockiness, I didn't even try it before jumping off a cliff. Arrogance is going to kill me.

That's it. Perhaps this was the messengers' plan from the start. Get me up here to die.

Focus, Zeon. I close my eyes and hold my breath. Since I was young, I've been different than other people in one aspect—I can think faster than anyone else. Usually, it just makes me do stupid things quicker than normal, so it's almost never an advantage. But sometimes, it means the difference between life and death.

I relax. Time slows to a crawl.

A 3D map of the world around me forms in my head, proving I'm not completely powerless. True, I can't fly, and who knows what else I can't do anymore, but I used to be able to modify cells and other matter microscopically, so perhaps I can do something with the see-through wall that stopped me here.

The barrier in front of me goes inland beyond the river on one side, while reaching out to the flat mountain on the other. But it doesn't go down through the island. I touch it with the palms of my hands and try to understand its structure.

Threads of energy woven into a net hold me here, but they're not made from anything I've ever seen in the real world. It's not physically possible. There's nothing solid about the net. It's the reason water and other things can get through, but not me. Not people. It must be tuned to detect consciousness, or maybe just brain activity. If I had time, I probably could do some experiments to actually unweave the threads, but I can't wait much longer.

As I start to lose consciousness due to the lack of oxygen, I concentrate. Focusing all my thoughts on my right hand, I press harder against the wall. My mind drifts to the point of contact and I panic for a second, wondering if this will work. A small ball of concentrated energy starts to form on my palm as I spread my fingers wide. Waves of pressure disturb the water around my hand, and the energy threads of the wall begin to rip as if disconnecting from each other.

But I don't have time to know if it works or not. Soon, my consciousness drifts away.

Chapter 6

REBORN

LOCATION: HYPERSPHERE

A horizon of small, flat rocks greets me when my eyes open, and I cough for what feels like minutes. How am I still alive? Muddy water still covers most of my body, so I must've ended up on the bank somewhere way down the river.

Exhausted, I lie half-submerged for a little longer.

My return to Pangea nearly took a deadly turn. Clearly, my last-resort attempt to break the wall worked, and I was able to cross the barrier. I just gambled my life on trying to split the filaments of an alien energy wall. This experience has definitely humbled me.

On the plus side, despite the fact I'm not able to fly, my mind continues to rush, and it seems I still can change the microscopic fabric of the hyperspheres.

After I take a long, deep breath, I stand up to enjoy the calming sounds of the bubbling current hitting the rocks, and the weapons firing nearby.

Wait, what?

The next explosion shakes the ground, almost

making me fall over. What do I do now? Most of my powers are gone. I can't fight barehanded, and who knows who's fighting whom?

The good news is the artillery isn't aiming at me, so the best course of action would be to move back and stay as far away as possible from the fight. This wouldn't be the first time in my life that I fled from violence, like when I misunderstood what the Burning Man festival was about.

Another explosion rocks the earth and I clench my jaw. The commotion is happening down the river, near the bank. Against all my natural instincts, I decide to walk nearer to the melee to observe it. If I want to survive, I need to know what's happening. And Jane might be in danger. With luck, no one is going to try to shoot me.

As I approach the fight, I take some time to observe the plateau's island. The river runs all the way around it, which makes no sense. It's as if the water goes around the rock, giving the appearance of a lake—except the lake behaves like a circular river. This is impossible. Then again, we're in the hypersphere, where the impossible is called "Thursday."

A few projectiles are shot in an arc from the island, but most are destroyed mid-air. The nearby explosions are from the few making it through. Actually, there's something odd about how most of them are destroyed while still in flight. Stopping in my tracks, I focus inward and visualize the terrain in my head.

Using my mind map, I can see the destroyed missiles all explode exactly where the island ends. I wait a minute or so to verify my theory, and a projectile that got through startles me, making me lose my concentration for a second.

Something is blocking most of the missiles right at the edge of the island. The more I pay attention, the more I'm convinced there's another one of those pale energy walls surrounding the island, as if protecting it from the riverbank. But why do some projectiles make it through?

I creep closer to the battle. The small bushes are no protection, but it's always harder to hit a moving target, so I cautiously plod ahead toward my fate.

As I move, the shots get stranger. I swear some projectiles are destroyed at exactly the same place where others came through. It's as if the barrier is failing in some spots for a short time, and the attacking force wasting ammunition on the off chance the wall is going to fail at the right time, in the right place.

If I walk down the beach, everyone will see me, so I take a trail heading away from the river. When I reach a small incline on the winding path, and the bank is at about 200 meters away, I'm shocked to discover two women within shouting distance.

I do a double take to check if I'm not imagining them. They shouldn't be there.

When I was in the hypersphere before, I was always able to sense people from kilometers away. But now, I almost walk into them. Luckily, the battle is too loud for anyone to hear me, so I crouch, hiding behind some unusually tall bushes.

It's time to take advantage of my special connection with the hypersphere, so I close my eyes and create a bird's-eye model of the engagement. Apparently, I can't see auras anymore, so must concentrate on the terrain and the actual shapes of the objects around me. Sure enough, a few dozen people are hiding on the tops of small hills and below trenches, shooting at something near the water.

The other times I was in Pangea, there was always an unmistakable glow around people and the messengers when I observed them in my mind map. Not anymore. They're no different than the rest of the landscape, except they're shaped like humans. And they're moving.

On the beach, a single beige armored vehicle is floating just a few centimeters above land. It appears to be carrying people. At the moment, half of it hovers above the water, and they seem to be preparing their retreat. Like everyone else on this battlefield, they don't show as anything special in my mind. No auras. It's as if I've been demoted in a virtual reality game.

Shots are fired at them, and some actually hit the armor harmlessly as they pull a woman inside. Three men in desert sand armor and helmets give cover fire from behind the floating vehicle. They aim at the people scattered inland. The personnel carrier has a turret, but it's smoking and inoperative.

The barrage of artillery—or missiles—keeps coming from the top of the island, with the odd one passing through the barrier and exploding in the forest inland. If I had to guess, the vehicle must belong to the people currently living on the rock, but how did they get here? And how will they make it back through the wall?

Things are getting complicated. I don't know who the goodies and baddies are. Perhaps if I get closer to the people on this side, I may recognize some of them so I can start asking questions.

Beating around the bushes, I sneak behind the two women. The dark-haired one wears ragged blue shorts that have seen better days, and a dark brown shirt that used to be white. She shoots nonstop toward the vehicle. The tanned blonde next to her just lies there face down, unconscious, her left shoulder badly injured.

I freeze, unsure of what to do. Usually it's a bad idea to startle people in the middle of a battle, and I don't know what language they speak. I'm afraid if I speak the wrong one, I'll be killed on the spot.

A nearby hit throws another cloud of dust in our direction. The woman shooting ducks down to hide, and I crouch again. That was close.

"Fuck!" she shouts before immediately moving back to her position and firing again.

A weak smile forms on my face when I see her. She was the first one I met in Pangea. At the time, my heart was still broken due to a failed relationship, and I thought I was dead. She changed that. Despite everything we went through in the hyperspheres, I've often missed the closeness we had during missions here.

Her unwavering faith in everything—the world, the messengers, life—was so blatant, so righteous, so attractive. And even though we kept lying to each other because we were supposed to be enemies and I'm sometimes a jerk, we fell in love.

That was years ago. Now we live in different Earths, and obviously we're not a couple anymore. Not for a long time. But we're finally not enemies.

So, moving even closer to them, maybe to about eight meters away, I shout, "Jane!"

The brunette's ponytail jerks to the left as she first peeks at her friend, maybe thinking her companion said something, but soon we make eye contact. Her eyebrows shoot up in surprise when she sees me, but they rapidly change to a furrow.

I get it. Based on her grimace, she's still not happy I lied to her. Boy, she definitely can hold a grudge. Still, this is better than what happened the second time we met in the hypersphere when she pointed a gun at me. Good times.

Jane rises to her feet in a rage, turns her capacitor around, and screams, "You motherfucker!"

Before I'm able to comprehend what's happening, she pulls the trigger. Time slows down as I enter my fast mode, but there are not many options. No matter how fast I am, evading a shot after the trigger is pulled is impossible.

I jump to the side to avoid the blast, but as expected, I'm not quick enough. A large chunk of my right thigh disappears, and a dull pain spreads through my leg. The shot barely misses the bone. Jane, in auto mode, keeps pressing the trigger.

And then, the worst possible thing happens. Her eyes go wide, and the shooting stops as a blast takes the back of her head out. Her weapon drops, and she falls like a doll.

Milliseconds later, her body disappears, a clear sign from the hypersphere that she's dead. I reach in her direction and scream. She's gone. While I'm still processing what happened, a lucky shot from the plateau gunners explodes too close, and the shock knocks me unconscious.

Chapter 7

NERVES

LOCATION: HYPERSPHERE

The raging water of the river, accompanied by an odd clicking sound from unknown insects nearby, wakes me up. As always, it takes some time for me to remember where I am and what just happened, but when I do, a wave of adrenaline hits me like a truck.

The battle is long over, but I saw Jane killed right in front of me. I might as well go ahead and say it—I killed her. It doesn't matter that she wanted to shoot me. The fact is I was the one who distracted her. Killing me was worth the risk of being hit by her enemies.

Rubbing my eyes in disbelief, my mind is flooded with memories of Jane. She was so unlike the women I used to date. She had principles and followed them to the end. Yes, perhaps she blindly trusted the messengers for too long, but that's part of who she is—who she *was*. She trusted people first and only shot them later.

But not today. I let out a sob. I had so much to tell

her, so many stories to share, and I was counting the days until our Earths could open a portal to meet her again. Never in a million years did I think she'd die like that, in front of me, with no closure.

As I swallow my sobs, my whole body feels numb. There's no time to mourn. People can still kill me, and I'm not ready to die. I want revenge. A primal rage starts to form. As always, anger is easier to deal with than sadness. So, I embrace it. Breathe it. The messengers will pay. The humans that shot Jane will pay.

Dry blood and dirt plaster my face, and I'm covered in dust. The fall also left a large scratch on my forehead. As I lean forward, a strong pain radiates from my thigh where Jane shot me. The plasma shot cauterized the remaining flesh, but I won't be able to walk very well with my leg like this. Which reminds me—I raise my head to have a better look. The place is deserted. Someone must have taken the injured blonde with them. Or maybe she died.

I decide to crawl toward the hill to observe the river and the place where the other people were shooting at us—at Jane—during the battle. Hopefully, no one's going to see and try to kill me again. My arms and legs are shaking as I drag myself to the hill where Jane was killed, and I stop to wait for the dizziness to go away.

Maybe she's still alive. My mind is still insisting this didn't happen, but there's no way she's back on Earth after that shot even if the rules in Pangea were lax like before—when we could survive if we didn't hurt our brains. *She's not coming back.*

I bend to one side to throw up. After several minutes, I force myself to keep crawling, because there's nothing else in my stomach even if I still keep getting the urge to empty it. When I reach the top of the hill, I see movement on the island. The armored troop transport is long gone, and Jane's friends are not around anymore. There's no one else here except me.

"Hmm," someone mumbles in pain nearby. The body is right next to me, and there's so much dust settled on top of her that she looks like part of the scenery. A glimmer of hope brings back my strength, and I drag myself the last few inches to the body. After I sweep off as much dust as I can, my heart sinks again. This is not Jane. It's Louise. She was the one Jane was trying to protect.

"Louise! Can you hear me?" I ask, but she doesn't answer.

Louise Bellaire was Ravi's girlfriend. Ravi, my best friend on Earth, was murdered, and a lot of people thought I had something to do with it. In truth, if it weren't for me, Ravi would be alive, even if I wasn't directly responsible for his death. Just like Jane.

Her shoulder is a mess of scrambled flesh and dirt, and her breathing quick and shallow. If I don't help Louise, she'll die. Except I'm in no shape to help her right now. I can't even walk. Fresh tears roll down my face, and soon I'm sobbing uncontrollably. Everyone I know ends up dead, and somehow, I'm always involved.

Louise rolls back a little, mumbling unintelligible words and bringing me back to reality. This is a hypersphere. There must be a way for me to help her. Everything that happens in Pangea is in our minds. Most people can't change hypersphere environments, but I can. For reasons still unclear to me, the messengers selected me when I was a child and trained me to manipulate Pangea.

Of course, as a neurocomputer scientist, I'm far

from being a doctor, but I did take several anatomy classes. I'm going to fix this.

I touch her shoulder, close my eyes, and concentrate. I can do this. Here, I'm usually able to change people's bodies to stop blood loss and even perform minor surgery. Granted, since I can't fly anymore, nothing is certain, but my powers *did* work on the barrier when I was drowning.

Most of Louise's tendons are destroyed around the affected area, as are her major muscles. This wasn't done by a plasma shot. It's shrapnel, probably from one of the projectiles. The ligaments there are just gone, and pieces of rock, metal, and dust are embedded everywhere.

Nodding to myself, I act quickly. First, I recreate the muscle fibers with my mind and then reconstruct the veins, just like I did years ago with Jane.

Saint Plehr, I can't believe Jane is dead. But I shouldn't be thinking about her right now.

I work on the cellular level to recreate the interior part of the blood vessels. Somehow, it's easier to do this than I expected. Whatever isn't allowing me to fly doesn't affect my ability to heal. Instead, the opposite is happening. It's as if my perception of smaller things has increased.

The bleeding quickly stops, and I start removing the most obvious piece of shrapnel and broken bones with my bare hands. There's no way for me to reconnect the large muscles and ligaments—they're too complicated—and no hope of rebuilding the bone structure. If she can't go back to Earth, Louise will still eventually die. But for now, this should do.

After she's stable, I do the same process on my own leg. Fortunately, my own injury is much cleaner and easier to deal with. Since the wound was cauterized by the shot, it's not bleeding, but I've lost muscle. My bones are intact, though, and the main arteries and veins are only scratched. Focusing, I recreate as much muscle as I can, but it's all botched work.

When I'm finally done, my face is drowning in sweat, and I think about my next step. I'll be able to walk, but only because I removed the nerve connections that communicate pain from my leg to the brain. But where to go, anyway?

Earlier, when investigating the landscape of the hypersphere, I noticed a few clearings and the remains of an abandoned city farther inland. There was no movement there, so it should be safe. It's about four kilometers from here. Maybe the deserted town will have something to help us.

Approaching Louise from the side, I crouch to lift her up over my left shoulder, keeping most of her weight off my injured leg. I leave her binoculars, weapons, and other gear here, so I have less to carry. She has definitely gained some weight since last I saw her. Maybe Ravi's death caused it. But she's still small enough that we're probably going to make it.

After she's balanced over my back, I slowly rise. Seconds pass, and I stay upright. This is doable. There's some wobbling, but nothing I can't handle. Once again, the lower gravity is on my side–although I no longer have feeling in my right leg. I may have overdone the nerve removal there.

The sun is getting lower in the sky, and soon it'll be night.

With a limp, I follow the faded trail toward the town. It's possible I'll meet someone along the way, and if that's the case, I hope they don't shoot me.

As we get closer to the trees—which have purple pulsating trunks—the bushes become scarce, and the diamond-shaped grass more prominent. There's a drastic change in vegetation here. Around the island and near the river, the climate is dry, with low bushes and even a few cácti, and I'm pretty sure I saw a blue kangaroo earlier. Here, however, the vegetation is greener, and the purple trees are getting bigger and bigger the farther inland we are.

The town is finally visible after more than two exhausting hours of walking.

I'm tired even after stopping several times to catch my breath. Paradoxically, it's easier to see the low buildings through the trees as the sun sets, because of their bright artificial lights. Perhaps there *are* people living there.

Dozens of small two-story gray apartments appear as I arrive at the main road. The external facades of the buildings still standing are mostly glass, but I can't see inside them. Based on the debris from the ones that were destroyed, I can tell they don't use any construction material known on Earth or Jora. It looks like reflective plastic.

"Hello?" I shout. "Anybody there? We need help!"

This place is eerily empty despite its inviting brightness. The rhombus-shaped grass is already taking over the road, spreading outward from the small lawns, and the only sound I hear is the chirping of something sounding like crickets but with a hard stop and a clacking noise between chirps. Occasionally, there comes a guttural sound that must be an animal.

After wandering the streets for about fifteen minutes, I decide to approach the concave door of one of the intact apartments. There's no visible knob or way of entering,

I extend my free arm to reach for the entrance. Just before I touch it, the door slides to the right by itself, a smell of decay wafting out of it.

"*Unit unassigned,*" says an incredibly soothing female voice. Despite her reassurance, I get the feeling this is not the best place to spend the night. I back away.

As I move along the road, the door of the next apartment catches my attention. To be more precise, I notice the *absence* of a door. Something inside must have exploded outward and taken down everything along the way.

Next to the unit rests a sad pile of black molten plastic or metal of some sort. It used to be an adjacent unit, but the only way I can tell it was the same type of building is that the remaining third of the destroyed walls is still connected to the one that's intact.

The apartment itself looks fine, as long as you don't care if you don't have a door or most of an entryway.

Inside, the walls facing the road are made of an impossibly clean see-through material. Although a passerby shouldn't be able to see us, the outside shines in as if there's nothing between us and the tiny lawn next to the sidewalk.

In the living room, blue floor tiles magically rise to transform themselves into fancy leather cushions, creating a long black couch. Gently, I lay Louise down. She moans but doesn't wake up.

I cross to the other side of the apartment, my head wobbling as I see myself reflected on the curved inside wall. My unbelievably young face—Pangea does that to you—is distorted and bloody, and the reality of what happened finally sets in. Reaching for the wall, I try to remain upright but instead fall to my knees.

The first time I willingly came to Pangea, I was greeted by Jane just as I saw my reflection on the glossy wall. Despite the fact she was mad at me, I always smiled remembering the odd situation she found me in—facing a wall, hands up like a criminal.

But not today. Not anymore. So, I let myself down on the floor, roll into a ball, and let the tears flow. Memories flood my mind, and I'm transported to the time when we were lovers and enemies, soldiers and scientists, healers and killers. I suddenly remember the smoothness of her skin, her citrus perfume, her pony-tail touching my arm as we embraced.

Eventually, I hear Louise sighing, and it brings me back to the present. For a brief moment, I look up at her and forget Jane even died, as if I'm trying to convince myself nothing happened. It's just a horrible mistake. A prank. Or a dream. It never happened. But soon, the feeling in my stomach takes over, and I sob again. I wish I had a bottle of tequila.

The thought of drinking something—anything—makes my mouth dry. I'm thirsty, and Louise needs water. So I stand, pull myself together, and enter the next room, trying to avoid seeing myself again.

An image flares in my mind and I freeze. I recognize the feeling. This is how we communicate with everything on Jora. But the system seems to be damaged, as if the house is trying but failing to communicate with me. After that, a faucet and a sink transform out of the wall, similar to how the couch was formed. When I move closer, a cabinet above the sink opens by itself to reveal several bulky glasses inside.

The crystal-clear water coming from the faucet

sounds like music to my ears, and I drink it after only a little hesitation. If this is going to kill me, so be it. It's not as if I'll be able to build a contraption to create water anyway.

When I'm back to the living room, I check on Louise and try to give her some water. Her forehead is hot. She has a fever. No matter what I do here, I can't fight an infection. My own leg is starting to hurt, and I'm sure it will soon be infected as well. As I'm thinking about our fate, still holding my hand against her head, Louise finally opens her eyes.

"*Enculé!*" she yells, and then she spits in my face.

Louise tries to move away from me, but she's too weak. She immediately screams in pain and reaches her hand to the afflicted area. Blood spills from the wound, soaking her hand. Just from this slight movement of her body, the damaged bones must have pierced her already-wounded shoulder. The more she moves, the worse it's going to be. She hyperventilates and becomes still.

"Please calm down," I tell her. "I won't hurt you."

Her eyes move around the room and come back to glare at me. "What are you doing with me?" Her eyelids begin to close, and her eyeballs move erratically. "You're a *monster!*" A groan escapes her lips. "A monster! You even killed your *best friend*—" And just like that, she loses consciousness again.

I can't believe it. These irresponsible messengers of the gods can't stop killing people, and I keep getting blamed. I did not kill Ravi. And Louise is getting worse by the minute. Yes, I can close wounds and stop bleeding, but I can't fight off whatever bacteria has set in.

"I need antibiotics!" I shout to no one in particular. Maybe there are some in the bathroom. And a surgery room, with real surgeons—and unicorns. But this apartment doesn't have anything to offer me. Perhaps some other house nearby has the drugs I need.

It's night when I hobble outside. Two beautiful moons—each one roughly the size of Earth's—shine above, and the streets are as bright as ever. It's not exactly cold, but the temperature has definitely dropped, and I shiver. Why is no one living here? Everything seems so convenient, except the parts that have been viciously destroyed.

I suddenly notice something has changed. To my dismay, a two-story house now stands in the middle of the road. With a triangular roof and a single chimney, it's shaped like many other homes I once saw on Earth. But instead of the usual plain façade, the outside is all white with a beautiful yet unsettling pattern of flowers, bees, kittens, and dogs. I am surely going insane.

Chapter 8

PRIMAVERA

LOCATION: HYPERSPHERE

After I climb the porch stairs, the old wooden door —painted with a large orange lion on top of a cliff—opens. An incorporeal female voice says, "Welcome, Zeon." Whoever is here must be expecting me. This could be a bad sign, but I must get help for Louise.

Reluctantly, I enter the house. The inner walls are also filled with images of cats, dogs, and nonsensical patterns. If I didn't know any better, I could be convinced this was a daycare and that I had brain damage from earlier.

In the kitchen, a small girl with long, straight brown hair is handling an iron kettle. She's wearing a one-piece flowery dress that goes all the way to her knees, along with pink sandals. Next to her, a circular table and a few chairs are set out as if she's expecting company.

"Hi, Zeon! Beautiful night, isn't it?"

Do I know her? She's familiar, but I always have difficulty with names and faces.

"Uh…" I limp toward her. My leg is in worse shape than I thought. A red-and-white checkered tablecloth tops the table, with two white ceramic mugs on it. They have teabags in them. That's it. I'm officially nuts.

"Please sit," says the girl. "And sorry 'bout the mess. I don't have many visitors." Her unnatural blue eyes watch me. She looks and acts like a twelve-year-old, maybe younger. It's a stark contrast to everyone else in Pangea who looks to be in their late teens, including me.

"Uh…" I say again as I pull out a chair and sit on it. "Who are you?"

"I'm Primavera. I'm so happy you're here." She giggles. "And now, you'll finally remember me."

She brings the kettle to the table and smoothly fills both mugs with boiling water. The tea bags bleed red.

"Remember you?" I ask.

After setting the kettle back on the transparent glass stove top, she slaps her hands to her face and blurts, "Almost forgot! Godfather asked me to give you something." Then she sprints into the living room.

Seriously, I wonder what game the gods are playing. The asshat messengers must be watching me, and she's probably bringing antibiotics. This is great, but that'll only help Louise in the short term, though it may be enough for my own wounded leg.

She comes back and holds out two objects, a sly smirk on her face. "He said you'll need these." It's like a slap in my face. Neither object is drugs. My cowboy hat is in her left hand and my sunglasses in the other. If she weren't so young, I'd probably yell at her.

Instead, I fidget. "Why do you call me Zeon? My name might as well be Bob for all you know."

Unexpectedly, her childish laughter fills the room,

and she tries to hide her small face in her hands. I can't help but smile back. Her reaction lifts my spirits.

She blushes and wipes a tear from her cheek. "You always crack me up, Zeon. So funny! You can only see my house if I let you. And we've met several times in your dreamspheres. But you always forget about me." A cute frown appears on her face. "But not today! This is a hypersphere." She grins again.

I don't take my things from her hands yet. "In my dreamspheres?"

"Yes. In your dreams. Unfortunately, people forget most of their dreams."

Perhaps noticing my hesitation, she drops the hat and the sunglasses on the table. Her mood also changes, her face transforming into a grimace.

"Who's your godfather?" I ask her.

"Ermey."

I take a deep breath. The name doesn't ring a bell. "Primavera, who are you, exactly?" The question I am thinking is actually *what are you*, but I don't want to be rude.

"What do you mean?"

I hold my hands up. "Well... where were you born? How did you get here?"

Confusion crosses her face for a second. "I was born here, in Pangea, like everyone else. You're from here as well!"

I laugh nervously. She doesn't know anything. She's just a kid. Maybe she's crazy, just like me.

"No. I'm from Jora, one of the Earths." I wave around the room. "The gods built this place."

She snickers. "No one created Pangea. This is just one of its many hyperspheres. And they're not gods.

They're just aliens—you know that, right?" She grins again.

I hold my breath for a moment. Maybe she does know something. "Is this... Ernie... a god?" I ask.

"It's Ermey. And no, he's not a god. He's a messenger of the... gods." She rubs her temples and sips her tea. The liquid must be really hot, since she stops drinking and blows on it.

I press further. "I take it you don't like them? The gods, I mean."

Her eyes show a flash of anger, and she looks down. "No. My godfather told me several stories about the gods. He likes them, but I don't think they're nice people. In all the stories, they're mean."

Interesting. Maybe this messenger isn't a fan of the so-called gods. I must meet him. Perhaps he can help us in this fight.

"Primavera, this house. It was not here earlier. Where did it come from?"

She raises her eyebrow as if offended by my question. "It's *my* house! It goes wherever I want it to go, to any hypersphere. Doesn't yours?"

She takes a bigger sip of her tea. I'm flabbergasted by her explanation.

"Uh... no?" I say.

She stares at nothing for a while. "Interesting." She drinks more of her tea and frowns at my mug, still untouched. "Why are you not drinking your tea? It's hibiscus."

Hibiscus? Pangea surely has some weird-ass names.

Primavera's eyes widen, and she stares at me as if reading my soul. "Of course!" A grin quickly forms on her lips. "You prefer coffee!"

Jumping up from her chair, she walks over to me.

Instinctively, I throw my arms up to protect myself, but she just eyes me curiously. You have to understand that people often try to kill me, regardless of what my prison-assigned AI therapist says. I slowly lower my arms as she shrugs and takes the teabag out of the mug.

Next, she walks back to her seat and closes her eyes. The result looks like magic. Without her touching my drink, the red liquid becomes black in the middle, and the blackness rushes to replace the rest of the tea as if an invisible pen is dropping black ink into it. The smell of delicious dark coffee hits me. I have found a new best friend.

"How—how did you do this?" The flabbergasting continues.

Primavera raises her eyebrow. "Do what? The coffee? Anyone can do this. It's so easy! I remember what I want—in this case, coffee—then I replace the molecules with my memory. The coffee molecules communicate the changes to the tea molecules nearby until everything is changed." She puts down her mug on the table and slides it closer to me. "Now you try."

Concentrating, I oblige her for a while, but unfortunately, I'm not able to do it. It probably takes some practice. "I'm sorry, but I can't do it. You've been here since you were born, so it's easy for you."

Primavera picks her mug back up and shrugs. Maybe I'm reading too much, but I think she's disappointed in me. I feel like I'm a level-one mage meeting a level-100 wizard in an online role-playing game I didn't want to play in the first place. At least I was able to break the barriers with my mind.

I look eagerly at her. "Primavera, do you know anything about those energy barriers?" I ask.

Ignoring the fact it's night, I finally start drinking my coffee. It's going to be a long time before I'm able to sleep again. My mind will just keep torturing itself with Jane's demise.

"The what?" asks Primavera.

She must've seen them. "The force fields that don't allow people to cross."

"Oh, those." She nods. "They're called veils. The gods' veils. The messengers put them there to protect the humans from themselves." Her face clouds. "It's so sad. They've been killing each other for a long time."

I set my mug back on the table. "Do you know what's happening here?" The coffee blend isn't right. I prefer dark, bold coffee, and this is mild. I'll let her know about it later. People love to have constructive feedback when they do something nice.

She grabs her mug with both hands. "There's a war going on, and lots of people have died. Ermey told me the messengers lost control of the situation."

"Aren't you afraid someone will hurt you here?" Great idea, Zeon. Let's make a young girl scared.

"No. They can't hurt me. Also, they can't see me if I don't let them."

"Why do you trust me, then?"

Perhaps I should shut my mouth and think before I speak. I'd be running for the hills if a stranger kept asking me these questions.

"Because I know you," she says. "More importantly, Godfather trusts you. And you don't even know how to make coffee. I'd turn you into a frog before you even got close to me." She laughs. I also laugh, not knowing if she's joking.

A spike of pain chooses that moment to jolt my leg.

It's swollen, and the damage must've reached an area that still has pain receptors. I grunt.

She stops her mug midway to her mouth. "Are you hurt?"

Before I can reply, she's already next to me, studying my wound. "You did a very bad job here..." She twists her mouth, assessing the result of my technique. "I thought you'd know more about Pangea." She gives me a disappointed look. I forgot to tell her my specialty is to let people down.

"Geez, thank you. It's not like I *grew up* here."

She flips her long hair—probably to get a better look at my leg. "Sorry. It's just the stories my godfather tells me. He said you saved billions of people."

"Well, this is me." I tap on my chest. "What you see is what you get."

Perhaps I should stop bickering with little girls.

"Sorry again. Let me help you." The way she says that gives me a sense of dread. She bites her lip.

"You can fix this?" I ask. "Like you did with the coffee?"

She sighs, taking a moment to gather her thoughts. "Not exactly. It's way harder with living things, especially people. And it can turn really bad. You know, your body is not actually here. Nothing is real here." She shrugs. "Coffee is just stuff. It has no mind." She points at the mug. "But your body in the hypersphere springs from your mind."

"Uh... what?" I'm slightly concerned I'm being lectured by a child. This younger generation is too smart. Soon I'll be homeless and begging for money on the streets.

"We must change your mind," Primavera explains. "It must *think* your body is fine. Then it'll be fine. But you'll have to help me find the right place. I know my own mind backward and forward, but not yours."

Fascinating. In the past, we could have been badly injured, lost limbs, or become paralyzed here, but every time we returned to Earth or Jora, we'd be fine, and we'd return to Pangea good as new. The same thing happened when I woke up here with my arm healed.

Now that Primavera mentions it, it starts to make sense. The brain is projecting our body, and feedback from the body changes it. So unlike in reality, where both body and mind are independent, here the body is a direct reflection of the mind.

Primavera takes this moment to tell me that the consistency, irregularities, and texture of the skin—and even of the flesh and bones—are somehow stored in our neurons next to the pain sensors. Of course, she doesn't use these exact words. She's only a little girl, after all.

When she touches my head, I shut my eyes to focus. Once again, I'm doing brain surgery on myself. On the plus side, I'm not doing it alone this time. I have a twelve-year-old helping me.

Finding the place in my brain that senses my leg is easy. They're the same neurons I had to numb to stop the pain in my leg. As soon as I detect them, Primavera's presence enters my mind like a dazzling bright ghost, making my head tingle. It doesn't hurt—quite the opposite. It feels warm, cozy, and friendly. But the unexpected sensation makes me gasp, and the connection is abruptly cut.

When I open my eyes, I find her eyes surveying mine. "Are you okay?" she asks, rubbing her hands.

I smile thinly. "It's okay. I'm just not used to this."

She places her tiny palm back on my head again. "Sorry. I'll do it slower."

Focusing on the parts of my brain that sense my hurt leg, I wait for her to reappear in my mind. Unlike before, now I'm prepared, welcoming her strong presence. With no hesitation, she quickly arrives at the areas in my left brain that sense my thigh and starts working on them.

A warm sensation spirals around my wounded leg as we both change the perception of my leg by my brain. Effectively, we lie to the neurons that the leg is okay. This, of course, would never work on Earth even if we had the technology to do it.

The procedure is painless, and doesn't take more than a few minutes. When I open my eyes, my thigh is back to normal, and the muscles, skin, and pain receptors are all in the right places. We did it. As I think about what happened today and about Louise lying unconscious next door, an obvious question forms in my mind.

"Primavera." I swallow before I continue. "Can you bring people back from the dead?"

She walks back to her seat, looks down, and takes a sip of her tea.

"No." She shatters my hopes with a single word. "Dead people are outside of the... hyperspheres," she goes on. "In a place called Entropia. Nothing protects you there. Your mind... scatters around. Disappears."

Then Primavera looks up, and her eyes search my face. "But Ermey was able to save me."

Chapter 9

SURGERY

LOCATION: PRIMAVERA'S HOUSE

I open both palms in surprise. "Wait a minute. You died?"

A glimmer of hope rises in my mind. I should go back and help Louise, but perhaps I can still save Jane as well. The idea seems farfetched, but this *is* the hypersphere, after all.

Primavera's face clouds. "That happened years ago. I don't remember how I died." She abruptly drops her mug to the table.

"How do you know about it, then?"

"Ermey told me the story." Her gaze is distant now. The jubilant girl I met earlier is gone. Our conversation has touched a nerve.

"What did he tell you?"

She closes her eyes and raises her brows while hugging the mug with her hands as if it's a long-lost kitten. Then, she brushes a strand of brown hair off her forehead.

"He said I was playing on a hill by the river and fell

off a cliff. The current stuck me to the rocks, and I drowned."

My heart pounds in my chest. "And then what happened?"

She shrugs. "The first memory of my life is of him holding me in his arms. He said we were in Entropia. It's a very dark place." Primavera looks to her side and whispers. "It's where the gods live." With her hands almost imperceptibly shaking, she pulls the mug closer for another sip. Whatever she went through, it's not for the faint of the heart. Too bad there are no counselors in Pangea.

I glare at her. "Primavera, a dear friend of mine died today. I'd do anything to bring Jane back. Do you think I can talk to your, uh, godfather so he can teach me how to do it?"

She stops mid-sip and shakes her head vigorously. My heart skips a beat. It's not taking this story very well.

"I know how he did it," she admits. "But I'm sorry, Zeon. It won't do her any good."

"But how did he save you?"

There's a way, and she's living proof. Without thinking, I start nibbling on my left index finger—a habit I stopped a long time ago.

"You must be in Entropia at the moment of their death," Primavera says solemnly. "Even if you're a few seconds later, it's too late."

The rollercoaster of emotions I'm feeling leaves me speechless. Then, I hide my face in my hands.

"The other problem is that if you're in there," she continues, "you're dead as well, and it's almost impossible to come back." Her words stab another knife into my heart. "Ermey died to save me."

It's several seconds before either of us says anything. My coffee is now cold and miserable, just like my life and my analogies.

Primavera breaks the silence. "I'm sorry, Zeon. I really don't like talking about it."

Well, Jane is gone, and there's nothing I can do for her. But Louise is alive. Ravi also died because of me, and I don't want to leave another friend to the same fate, even if she hates me. And although Louise is unconscious and won't be able to help us, I have an idea for healing her shoulder.

After Primavera promises she won't turn anything into a frog, we walk to my apartment. Outside, the noise of unknown critters is suppressed by a sudden wind, and the abandoned road gives me the creeps. A chill goes through my spine and I finally sprint the rest of the way, leaving the little girl all by herself. Primavera follows, taking her time and eyeing me with a bemused smile.

"It's cold outside," I say defensively.

She wrinkles her nose at the mess I left in the living room. A trail of dirt highlights the path to the couch, filthy clothes on the floor and dried blood stains decorating much of the room.

"Sorry. I wasn't expecting visitors."

"It's not that." She shakes her head. "You've been careless. I had to disable the traps. You could've died!"

Traps? Before I can ask what she means by that, she walks toward Louise, who hasn't moved since I left her. Primavera kneels down next to the tiny woman, who's barely taller than herself.

As she caresses Louise's arm, Primavera's lips tremble, and her eyes water. "It's barbaric." I'm pretty sure I didn't know that word when I was her age. "All the violence. All the deaths."

I keep my mouth shut because I don't know how much Primavera trusts or interacts with the messengers. For all I know, her godfather may just be a wolf in sheep's clothing. Humans are violent, yes, but the messengers are the catalyst in the hypersphere. The deaths in Pangea are all on them.

"Her name's Louise," I tell her.

Primavera looks at me sidelong. "Louise? Do you know her?"

"Yes. We're friends." Well, we *were* friends. No need to elaborate.

I observe her deformed shoulder and the bloody mess I left behind me. Thankfully, blood in the hypersphere doesn't bother me the same way it does on Jora.

Primavera's lips tremble as she touches Louise's arm. "It's bad, Zeon," she says, her voice wavering. "They're going to die!"

Children crying has always unsettled me. I don't know how to react. On one hand, there's the urge to hug her close and comfort her. On the other hand, I want to know what the hell she means by "they."

Before I can ask, Primavera touches Louise's belly with her other hand.

Saint Plehr, no. My eyes widen as understanding fills my mind. Louise is pregnant. I begin to hyperventilate, but the number one rule of panicking is that only one person in a pair may freak out at any time. It's unfair the little girl called dibs on it, but as the adult in the room, I must remain calm.

"It's okay, Primavera," I lie, my voice breaking. Kneeling before her so I don't look like a giant, I open my arms, and she hugs me, her body shaking. "It's okay."

After a while, Primavera pulls herself away from me. "I can't help her. I don't know her brain!"

I lay my hands on her shoulders and stare into her light-blue eyes. "We can do this," I say with more confidence than I actually have. "Do you trust me?" I ask.

She nods, her chin shaking. She's a strong kid.

The reason she can't change other people's minds on a whim is that she doesn't know the anatomy of the human brain. I know, shocking. Kids don't learn anything in school nowadays. Without me helping her to heal my thigh, she wouldn't have been able to do it. I, in contrast, have specific knowledge of what a brain looks like, how it functions, and what parts respond to external stimuli.

This was part of my education in becoming an expert in neurocomputers. It turns out that connecting your brain to peripherals to make you think you're in a virtual world requires the professionals to know the brain inside and out. I know all the nerves and pathways to the human brain. It's my day job—or used to be.

I stand up and walk behind the couch, looking at her with a serious expression. One way or another, we're going to fix this. My only fear is that—if this ends badly—it'll traumatize Primavera even more.

When I'm next to Louise, I gently touch her cheek with my right palm. Following my lead, Primavera presses lightly on our patient's head. I'm still new at this, and need her help. Primavera doesn't know where Louise's shoulder is located in her brain, but I have a good idea of how to find it.

Primavera's presence and mine both meet inside

Louise's brain, and I know exactly where to go. As luck would have it, the two sides of our brains are similar in the motor and somatosensory cortexes. This means comparing one side to the other should help us to identify what's wrong, and the fix should be to mimic the neuronal charges and shapes of the healthy side.

As we search for the right neurons to change, I wonder if the messengers do something similar when they bring us to Pangea. For starters, our bodies here look like they're barely out of our teens. Louise is completely blind on Earth, yet here she sees perfectly. Maybe I'll understand the process of creating someone's body from their mind someday and get better at it.

After ten minutes of painstakingly studying Louise's brain, we're ready to alter it. I found the neurons that sense Louise's left and right shoulders. We only need to copy their electric states and configurations to the other side. How hard this can be, right? I open my eyes to check on Primavera, and she opens hers a fraction of a second later. Her fingers shiver, but she gives me a weak smile.

Closing my eyes again, I enter my fast mode. For a moment, I'm worried Primavera won't be able to keep up with me, but she does so without hesitation. She's back to the place we need to be seconds before me. Really, it shouldn't be a surprise. I have abilities in Pangea because I spent a month here as a child. Primavera has lived in the hypersphere all her life. If anything, I'm slowing *her* down.

Primavera's presence in Louise shows as a bright, soothing purple light. Mine shows as a faint yet intrusive white blob. The little girl follows my dim glow obediently. As I show her the neurons for the healthy shoulder side, she uses it as a guide to alter the brain cells on the other side. Easy as pie.

When we're done, it feels anticlimactic. We open our eyes and look at Louise. Her breathing stabilizes, and her shoulder, chest, and upper arm are perfectly—magically—fine. Her shirt, though, is still completely ripped. Primavera rises and brings me a baggy t-shirt from another room. Oddly enough, it has the picture of—based on the description—*Juan* Bon Jovi on it. It's too big for Louise, but should do for now.

"What now, Zeon?" Primavera asks, washing her hands on a circular white sink formed from the floor right in front of her, literally in the middle of the living room. Seeing something so mundane brings my mind back to Jane. Taking a deep breath, I try to think of something else. There's nothing I can do about her death now.

"I need to take Louise back to her people," I say, "but everyone there seems to hate me."

As I consider what to do next, an obvious solution comes to mind. "Primavera, do you have tweezers?"

Chapter 10

OF BEARDS AND HORSES

LOCATION: HYPERSPHERE

Primavera brings me tweezers from a hidden cabinet in the bathroom and leaves me to it. Several hours later, the sun is already rising, and we're standing outside looking at each other in amusement.

While she was out, I plucked hairs from my five-o'clock shadow in equally spaced spots. It hurt like hell, but the pain helped me map part of my body—in this case, my beard—in my brain. Then, I worked on those neurons until I had a respectable beard that would've taken me more than a month to grow naturally.

Despite all my work, Primavera doesn't even flinch when she sees me. Perhaps my idea isn't going to work. Meanwhile, she has a towering surprise of her own following behind her.

Primavera puts her hands on her hips. "I see you've been busy." She grins.

"And how about you?" I gesture at the creature she brought with her. "Don't you ever sleep?"

A majestic chestnut horse, about a meter and a half

tall, trots exaggeratedly behind her. Primavera herself can't be more than one meter and thirty centimeters tall, and her head doesn't even reach the back of the horse. The large animal has fluffy white fur below its knees and a patch of white on its face between muzzle and forehead.

She doesn't have to lead the horse; it happily follows her as she gets nearer. "I don't need to sleep," she says. "I just move between hyperspheres and dreamspheres." She chuckles. "I can go skiing, meet new people, and play-fight with giant grasshoppers. Don't you?"

I grin back. "No one fights with grasshoppers, Primavera. You're... special."

But it does make a little sense that she doesn't need sleep. When this all started years ago, I'd spend the day on Earth and the night in Pangea, and still wake up rested. But jumping between hyperspheres is unheard of, and I had no idea dreamspheres existed until Dooria told me about them.

The mare behind Primavera kneels down on one leg and gently headbutts Primavera, reminding us of its —of her—presence.

I put my hands on my hips. "I didn't even know we could have horses here."

Primavera turns and pets the horse. "Her name's Dorothy. You can keep her for a while, as long as you take good care of her."

Dorothy lies down and begins rubbing her head on Primavera like a cat. The little girl grooms the horse's hair happily and absent-mindedly.

Scratching my nose, I try to hide my face from the girl. "She'll be in good hands," I tell her, but in truth, I have no idea how to take care of horses. Considering my luck with the people closest to me, Dorothy's chances of surviving the week are pretty low.

Trying to avoid thoughts of Jane, I walk over to the mare and raise my hand to touch her. Dorothy lowers her head, letting me caress her crest and forehead.

"Good girl!" I say, feeling the warmth of her skin below her coat. She nickers softly at me and twitches her tail.

"She likes you." Primavera giggles. "Even though you have this silly beard. Why did you do it?"

"I'm hoping the others won't know who I am. They're mad about something, and I still don't know why."

My facial hair is completely different now, not just the beard. The eyebrows are thinner and delineated after more careful, painful plucking. This is all I can do, considering the circumstances. I hope this hare-brained plan works.

"It won't work," Primavera says. "Your aura is brighter than the sun." She points her small index finger at my beard. "As you know, Bob," she jokes, "we recognize people here by their auras, not their faces."

She's right—I forgot I had an aura. Closing my eyes for a second, I focus on myself for a change. The brightness around me is like a flare. This is how I visualized people in Pangea in my mind map in the old days. Everyone had a bright light, including the messengers. So, mine, at least, is still there.

And how interesting. When I follow the path of my auras into my head, they converge into a small cluster of neurons. I'm pretty sure this is what connects us to Pangea. Maybe I can use this knowledge to send people there and back.

And yet, neither Louise nor Primavera has an aura

I can detect. Someone must've deliberately changed my perceptions and abilities in the hypersphere, making my job harder.

"Primavera, most people can't see auras." I chuckle. "And even if they did, I doubt they'd know it was me."

It's clear that spending her whole life here has probably made her aware of auras and how they differ. But humans live on planets, not in magic holodecks and wandering houses. Other than the two of us, I don't know anyone else who can see auras.

"Oh, well." She shoots a worried look at Dorothy. "Don't let anyone hurt her."

The rest of the morning, Primavera spends some time teaching me how to ride a horse. Although I own a cowboy hat, I've only seen a horse once in my life in what was a very awkward wakeup call the day after my twenty-first birthday. During the practice, Primavera looks so disappointed in me. I tell myself this should be a good lesson for her. Adults often don't know what they're doing.

It's mid-morning by the time we're ready to go, and I'm already tired from my second sleepless night. Luckily, Primavera brings me a large cup of coffee—which hits the spot—followed by a pink backpack full of supplies.

The pair of jeans I found when Primavera was out fits me perfectly. I briefly consider wearing an odd white t-shirt with the words "Kirk Cobain" and "Moksha" on it, but my spider t-shirt reminds me of Jane, and I'll keep it even if it's dirty.

The next thing is to decide what to do with Louise. We gave her water when she woke up earlier in the day, but her mind was still in a haze, and she immediately went back to sleep. She'll hurt herself if she wakes up scared in the middle of our journey.

So, I sling her body over the saddle, face down, and we cautiously tie her up with some rope Primavera brought. And by "we," I mean "she." What hurts me the most is the look of disdain Primavera gives me as she works on the knots.

"I don't know how to make knots," I tell her. "I'm used to plastic zip ties. Not that I'm in the habit of zip-tying women up." I laugh nervously. She frowns and shakes her head at me.

Thirty minutes later, I'm mounted on the horse behind the saddle, sporting my cowboy hat, my sunglasses, and a respectable beard. To be honest, Primavera tied Louise up in only five minutes. The rest of the time was wasted trying to get me onto Dorothy with another person already draped over the saddle.

When I'm ready to leave, Primavera points her index finger at the forest. "Just follow the trail heading west out of town and through the forest. I often see humans there."

Frowning, I ask "West? How do you know that's west?"

She shrugs. "They're cardinal directions. You know, based on how the sun moves in the sky." She crosses her small arms and nods her head in the direction of the plateau. "The river is north from here."

"Right, of course," I say, feeling stupid. "Twelve kilometers? This is going to take a while. The pace through the forest is going to be slow."

"Be safe," she tells me solemnly, caressing Dorothy's nose. "But more importantly, keep *them* safe."

"I will."

"And please don't tell anybody about me." She looks at me with her young, beautiful green eyes. "Ermey said I'd be in danger if other people found out."

Well, explaining how I healed Louise without mentioning Primavera is going to be hard, but it's impossible to say "no" to her. No decent human would want to break her heart.

"Don't worry, I won't say a word," I say. "And it's not like anyone would believe a little girl helped me, anyway." I laugh, and immediately she pouts her lips. "No, Primavera." I chuckle. "Not because of you. You're awesome!"

Her face brightens, a big smile lighting her features. Oh, the joys of being young and naïve.

Then, as if guessing we're done here, Dorothy begins her weird trot by herself. The lower gravity is probably responsible for her odd walking. The mare doesn't seem to respond to my instructions, but luckily, she's going in the right direction.

As we move into the forest lining the town, the tall trees with purple trunks remind me of my first encounter with Jane. That day, I was able to carry her out through the canopies and fly like a superhero. She thought I was an angel, but she couldn't have been further from the truth. Unless she meant an angel of death.

The trail is sometimes uphill and sometimes down, never making up its mind in one direction or another. Although the trees are thick around us, once in a while I can spot the flat mountain in the distance, making me wonder who's there and why they're fighting. There's no battle going on today.

Considering how dense the forest is, this trail

through the middle looks too perfect. Someone spent a long time cleaning it up. The ground is mostly dirt, with a few irregular roots as thick as my arm sprouting up along the way.

Two hours later, we're still surrounded by forest with no signs of civilization, and one of the energy walls they call veils is only a few trees ahead of us. It's the end of this sector. Perhaps Primavera was wrong, and the people I'm looking for are somewhere else.

Meanwhile, Jane's no longer on my mind. Instead, an animalistic desire to pee is pushing me to the edge. As always, I had too much coffee. Resigning myself to the fact I'll have to climb back on Dorothy later, I step down from the horse to hide behind a tree and do the deed.

Despite the way she's awkwardly slung across on the top of a horse, Louise remains asleep. During her unorthodox surgery, I took some time to check on her belly. If memory of my biology classes serves me, the size of the fetus indicates it's about two months old.

It's almost funny. Although Ravi has been dead for two years, I have an unreasonable anger toward her. It's as if she betrayed him somehow. But I know it's an irrational feeling. She deserves to be happy, and it's not as though Ravi could drop from the sky to be with her.

At that moment, someone drops from the sky, taking me by surprise. He lands on me and throws both of us to the ground. My hat flies away, and the fall knocks the wind out of me. I wasn't even able to finish relieving myself, and I fidget for a moment, trying to get my pants back in order.

As the dark-skinned man pins me to the ground and starts yelling, the face I see makes absolutely no sense.

"What did you do to her?" Ravi shouts, waving the dagger in his hand.

Yes, Ravi. My dear friend, who was murdered on Earth right in front of me, is going to kill me. His right cheek has a large slash-shaped scar, and he looks like a homeless guy with his fraying dark-blue shirt and dirty flat-front navy pants.

"Let me talk!" I shout back at him, but it comes out way weaker and more high-pitched than I wanted. I show him the palm of my hand as if it could stop me from being stabbed. A wheezing sound comes from my lungs, so I take some extra breaths.

Out of the corner of my eye, I see shirtless John using his massive muscles to pull Louise off Dorothy as if she weighs nothing. The horse ignores the commotion and grazes on a small patch of grass which has thrived in the shadows of the trees just long enough to be eaten without ceremony. Louise, still unconscious, is taken away.

John is a young black man, and he's clearly in better shape than the rest of us. On Earth, he's in his sixties and in a wheelchair. Regardless of where you meet him, however, he's always so alive and in charge. Today he looks like a black Hulk, including the ragged shorts. Stupid sexy John.

"She's fine!" I say, recomposing myself. "I was bringing her back to your camp, I swear!"

When I'm about to sit up, ropes drop all around us, and several of the old protectors of Earth slide down. Even Frederico with his ugly mustache is here. I look up and find a complex system of planks and tree-houses above us. So that's where they are. Too bad I can't see auras anymore.

Ravi takes this moment to leave me to his friends

and go after Louise, who seems to be regaining consciousness. Meanwhile, Vladimir, a lieutenant captain in the Russian navy, steps on my leg, hard. He gives me a sadistic smile. Like John, his clothes are worse for wear, but I have never seen Vladimir with a dirty sleeveless shirt and ripped jeans until today. His battered outfit makes him look even more dangerous.

John stands by his side, eyeing me with suspicion. He's carrying a large rifle-like capacitor on a strap—an energy weapon from Pangea. Luckily, they don't seem to recognize me—if they did, I'm sure I'd already be dead. Granted, getting knocked down by a ghost wasn't in my plans, but as long as they don't know I am Zeon, their supposedly former friend, I should be safe. My hairy disguise seems to be working so far.

"You look familiar," John finally says. "What's your name?"

You don't want to be John's enemy. I'm so glad I have him by my side again and that they don't know who I am.

I open my eyes, smile, and say the first thing I think of.

"My name's Zeon."

PART II

To know your Enemy, you must become your Enemy.

—Sun Tzu.

Chapter 11

ANTONIA

LOCATION: HYPERSPHERE

"Goddammit!" I shout, mad at myself, and Dorothy snorts in response. I close my eyes and clench my teeth, waiting for the inevitable.

Oddly enough, John doesn't shoot me. Not yet, anyway. When I open my eyes, I see him frowning. "Zeon? What a strange name." He waves at Louise nearby. "Where did you find her?"

Vladimir steps harder on my leg, and I yell in pain. Perhaps they don't know who Zeon is. But how is that possible? Primavera said this was a hypersphere, but maybe she's wrong. Perhaps this is a dreamsphere where nothing is real. This might explain why I don't see their auras and why I'm always caught by surprise.

"There was a battle going on," I explain. "An explosion knocked me down. When I woke up, everyone else was gone, and I found her wounded and alone." I gulp. "I mean, not alone. The horse was next to her." I nod rapidly. "No one brought a horse to us."

Vladimir and John stare at each other for a while,

and John turns back to me, grabs his capacitor, and touches my face with the end of the double barrels.

"Listen to me, you goddamn little prick. I'm going to ask you a few questions. If I'm not satisfied with your reply, I'll pull the trigger and blow your head off. It's as simple as that."

I gulp. I'm bad at these games even when I know the correct answer.

"What country are you from?" he continues.

"The United States," I lie. They probably have no idea what the Atlantic Alliance is. Also, saying I'm not from Earth is definitely the wrong answer. "Why are you asking me these questions? I saved Louise's life!"

John narrows his eyes at me.

"Shut up!" Vladimir says in his strong Russian accent, pressing my sore leg again. I moan in pain. My brain still remembers the damage to that thigh, and his aggression is not making it any better.

"Give me a description of Antonian football," John demands.

My mouth opens, and I stare at him. Now they're making up words.

Wait, I know what's happening. This is a test. Taking a deep breath, I go into my fast mode so I can think. Obviously, this is some kind of code. They must be checking whether I'm from Earth, but perhaps using the name "American" would be too easy. Antonian sounds like a college. Maybe from San Antonio, Texas?

I try to buy time. "College or professional football?" This questioning is so surreal it reminds me of Monty Python.

John laughs and brings his weapon up a bit. "Ah, great question!" But the cartoonish lime-green double ellipsoids on top of the gun are still pulsating with energy, ready to fire. "I don't think anyone not from the U.S. would even know the difference. However..." He frowns, and the barrels of the weapon are again pointed at my head. "Since you asked, what *is* the difference between college and professional football?"

I look cross-eyed at the exquisite square barrels right in front of my face. "Uh..." In hindsight, I should've paid more attention. "I don't know. I thought they were the same."

John relaxes again, puts away his weapon, and nods at Vladimir. The Russian captain hesitates, his eyes shifting from me to John, but he finally takes his shoe off my leg, although not before stepping on it a little bit more.

"It makes sense," Johns says. "Few people know the difference, and if you did, I'd have to shoot you." He grins. I think he's joking, but I'm not sure. "You're definitely one of us."

I sit up and take my time to inhale, exhale, and rub my leg. What an odd way to verify my planet of origin. And it obviously didn't work, since I lied.

Ravi joins us and walks right next to John, looking at him with death in his eyes. Ravi's head is at the same level as John's enormous chest, but the shorter man doesn't even flinch. He just looks up at John, invading his personal space, unafraid of him.

"She's *fine!*" Ravi finally says. "No sign of any wound. Zeon didn't do anything with her besides tying her." He gives a quick glance in my direction, but his anger is directed at John, not me. "She was still alive after all, just like I *told you*, Jonathan."

Funny, I never knew John was short for Jonathan.

John, as always, stands his ground. He looks Ravi

up and down before eyeing me. "Zeon, did you see any other woman with her?"

My heart sinks. "Yes. Jane." My mind takes me back to that horrible moment, her head exploding in front of me. "The guys on that transport, I think—they killed her." I hate that I have to relive it again.

John steps in front of Ravi and turns his back to him as if taking the angry man out of the conversation. "You mean Jean. When it happened, we were too far away to help her. And we thought Marie was dead as well, despite Raj telling us we should go back and look for her."

Ravi walks around John, his thick eyebrows furrowing. He must be as confused as I am.

"Uh..." I say, unable to formulate a thought at first. If I were a superhero, this would be my one-liner.

I resume eye contact with John. "Could you repeat that?"

John chuckles and extends his arm to help me stand, but instead, I just look at him as if it's a trap. "Come on, Zeon. Are you trying to be funny? You have a lot of explaining to do."

Reluctantly, I grab his hand and rise to my feet, trying to understand what's going on. They're so close to me that I have to move my head from left to right to take everything in.

"John, what's your name?" I ask, again without thinking.

He frowns and crosses his broad arms. "Please don't call me Jon. I hate that. I'm Major Jonathan Tuyson from the United States of Antonia."

Slap my ass and call me Freddy. These people aren't from Earth. The fictional character Sherlock Holmes once said that when we eliminate the impossible, whatever remains, however improbable, must be the truth. Or maybe it was Surelock.

Still, these people are definitely from *an* Earth. The messengers mentioned the possibility of more than two parallel Earths, but I never gave that possibility a second thought. I wonder how many Earths are out there. And more importantly, who in the tickle was Antonio?

"I'm sorry, I'm a bit lost." I force a smirk.

Then it hits me—I didn't kill Jane. My arms and legs go instantly numb, and I lean against a nearby tree. Bittersweet emotions rush through me. I killed someone else. They called her Jean. Saint Plehr, I'm so relieved.

Except someone *just* like Jane has died. Whoever she was, she must've shared a lot of the characteristics making my Jane special. Now she's gone, and I'm still the reason.

After a long pause, I continue my lying. "I don't know what's happening here. I woke up in this place and found Louise—I mean, what's her name again? But I have no idea where I am."

Ravi—Raj, actually—remains silent, glaring at me.

"Marie Belliveau," Jonathan replies, unfolding one of his arms and gesturing at the trees behind us to where they're keeping her. "She was badly hurt in the battle yesterday. Now she's completely fine and with a different... wardrobe. What happened to her?"

I rub my forehead, thinking quickly and lying yet again. "I don't know. She was like that when I woke up."

He squints his eyes. "So you told us. And she had a horse next to her. Despite the fact we've never seen a horse here."

"That's... odd," is all I manage to say.

Raj bares his teeth at Jonathan. "I'm going to check on Marie. This is *not* over!'

The large man completely ignores him. "Do you know anything about Pangea?" Jonathan asks.

An award-worthy fake expression of concern crosses my face. "Pangea?" I shake my head.

Jonathan looks at the one who's supposed to be Frederico. "Alfredo, is this even possible?" He's Alfredo now. My head is going to explode. "You know," Jonathan continues, "him waking up only now, not knowing anything about what happened to Terra?"

So, they call their Earth "Terra." Interesting.

Alfredo scratches his pretentious mustache. "There may have been a few survivors on Terra." He has a thick Italian accent, exactly like Frederico. "But I'm surprised someone from the United States survived."

"The last memory I have is when I was driving and another car hit me," I lie, thinking on my feet. "And next thing I know, I'm here."

"Hmmm," Alfredo says. "Perhaps you were in a coma."

The long sleeves of his denim shirt are rolled up his arms, and the unbuttoned top of the shirt shows too much of his unsightly hairy chest. He's also wearing khaki shorts with a brown belt. The whole ensemble—plus his aforementioned mustache— makes me want to punch him.

"Yes, that's probably it. I had an accident and I'm in a hospital. And I'm dreaming." I breathe a sigh of relief.

Jonathan walks behind me and forcefully removes my pink backpack, no questions asked. "There are no hospitals anymore," he says, adjusting his weapon on his shoulder as he browses the contents of my backpack.

"Uh…" I mumble again. No hospitals? What the hell is happening on Terra, their planet? I try to think, but always forget my fast mode doesn't work well when I lie. "Are you sure? There must be an explanation…"

Alfredo scratches his forehead while holding his bare, unnaturally white elbow in the other hand. "Maybe you were visiting another country? One that still has hospitals?"

"Yes, that's it. Thanks, Alfredo!" I change my mind. This version of Frederico seems nice and smart, even though I want to hit him. "I was traveling, visiting New Zea— " I stop myself just in time. Who knows what New Zealand is called there? "You know, the island next to the big one in the middle of the giant ocean? I'm sorry, my accident must be making things hazy."

Jonathan wrinkles his forehead. "Obviously." His eyebrows are now so low they're actually covering his eyes—"since you forgot how to use your big words. You should know first impressions are the most lasting."

Alfredo's face lights up. "New Holland?" he asks with wide eyes. "The one near Australia, in the Pacific Ocean?" A pleasant smile appears on his face.

Hmm. Some names are still the same. I'm *so* going to screw this up.

"Yes! They drive on the wrong side of the road, right?" I laugh. Wait a minute. What if they don't drive on the left side there on Terra? "Or maybe not. Sorry."

Alfredo nods. "And your name is weird because your parents are from there."

"Yes. That makes complete sense. Thanks, Frederico—I mean Alfredo." The words 'thanks' and 'Frederico' should never be in the same sentence, not unless he's hitting himself.

Jonathan makes a throat-slicing gesture at Alfredo. "They speak English in New Holland. Clever liars give details, but the cleverest don't!"

"Uh..." I mumble again, not knowing what else to say. I take my sunglasses off to rub my eyes. It's been a tough day.

Alfredo comes to my rescue again. "I meant the indigenous people. The Māori. I spent a year there during my graduate studies."

The major shakes his head. Either he's not convinced or he's mad at Alfredo for helping me out. I'm not sure.

Meanwhile, Louise—or Marie, I guess—shows up, her arm slung around Raj's shoulder. She has a look of determination on her face, despite her red eyes and dried tears. Someone must've told her about Jean already.

With her body shaking, she moves away from Raj, and wobbles toward me. When she's close enough to slap me, she points an accusatory finger at my chest.

"It's *him!*"

Chapter 12

AFTERLIFE

LOCATION: HYPERSPHERE – TERRA'S SECTOR

Jonathan raises his eyebrows. "What do you mean?"

Her gaze lingers on my jersey for a moment before she looks at Jonathan. "Yesterday, during the battle, I saw someone in the river through my binoculars. That's why I left my position. I wanted to take a better look at him." Marie's voice breaks.

We can all guess what she's thinking. She broke formation when she saw me, then she got hit by shrapnel. Because of that, Jean came after her and ended up getting killed. And she must feel responsible, although I'm still the catalyst.

"The spider stamp on his black t-shirt gives it away." Her eyes drop down to the ground and Raj hugs her, keeping his angry stare on me.

"Zeon, I don't think you're being forthcoming with us," Jonathan says, "so we'll take you to one of the treehouses while we decide what to do with you."

Glancing up, I observe the canopies of the trees. A web of ropes and wooden structures is connected high above us—so high they look tiny from here. I'm confused. Instead of living in the not-so-small town nearby, with its advanced amenities and full wardrobes, they prefer to stay here like savages, with battered clothes.

At first, they try to make me climb a tree near the veil. However, I'm the worst climber ever, and I just can't do it. Reluctantly, they drop a basket barely large enough to fit my butt and pull me up in an undignified manner.

Not surprisingly, the fear of heights is one of my many phobias. Once I'm about fourteen stories from the ground, sweating, Raj leads me over planks connecting all the structures until we reach an empty platform touching a pale energy boundary. There, he drops my pink backpack and pushes me to the ground.

Raj is already walking away when I look back at him.

"Hey!" I call out. "What if I have to, you know, go?"

He turns his head back and smirks. "Then you just walk to the edge *carefully* and do it. This is not a hotel, Zeon." His angry grin reminds me of Ravi. Really, Raj is just like an extreme version of Ravi—one that's always mad at me.

But instead of leaving, Raj walks back to me through the planks, crouching. "By the way, Marie said she had a dream where she saw... someone. Did you see anyone else on the way here?"

I avoid his eyes. "No, of course not. It couldn't be me, though. I'm not a monster."

Raj grabs my left arm and pulls me up. Only now do I notice his impressive biceps. War and living like Tarzan apparently change a person.

Pulling me so close I can almost touch his scar with my chin, he shouts, "What did you say?"

"It's not what you're thinking!" I quickly reply. "She was delirious, probably having nightmares. She called someone a monster in her sleep."

He pauses, as if taking in what I just said. Then, with a grunt, he lets me go and walks across the plank to another tree. When he gets there, he pulls the wooden bridge toward him, leaving a gap so large it's impossible to jump.

"What about toilet paper?" I shout, but he's already walking away.

The wood cracks as I turn back to study my impromptu jail, giving me goosebumps. The platform I'm standing on is different than the others. Like Raj said, this is not a five-star hotel, but the other so-called rooms have the bare bones of civilization: roofs made of leaves, makeshift tables and chairs, and even some closed quarters for what I can guess is private stuff. The space where I wait is just a simple wooden platform made of smaller trunks tied together with ropes.

Unfortunately, I can't just power walk to the trunk of this tree and climb down. The branches supporting this platform stem from a tree across the energy barrier. For all intents and purposes, this is a jail surrounded by a plummeting death behind me and a light, transparent veil in front of me. And even if I somehow manage to open it, I wouldn't be able to climb down the tree on the other side by myself.

There have been so many revelations today, and I try to process them all. There are several Earths, and they're all fighting here. But I still don't know if the necromantes are here, or why we have these veils. And we never know exactly what's true in this place. No one has ever seen the gods, since they're just energy, and the protectors and messengers are unreliable narrators.

But I'm too tired to think about this. Coming to terms with my situation, I have a quick snack from my backpack before lying down on the hard surface. It's still about an hour until the sun sets, but after spending the night awake, I'm exhausted. Whatever betrayal or lying is left for me can wait until morning.

WHEN I OPEN MY EYES, it's dawn, and one of the annoying crickets is perched on top of my hand, right next to my face. While we can hear them all the time, I had never seen them before. The clacking sound must have woken me, and now I finally understand how they make it. While the chirp itself comes from the wings rubbing together, the sharper noise is their spider-like fangs snapping. The cricket is nearly the size of my hand, and I'm sure those fangs aren't just for show.

Because of that, I scream.

It's my typical reaction whenever an unknown insect is within striking distance of my nose. Frightened, I jump to my feet, and it flies away without doing any harm.

After removing all its siblings from my head, chest, and legs—and doing a unique ritualistic grunting dance to make sure they're all gone—I carefully pace toward the wall that's part of my prison. It's still early and fairly dark, so the perfect time for experiments.

There's a small gap between the last plank of my platform and the undulating energy boundary where only the branch of the tree goes through. The veil vibrates when I extend my arm to touch it. My hand moves back and forth with its movement.

With my eyes closed, I study its throbbing inner structure. The strands are woven in a plain diamond pattern, like a basket weave, appearing as fiber optics in my mind.

Next, I try to mimic what Primavera did with my tea—and I add a new set of threads to the veil. The new filaments emerge near the palms of my hands, slowly at first, but soon replacing the weak ligaments on the wall for dozens of meters in all directions.

Surprised, I take my hand off the wall. It becomes brighter and more opaque, and even its oscillating pattern changes as if it's responding to the new threads.

I look around me. There's no movement in the nearby treehouses. Whoever's on watch must've seen it, and I'm at the epicenter of this phenomenon, but I don't think there's a way to trace it back to me due to the trees around us. It probably just looks like the wall did something weird.

Taking a deep breath, I touch the veil again. I won't try to undo what I just did. Instead, I need to go deeper. It's odd—I can't fly or move objects with my mind anymore, but in Pangea, I now have a better understanding of the microscopic world.

There appears to be no limit for how high the veils will go—probably into space and beyond—and, similarly, there's no end in sight underground. Perhaps they're infinite in both those directions.

Next, my mind follows the fibers laterally, all the way to the plateau island, where they become a circle —actually, a cylinder—surrounding it. Soon, I have a top-down view of the whole battlefield. The energy veils light up in my mental map like an enormous wagon wheel with eight spokes ending at a hub, and the hub encircles the island.

The messengers must've divided the hypersphere into eight octants plus the area in the middle. If I remember correctly, I must have arrived in Pangea to the east of the southeastern spoke, gotten caught by it in the river, and woken up on the shore in another sector, where I met these people.

Eight octants, plus the island. Perhaps each of them is the spawning area of a different Earth. The messengers, yet again, lied to us by omission. If I'm correct, at least eight Earths exist out there. I have evidence of at least four: Earth, Jora, this one—Terra, with a creepy but nicer version of Frederico—and their enemies on the plateau. Assuming those people aren't from Jane's Earth.

Another oddity is the waterway I fell into. As I suspected, it surrounds the island, and there's neither a source upstream nor an outlet downstream; it just revolves around the flat mountain and if it weren't for the strong current, it would just be a lake.

I'm not going to ask them if they know about all the veils and the parallel Earths. Based on my fake story, I just got here and am none the wiser. If I did ask, they'd try to figure out what else I know, and I don't respond well to torture.

Eventually, the noise of the plank extending back to my platform snaps me back to my immediate surroundings. Instead of Raj, Alfredo's the one who comes to rescue me. Loud voices are shouting below us.

"Good morning, Alfredo." I glance at the veil.

Thankfully, it's back to normal, with no signs anyone changed it.

Alfredo extends a long piece of wood—or plastic, maybe—and reconnects my platform to their intricate tree system. "We have to go," he says, checking to make sure the thin bridge is stable.

I tiptoe across the plank toward him. "What happened?" There's a lot of movement below, and Jonathan is yelling at someone.

Alfredo also looks down at Jonathan. "Ivan just saw movement on Fortress. We're preparing for battle."

"Fortress?"

"Yes, Fortress Mesa. You must've seen it. It's on the island."

I have no idea what a mesa is. I thought it was just Spanish for table. Perhaps I should work on my English vocabulary.

"But why do I have to go with you? I'm your prisoner. I'd rather just make license plates."

Alfredo laughs. "We're nomads. That's the only way to stay alive here." His Italian accent gets thicker the longer he talks. "This is only one of our bases. Considering we may take a long time to come back, you'd be in trouble staying here by yourself." He waves at my improvised cell.

"How are we going to get down?" The basket that brought me up is nowhere to be seen.

Alfredo grabs one of several ropes they have hanging from the branches, drops one of its ends down, and wraps his legs around it. "Like this." Then he slides down, firefighter-style.

Saint Plehr! I really hate heights.

"The rope almost never breaks!" he shouts from the bottom.

Several minutes later, I make it down, but not after cursing them from above—I feel more courageous if they can't touch me—and burning the palms of my hands. It'll be a long time before I'm able to unclench my teeth. I hate to admit it, though—it was fun.

When I land, Jonathan is nearby, pressing a button on his large double-barreled capacitor. Capacitors are the energy weapons I've seen before, the ones with football-shaped cartridges on top. He's releasing the safety and it buzzes like a blender for a few seconds, and the trigger lights up green. This is a terrible design for battlefield use since it gives away your position at night, but then again, I'm not the architect of the hyperspheres.

"Everyone's getting ready," Jonathan says. "Ivan, how many vehicles are moving on Fortress?"

"All they can handle," Vladimir's doppelgänger says, holding his knees, seemingly out of breath.

"Okay," Jonathan says. "We'll have to spread out, so we don't all die together if they hit us."

A bag the size of a bed falls from the sky near us, and Raj drops down from another rope. Soon he and Jonathan begin to give everyone capacitors—everyone but me. But I don't actually care. Unlike them, I don't kill people. I won't let the messengers change that about me.

"Well, good luck to you guys," I say with a forced smirk. "I'll head somewhere else and get out of your way."

Jane is probably alive, and I must find her. I start to walk toward Dorothy, but Jonathan stops me midway with his incredibly large hand on my chest. Well, better than a weapon, I guess.

"No, Zeon. You're coming with us. And leave your

horse." He nods at Dorothy. "We don't want to attract any attention."

Dorothy calmly drinks from a bucket. At least someone's taking care of her. But Primavera's going to kill me. "We're abandoning her?"

"If we don't come back here, we'll search for her later. A horse is better than anything we have here." Oh, I see. She's just a weapon to him.

Alfredo gestures at the pile of capacitors next to Jonathan. "Should we give him a gun?"

Jonathan chuckles. "No. An ounce of prevention is worth a pound of cure." Okay, I've got to admit, this nonsense from him is starting to annoy me. "Zeon, stay with Alfredo and Ivan."

Vladimir—or should I say Ivan—smiles broadly when he hears that. Got it. He's the psychopath in this group.

"Raj, you stay close to Marie," Jonathan continues. "You'll approach the enemy from the south."

I give Jonathan an accusatory frown. That was odd. "Why is Marie going?" I say. "Don't women in her condition usually avoid combat?" I keep sticking with my habit of not thinking before I speak. Dozens of eyes turn to Marie for a reaction and she doesn't disappoint —her jaw drops.

Jonathan turns back and shouts, "What the hell are you talking about?"

"Uh... sorry. I meant to say she's hurt. *Was* hurt. Not pregnant or anything."

Marie remains silent. Raj, looking nothing at all like Ravi, steps toward me, but not before throwing a quick glance at her.

"Marie can take care of herself. But watch your mouth, *Zeon*." He says my name the same way Ravi used to whenever I ordered food sans peppers. "When I get back, I may kill you."

Without waiting for me to give a witty reply, Ravi and Louise—no, Raj and Marie—take the trail going east. Soon, everyone's on the move, each taking a different path through the forest.

Meanwhile, Alfredo, Ivan, and I take the only path following the veil. It doesn't take a genius to realize they're taking me as far away from the battle as possible.

Alfredo chuckles. "I'm surprised she didn't punch you on the spot. Marie's hit people for less—like saying Calafia's wine is better than Provence's."

I sigh. Anytime I come back to Pangea, the situation is always more complicated than I expected. Who are these people, and whom are they fighting? At least Raj is not my deceased friend Ravi. Don't get me wrong —I'd love it if he hadn't died—but talking to dead people creeps me out.

"So, Alfredo, what happened on your—I mean, on Terra? And what the hell is 'here,' anyway?"

"This is going to sound ridiculous." Alfredo exchanges glances with Ivan. "But everyone you met today is dead."

Chapter 13

KHOF

LOCATION: HYPERSPHERE – TERRA'S SECTOR

Ivan takes the lead, and I laugh nervously as we stride through the forest. It's not that I'm against fighting side-by-side with zombies. If you think about it, it actually sounds cool, as long as they're not trying to eat your brains.

But once you're in a situation like this, you begin to think you're crazy—and in case you're not, you start looking for escape routes.

"You don't look d-dead to me," I say.

It's impossible to run on this pseudo-trail due to the unpredictable roots and the winding nature of the path. Despite the conspicuous purple of the tree trunks, the pulsating roots themselves are covered in packed dust and thus indistinguishable from everything else on the ground.

"It's a long story," Alfredo says.

As we move forward toward the river, he takes this time to explain. The so-called gods, he tells me, made a mistake and accidentally created a parallel Earth. The only possible way to fix it was to get rid of one of those worlds. To keep it fair, the messengers sent moles to both Earths to destroy them, and the first to finish his mission would keep his own planet safe. Allegedly.

Anyway, about a year ago, someone on Terra took control of the arsenals of both the U.S. and Rossiya—I assume Russia—and initiated a nuclear holocaust. However, since they were asleep at the time and fighting in Pangea, their consciousnesses remained in the hypersphere.

We're not exactly running, but the pace is faster than walking. I slip a little to one side because of the loose rocks but manage to stay upright. "But did you go back to Earth?" I ask. "I mean, Terra—after the holocaust? If you didn't, how can you know Terra was destroyed?"

Alfredo walks with his capacitor pointing upward, scanning the horizon. "No, no one went back. Most of us were in Pangea when it happened, but Ivan was still on Terra because of his time zone. He managed to go to sleep in the middle of the nuclear war, and woke up here, telling us what had happened."

Frederico's lookalike stops walking and turns toward me. Putting one hand over his mouth, he leans closer. "Unlike us, he has no family," he whispers, eyeing Ivan. I shiver. The protectors that weren't in Pangea probably decided to stay on Terra and die with their loved ones. But how the hell do you sleep during the end of the world?

"How do you know you're dead?" I whisper back for no reason.

He shakes his head. "Oh, you know. Believe me!" He chuckles sadly. "Also, one of the messengers confirmed our worst fears later. If we leave the Wheel, we die."

"The Wheel?"

"That's what we call this hypersphere. The land is like a ring around the island. And the gods' veils are arranged like a spoked wheel."

"*Vat* are you doing?" Ivan shouts, about fifty meters ahead of us. "Battle's that way!"

After exchanging a guilty look, we restart our journey. I always assumed if we died on Earth, our bodies here would just disappear. If what Alfredo is saying is the truth, however, then when we die on our planets, our consciousness remains alive in the hypersphere until we try to exit it. The moment Pangea attempts to download a brain back to a non-existent body, real death happens.

Alfredo and his people avoided this fate by staying in the hypersphere all this time. I'm amazed by their situation. Then I wonder if the hypersphere has the familiar flashing end-of-the-game circle that resets it, like I've seen before. If someone triggers that, everyone here will be dead.

We keep following the path along the energy boundary. The trail following the veil isn't fancy, so my guess is that people walking next to it over and over created this visible track, though it's only wide enough for a single person. Often, the path goes around a tree that's too close to—or sometimes partially inside—the veil.

I crouch to avoid a fleet of large bees carelessly flying nearby. "So—did the other Terra win?"

He stops and rubs his forehead. "They didn't technically win. Their planet was also destroyed. Poor Mark. Do you know what Khof did?"

Mark must be their version of Mike. On Earth, Mike and I switched bodies.

"No."

"He murdered Amy. Mark's daughter."

Saint Plehr. Amy must be like April, *Mike's* daughter. My heart drops to my stomach. The messengers asked me to do *anything* to reach their goal—even kill people. The guy they picked to destroy Terra apparently had no qualms about that, if he murdered a child.

"How old was Amy?"

"She was seven or eight years old. Mark snapped after that and destroyed Khof's planet. The rest is history."

I see. On Jane's Earth, April died when she was four. Swerving to avoid a low branch, I try to keep pace with him. "What happened to Mark?" I ask, dreading his answer.

"He must've been killed. We never heard back from him."

Unlike Mike, it sounds like Mark actually went through with the messengers' original plan. So, he either died when he destroyed the other planet, or he was killed in Pangea. No one would let someone who murdered a whole planet go unpunished.

As we get closer to the river, we stop to rest and observe the landscape. Based on the sun's position, noon is two hours away. The enemy's trucks and tanks are waiting on the island's beach. They're visible even from here, through the island's veil. Alfredo gives me his binoculars so I can take a better look at them.

"I see a lot of vehicles but no one nearby," I say. Fortress has a sloped road winding down into the mesa's middle section. There, I see trucks, transports, tanks, and missile launchers lining up.

"Oh, but they're there. It's the gods' veil," Alfredo

explains. "Not only can't we cross it, but we also can't see people or animals through it. Large or inanimate objects are fair game, though."

"Why do they have armored trucks and you don't?" It seems unfair.

"The top of Fortress has the prize of this battlefield —trucks, tanks, artillery, troop carriers. But the river is filled with traps. It was less than a day after the Wheel hypersphere opened when those people conquered the island, and then the walls went up." A sad smile shows on his face. "Seriously, nothing appeared out of the ordinary. Yes, we were losing to Khof, but we thought it was just another one of the messengers' games. You know, some people would die, the hypersphere would restart, and another environment would show up. But soon after that, Terra went into Armageddon."

Beside us, Ivan frantically clicks on a pen-sized laser-pointer device. He points at the edge of the forest, probably communicating with someone. "The enemy's vehicles are ready to cross the island's veil," he tells us. "It's been months since we had to fight that many. They must be upset we killed one of them yesterday."

An expression of panic crosses Alfredo's face. I wonder how many casualties they had that same day.

"This is going to be a big one," Alfredo says somberly. "We're retreating and forming three groups inside the forest."

Interesting. When Jean died, their tactics were different. They took the initiative and kept the enemy at the shore. "Yesterday was only a scout party," Alfredo continues, as though guessing my thoughts. "We can take one armored transport, but not an army."

I wave at the island. "But the war between the planets is over. Why are they still fighting?"

"They want revenge," he tells me. "And we're pretty sure they're working for someone."

"Right." I gaze at the plateau. "They're trying to take over Pangea from the messengers. And they'll kill every sentient being in the universe if they succeed."

Ivan's weapon touches my back before I even finish my sentence. Alfredo stops in his tracks and stares at me, his mouth hanging open.

"And how do you know that, *cyka blyat*?" Ivan asks.

Before I can say anything, the veils flicker for several seconds. Then something—or someone—crosses the island's veil as if it isn't even there. This in itself is already impressive, but what's more remarkable is that the unknown entity is flying.

It's too far from us, and even when I squint, I can't tell what it is. Then I remember I have a pair of binoculars hanging at my chest. When I'm finally able to focus and follow the airborne object, I find it's a young man, approaching us low over the river.

"Weapons ready!" Ivan shouts, and we all drop to the ground. They both aim at the moving target. The person flying doesn't get closer than the middle of the river, however, probably afraid of getting hit. It's clear he's surveying the battlefield.

"Who is he?" I ask, my mouth dry. He's about two kilometers away, and even with the binoculars, his face is unrecognizable.

"He's the genocidal bastard responsible for our deaths," Ivan tells me. "His name is Khof."

A sinking feeling of dread makes my stomach curl. I know exactly who the handsome gentleman is. This is why Jean tried to kill me.

"And he can fly?" I press. "How?"

Shots are fired at the flying man from our side of the beach, but the target is too far away. My legs start to shake. There's no sugar-coating this. Khof is my doppelgänger. A beardless, hatless, joyless me with raw eyebrows. Somehow, he can still fly. Perhaps all the time he spent here allowed him to re-learn the skill. But he can't be stronger than I am, right?

"Oh shit," I say.

Inland, a boulder the size of a car detaches from the far east hill. We all turn our heads to watch as it slowly breaks from the rest of the ground. It's near the spoke of the energy wall opposite ours. As it moves up, chunks of smaller rocks and dirt fall from it like sand. Soon, it's completely separated from the hill, leaving behind the beginnings of a mudslide that take out the nearby trees and bushes as it moves.

Above the impromptu avalanche, the boulder also moves, except it's flying. It gains speed as it heads toward the origin of Terra's last shot. Whoever is there is going to be smashed by a freaking boulder.

Seconds later, it hits the ground with a loud thud we can hear from here. The impact creates its own mushroom cloud of dust.

Khof just did all of that from the middle of the river. When we finally look back at him, he's already gone, hidden behind the veil. How the hell can we fight him?

"Now they'll start an artillery barrage," Alfredo says. "They're precision-guided missiles, but we have jammers that confuse their sensors. So, they act just like dumb shells."

As he predicts, the veil around the island flickers

again, but this time, Khof doesn't show up. Instead, the first projectiles begin to hit our side.

"They need to hit the veil with a lot of missiles to weaken it so the vehicles can cross it," Ivan says. "Sometimes Khof throws boulders at it from the other side for larger tears."

Trying to be discreet, I lean toward the nearby veil and extend my arm back, touching it with my palm. Pressing my eyes shut, I examine its pulsating fibers. They're made of a solid energy core encircled by a stream of interlaced particles, like ethereal ropes.

"Who's staying?" Alfredo asks Ivan in a worried tone.

"Jonathan. If he survived that big rock." Ivan shakes his head. "They'll try to kill as many as they can before they attack with armored vehicles."

As he speaks, I concentrate on the wall. The threads in the energy veil around the island are being torn by brute force. The broken filaments create temporary gaps, and a few missiles get through unharmed. But the energy strings soon reconnect, wasting most of the other side's effort to break them in the first place.

If Khof is truly like me, shouldn't he be able to open the barrier with his mind? The lines are malleable, and it would be easier to ask them to change and move out of the way instead of attacking them directly. Even the dumb thing I did when I was underwater—using a ball of energy—would be better than this. But he's been here for a long time. Despite Khof's superhuman abilities, I doubt he knows what he's doing.

For now, the incoming projectiles are harmless to us back here, but they're increasing the cloud of dust that formed when the boulder hit the ground, and a mass of floating dirt begins to cover us. This gives me an idea.

"Let's go!" Ivan yells and bolts toward the trees. There's too much dust in the air, and the wind keeps blowing more our way. I hear his and Alfredo's footsteps as they run away.

"I'm right behind you!" I shout back. But instead of running back to the camp, I do what no one in their sane mind would do—I sprint in the direction of the river, where the enemy will soon arrive if they manage to penetrate the veil and cross the river.

About five minutes later, I reach the beach and drop to my knees beside the nearest veil, panting. As far as I can tell, neither Alfredo nor Ivan has followed me. They won't see what I'm about to do.

Without much time left until they cross, I touch the energy wall and concentrate. My mind again recreates the boundaries of this world as a giant 3D wagon wheel. Keeping my eyes closed, I instruct the veil to create more and more threads to increase the strength of the weaving, and I send this instruction to the next filament, which should then repeat the command. The effect starts slowly, like before, but it soon speeds up and spreads like ripples on a lake, moving forward toward the island, and backward through the forest behind me.

Half a minute later, the threads of the veil around the island finally get my message and begin to strengthen the diamond-like mesh twofold, then threefold. Soon, there are at least ten times more energy lines woven into the original pattern.

Next, as if someone flipped a switch, the noise of artillery is gone, and there are no more rips in the veil.

The cacophony of war is replaced by the soothing, bubbling sound of the river. The crickets are still too shy to discuss the situation.

When I open my eyes, I'm startled to see the result of my work. The veils are fully opaque and sparkling yellow, like impossibly tall theater curtains covered by glaring gold sheets. It's as though they're reflecting sunlight, except the sun could not be reflecting like that from all the boundaries around us. The light comes from the veils themselves.

The sight makes me smile.

"What the hell?" Alfredo says, from behind me. When I turn to face him, both he and Ivan have their weapons pointed at me.

Chapter 14

ARRESTED

I awkwardly hug the small purple trunk behind my back as I sit in an uncomfortable position back at the camp. My hands are tied together with rope on the other side of the tree. The smell of grilled rodent with long legs makes my stomach grumble, but nobody brings me a piece of the blue alien meat.

As they cook dinner, Terra's protectors discuss what to do with me. I can see them in my mind map, gathered together on a nearby tree. It's the largest platform they have. True, I can't see auras anymore, but their shapes are obvious from this distance.

What's probably delaying them is that Jonathan is one of the victims of today's battle. Although he's still alive, his right leg was in shambles when Raj and the others brought him back hours ago. He was the one who gambled a shot at Khof, missed, and was rewarded by a giant flying rock. Based on what I overheard, the only solution is to amputate it, and it's not like they have advanced medical facilities here.

While they debate my future, I decide to practice

Primavera's trick. Unlike her, I have to touch whatever I want to change, but the rope is already on my skin. I just have to focus. To my surprise, the trick works perfectly. The strings decompose around my wrists and drop to the ground as dust.

As luck would have it, this is the moment someone meanders around the trees toward me. There's no time to flee. I keep my arms in their agonizing position around the tree, pretending my hands are still tied.

Finally, Marie appears in my field of vision, her eyes focused on my face. Her expression is calm and thoughtful. She wears the same t-shirt Primavera found for her. It has a list of songs like "Fuego de Glory" and "Never Say Adiós."

"So." I break the ice. "You like Juan Bon Jovi too?" I grin.

Marie laughs, her eyes lighting up. She doesn't act at all like her doppelgänger from Jane's Earth. I could never tell what Louise was thinking, especially not from her eyes. Louise's vision in the hyperspheres was secondary, and she usually relied more on scents, vibrations, and sounds. On Earth, she was completely blind.

Marie's eyes, on the other hand, are a reflection of her soul. Perhaps she was sighted on Terra.

"As a matter of fact, I am." Her face brightens again. "My favorite is 'Wanted: Vivo o Muerto!'"

I frown. This is not funny, considering my situation. Her face turns red, and she looks away. Things are awkward, and I almost scratch my nose, but that would give away that I'm actually free.

After a while, she looks at me with purpose. "Zeon, we have to talk."

Uh-oh. I've had more than my share of conversations of this type, and they all sucked.

"I'm not stupid," she continues, and I bite my lip. Flashbacks from a few romantic dinners with former girlfriends cross my mind. "I shouldn't have survived yesterday." She rubs her now healthy shoulder. "And nobody knows I'm pregnant."

Unbeknownst to her, we're recreating a discussion I had in college word for word, except that one was in Dïnisc. She shifts her weight from one foot to another and leans on a tree for a second.

"They'd try to stop me from fighting," she explains, "but we're all dead anyway."

Okay, *now* we have something original.

After a quick pause, Marie sits down on the dirty ground, folding her legs toward her body with both ankles on the floor. "You have to help Jonathan, or else he's going to die." Her eyes fixate on me. "I don't know how you saved me, but I doubt magically fixing the veils is the only thing you can do here."

And that's why everyone should keep their superpowers to themselves. When I healed Marie, Primavera was right by my side, helping me along the way. There's a chance I could save Jonathan, but what if I fail? I could kill him in the process.

"I didn't do anything with the veils," I lie. Seriously, I'll deny everything they ask me, including having fixed the energy walls. It's all fake news. I cannot afford them figuring out I'm not from Terra. "And even if I did, why would I hide it from them?" I nod in the direction of the others.

"<Because you're not from Terra,>" she says, not in English but Dïnisc. Damn it. I keep forgetting Pangea is having an angel conference. "<And although Raj can't

remember faces, I'm pretty good at it.>" She glances away for a moment, but quickly stares back at me. "<Your beard and eyebrows don't fool me>," she continues in Dïnisc. "<You look *exactly* like Khof.>"

I shift my eyes from side to side as I think how to lie my way out of this.

"<I'm sorry. I can't understand a word you're saying,>" I lie through my teeth—in the same damned language. "<Ah, shit,>" I say, still speaking in Dïnisc.

Marie remains quiet as I pause to consider my predicament. She must be—or was—an angel of the messengers. This is why she speaks both languages.

"<Do they know you're an angel?>" I ask her. Since they're all dead, I bet they wouldn't welcome with open arms anyone close to the messengers of the gods.

"<No. I'd be in danger if they learned about it. So, your secret is safe with me. For now.>"

"<Why? If I look like Khof, I may also *be* just like him. Why are you keeping this secret?>" Seriously, why do I keep saying these idiotic things?

Marie takes a long, deep breath before answering me.

"<You look like him, but you don't act like him. Khof killed Raj in his sleep just before Terra entered a nuclear winter. He wouldn't have saved me in a million years. And he definitely wouldn't have closed the veils.>"

She risks a look back toward the camp, probably to check if anyone's listening. Who knows who else is an angel here? Perhaps they should've distributed badges at a registration counter. "<So, obviously, you're not from Yora. But you're also not from Terra.>"

I see. Yora must be Khof's version of Jora.

Marie presses her hair back with both hands, her

eyes staring into my soul. My life is in her hands. I've met my share of angels, and they range from insane murderers to misguided fanatics. Perhaps Marie belongs to a third group. But right now, I can't tell.

"<So, Zeon, what happened to your... Terras?>"

My ears flush red. "<We rebelled. Our planets joined forces in the end. They both survived.>" I feel a little guilty saying this, since her version of events ended badly. Also, I'm not sure how much I can share with her.

Keeping her eyes down, Marie runs a hand through her hair, lost in thought. Meanwhile, I absent-mindedly mimic her and brush my own short hair with my fingers. Marie jumps back, startled, but to my relief, she doesn't go away.

Instead, she stands, and I do the same, albeit slowly. No need to frighten her even more. Bringing my hands down, I look at them. I forgot I was supposed to be tied to the tree.

"<Let me explain. It's not what you're thinking.>" I temporarily avoid her eyes and mentally cringe. It occurs to me this is exactly what my ex-fiancée Nia once said.

But we don't have much time to delve into my transgression. The noise of quick steps approaching makes us stare at each other like deer caught in the headlights.

Busted.

Raj leaps in between us with a curved dagger in his right hand. "What are you doing?" he shouts.

Marie's eyes dart from me to Raj, clearly uncertain of what to say. I'm out of ideas as well, and usually make things worse, so I stay silent for a change. Let her explain our shenanigans.

"Raj, I untied him," she lies, speaking English again. "He's the only one who can save Jonathan."

He chances a glance at her, but then he shakes his head. "Are you kidding me? We don't *trust* him." He points his dagger at me. "He could've killed you just now."

Great. She just lied for me, and I'm making them fight. Because of me, they may separate, and their kid will have to be raised in two different homes—or, to be more precise, two different trees.

"But he didn't kill me," she counters. "More importantly, he was the one who saved me yesterday. And he's right, Raj." Her lips tremble. "I'm pregnant." She lets out a sob and smiles. "*We* are pregnant! But I don't want anyone else to know. Otherwise they won't let me fight."

Raj stares back at her and falls silent, his face expressionless. This is the moment that can make or break a relationship. I've seen it many times—no, not *personally*. I saw it on soap operas—Earth's best TV shows. This declaration was usually followed by tears of happiness or unexpected anger. At least one time, someone ended up getting punched in the face.

Considering I've messed up their lives and their parallel versions of each other so many times, I feel I should say something to help this end well.

"See, Raj?" I wave my hand at her belly. "She's not fat. I mean, she's heavier now, but it's for a good reason!" I grin.

And then Marie punches me in the face.

Chapter 15

AMERICA

At first, most of them don't want me anywhere close to Jonathan, who's unconscious by now. But Marie vouches for me, and under the threat of blowing my brains out if I even sneeze, I perform a successful operation. Jonathan's leg is as good as new.

Now it's early evening and we're sitting around a small campfire, having dinner near the largest purple tree in the vicinity. Thick purple sticks wrapped with oil-soaked cloth illuminate the immediate area. I finally have the opportunity to eat the weird rabbit, but I wish I hadn't. It tastes and chews like brand new tires.

While I surreptitiously check to make sure we're all actually eating the same thing, I catch Alfredo eyeing me intently from the other side of the circle. The flickering of the flames illuminates his blank, lifeless face. And he was so cheerful when we first met.

"Where are you really from, Zeon?" Alfredo finally asks in a hurt tone. He's wearing a battered pair of jeans and a long-sleeved black blouse with visible holes.

I inhale deeply before lying to him. "I'm from the United States of America." I'm afraid if they figure out I'm another version of Khof, they'll kill me. I get that Khof is to blame for their deaths, but the real enemies are the messengers. Just like when we battled in the hyperspheres years ago, they're fighting the wrong enemy.

My statement causes bedlam. While some of them chuckle, others are outraged.

"America!" Raj exclaims. "How dare you?"

"You're insane!" says Alfredo.

Marie tilts her head at me, confused. Since Khof looks exactly like me, it's probably obvious to her that I don't come from an Earth like theirs, but that I was actually the mole there. If she's going to expose me, this is the time.

After the commotion dies down, I continue. "There are many parallel Earths—or Terras. I'm from one that wasn't destroyed, and neither was our counterpart. The messengers played the same games with us, but we survived."

Hungry, I reluctantly grab what looks like a long, leathery rodent thigh. As I gather the courage to eat it, a thought crosses my mind. "By the way, if the Wheel started as a feud between your two planets, why are several Earths now involved?"

Marie shrugs. "We don't know." For a moment, I watch her removing pale leaves from a thin branch, grinding them between her fingers, and dropping the dust on top of a large leaf. Then, she breaks the stick into smaller bits that she throws into the campfire one by one.

"Maybe the necromantes are involved," she finally adds.

An awkward silence follows this statement. It's as if someone just mentioned He-Who-Must-Not-Be-Named. No one makes eye contact with me.

"Necromantes?" I ask, pretending I haven't heard of them. "Who are they?"

I'm suddenly very aware of the cracking and popping noises from the fire. Bodan and I used to share scary stories around campfires like this one; I usually wasn't able to sleep well for days after.

Marie frowns and looks at me. "Nobody knows. No human has seen them and survived. But how would you not know this? You're a protector!"

Ivan conveniently takes this moment to walk around the circle and lean on a tree behind me, just out of sight. I hear the metallic noise of a weapon.

Meanwhile, Alfredo looks at me with a blank stare. "Yesterday, when we met you. Why did you lie to us?"

Anger brews inside me. "Because that's what you do when you're trying to survive a deadly trivia game." I regret nothing—except maybe eating this awful piece of dark meat tasting like cleaning supplies.

Jonathan finally joins the group, walking with a faint limp and sitting down next to Alfredo. Although his thigh is good as new, his brain still has a faint memory of the injury. This happened with Marie as well, but her wound was way worse.

"Ask no questions and hear no lies," he says. I nod back at him. Despite his annoying sayings, he's right.

The fire flares up when Marie tosses in a bigger piece of wood, which ignites like a firework. The sudden brightness draws our attention back to her. It's clear she's not listening to our bickering.

"A long time ago, the gods made a horrible mistake," she begins in a reverential tone. "They created a race to be their servants. They were given several different names—dragon mantises. Fire snakes. Boitatás. Killers of the Worlds." She scoffs at her own words. "The messengers lost control of them thousands of years ago. That's when the Pangea wars started. The gods and the necromantes have been fighting for the control of Pangea for millennia. And if we lose Pangea..." She pauses and looks at me, expectantly.

All eyes are on me as I'm caught in a flash quiz mid-chew. It's like I'm back in high school, or the equivalent awkward teenager years on Jora. I swallow.

"Everyone dies?" I finally say. "Because no one can sleep anymore?" No one told me this would be on the test.

Marie turns around and grabs another dry branch from behind her. "We're not the protectors of Terra. We're the protectors of *Pangea*. And if we lose it, yes, everyone dies."

I've heard this before. This is the messengers' official speech. To be honest, I prefer when my politicians have a platform of hope and not fear. Now I know where Dooria gets her campaign slogans.

Jonathan sneers. "As if it matters. Terra is no more."

The work Marie has been doing on the leaves finally pays off. The constant rubbing of the leaves with her index finger and thumb has created a pile of gray particles.

Without looking at Jonathan, Marie says, "We all need to sleep, Major. Even here."

When she's finished with the last leaf, she grabs the pile of dust with both her hands and throws it at the fire. I swear the particles drift above the flames for longer than they should, like a cartoon, but no one seems to notice or care—not even Marie. Eventually, gravity wins, and their fall violently ignites the flame, causing the biggest flare of the night. A smile finally appears on her face. Playing with fire is dangerous, but fun.

"So, *tovarishch*," Ivan says from behind me, startling me. I forgot he was there. "Why should we believe anything you say now?"

"Well, I don't care if you believe me. After tonight, I'll start looking for my friends." I turn and glare at Ivan, as if daring him to say otherwise. He keeps quiet, but he and Jonathan glance at each other.

"So, how many parallel Terras exist?" Alfredo asks me in between bites, seemingly back to his happy self. I'm glad he's changing the subject, defusing the situation. How different he is from his counterpart on Earth.

I use my teeth to clean the rest of the rubbery meat from the rabbit's hilariously long femur. Using it as an instrument to scratch the packed dirt in front of me, I draw a wagon wheel with eight spokes and a circular central hub.

"I can't say for sure. The Wheel is divided by the veils into eight octants plus the middle." I use the bone to point at the sector between south and southeast. Like Primavera did, I'm inferring the directions based on the sun's rotation. "We are here."

The long bone now points to the area between the east and southeast spokes. "But when I showed up in Pangea," I continue, "I was in my own sector, to the east."

I look at Marie and try to smile, but my face throbs where her fist connected, and I immediately look away. "I almost drowned crossing the southeast veil," I continue, "so Marie *did* see me when I left the river."

In between bites, Alfred speaks with his mouth full. "Eight Terras, then. Unbelievable!"

~

THE NEXT DAY, Jonathan and the others hold a small service for Jean. Like Jane, she was an important member of the community, and everyone liked her. Most cry, but Marie sobs like no one else. I try to keep my chin steady, but it never stops shaking, so I excuse myself from the ceremony. I can handle anything but grief, especially if I feel responsible for it.

Nearby, Alfredo hugs Marie as Raj observes them in silence. I don't think they've noticed me.

"Are you sure you're okay?" Alfredo asks Marie, shooting a glance at Marie's belly. Alfredo, the better version of Frederico, must know about the pregnancy. Marie nods quietly in response. When they catch sight of me, I look away, embarrassed to have overheard them.

"Zeon, I don't know what part you played in Jean's death," Alfredo says, "but thanks for saving Marie. And her baby."

Reluctantly, I approach them, checking to see if anyone else is nearby. Raj crosses his arms and steps closer to Marie.

"It's okay," I say. "By the way—" I smile at Raj, trying to be friendly—"do you want to know the sex of the baby?"

His eyes widen. "What the hell?"

"When I do the... surgeries, for the lack of a better

word, I see inside people." I point a finger at my head. "Or inside *things*. That's how I fixed the veil yesterday."

Raj wraps his right arm around Marie's waist, looking intently into her eyes. Marie gazes back at him and shakes her head slightly.

"No," she says with a weak smile. "We want it to be a surprise."

Later in the day, I finish my preparations to cross the veil. My pink backpack is again filled with supplies, including the blue rodent meat. Ivan didn't want me to go, arguing that I could help them fight Khof. I explained that we should search for more people to help them and, more importantly, that they probably wouldn't be able to keep me from fleeing, considering what I could do. Luckily, they didn't consider the possibility of killing me—at least not out loud.

As far as I know, no one is going with me. Who knows what kind of people I'm going to find on the other side? Based on my experience, they're likely to shoot on sight. Also, the Terrans' group is already small as it is—they have fewer than thirty people here —and they should be looking after each other. I don't blame them. Meeting someone whose Earth survived must be depressing.

I'm not going back to the sector where I showed up. That's where my people, the Jori, must be. But Jane was the one who asked for my help, so I'll search for her instead. She must know if Pangea's in danger or if it's just a plot by the messengers. I'm going to walk the map clockwise, starting by crossing the south veil.

Jonathan questions me about it, and I just tell him my friend is from a different Earth, so going back to my own sector isn't an option. There, I'd probably only find Nia and the others, including Bodan. No, thanks.

Then Raj shows up with a backpack of his own and a large double-barreled capacitor. Marie walks next to him and kisses his cheek.

I look at him in surprise. "I thought I was going alone."

He laughs. "No. I'm going with you."

"This could be dangerous. Are you sure you want to leave her in her, uh—" I steal a glance at Marie —"condition?" He's leaving a pregnant Marie behind. It seems irresponsible.

"This is exactly why I have to go with you, Zeon," he replies. "If there's any chance of us surviving this, it'll depend on you."

~

Dawn is an hour or two away when we finally approach the veil. The idea is to take advantage of the dark to scout out what kinds of people are waiting for us. Who knows if Jane's Earth is the one we'll find? Jonathan, Ivan, Marie, and the others accompany us, just to see how Raj and I are going to cross. Unfortunately, Dorothy disappeared during the previous battle. I just don't know how I'm going to explain this to Primavera.

It's a cloudless night, but we still can't see the stars because of how compact the trees are. Luckily, the two moons are both on top of us, and their bright light allows us to see enough to move without tripping on the devious roots. Maybe I'm misremembering but the moons look closer to each other tonight.

I'm glad we're not in total darkness, but the dimness makes everything look creepy, and the number of insects in this forest gives me the impression everything on the ground is moving. Stepping on bugs quickly becomes commonplace.

Although the crickets remain harmless, some of the other bugs sting, leaving itchy rashes in their wake. I kick my feet as I walk, attempting to throw the critters away. Raj finds this hilarious.

When we finally reach the wall, Raj leans his weapon against a tree and embraces Marie. Meanwhile, Jonathan limps toward us, approaching me for the first time since I healed his leg. My guess is he's going to thank me.

"Listen to me, you goddamn little prick," he says gruffly. "If Raj doesn't come back, I'm going to hit you so many times even your voodoo won't save you."

Shaking my head, I approach the veil, and the former protectors surround me in a semi-circle. Then, I carefully touch the energy field with my open right hand and close my eyes, feeling the wavy strands of energy pulsating below it.

The extra filaments I added during the battle are long gone, and the barrier is back to normal. I don't know what Khof is thinking by attacking it head on every time he wants to cross it. It's so much easier just to ask them to split and fold.

When I open my eyes, a diamond-shaped entrance twice my height is highlighted by the bright lines now clumped together around it. It looks like a portal to another world, except the "other world" is another section of the Wheel. The south-southwest octant, to be exact.

Although the Terrans knew I changed the wall yesterday, they still had not seen it firsthand. Alfredo gasps, but Ivan rolls his eyes.

Before we cross the barrier, Marie puts her mouth

to my ear and whispers in Dïnisc, "<Please keep Raj safe.>" I find it odd she doesn't say it in English, but I brush it off as her being cautious. I nod.

After that, I turn to face the others. It's time to go.

"<I guess I'll see you guys later,>" I say, and a flash of anger crosses Jonathan's face.

As soon as the words are out of my mouth, I facepalm inwardly. I didn't speak in English. This is a common problem with people who are bilingual. There's some kind of switch in our minds that changes as soon as we hear someone speaking a different language, especially if it's our first one.

With the exception of Marie, the people here probably don't speak Dïnisc—unless they're angels too. But they probably *have* met people who spoke Dïnisc several times during the battles in the hyperspheres. So, they know exactly how Dïnisc sounds, even if they don't understand it. They've heard it from their worst enemies.

"What did you say?" Jonathan asks, beckoning Ivan with his hand. The Rossiyan moves a step closer to me.

I gulp. Time to engage in my fast mode. As always, I'm my own worst enemy, and this time I don't mean Khof, my lookalike.

"Well, I don't know how you haven't noticed it, but you're all surrounded." I adjust the backpack on my back and point at a dying bush next to Marie.

As they all turn to look at it, I touch the wall, ordering it to start closing. In less than a second, I'm through the opening and out in a field, running for my life. Luckily, I'm as fast as I am dumb.

Chapter 16

AURAS

After I cross the barrier, I realize I may not have made the smartest decision. A sudden drop waits in front of me, so I stop. The forest ends at the edge of a respectable cliff, and the trees continue down a long slope to my left. Fifteen or more meters below me, small, sparse bushes dot an otherwise empty landscape. I could jump down and try to survive the impact, but I'd still get seriously hurt, even with the lower gravity. Best-case scenario, I'd break a few bones.

Someone tackles me to the ground as I try to turn, and my hat flies away. I hit the back of my head on the ground when I crash. The world swirls as my vision blurs, but the attacker is still unmistakable. All I can make out are thick brows and dark skin, but there's no need to see the scar to know it's Raj.

Just like when we first met, he stands over me, his knife reflecting the feeble light.

"Who are you?" he shouts, and the occasional flicker of white on his eyes makes him look even more threatening.

"I'm your best friend." For once, I'm not scared. "At this moment, anyway." I gesture at the barrier behind him. Now it's closed, Raj is trapped in this sector, and can't go back without my help.

"You're one of them. I should kill you right now!" He presses his curved and unusually sharp knife against my throat.

"You know, you shouldn't judge me just because I speak both languages." If he only knew. I could throw his girlfriend under the bus. I won't do it, though, because of my aforementioned disturbances with Ravi-and-Marie-like relationships. If anything, he's the one at risk here.

Sighing, I melt the knife's blade as though it's nothing. Practice has been improving my skills. Next, I push him away as his hand slips harmlessly across my throat. His body falls sideways onto the brown roots of a tree that reminds me of deformed tapioca.

"What the hell?" He holds the bladeless handle between his hands, ignoring me for a second. I don't blame him. Despite all his time in combat, the outlandish phenomenon makes Raj lower his guard. If I were his opponent and knew what to do, I could kill him. Luckily for him, I'm not his foe, and don't have the stomach for killing someone anyway.

I adjust myself to a sitting position. "I am not your enemy, Raj."

Some kind of liquid drips down my neck, and the thought of blood startles me. Quickly, I touch the substance with my fingers and bring my hand closer to my face to examine it. Even in this low light, I can tell it's definitely not blood because of how shiny it is. Perhaps I made a mistake when I transformed the steel blade into liquid. It seemed like the right thing to do at the time, but now my neck and my spider t-shirt are both covered with silver stains.

"How... how did you do it?" Raj is still entranced by the missing blade.

I pause before answering him. "I can do things here that no one else can. I already helped Marie and Jonathan, so you should know." I dust the dirt off my pants with my dry hand, angry for a change. "For now, though, I'm looking for a friend of mine. You can either help me or go back." I nod at the energy wall. "I can open the veil somewhere else so you can return if you want."

Raj rolls over and sits up next to me, still eyeing his useless weapon. I cross my arms; he's about to apologize. I'm pretty good at reading people.

"You *idiot!*" he says. "We have no weapons now. What happens if we find hostiles with guns?"

I pick up my hat and glasses that are scattered next to me. "What are you talking about? Didn't you get a weapon just before our trip?"

We both stand up and glare at each other.

"I was *about* to grab it when *someone*—" he pokes at my shoulder, hard—"decided to speak gibberish, trick us, and leave!"

Glaring at his fat finger, I push it away with my hat.

"You guys didn't give *me* any capacitors. And *anyway*, I wouldn't have had to leave if people weren't trying to *kill* me!"

Raj grabs both of my shoulders and pulls me closer to his steaming face.

"Well, *Zeon*, if so many people want you dead, there must be a good reason!"

His head suddenly comes into shiny focus, the deep, devilish scar dominating his facial features as it reflects the intermittent, bright-red light hovering above us.

Uh-oh.

We both look up to see a red flare that appears to hover in place for a moment. Soon it starts its downward trajectory. Whoever threw it must've seen us. It came from the inland flats, east of the ridge. So much for sneaking in.

When our eyes meet again, we whisper at the same time, "Run!"

Raj takes the lead, racing south into the forest to follow the trail away from the edge of the cliff. I'm right behind him. Even if we were sighted, it would be tough for them to find us in the forest. This is, after all, the strategy Terrans have used successfully for a long time.

We run downhill along a small path that more or less follows the veil. A few moments later, even the vivid light from the double moon system above us fades to an almost pitch-black luster. From there, we proceed cautiously, tiptoeing around fearless root segments.

"We can't stay on this trail," Raj says, breathing hard.

He's right, of course. A clear path from where we came will lead us to the people who spotted us with the flare, and if they have half a brain, they'll know we're coming through here. I glance into the darkness as if I can see anything, but to no avail.

Wait a minute. I keep forgetting my abilities here. True, I can't easily identify auras with my mind map anymore—mostly because these people don't have them—but landscapes and buildings are fair game. And people are still shaped like people, so if I pay attention, I'll be able to detect them.

Concentrating, I quickly study the environment around us. As far as I can tell, nobody is nearby yet. But I do find a place that can keep us isolated and hopefully safe for the moment.

"Raj, I know where to go. Follow me."

Thirty minutes later, we're in a small opening surrounded by trees. There are even a few strands of grass on the ground, and we could probably see the stars through the trees if the moons weren't so bright. The twilight glow illuminates us through the canopies, making us look like ghosts.

We decide to wait until morning to scout along the edge of the forest, less than ten meters away. Since we were spotted in front of it, we need to stay away from the veil for a while, but there's no reason not to stay near the flatland. This place is huge, and due to the vegetation, they can't see us unless they're right next to us.

After staring at the sky for several minutes and drinking the water he brought with him, Raj pulls out a round object looking like a brass knuckle.

He shows it to me on his palms as if cradling a baby, glaring at me accusingly. "How did you do this?"

I now recognize what he's holding as the handle of the knife.

"It was my favorite Karambit," he says, and for a moment, I think he's going to cry.

"I'm sorry." In my place, he'd have done the same. "You were threatening to cut my throat."

With a slow, careful motion, he drops the thing to the ground as if it's sacred.

"Raj, I forgot to ask you something. If this is like the other battlefields, there must be a place to end it." To end the battles we used to fight, we always had to touch a designated target, like a capture-the-flag game. "It used to be a large, flashing red circle. Is there one here?"

I'd planned to find this trigger from the beginning, but now, there's an unforeseen problem. If one of the protectors touches the target, the Wheel hypersphere will end, and everyone here will be sent back to their planet–except for the people on Raj's team. Without their Terran bodies, they would all die.

Raj shrugs. "Supposedly. We searched everywhere inside our sector, but never found it."

Instinctively, I scan the area around us. This is a new octant, after all, but I don't think we would just stumble upon it. So, I look back at him. "Aren't you afraid someone's going to find it and end this hypersphere?"

He draws a slow breath. "It's our biggest fear. We hope if the Yori find it, they won't touch it either, since their planet is gone, and they'll all die too."

"But it's worse now than before," he goes on. He presses his lips together. "The rules have changed. Only the winning team is supposed to go back."

Looking down, I consider their plight. This game may end at any moment, and the only thing they can do is to hide in the trees. Then, I focus my eyes back on him. "Why do you live in trees and not in the town? It's more than big enough to accommodate everyone."

Raj rolls up his sleeves absent-mindedly. I wonder if they have winters here. His outfit is not the best for warm, humid places, and I finally understand why his clothes are dark. White clothing does not agree with fighting in a dusty place.

"We lost William in one of the apartments," he said. "The door exploded when he tried to open it." He slumps his shoulders. "They're all booby-trapped. Sometimes, the door opens and you think everything is fine, but the traps can be anywhere inside. We used to send small animals to check it out. There's one that looks like a deer-kangaroo mix but without ears." He snickers before frowning. "We take any food and clothes remaining undestroyed after the animals trigger it, but the traps reset quickly. Alfredo almost died when we found that out. It turns out deformed kangaroo meat is better than dying over parmesan cheese."

Before I can picture eating kangaroos, I sense someone. The hairs on the back of my neck shoot up, and adrenaline rushes through me. I concentrate on the nearby fields, watching for movement.

Half a kilometer away, someone approaches us in slow but steady movements.

I thought I couldn't see auras anymore, yet here's one aura as bright as mine. I don't know who she or he is. But Saint Plehr, it's so bright! After all this time of noticing no auras, I'm startled by its sudden appearance.

"Raj," I mumble. "We're not alone."

Chapter 17

STRANGER

LOCATION: WHEEL – UNKNOWN SECTOR

R aj and I hide behind nearby trees, watching the intruder approaching us on top of his—or her—small horse. The sun will soon indulge us with its presence, and the spread of red and orange rays of the atmosphere bathe the scenery. Far behind the newcomer, the shadows outlining Fortress loom upon the horizon. The horse walks elegantly toward us. Its rider knows where we are.

Without warning, Raj climbs a tree like a professional, disappearing before I can say anything. If the person coming here is a threat, it'll be two against one, and he's pretty good at surprising people from above.

While the stranger approaches us, I close my eyes to admire the radiance of their aura. It feels warm in my mind, and instinctively, it draws me closer, as if tricking me into thinking we're friends.

When they're about thirty meters away, the horse stops, and a short, feminine figure wearing a long gray hoodie dismounts skillfully. The single-barrel ellipsoid of her capacitor looks cleverly dull, as if some kind of black pigment has been applied to it.

She lets her weapon hang from its strap, her hands moving freely as she walks. She stops about eight meters away, too far for Raj to attack.

"Zeon? Is it really you?"

Her voice sounds distant, contained, and I recognize it. She was a friend, but not anymore. I step from behind the tree to look at her. My hat and glasses hang uselessly in my left hand. No need to hide myself anymore.

As always, she doesn't look directly at me, but it's close enough. I grin at first, but then frown as I realize she's about to get the biggest surprise of her life. Louise pulls down her hoodie, revealing a concerned face.

As if on cue, Raj drops from the tree. He throws up his arm to protect his face, and the arm nearly breaks on impact.

"*Traître!*" Louise shouts, grabbing her weapon and aiming at him. Luckily, she doesn't ascribe to Jane's "shoot first, ask questions later" motto.

Raj must be in pain, but he just rolls toward her to get a better look. The weapon she's carrying quivers as he pulls himself up to a kneeling position. "Marie?"

I cringe as I wait for the meeting to unfold.

Louise takes a step back. "Who are you?" Then her mouth opens wide.

Confusion also crosses Raj's face as he eyes Louise and her four-legged companion. He doesn't say anything, but I suppose he's wondering what the hell she's doing here, where she got a horse, and what happened to her clothes—basically, a repeat of me waking up after my twenty-first birthday.

"Ravi?" Louise's voice cracks, and she trembles.

The capacitor falls from her hands, hanging once more from its strap. "I can't—couldn't—see you. You're alive?"

"What?" he says, finally standing up, and Louise treads cautiously toward him with watery eyes. When they're so close she could kiss him, she pulls her hand up and caresses his scar.

I cautiously pace toward them, trying not to get too close. "Louise, he's not Ravi."

Raj squints and Louise's mouth shakes. She chances a quick look at me, but soon she's fixated on Raj again. Her eyes widen, and she steps away from us, watching him as if he broke her heart.

The couple doesn't say anything as they study each other. Taking advantage of their hesitation, I step in between them to rip-off this Band-Aid as quickly as possible. Or maybe to apply it with an antibiotic cream. Evidently, I'm also bad at metaphors.

"Raj, this is Louise. She's an old friend." I turn to face him. "She's not Marie." I turn back to Louise. "And he's not Ravi." I wave my hand at Raj. This is the weirdest introduction I have ever done.

Tears roll down her face as she stares at him.

Raj nods. "From another Terra," he says. "I'm sorry I scared you. You look exactly like Marie."

Her emotions change from sadness to anger, and she glares at me like Bebe does when I open the cabin door and it's raining outside—as if I'm responsible. Jane once told me that rushing to blame someone was one of my least attractive attributes, second only to jumping to conclusions—but it looks like all Jane's friends have similar traits.

"I'm sorry, Louise. I know exactly what you're feeling," I explain.

Somehow, she manages to intensify her frown. Leave it to me to say the worst possible thing in any situation. She breathes in and out slowly, her eyes closed, and when she opens them again, her face is stern.

She purses her lips. "It's okay. I thought you were alone."

It's completely understandable. Our brains often play tricks on us, and we're the easiest people to fool. She obviously never realized the existence of other Earths might mean she'd eventually meet someone looking exactly like Ravi, without actually *being* him.

"Sorry, Raj." Louise says. "I mistook you for... someone else." She sounds more hurt than disdainful.

"And I'm Zeon," I add, "in case you don't remember my name. Not Khof." I laugh nervously and wink at her. Raj looks at me funny.

"Khof? That's his name?"

I smile. Louise was always quick on her feet. As she's about to address the elephant in the room—that I look exactly like Khof—I slowly shake my head, hoping Raj doesn't notice it. Based on her initial reaction, she probably thought Khof was me before meeting us in the forest, and now she must make up her mind whether or not I'm the one who's their enemy here. Meanwhile, Raj has gone back to admiring her, since she does look a lot like his partner.

After a long, pregnant pause, Louise says, "Of course I know you, Zeon." I stop holding my breath. "I mean, if you're *really* Zeon."

I must be very good at convincing people. Even though they've been fighting Khof all this time, probably thinking he was me, she totally bought my story. Yes, it's the truth, but even I am having trouble believing it. For all she knows, Raj could be Khof's hostage, helping him infiltrate their camp. If I were her, I wouldn't believe me.

"It's the beard. Makes me look like a bad-ass." I grin. Louise just sneers.

After Raj goes back in the forest to grab his back-pack, our little group begins its journey to Earth's headquarters in the Wheel. We slowly walk beside Louise, who stays on foot and leads her horse, a finicky white-and-black paint stallion who snorts often and looks away every time we approach him. Louise is the only one he trusts, and he follows her obediently.

"His name's Pierre," she explains when she sees me watching him.

As we move through the forest, something that's starting to feel commonplace here, we exchange our stories. Louise learns about the fate of Raj's and Khof's Earths, while she corroborates my original story to Raj. He still doesn't know I'm Khof's version here.

Something worries me, though. Instead of heading deeper into the trees, it's clear we're going to a town. The units there must be a minefield as well.

"We can't go to the apartments," I tell Louise. "They're booby-trapped."

She shrugs. "They were dangerous, but not anymore. We figured out the system. One unit is assigned to each one of us, although we don't know which one, and only that person can enter the house and disable the mechanism. It took us months to figure out the right houses and to solve the puzzles, but we did it with almost no losses."

Stealing a glance at Raj, I wonder if he's feeling stupid right now. Unfortunately, his eyes meet mine, and I'm sure he's guessing my thoughts.

Either way, I'm the fool here. Primavera saved Marie and me when she disabled the traps in our unit, and I didn't even realize that had happened.

We enter the city from higher ground, the apartment units getting denser down the hill. The clatter of Pierre's hoofs on the paved street makes me fear someone is going to hear him, but there's no one nearby. The beautiful road we now travel is paved with square cobblestone, and it's wide—about ten meters from side to side. It winds its way down to the center of this large settlement.

Turning to face us, Louise says, "All the units here are unassigned. I'll take you to someplace safe before I talk with John and the others."

I narrow my eyes, but nod. There's no way John would not be watching all the entry points of his headquarters. But maybe because she and Pierre are with us, and my outfit plus the beard are disguising me, people will leave us alone.

As we move deeper into the town, we begin to see its inhabitants. This place is way bigger than the town in Terra's sector, and it's packed with protectors and animals. A crowd of horses and people are mixed together, and I wrinkle my nose when the stench of manure hits me.

"Morning, Louise!" a man says as he sweeps the entrance of one unit—his apartment, I assume. Louise ignores him, but he seems unaffected. I'm pretty sure he's whistling a Madonna song.

Everywhere around us, men and women enter and exit the units. Some of them are carrying boxes. I estimate there are at least two hundred people and hundreds of horses picketed or in stables, and these are just the ones in the part of the town I can see.

"Stables?" I say. "Did you have stables, Raj?"

He shakes his head. "No. We don't have horses, either."

As we admire the view, I concentrate, studying Earth's protectors with my mind. My jaw drops to the ground. Everyone in my mental map shows as incredibly bright bulbs of light. They're not at all like Raj's people.

Then my heart sinks as I understand the situation. Raj, Jonathan, and the others are dead, and that's why they don't glow. But seeing the warm points of light moving about and around us makes me really understand Raj's plight. Unlike the Terrans, the bodies of the people here are still alive on Earth. I feel for him.

Louise stops in front of an oval-shaped flat console and presses her palm on its black surface. "House," she says out loud. "New occupant. Zeon." The concave door right next to the console slides open.

"*New occupant,*" the house answers. "*Welcome home, Zeon!*"

The blonde crosses her arms. "You can stay here. I have to... uh... clear up some things with them. No reason to alarm anyone." I know what she's talking about. I'm tired of being greeted by people pointing weapons at me.

Before we can hide in the apartment, the wind changes, and I sense something, a presence nearby. Quicker than ever before, I enter my fast mode and close my eyes. Someone is on a second-floor balcony in the next unit, aiming a long-barreled capacitor at us. I immediately throw myself on top of Raj to move him out of the way. I don't touch Louise since I assume whoever is there is one of her friends, and they wouldn't want to harm her.

Energy beams shoot the exact place we were standing just a few seconds ago, creating equally spaced bucket-sized holes on the road. The shooting itself is silent, but the violent impact vaporizes part of the cobblestones, causing an immediate vacuum that the air rushes back into. The result is loud enough to hurt my ears.

People that must've heard the shot run away through narrow streets or take cover in the units. Some have their capacitors pointed in our general direction. Louise walks in between us and the main attacker, who stops shooting.

"Get away from her!" a female voice shouts.

I smile when I finally see Jane. As usual, she's pointing a weapon at me.

Chapter 18

LOUISE LANE

L ouise raises her hand. "It's not what you're thinking," she says. "I can explain." I've lost count of how many times I've heard and said these exact sentences.

"He's a monster!" Jane says. She's peeking at us from inside the unit, so I still can't see her very well. The barrel of her capacitor is in plain view, though.

Not taking her eyes off the balcony, Louise moves around behind us. Raj and I sit up and exchange glances. I don't think he—or Louise—have yet recovered from the shock of seeing each other. I've never seen him—or Ravi—stay quiet for this long. Seeing Jane here is also going to be weird for him, even if he's expecting it.

Once Louise is behind us, she touches the back of my head with the barrel of her gun. I shake my head inwardly.

"You can come down," she tells Jane. "He won't be a problem. But hear me out first. Don't shoot!"

After scanning the street for a quick moment, Jane

climbs over the balcony railing, facing forward, and jumps. When she finally hits the ground, falling onto one knee, I can't help but grin. She's alive. In the last few days, I've kept having nightmares where she gets killed over and over as she shoots at me.

"We should kill him now." Jane gestures at me. "It will end this stupid war."

Her outfit is breathtaking, and I feel guilty for the sudden lust it causes. She wears a black tank top and shorts with military-style boots, and she's sporting her trademark ponytail. Memories of Jean dying—when I still thought she was Jane—surface and mess with my emotions. Our brains were not designed to handle this.

Besides the single wide-barrel light capacitor she carries on a strap, similar to Louise's, she also has a smaller pistol-like gun on her thigh, with a mini-football energy pack on top of it. She always had a thing for small, practical guns.

"Good morning, *Louise* Lane!" I say as Jane joins Louise behind me. An unexpected kick to my right kidney makes me wince in pain, and I bring my left hand around my stomach to feel it. Somehow, her kick also manages to reignite the pain in my face, where I got punched by Marie.

"Don't *fucking* do this!" Jane shouts as I start to get angry. Granted, my dreams of being received by Jane's friends in a parade on top of a fire truck are long gone, but this is ridiculous.

"Jane, calm down," Louise says. "I know how bad this looks. But take a good look at the other one." My mental map shows that behind me, Jane studies Raj's face, and no one says anything for a long time.

"Ravi?" she asks, her resolve finally faltering. "But what does it mean?"

"No," Louise says. "His name is Raj. He's from Terra, *another* parallel Earth." Louise waves at the bewildered brunette. "Raj, this is Jane."

I take this touching moment to rub the dust off my pants, grab my hat, and push myself up. For once, no one shoots at me. I extend my hand to Raj, who takes a while to even understand what I'm doing. He eventually grabs it, and I pull him up.

Jane rubs her face with her left hand. "I—I knew about the other Earths. But I thought they had different... people." Her eyes tear up. "So, you're saying Zeon—"

Louise finishes Jane's sentence. "Zeon's not our enemy. The one we've been fighting all this time is called Khof. He looks exactly like him."

Raj tilts his head. His eyes narrow, and his thick brow furrows. "You son of a bitch!" He points his finger at me, eyes wide, and his anger quickly changes to confusion. "You *are* him! I can see it now!"

For once, he doesn't try to attack me. If Louise knows who I am and doesn't feel threatened by me, he must realize my story is true.

It's Jane's turn to blush, but she avoids my glare, probably—or better, hopefully—because she's embarrassed.

"Are you sure, Louise?" Jane's voice cracks as she says her friend's name. "If you're—if you're wrong..."

"I'm sure of it," Louise says firmly." He's not our enemy. I knew the moment I set my eyes on him."

It's nice to have someone on my side, but Saint Plehr, everyone is so quick to jump to conclusions. Just because there's a copy of me running around and killing people doesn't necessarily mean it's me. I doubt Khof can match my sense of humor.

Taking a deep breath, Jane finally turns and gives me an intense gaze. While her eyes survey my face, her hands clutch onto her weapon as if it's her baby.

She places her gun-free hand on her neck. "I guess I'm—I'm sorry, Zeon. But you have to understand..." She doesn't finish the sentence, and I don't help her. I get it—it's hard for them, but hard for me too.

I look up at the sky. It's mid-morning, everything is really bright, and it's already too warm. So, I put my hat back on and adjust my glasses.

"It's okay, sweetheart," I say, tipping my head and winking at her. "It ain't my first rodeo."

Jane shoots me a broad smile for a moment, but then her brows come close together, enhancing her pretty and incredibly young face. I always love when she looks angry like that.

She crosses her arms. "Keep the shades. But the hat, the beard, and the attitude gotta go."

I smirk. Jane always composes herself quickly. There's a war going on, and not much time to reminisce. But she's going to hear about this later. Probably the next time I have to win an argument.

She puts her hand to her mouth and whistles, and soon a familiar large, reddish-brown horse gallops from a side street, nickering as if laughing at us—or at me in particular. Jane caresses her snout—the horse's, not her own—and smiles.

"Tsk, tsk, tsk," I say, staring at the horse in disbelief. "Dorothy." The beautiful mare snorts in reply.

"What did you say?" Jane asks, her hands dangerously near her weapon. "How did you know—" She gives me a concerned look, eyeing me as if I'm from another planet. Louise tenses.

"There are lots of things you don't know," I say,

shooting them an annoyed look. "But you should at least give me the benefit of the doubt."

The girls—only around nineteen years old here, like me, despite our real ages being much more varied—stare at each other for a moment, blush, but don't move their hands away from their capacitors.

I sigh. "Do you know where Dorothy was the last two days?"

Jane shakes her head. "She disappeared. I thought I'd lost her. I had to use one of the younger stallions, and they're skittish."

Pierre whinnies and stomps in response to this. Louise walks over to comfort him.

"Well, somehow she was all the way in Raj's octant," I explain, "and she helped me transport someone that was hurt."

Then, I explain the whole story since I showed up here in the Wheel. Jane is shocked by what happened with Jean, and appalled but not surprised by the existence of Marie.

Of course, I don't mention Marie's pregnancy. It's too much for them to take at this moment. And Primavera asked me to not tell anyone about her. Therefore, I lie and tell them Dorothy just showed up at the right place and the right time after I healed Marie, supposedly by myself.

"But how did you learn Dorothy's name?" Jane asks, her expression clouded with suspicion.

Goddamn it. This is another reason I hate lying. I don't know how to do it.

"Uh..." I brush my hair with my fingers, trying to buy some time to think.

"Her name's engraved on her bridle," Louise says, watching me closely.

I nod emphatically. "Obviously! Her bridle!" I wave at Dorothy, encompassing her whole body with my gesture. I have no idea what a bridle is or where it goes on a horse, and I didn't see her name engraved anywhere.

"Anyway," I continue, changing the subject, "how did you recognize me?"

Jane brings Dorothy about and mounts the mare in a single smooth movement. "It's the way you walk," she says. "Your mannerisms. Your body language." She grabs the reins without looking at me. "Once you fooled us on Earth by taking Mike's place, I started paying more attention to *you*, not what you look like."

As for me, I can't stop staring. Seeing her here, riding a horse like an Amazon, reminds me of the time we spent together in Pangea. Minus the horse.

With a final glance at Louise, Jane says, "Follow me. I'll be waiting for you at headquarters."

Before I can say anything else, Jane and Dorothy race ahead, probably to warn the trigger-happy towns-folk. Clearly, Louise doesn't have much tact in these things, considering we were still almost shot despite her efforts. She's definitely a different woman than the one I met years ago. Ravi's death has made her bitter and direct.

Louise explains more of the Earthlings' situation as we resume our journey toward downtown. They know there are eight Earths. Apparently, the messengers briefed the protectors who arrived here after Khof took over and they lost control of this hypersphere. According to them, the numbers start at sector west-northwest and go clockwise on the wagon wheel created by the veils. Jane's Earth, the one with American football, is Earth seven. Terra is number six. My own planet, Jora, is number five.

Other than this, they have no data on the alternate Earths, and we're the first ones to confirm any of it. More importantly, they didn't know we could have humans looking exactly like us on other planets; they thought they all would be different people, like those from Jora and Earth.

The only information we know with certainty is that Earths five and seven, mine and Jane's, were selected to battle each other years ago, and both survived, while Terra and Yora, Khof's home, fought each other and were both destroyed.

"When we were drafted," Louise says, "the messengers told us that Zeon—I mean, the people on the island..." She glances at me but looks away. "They had made a deal with the messengers' enemies. Have you heard of them?"

I briefly scratch my nose. "The necromantes."

"*Necromantes*," Louise says, emphasizing her French accent. "How do you know this? Have you seen them?"

My muscles tense just hearing their name. "I just heard stories from Dooria. Raj's people also know about them."

Raj clears his throat. "But you have more information than we have. No messenger talked to us this time. We only speculated based on what Mercury told us years ago." Mercury is one of the messengers.

After we follow the street for several minutes, we finally find Jane inside a wooden gazebo. As we expected, she's not alone—John and Paulo are next to her. The small structure is in a cute little park that works also as a roundabout for this part of the town.

The roads around it are all empty. Snipers lie in wait on the tops of nearby apartments, weapons at the ready.

Stopping a few meters away from my welcoming party, I take a good look at them. Jane's eyes are swollen, her expression wary but firm. Beside her, John's army-green combat uniform seems inappropriate for this climate, but he doesn't seem bothered by it. His hands are on his hips, and as always, I can't tell what he's thinking based on his deadpan face.

In contrast to John's battle-ready attire, Paulo wears black pants, boots, a khaki shirt, a silver sheriff star and—of course—a small but still unmistakable black cowboy hat. I swear it looks like a sheriff's Halloween costume—and a very tall sheriff at that.

To my surprise, Paulo is the one who breaks the spell and walks up to me with a big smile on his face. John extends his arm to stop him, but to both his and my horror, he fails.

Paulo open his arms wide and says, "Howdy, partner!"

Seeing his outfit, I realize the bossy woman is right. It looks silly. My cowboy hat's gotta go. Meanwhile, Paulo embraces me in a long, uncomfortable, but paradoxically soothing hug.

Chapter 19

DEBRIEF

When I first entered one of the living units in Terra's sector, where Primavera and I healed Marie, I thought they were all the same size. My assumption was incorrect. John's apartment must be the size of a ballroom.

It must have been a daunting task for them to figure out who owned which unit here, so they wouldn't get killed. There are thousands of residences in this place, all of them interspersed with roads, trees, grass—not to mention gazebos and stables. I even see a fountain as we enter John's apartment.

We gather in his dining room around an oval mahogany table—don't ask me why, but it's always mahogany. There are eight wooden chairs so polished I'm surprised we don't slip from them, each one sculpted from a single section of a tree. The wood is definitely not soft, but the smooth curves feel comfortable.

John prefers the formality of sitting at the table,

with him at its head. Raj and I sit on his left, and Paulo, Louise, and Jane are across from us.

Mike's not in the Wheel. Like me, he was a mole, and after our final errand with the messengers, we don't have to come here if we don't want to. I'm told he stayed on Earth to work on the portal between our planets.

I repeat the story of how I ended up here to John, bypassing the part where I was in jail and watching fireworks with my pet robot, but something's bothering him. He keeps asking the same questions in different ways.

"So, when this woman—Jean—died, she shot you in the leg. I understand you healed it in the same way you helped Jane years ago"—John waves at Jane for emphasis—"by stopping the bleeding, closing the veins, and the like. But then, hours later, you magically figure out how to completely remake your thigh and Marie's shoulder." He rests both of his palms on the tabletop. "Doesn't it sound odd?"

"Um..." I scratch my beard and avoid eye contact as I work on a lie. I'm not going to let them know about Primavera. "There's nothing *magical* about it. I just needed someone to teach me." Wait, I need to be more careful about what I say. "I mean, I just needed time to teach *myself* how to do it." I nod at John for longer than I should. "*Someone,* in this case, is me." I chuckle, looking at Jane, hoping to get a sympathetic nod back. Fat chance.

"And what about your black eye?" Jane asks. "How did you get it? And why isn't it healed?"

Earlier, John forced me to take my "birth-control glasses" and the hideous hat off—his words—so I can't hide anymore. I wish I could lie and tell them the black eye was due to fighting a dozen enemy combatants, but Raj is in the room to contradict me.

"I accidentally made someone mad."

Raj scoffs at me. "It was Marie." He chooses the worst time ever to relearn how to speak. "Zeon called her fat." His head bobs, and he looks even more like Ravi when he does that.

But when Raj's eyes meet Louise's, his face becomes grim. Earlier, I told Raj what happened with Ravi and Louise, and about Ravi's unexpected death. I failed to mention Ravi was pointing a gun at me when he was killed, though. I was—and still am—tired of defending myself.

"*Accidentally*," I repeat. "I never said the word fat."

Jane exhales and adjusts her ponytail, a faint smirk on her face. "I guess you haven't changed."

"Oh, really?" John says. "And why don't you just go ahead and heal your ass-ugly face like the savior you are, Zeon? Maybe using your inner chakra or something?"

His ridicule makes my blood boil. "Major," I reply, "with all due respect, you don't have to be a fucking doctor to know that messing with your neurons unnecessarily risks damaging your brain."

And becoming stupid like you. I don't actually say the insult out loud. There are other ways to hurt your head, and John looks like he'd be happy to demonstrate them on me.

"Where were you, Zeon?" Jane interrupts, in a voice louder than normal. I look at her, confused. "All this time?" Her chin is trembling, and before I can answer, she slams her hands on the table, startling everyone but John.

"Where the *fuck* were you?" she shouts. "People are dying here!"

It's funny both she and John are angry after they finally believe I'm not Khof—or more importantly, that Khof isn't me. I'm no neuropsychiatrist, but this feels exactly like when your mother finally finds you after you went missing as a child—relief followed by anger. In this case, I've been upgraded from psychopathic murderer to indifferent coward.

"I thought we were done with the messengers, and with Pangea," I say. "I had no idea you were fighting here. And I was all alone and in jail because of what Mike did on Jora." I frown. "You can't possibly blame me for this."

Jane stands up and paces around, still keeping to her side of the table. Everyone stays quiet, giving her some time. She watches the movement outside, staring through the implausibly invisible glass. The only hint it's there is because of the abnormally silent people on the street beyond it.

After a while, she walks back to her chair, rests her hands on the back, and turns to face us.

"What made you come here, then?" she asks me. "And why now?"

I scratch the back of my neck. This is one part of the story I glossed over.

"It happened when Dooria showed up," I tell her, following this up with a quick explanation of who Dooria is and her role in my personal life. Jane knows about my ex-fiancée Nia and her illicit relationship with Bodan, so at least there's no need to explain that.

"Dooria said you needed my help," I explain. "I didn't believe her at first—the messengers are full of tricks—but she told me you'd sent a message. Something only you and I would know."

She turns her head to the side, still looking at me. "I did nothing of the sort. What was the message?"

I clasp my hands, measuring my words, a half-smile forming on my face. "She said *Louise* Lane needs spider guy's help. This is why I'm wearing this." I point both thumbs at the spider decal on my t-shirt and grin. Jane used to mispronounce Lois Lane's name all the time, and I always thought it was funny. And only she knows that.

"But Louise Lane is Superperson's girlfriend, not Spider-guy's," Raj says, frowning. Well, I'll be damned. Jane's mispronunciation actually means something on Terra.

Louise—who's definitely *not* Louise Lane in this analogy—gives a knowing look at Jane, but neither of them says anything. John's eyes dart between all of us. He's clearly waiting for an explanation.

"C'mon, Jane," I say. "You must know what I'm talking about. Remember when we had the best, most memorable—"

Jane's eyes widen, and she shakes her head, reminding me she's from Earth, the planet of the prudes. I catch myself just in time, clearing my throat.

"I mean, when we had the most extraordinary talk we ever had?" I force a chuckle. That was close. "Definitely not sex." She rubs her palm on her face.

John grunts at me. "Let me get this straight. Someone lied to make you come here, and all of a sudden, you're back in Pangea, able to heal people and who knows what else." He pauses. "And yet, you can't fly like Khof or do the things he does. Why is that?"

"I don't know. It was a shock to me as well. Clearly, Khof is stronger than me."

A timer-like ping interrupts our conversation. John waves his right hand above the table, and a floating, semi-transparent user interface wheel appears. It vanishes as John reads a message and touches it.

The main entrance opens, and Vladimir steps inside. I usually don't remember what people wore even hours before—it's one of my blind spots—but not in this case. Vladimir always wears the exact same attire—an impeccable sleeveless shirt, denim pants, and matching brown belt and flashy boots.

After a short glance at everybody at the table, Vladimir gives a quick "*tovarishchi*," but he doesn't wait for us to acknowledge. Instead, he talks directly to John as if we're not even in the room.

"Bastard was scouting but flew away." He gives us an evil grin. "Sniper arrangement is working."

Avoiding my eyes, Jane sits at her chair again. The last vestige of doubt is gone. The enemy she's been fighting for so long is not me but disassociating him from the person in front of her, the one she dated and loved in the past, must be hard. Especially after so much time thinking otherwise.

"Did you get a good look at his face?" John asks him.

"*Da.*" He waves at me. "Ugly *blyat* looks like him but no beard." He sneers. "No offense."

I can almost hear a collective sigh of relief from the room. Vladimir did insult me, but it's better than the alternative of killing me on sight. I suppress a chuckle. This whole evil twin thing reminds me of my favorite episode of *Days of Our Lives*.

"Okay, so you're not him," John says. "But how do

you know you're the same one we met and not some Zeon from a parallel-parallel Earth?" He smiles at his own joke.

"Well," I wave at Jane, "she should know. I mean, you all know now about our—ahem—exchange of ideas." Jane just rolls her eyes.

"This happened here, I'm guessing?" John asks her. Jane buries her face in her hands before nodding. "The messengers know about it," he continues. "How else would you get that message from your mother?"

I snort. "Dooria is a mother-like *figure*. My friend's mother. Seriously, Major, I don't know what else to say."

But John is right. The messengers were the ones who sent the message. I'm not even surprised. The only unknown is whether Dooria was aware of this.

"Well, I have an idea, a question that will prove if you're Zeon or not. Remember the eve of our final battle with the messengers?"

"Of course." How could I forget? It was the day after the messengers tried to kill us all. He met me at the hotel for a cup of coffee. News vans were outside broadcasting the story that Ravi had been murdered, and most people thought I might be the culprit. So, I'll be able to remember anything he throws at me.

"Can you describe what I was wearing that day?"

You gotta be kidding me.

Chapter 20

REPARATIONS

LOCATION: WHEEL – EARTH'S SECTOR

Then he laughs. John's question makes me doubt for a moment that he's the same person I met years ago, the one who never cracked a joke. It turns out people can change.

"Jonathan," Raj says. "I'm sorry, I mean John. We need to go back and bring my people here. You have better resources than us, and it's better if we fight together."

John gives Raj a non-committal nod. "We'll get to that. But not now. Tonight, the two moons are going to be aligned."

"What does that even mean?" I ask. Even if the moons have been slowly coming into alignment over the last few days, how that would help us is beyond my comprehension.

A wide grin shows up on John's face. "It means, if you don't know how to swim, you should learn fast. Louise, can you show them?"

Louise makes odd gestures on what I can only assume is an invisible floating interface. "The river slows down and becomes a lake for several hours," she explains as a 3D map is projected onto the table out of nowhere. It shows the island in the middle and the river coming to a stop as two bright spots align high above it.

I keep forgetting how awesome hypersphere audio-visuals are. Yes, we can do something similar by projecting images onto our brains on Jora, but here they do it out of thin air. On top of a mahogany table.

"You cannot possibly expect me to open the veil for you," I say. "When I do that, the barrier lights up like it's Christmas. It's going to be a giant 'Look at me!' sign."

"No need for that, Zeon," John says. "Not yet." Responding to the movements of his arms, the projection zooms in to the island's veil. "When the moons align, the force field also weakens in a few spots, allowing people—though not vehicles or large ammunition—to cross through. Those spots are hard to find."

He points at specific areas where supposedly the barrier is weaker, but I can't tell the difference. I guess it will be even harder to find the crossing points in the dark.

"We speculate that this is a part of the Wheel puzzle originally created by the messengers," Louise says. "We only noticed it during the last alignment after we crossed the river, but it was too late to take advantage of it."

The messengers' hyperspheres were always designed for battles between humans, and most of them also had intricate puzzles for us to solve. They were testing us, trying to figure out if humans were worthy fighters for the gods. It seems this one is no exception. Well, except the messengers can't access it anymore.

"This must be another test," I say.

"You're probably right," Jane says. "But it doesn't matter. We have no other choice but to take advantage of it." She waves her hand at the floating map. "Are you going to help us or not?" Jane asks.

At her question, I hesitate. Jane has already complained twice that I didn't go back to Pangea to help them. In both cases, I had no idea what was happening here. This time, though, I don't have that excuse. People are dying. Khof is outnumbered, but he's the only one who has high-powered weapons. And if he wins, the so-called necromantes will take over Pangea, the land of dreams.

"There are no habitat rings to go back to like last time," John says. "They were destroyed by Khof. So, there's no going back to Jora right now. You're stuck here with us."

Maybe John thinks my hesitation is because I'm thinking about fleeing. In reality, I hate when a decision is made for me, even if I was going to do it anyway.

My chest rises with a deep breath, and I shut my eyes for a second, taking everything in. I'd never forgive myself if I did nothing.

I open my eyes. "Where do I sign?"

THE TOWN in Earth's octant reminds me of the hilly, narrow roads of Catalonia, where relatively short structures are built to follow the terrain rather than make it easier for humans to walk around. The difference here is that the buildings have no straight edges or corners, and they're all dull gray, making them appear futuristic. They could easily be the dorm area of a Starfleet academy.

After assigning an apartment to Raj and dropping him off, Vladimir takes me to the one Louise had set up earlier for me. The available empty units belonged to protectors that aren't around anymore. The previous occupants were all Khof's victims.

Once we're inside, he waves at the unrealistically spotless living room inside the front door of my new home. "Here you are, Zeon."

I survey the place in awe. I wish we could live here forever. The units are self-cleaning, and I'm told there's a laundry chute that returns your clothes clean and ironed in less than an hour.

"Enjoy your free time," he says, chuckling. "Eat a worm. The battle is tonight!"

"A worm?" I ask, confused.

He slaps my shoulder. "*Da!* Take a bath. Rest. Eat. Drink!" A big grin appears on his face. "I was told to give you this garbage." He hands me a bottle of white Zinfandel.

Without waiting for my answer, he turns around and walks out the door. It automatically opens and shuts as he leaves, and I can clearly see through the transparent walls as he jogs down the street, whistling.

Half an hour later, after the most thorough shower of my life—the water pressure seemed to come from everywhere, making sure I was clean inside and out— I'm finally dressed. Whoever lived here before was really into soccer. A rainbow of more than a hundred soccer jerseys takes up most of the closet, complete with socks, boots, and even cleats.

My choice of attire is Seattle's somewhat discreet

deep-blue away jersey, jeans, and a nice pair of turf boots. I don't want a shoot-me-first style when I go into combat, and the Sounders' jersey was a rare find amongst the bright yellow, orange, and other equally scandalous color selections.

In the kitchen, I find wine glasses in a cabinet that pops up from the wall, almost hitting me in the face. It takes me longer to find a wine opener since the drinks here are automatically generated and poured into the glasses. The system keeps trying to fill my glass with Chardonnay. Sweet wine is frowned upon even in Heaven, it seems.

Once I get the bottle open, I sit alone on the comfortable black couch and hold the glass high, looking through the rose-colored liquid. No one is going to see me drinking this tacky beverage, so it should be fine. And it's only considered tacky by experts because its sweetness masks the delicate bitterness of my life.

A tri-tone text alert breaks me out of my reverie. It's been years since I last heard it—we don't have phones on Jora—and it brings back conflicting memories from my time on Jane's Earth. I glance around the room—mostly bare—and the alert sounds again.

This time, I identify its origin. It comes from the entry door. Jane is outside, one hand running through her wet hair, the other on her hip. Since Louise made the housing unit identify me as the resident, people outside have had to knock to get in—or ring the text-alert bell, I suppose. I set my drink down on the glassy table and stride in her direction.

As I approach the door, she lowers her eyebrows, tapping her foot nervously. Before I get there, she rotates her hand clockwise and the doorbell rings again. This makes me smile.

The door opens by itself when I get close enough.

"Hey, Jane!" I grin. "You're really sexy when you're mad."

Her new attire is a loose gray blouse with short sleeves and cropped tight black pants that leave her calves out in the open. She smiles at first but quickly narrows her eyes. This is progress. The last time I said that, she punched me in the arm.

"You haven't shaved." She bites her lip. Jane's complaints never bother me because I know they're not out of malice. She just says whatever's in her head. I like that.

"No, I haven't. I've heard that a Khof-like beardless chin is not in fashion here." The last thing I want is to look like him in a battle.

"Good point."

Her odd choice of pants highlights her smooth, attractive legs, but looks like a compromise for people who can't decide if they're going to wear shorts or normal pants. Not that I'm complaining—she looks great in them. When my eyes meet hers again, she grins, having caught me in the act of admiring her. Smooth move, Romeo.

"They're Capris," she says.

I haven't met Capri yet. She must be one of the new protectors. It's odd that Jane's wearing someone else's pants though. "They look great on you."

"May I come in?" She looks at the hallway behind me.

Turning around and walking back to where I was before, I say, "Of course! But you should know this is a gun-free house." I chuckle.

Clutching the handheld capacitor hooked into her holster, she follows me. "Maybe you shouldn't do jokes like that. You still may be an impostor, right?"

She's right—it was a joke, but Jane definitely loves guns more than people. I wave at the floor. "Beware of the step between the kitchen and the living room."

Jane relaxes. "I know. Most of our units are like this. You can change it to be a smooth slope."

"Raj is still in awe that you were able to get inside them."

Looking around, she rubs her forehead. "Maybe it was persistence? It took us a long time to figure it out, and Khof wasn't attacking us on a daily basis at the time. Louise helped us the most. She has a way of seeing things that aren't obvious to the rest of us."

It makes sense. She's blind on Earth, so she definitely has different perceptions.

When I get around the small table, I grab my wine and lie down on the couch, gesturing at Jane to do the same. Jane eyes my glass and frowns. I take it personally and jump to conclusions, frowning back.

"Um... it should be no one's business that I like sweet drinks."

For all I know, a bunch of pretentious jerks met one day on Earth and created an arbitrary rule against sugary drinks, and now everyone has to follow it. If I were the jerk in charge, the rule would be the opposite.

She shrugs and sits down on the couch next to me. "It's fine. I just thought it wasn't a good idea to drink before a battle." Then she pauses. "You know what? I'll join you." The coffee table in front of us magically produces a wine glass. There's a lot for me to learn here. I thought we had to go to the kitchen for that.

After I pour the wine into her glass, she takes a

large sip and looks down. There's an air of reluctance about her. We have a lot of baggage.

"Zeon, I'm here to apologize." She bites her lip and looks away. I wait for her to continue. "I thought you were a psychopath. I thought Khof was you. But I should've known. I'm sorry." Her eyes meet mine again.

"It's okay. I can't blame you. He has my beautiful body," I joke, "and we didn't know about the other Earths."

She looks down and takes a deep breath. "And the last time we met... you were right. The messengers—some of them, anyway—they betrayed us." She swallows hard and looks back at me.

Like many other angels, she was indoctrinated in Pangea from a young age. The fact the messengers wanted to kill all humans was too much for her to take.

"It's okay, Jane. But I have to ask you something. About that day. And I don't want you to feel worse about it."

During our final fight with the messengers, she used a weapon that, at first, hadn't been in her hand. She did something I thought only I was able to do, and only under stress—move solid objects with my mind.

"Remember how you got your capacitor when we were on the floor? How did you do it?"

Her wide eyes focus on me, her eyebrows scrunching together in puzzlement.

"Me? I thought it was you!"

Interesting. So, she didn't do it on purpose. It seems other people can affect hyperspheres, but maybe it doesn't come as easily for them. They were never trained for it like I was.

"You must've done it accidentally, then. But it

doesn't matter. It's all in the past. We're here now, fighting together again."

She grabs a disposable tissue from a metal box magically appearing from the couch's arm. Then, she sniffs loudly and cleans her nose with the tissue. "I thought you were the monster." She gives me a sad chuckle. "I'm so sorry."

Yes, she believed in the messengers, but her faith was misplaced. She didn't know better. Jane thought she was doing the right thing. Saving lives. Her heart was in a good place.

Tears are flowing freely down her face now, and I touch her arm to reassure her. It has the opposite effect, though. She starts sobbing, shoving her face into her hands to get away from me. But I don't let her do this. Instead, I shift closer and cautiously pull her into a platonic embrace. Her arms wrap around my back, and her face touches my shoulder as she continues to cry, her body shaking.

The contact of her bare neck on my cheek and the slight perfume of roses from a recent shower temporarily bring me back to a time when we were a couple. A chill runs down my back. That life is over.

During our embrace, Jane leans on my chest, forcing me to lie down on the couch. Her eyes close and her breath eases. To my dismay, before I can say anything, she falls asleep. How funny. I haven't realized how tired I am. And then, just like that, I drift to sleep too.

Chapter 21

SWARM

When I open my eyes, the couch is nowhere to be seen, and we're both lying on the grass. The whole apartment is gone. Above us, a red giant illuminates the landscape.

Jane throws her hands up and glares at me. "What did you do?"

I stare at her. "It wasn't me!"

Pushing herself off me, she stands up. With her help, I follow suit. We're on top of a hill covered in diamond-shaped grass, surrounded by low bushes. A valley can be seen far ahead.

Jane temporarily forms a ponytail with her fist, but she has no hairband. The hair falls back down her back. "We're not in the Wheel anymore."

Instinctively, I sweep the dirt off my clothes, except there's none. They're completely clean. Everything here looks really odd. It feels like I'm inside a double-exposed photo; anything in my peripheral vision is out of focus. Things are only sharp if I look at them directly.

"What is this place?" I ask. Clearly, it's a different hypersphere, but why does everything look blurry?

Jane points to the sky. "Look!"

Above us, the sun's brightness seems to blink in a few spots, as if thin clouds were passing in front of it. Using my arm to shield my eyes, I squint. *Those can't be clouds. Clouds don't move that fast.*

And then we see them, swarming the skies, flying around us in the form of a misshapen arrow. I rub my eyes to be sure I'm actually seeing it.

"What *is* that?" Jane asks.

A dark gray swarm of bugs flies above us, but they're too far away. There must be thousands of them. I glance behind us, and the tall trunks of a forest immediately come into focus. It feels like I'm under the influence.

"Uh... maybe we should run?"

"Wait!" Jane says. "Who are they?"

She points at the valley ahead where a large army of humans has gathered. I hadn't noticed them but there must be thousands of beings there. They're carrying rifles and capacitors. Some ride on trucks with missile launchers. The swarm is not heading in our direction. It's going to attack them.

"How is this possible? Those look like humans." Because of the distance, I can't be certain.

Far off, a single bug leads the enemy attack, and the swarm stops just behind it, forming a sphere made of thousands of tiny points. Nothing happens for a couple of seconds–and then the humans start firing, all at once.

Jane brushes a strand of hair away from her eyes. "Could they be from another Earth?"

"I don't know. Maybe. Each of our planets has

billions of people, and there are eight Earths, so who knows?"

The projectiles reach the flying army but explode harmlessly against invisible bubbles. Energy shields protect every single individual in the swarm.

As we watch, the humans keep firing, but the bugs just wait there, taking the hits. The sky is lit by the exploding shells. It's a beautiful yet frightening sight. What those people are doing is not sustainable.

"They're doomed," Jane says.

As she predicted, the humans soon abandon their attack and begin to run for their lives. *This is it. They'll be slaughtered. I can't let that happen.* So, I take a step toward the melee, but Jane grabs my arm.

"No, Zeon. This is suicide! Are you crazy? They'll be dead before you even get there."

"There must be something we—or I—can do."

She moves her hand down to touch her holster but stops before reaching it. "No. We can't win against that many, Zeon."

The swarm slowly starts to move toward the people. The formation changes from a sphere to a long narrow cone, speeding up.

"Why are the bugs moving?" I ask. "Why don't they just fire back? It'd be like shooting fish in a barrel."

Ranged weapons would make their job easier, but they don't have to use them. When the needle of the cone reaches the people, the bugs slice through human bodies, over and over again as the whole cone sweeps through them.

Blood sprays, painting the vegetation dark red.

The swarm spreads in all directions from the first contact point, and the battlefield is blurred by shades of red and gray. In seconds, there's no one left alive, and no sign real people were ever there.

No sane person would think the large blobs of red marking the valley were once part of real humans, not unless they had watched it happen. I feel sick.

"Oh, my God!" Jane whimpers. "They're all dead!"

We remain motionless for a moment, stunned by the violence. The bugs rush above the field like a tornado, maybe looking for survivors. After that, they fly upward and once again form a gray cloud that dims the giant sun. If they see us, we're toast.

There's no need for anyone to tell us to retreat. Once the enemy is again airborne, Jane and I turn around together and run toward the nearby forest. Maybe we can hide there.

"It's too far." Jane says. "Can you find another place for us to hide?"

I concentrate, looking for a way out. The hyperspheres are never the same, but the messengers always leave hidden passages and secret hideaways we can use. But I can't find anything here. Even in my mind, things are out of focus. What a weird place.

As I try not to panic, my virtual search continues down the hill until it suddenly stops. Well, that's strange. Unlike all the hyperspheres I've been to, this one ends—it has a boundary. There's nothing but darkness after that, so the forest is our only option.

I grab Jane's hand. "Come with me. If they don't see us, there's a chance we can make it."

And then, we run for our lives.

Just like a knight in shining armor, I wonder, but all of a sudden, my foot is trapped by vines. They're impossible to see when everything is blurry. We fall face first to the ground, deforming some low bushes nearby.

High-pitched screeches announce we've been seen. The calls continue, the swarm getting nearer.

Again, Jane is the first to lift herself up, grabbing me up by the arm in the process.

There's nothing else to do. The chaotic mass of assassins assembles above us, forming another sphere. It's the same formation that attacked the others.

"They're... so tall!" I say.

When we watched the battle from afar, they looked like small bugs, and the fact they were in a swarm didn't help. But now I can see them better. Far from being tiny, the leading bug is a giant, skinny creature with a triangular face covered in eyes, like a gray praying mantis twice the height of a human.

However, their bodies aren't at all like bugs. They have muscles, and wear a tight black fabric delineating their long torsos. A single belt around what I assume is their waist carries what can only be described as an array of holstered sidearms. They're energy weapons, but we didn't see them using them.

Then, instead of pulling her capacitor out of its holster, Jane grabs my hand. True, the small gun wouldn't do anything to protect us, but I appreciate the gesture. Maybe she likes me more than guns.

I feel a slight wobble in her fingers, but her expression isn't one of fear. More like defiance. I gulp. At least we'll die together. We both take deep breaths, and my panic paradoxically subsides after I accept our fate. I just hope we die as quickly as the others.

"Why do they all have backpacks?" Jane asks.

The swarm is close enough that I can feel them in my mind map, study their inner bodies. I blink.

"They're not backpacks, Jane. They're brains."

"But they're huge!"

Tell me about it. Their brains are four to six times larger than ours, and they outnumber us. We thought they were bugs, but in reality, *we're* the bugs here, ready to be crushed.

"That can't be natural," I say.

The leader of the pack stops, as it did in the previous attack, and extends its extra-long arms, one carrying a sword as long as the creatures are tall. Even from here, I can tell it's not a regular sword. The blade glows red along the edges. It has a power source.

And just like that, we're in the shade. From behind each one of the creatures' arms, something extends to block the sun. I wonder at first if it's fabric, but it's not. It's part of their bodies.

"They have *wings!*" Jane says. This is so odd. Instead of thinking about our impending doom, Jane seems to be struck by the amazing shape of the aliens. This is what I've always liked about her. It's not that she's unafraid. It's that she's better at acting. Maybe today, I can be a little bit more like her.

"Don't worry," I lie. "We're going to make it." I let her hand go, hug her with my left arm, and pull her closer, pretending I have a plan as we wait for the onslaught.

It doesn't take long. Just as before, the swarm moves into a cone formation and comes at us. I put my free hand over my head, close my eyes, and concentrate, ready to fight. Maybe I can do some damage when I touch them. But nothing happens.

Except that something—or someone—hits the ground just in front of us. I detect a being with an aura ten times brighter than humans or messengers, and I open my eyes with my mouth open.

The other bugs have disappeared, and a single

creature towers over us. It must be at least four meters tall. It folds its enormous wings as it lowers its arms, and everything gets brighter. The gray giant was literally eclipsing the sun.

Now the monster mantis is turning its multi-eyed face to Jane. Despite its body size, its head is smaller than a human's.

"Ms. Engel," a voice addresses her. The creature's mouth doesn't move, but I hear its voice in my head. It's a telepath.

Jane and I look at each other. She must've heard it too.

Next, it's my turn to be examined by the tiny head. "Mr. Zeon. Expecting you."

Chapter 22

NIGHTMARE

LOCATION: SOMEWHERE IN PANGEA

The way the bug communicates is much better than speaking. Thoughts form in our minds that tell us its precise intent. However, when I put the message into words, it sounds like broken English.

"Am Haides. Necromantes Brotherhood. Underworld general." The word "underworld" appears in my mind with a hint of death, despair, and destruction.

I've got to hand it to them—they have incredibly cool titles.

Jane hasn't let go of me in the meantime, so we remain embraced, looking up at the bug general. "Where are we?" she asks.

Haides' several tiny eyes blink simultaneously when he turns to look back at Jane. He can hear us. "Dreamsphere. Brotherhood banished. Dreamspheres allowed."

I see. They were banished from Pangea many years ago by the messengers. Dreamspheres are the only places they can show up here.

"What about the people that died?" Jane asks. "Is this just a dream?"

Haides bends his knees to crouch in front of us, the way people do when talking with little kids. We're at eye level with him now, his head slightly above ours.

Even sitting, he's still taller than we are.

"Gods. Created mantes. To Fight enemies, kill humans. Long ago." I swear Haides just sent a scorn emotion, just like we do on Jora when our augmented sensors are enabled. "Three planets. Gone."

It takes me a couple of seconds to parse that one. So, the battle we saw happened a long time ago, and they killed all humans from three Earths. I gulp. It was a triple genocide.

Haides continues. "Humans. Mantes. Pawns." According to him, they were under orders by the messengers. He's arguing we're being used by them, just like they were.

"But why are we here?" I ask.

Knowing why is more important than how. I have a pretty good idea of what happened—*in vino veritas*.

"Ms. Engel. Mr. Zeon. Brought you. Have request." Haides' arms touch the ground and move aimlessly. I don't think they're used to staying in this position for long. "Join Khof. Brotherhood returns. Godsland Entropia destroyed."

My eyes fixate on Haides as I think about what he just said. Haides has just confirmed that Entropia *is* the place the gods live. Primavera said it's also where our minds go when we die. I'm not a fan of the messengers but allying with Khof doesn't seem the best solution. If we do that, Haides and the necromantes will invade Pangea. But—according to the protectors—if this happens, a lot of people are going to die. Why does everything in Pangea always involve mass murder?

I step in front of Jane and clear my throat. "This is nice and all—kind of the classic hero journey, if you ask me." I draw a circle in the air with my hands. "But there's a small problem vis-à-vis destroying Pangea." I laugh and glance at Jane, who frowns. "Uh... if you do that, I think, the dreamspheres are going to be destroyed, and we're all going to die. Including you."

Like a fly, Haides' giant hands rub his face so fast that for a moment, I doubt it even happened. "Dreamspheres gone. Allies safe. Mostly."

Haides confirms they'll destroy the dreamspheres, and almost no new dreamspheres will be allowed as the war with the gods rages. While hyperspheres are playgrounds created by the gods to—apparently—torture humans, we create our own dreamspheres every time we sleep. But he'll make an exception for some humans that fight with him, and let most people survive.

The problem is he said 'most.' What does it mean?

Haides' mouth opens and closes, and a drop of black liquid forms on his lips. The movement makes a high-frequency noise. "High cost. Mantes. Humans. Many deaths."

I look away for a second. His comments prove he can read my mind. Great. There'll be collateral damage, and many will die. Still, the emotions sent in his message indicate his Brotherhood did not make this choice lightly. With the systematic destruction of Pangea and the dreamspheres because of the upcoming war, they can't control which ones will be destroyed or allowed back. There are too many of them. A lot will die, including their own. Necromantes also need to sleep.

"Mantes planet," Haides says. "Supernova. Need Pangea."

I force myself to not glance at Jane. So *that's* why they're fighting. The star by the necromantes' home planet will soon become a supernova, killing them all. Their only hope of survival is a bodiless life in a hypersphere, exactly like the people from Terra are doing now.

But the messengers of the gods won't allow this. So Haides isn't a run-of-the-mill genocidal maniac. More like someone who will do anything to save his people. I can empathize with that, but not with the murdering.

"But Haides," I say out loud, for Jane's sake. She can't hear my thoughts. "Most people on Earths—well, most beings in the *universe*—won't even know what's happening. How is that fair?"

Again, his hand scrapes his eyes in a blur. "Mr. Zeon. Unfortunate." I swear he moves his tiny head side to side as he pauses. "No species. Enemy hands."

They don't want other races helping the gods. But I've heard enough. This whole conversation reminds me of a similar speech from none other than the messengers themselves. I wasn't convinced that time, and I'm not convinced now.

Therefore, there's only one way to handle this.

I'm about to lie and accept his proposal—so we can get out of here—when Jane speaks up.

"No." She shakes her head, which I think is ill-advised. Who knows what that means to an alien creature? On Jora, it means someone is soliciting no-strings-attached sex. "We'll never join you."

I move to stand between Jane and Haides with my

arms extended, palms outward. "Wait, what are you saying?" I guess Jane is not as good at lying as I am. This is the wrong thing to say in front of a monster with a giant brain and insect-like muscles.

"Zeon, do you know why I'm attracted to you?" Jane asks.

I tilt my head in confusion at her, but she doesn't elaborate on what in the tickle she's talking about. This is not the place or the time to discuss this. So, I roll my eyes toward the huge alien. "Because I know which battles to fight?" I wink several times.

She grabs both of my hands, and our eyes lock. "No. Because you trust no one, while I'm not that cynical. We're so different yet so similar in one way—we stay true to our principles."

She smiles. This would be nice to hear if not for the fact we have a necromantis so close that it could—and probably will—kill us.

"And I know you're not going to like this," she continues, "but you must trust me. We have to fight for the gods this time. Even if you don't agree with me."

Before I can reply, Haides' right arm grabs my neck and stands, pulling me up. Each one of his hands has five fingers and two thumbs, and he uses his thumbs to start choking me.

"Stop it!" Jane says. "You can't kill him. This is a *dream!*"

Haides ignores her and brings me closer to his face, looking into my eyes. "Thousand years. Only here." All his eyes blink for longer than I was expecting. "Learn to kill. No wake. Certain death." He's saying if we can't wake up when we're killed in a dreamsphere, we'll die. And, somehow, he's orchestrated this exact situation.

Jane draws her small capacitor so fast it looks like

she's unsheathing a knife, and she immediately starts shooting the necromantis point-blank. The shots flare against the creature's skin, clothes, and armor, but he doesn't even blink his multiple eyes; they must have body-tight shields.

Haides' face slowly turns to her as she keeps firing. "Sorry. Kill Zeon. No alternative. Send message. Tell others."

Then a feeling of guilt appears in my mind, and I almost feel bad for him.

She may not remember—this is just a dream.

Haides looks at me again. "Nightmares. No forget."

An expression of horror dawns on Jane's face. For a change, she's the one that made the wrong call. She should've lied that we would help them.

"No!" She drops her gun, jumps on his long, thin leg, and begins punching whatever is closest. I want to say something, but can only make awful choking sounds. I try to concentrate and do some damage to the alien creature, but there isn't much time. Maybe I'm going to die after all?

Suddenly, a bright blue light explodes from Haides' long vertical chest. My head is right next to it, so the smell of burning meat hits my nostrils as buckets of green blood splash all over me. The object that pierced him looks like one of the swords the necromantes were carrying earlier, but this one is smaller, maybe a third of its size. Sound comes out of Haides' relatively tiny mouth in the form of a horrible shriek.

I hear his final words in my mind. "Find you. Mr. Zeon. In nightmares." And just like that, his body disappears.

"Gotcha!" says a little girl's voice.

As I hit the ground, not able to cough yet, I see

Primavera hovering above us. The same blue glow of the sword also surrounds her, and her deep black eyes would be scary if it weren't for the large grin on her face.

Her hair is loose and moving with the wind, and the sword seems too big for her. She's wearing a freaking cape and even has a butterfly logo on her chest.

Despite her fantastic appearance, Jane ignores her at first and rushes to my side. We're both stunned, but probably for different reasons.

Primavera takes this time to float down to the ground. The glow around her and the sword fades. "I thought you didn't play with grasshoppers," she says.

Jane caresses my throat, maybe checking for cuts. I'm still unable to speak. When she seems satisfied with my overall health, Jane turns toward Primavera. "Grasshoppers?" is all she manages to say.

The girl points her longsword at Jane, oblivious to my near-death experience. "Who's she? Are you sleeping together?"

Still speechless, I shake my head too fast, and the movement hurts my neck.

"What?" Jane says.

"You know, shared dreams," explains Primavera. "Two people in the same dreamsphere. It rarely happens."

Jane gestures at the now empty space where Haides was just a few seconds ago. "Did you kill him?"

An expression of horror appears on Primavera's face. "Of course not! You can't kill anyone in a dreamsphere. Most of the time, anyway..." She gets lost in her thoughts for a moment. "He woke up. I've beaten him many times."

This is getting complicated. Primavera pierced his brain with her sword. If this were a hypersphere, he'd be dead for sure—just like Jean. But apparently, dreamspheres' rules are laxer. As long as you're able to wake up, you're fine. Maybe there's not a complete upload of the brain here, like there is in a hypersphere. This means—if Primavera is right—Haides was probably able to wake up.

Once I finally get my voice back, I blurt out what I've been waiting to say since Primavera saved me. "Green!" I choke a bit and cough again. The girls look at each other, puzzled. "Grasshoppers are green, Primavera." I take a deep breath. "Not gray."

The kid shakes her head. "No. They can be gray, or green. Or even brown. Any color, really."

Well, she's right. I don't know what I was thinking. But I stand my ground. "C'mon. They *clearly* look like praying mantises!"

Primavera puts her left hand on her hip and points at the ground. I flinch, looking down and searching for bugs. The last thing I want to see now are real praying mantises.

"Where can you even find mantises with fingers and thumbs?" she says. "And a short neck?" Her head bobbles. "And I can call them whatever I want."

"Quit it, Zeon." Jane grabs my arm, and for the third time today, she helps me up. "Can one of you explain to me what's going on here?"

Leave it to me to fight with the person that just saved my life. So, I sigh and introduce the two of them, including why I didn't mention the kid before. It wasn't my secret to tell.

I also let Primavera know they're actually called necromantes. It takes a lot of effort to not rub in her face that—due to this very important detail—I *am* right about their closest relatives. Who's the grown-up now?

"Necromantes?" the kid asks, frowning. "What an awful name. I didn't know. They never talk to me when we play." Her eyes brighten again. "And it's *so* hard to find them. Half the fun is finding the right dreamspheres. There are trillions."

"So how did you find this one?" I ask.

"I was visiting Dorothy and found you sleeping, so came here to look for you. Your dreamsphere is one of the few I can find because—" She trails off and scratches her ear. "Because of what happened when you were sick as a child. Ermey told me." Primavera is an awful liar. We'll have to talk about this at some point.

Jane folds her arms. "The necromantes are dangerous, Primavera. I don't think they're playing with you."

Primavera frowns again, and her sword swings dangerously when she opens her arms. "But I thought we were friends! We've been playing together for so long."

A thought comes to my mind. Maybe Primavera can help us? "How many of the mantes can you fight at the same time?"

Jane's jaw drops, and she vehemently shakes her head. "Zeon! She's just a kid! You can't possibly consider—"

"'bout three or four," Primavera interrupts, dropping her sword to cross her little arms. "If it's more than that, I just fly around teasing them." She looks at us with an endearing smile.

Jane glares at me with a 'You have a lot to explain but we don't have time right now' face. "Let's go back," she says. "We still have to fight. We cannot let Khof win."

I shake my head. "We can't go back now. There was probably something in the wine Vladimir gave me. It may take a day for us to recover from it."

Primavera shrugs, holding her sword higher. "Not really. I can pop the dreamsphere and take you back!"

"Pop?" I ask. "How?"

Her eyes become wide. "Ermey doesn't let me do it because anyone inside wakes up startled. And, oh boy, they remember the dream."

I look at Jane, who's still frowning, but she nods. The kid knows what she's doing. Well, except the grasshopper thing.

"We don't mind, Primavera," I tell her. "Let's do it!"

Primavera grabs the sword from the ground and points it upward. "Brace yourselves!"

I take a last look around, taking in the out-of-focus world. After Haides' warning, it's going to be difficult for me to fall asleep again.

The girl closes her eyes and jumps into the air. The bright blue glow reappears around her and the sword, and the wind starts making whistling noises.

Paradoxically, her eyes become darker. When she gets about twenty meters up, she points her glowing sword down and drops quickly.

With something that looks like an evil grin on her face—she's really having fun with this—she stabs the ground. When the sword is halfway buried, everything goes dark around us, and Jane and I are jolted back into my apartment, gasping and hugging each other.

Still groggy from whatever was in the wine, we find ourselves entwined on the couch. But there's no time for cuddling. There's a battle to fight.

Chapter 23

ALIGNMENT

After we tell everyone what happened, the protectors create a search party for Vladimir. Soon, he's found lying on the floor in an alley between the main units, naked, unconscious and with a concussion. When he finally awakes, he denies spiking our bottle of wine, arguing that he doesn't remember his last hours or who the *blyat* was that hurt him. He has no recollection of Raj and me showing up earlier. Meanwhile, John refuses to arrest him. The major trusts Vladimir with his life.

To be fair, John is the military leader of the Earthers, and everybody has faith in him. There's a good reason for that. I was told that Khof—who they thought was me—hasn't made a lot of progress here. They've had some losses, but they always made Khof pay for his victories dearly, with similar casualties on his side.

Khof's strategy of sending a few motorized units at a time just can't beat more than a thousand well-trained humans under John. And Khof cannot have more than forty protectors on his side at the moment —that's the original number of protectors every Earth had years ago.

When the sun is setting, John starts gathering his army near the beach. The plan is to divide us into five columns of about two hundred people. No one should be able to see us through the barriers. Every protector carries a small capacitor of some sort and nothing else.

One of John's people approaches me, yelling "Go timbers, army!" to my face and pointing at my Sounders jersey before joining his platoon. It must be our battle cry.

While we prepare for our assault, I get bored and decide to do some exploration. There's an abandoned brownish armored personnel carrier about a hundred meters away from the beach. It made a lot of progress inland before John's forces destroyed it. The damaged vehicle is the same model I saw two days ago when Jean was killed. However, only the front half remains intact.

"Remember the days you could die in the hypersphere and still go back to Terra?" Raj asks. He's following me, glued to my side and watching everyone, wide-eyed. It must be confusing to see so many familiar faces that don't actually know him. So, he stays here, bothering me.

"Yes. The messengers changed the rules when... uh... something happened." My cheeks flush red. They changed the rules because of me. Before that, you'd only actually be dead if something damaged your brain in the hypersphere. After what I did to save my friends, *any* type of death in Pangea became a real death on our planets.

When we reach the transport, we step onto its

back, but we have to bend our heads to get inside. The ceiling is low, and it would reach my nose if I were able to stand up straight. I do a quickly microscopic scan with my mind. The armor must be strong enough to protect the soldiers inside from hand-held energy beams.

"During those days," Raj continues, "we would die and go back to Terra." He slumps his shoulders. "Dying in the hypersphere is unsettling. You wake up there sweating and feeling a lot of pain where you were hit. But dying on Terra when your mind is here is way worse. It's the stuff of nightmares. Or horror movies."

Raj looks at me expectantly. I pause, taking it all in, then ask, "What happened to you?"

He touches the ceiling, also staring at the vehicle's veins. "I don't exactly know. It happened when I was having breakfast here with Marie. I dropped to the ground and saw both Marie and Khof watching me as my body died on Earth. Marie was in the Wheel, and Khof was on Terra, killing me. Blood came out of my mouth and nose. I thought I was going to die here as well."

"Sounds awful," I say, meaning it. Raj nods in silence.

Despite being half blown apart, the transport is still partially working. The pulsating arteries on its dark red deck make it look alive. It has two rows of seats with a lot of space in the middle. If Khof only has the original protectors, two of these transports would be more than enough to carry all of his people. But you never leave all your eggs in one basket, and Khof needs others to drive the tank crews and the heavy artillery.

Raj sits in the first row and crosses his legs. "It's worse than it sounds. I was instantly depressed, as if my will to live had gone. Suicidal even. Marie was the one who saved me from myself that day."

I walk past him to check on the driver's cockpit. "It was as if your light had gone off," I say. Literally. Their deaths turned off their auras, their connection to Terra.

"Exactly."

The front of the transport has a single seat surrounded by a transparent bubble. Their systems here have the exact same interface as the ones we currently have on Jora. Similar to what happened years ago, they wanted people like me to win, the ones trained from infancy to use this technology.

"Hey, princess," John shouts from outside. "Get your shit together! We can't take this transport."

As I leave the vehicle, John grabs me by the arm and pulls me to the front of his column, immediately behind him. I quickly recognize Louise, Jane, and Vladimir in the same group. John's trusted colleagues. Vladimir doesn't look sorry at all for his part in what happened earlier. Raj is sent to one of the other teams.

I'm supposed to be in the first wave, to work as a medic and do whatever "stupid magic trick" I can to help, according to John.

"Timbers army!" I shout, raising my fist, but they all look at me funny.

John rolls his eyes before addressing us. "In ten minutes, the river is going to slow down enough for us to cross it. We have three hours to swim there, kill as many of them as we can, and come back. The peak of the alignment is in an hour and a half."

Great. Here we are again on the verge of killing people. I don't want to do that. They can say whatever they want about me, but I've never killed a single person. The protectors, on the other hand, have been killing from day one. Maybe it gets easier with time.

With the plan in place, we begin our march down the beach. "Why are we swimming?" I ask. "You don't know how to make boats?"

"Because they can see everything but people and animals through the veil, you moron." He's not able to hide his contempt.

"Oh really?" Then I put my foot in my mouth. "And what about our clothes? Shouldn't we all be naked?" I accidentally wave at Jane, who looks offended.

John stops, and since we're walking in line, my question results in all two hundred people in our column halting. He turns around to address my perfectly valid question, his face expressionless.

"Clothes and weapons are fine. If you're wearing them, people from the other side of the wall can't see you." He nods. "It's stupid. This is a *stupid* place. But you of all people should know we don't make the rules here." His words almost make me believe he isn't mad at my question. His grabbing me by the neck of my shirt and bringing me so close our noses touch as he answers, makes me think otherwise.

Despite his awful way to deliver this message, John is right. At the end of the day, Pangea is not real. It's all in our minds.

We get to a sandbank that protrudes into the river, making it the narrowest point to cross, at about 300 meters. There's enough space for all teams to congregate here and swim to their designated areas of the energy wall. Our team has the shortest swim to arrive at the bank on the island, reaching the only beachhead there that's not behind the veil.

Other teams aren't so lucky. In most places, the

wall barely leaves enough space on the island's beach for one person to stand up.

The flow has already slowed enough for us to cross. John rotates his capacitor around, holding it against his chest, then jumps into the water.

The energy ellipsoid works as a flotation device, and soon he's moving ahead. Louise pushes me down as the others dive around me, and just like that, I'm back in the river that nearly killed me when I fell off a cliff in what feels like ages ago.

The water's chilly, but not too much, and Fortress Mesa slowly approaches as we cross the now motionless river. The moons above us are a single light in the sky, dimmer than when they were both contributing light. What happens now is odd, one moon blocking the other from reflecting the sun's light to us in a lunar-lunar eclipse.

Starting across the river earlier than most doesn't help me much, and I'm one of the last to arrive on the other side. In my defense, I'd been enjoying a long vacation in paradise prison while they fought here. I'm just not used to physical labor yet.

John looks at me and shakes his head. "I'm beginning to think you won't be any help at all."

The others are already touching the veil in different places, looking for a way in. Once I finally approach the barrier, I put my whole hand on it and start searching. I'll show him. In no time, I'll find the right place before anyone else. My mind is fast, especially here.

"I found it!" Louise says in a low voice.

The nearby threads ripple, as if a curtain has been opened. This is strange. The veil doesn't seem weaker anywhere. Louise must've been really lucky.

Someone grabs my arm—John?—and pulls me closer to her. By sheer luck, Louise was right next to it the moment it opened. And it happened elegantly, better than when I compress the threads to make a diamond-shaped hole, the only way I know how to do it. I make a mental note to do some experiments in the future to see if I can replicate the process.

John pushes me toward the opening in the veil. "You first."

Sighing, I walk through the curtain-shaped hole, and everybody else positions themselves behind it. Dead silence fills the air around us. Even the crickets are holding their breath. Taking a few steps in, I observe the area. This place is large. The foot of the mesa is still 300 or 400 meters away, so I tread carefully, walking in between the bushes that are more common in this area than on the other shore.

A quick glance behind me shows the dim silhouette of the barrier's opening, but it's only visible because John's forces are right on the other side. From here, it looks like the fabric of space was ripped in one place, and ghostly arms, half-torsos and parts of weapons hang behind it. It works as a triangular window to the other side, allowing me to see them.

After about a minute of seeing nothing on this side, I close my eyes to get a bird's eye view. Since everyone from Khof's Earth is dead, just like Raj's people, I don't expect to see any bright auras, but it's possible I can still detect movement or any human shapes before anyone else spots them.

I freeze. A dozen crouching shadows move around the base of Fortress in our direction. They'll be here in seconds. Meanwhile, vehicles just out of sight on top of the mesa are plodding ahead, ready to fire. They're waiting for us.

Perhaps there's still time to go back. I turn around as silently as possible, but before I can run back, I see a large group of John's soldiers already on this side. Saint Plehr! They should've been waiting for my sign.

"It's a trap!" I shout as I race back to the shore. There's no reason to be subtle.

My warning creates a hubbub, and everyone scrambles for their lives. Khof's army abandons their attempt to be stealthy and begins running at full speed after us.

While our team retreats, John remains at the veil, yelling like a sergeant. To my surprise, Jane stays, watching me sprint back to the wall. Acting as if she's in no danger, she kneels down and steadies her weapon, adjusting the barrel slightly in my direction. What the heck is she doing?

As I run toward her, I chance a quick glance toward whatever she's aiming at. One of Khof's team—a short, dark-skinned woman in green camouflage—is next to a man-made hole closer to the shore, ready to shoot me. At the exact moment our eyes meet, Jane pulls the trigger, and the woman drops to the floor, grunting in pain. Jane saved my life once again.

Moments later, an energy blast originating from someone to my left hits Jane high in the hip, vaporizing a third of her pelvis, one of her kidneys, and a large part of her intestines. She drops down on her side, on top of her weapon, her ghastly scream slicing right through me.

Chapter 24

DEATH

Everyone else from John's army has made it back to the other side of the veil, leaving just Jane and me.

Focus, Zeon!

There may be time to save her. Perhaps if I just grab her body, I'll be able to get away before anyone gets here. They're too far away. Maybe I can do this. Time to enter my fast mode.

When I'm about two meters away from her, someone's foot hits my head, and I fall hard on my left hand, instantly breaking my wrist. The rest of my body hits the pebbly shore of the river soon afterward, but the sacrifice of my wrist wasn't in vain. My head hurts like hell, but it could've been worse.

Jane lies an arm's length away, drawing quick breaths. I crawl forward and grab her hand with my uninjured arm, and she slowly tilts her head to look at me. The smell of burnt flesh makes me nauseous. The fear in her eyes makes my heart miss a beat. The damage is too great. Her death is imminent.

The trucks on top of the mesa start shooting at the veil. With no computer-aided aiming system, it takes several seconds for them to actually hit the rippled part where we invaded. At first, their shots flash against the veil several meters away from where we crossed it, but they soon close in on the right place through trial and error. Now no one else can cross it there, or they'll be blown to bits.

I may not be able to save Jane in this chaos. And since the messengers changed the rules years ago, any death in a hypersphere is a real death on Earth.

The truth is, I've made a huge mistake. While most enemy troops are on the ground, with some on the top of Fortress, the biggest threat comes from the sky. The unexpected ambush made me forget that although I can't fly here anymore, Khof's not bound by the same limitations.

I turn around to see myself—or someone that's my mirror image, sans beard—inspecting us. When I notice what Khof's wearing, I almost throw up in my mouth. Besides the short shorts that legally give any passerby permission to punch him without conse-quences, he's wearing our soccer team jersey—the Red Angels. Except instead of bright red, it's blue. My team wears a fucking blue jersey on Yora. Someone please just kill me.

He raises his right hand with an open palm, and the artillery stops firing, leaving my ears ringing. Now they have the right place pinned down—the hole where we invaded the island. Anyone showing their face there will be instantly hit by an energy blast.

No one is coming to help us.

Khof floats down, landing just like Primavera did, and walks toward Jane and me. For what feels like an eternity, he stands over us with a look of concern on his face.

"Why are you fighting us?" he finally asks. "The gods are the enemies. *They're* the murderers. How can't you see this?"

He grimaces when he takes a good look at Jane. It clearly takes the wind out of his sails, and for a brief moment, he looks shell-shocked. "You're hurt..." Crouching down, he stops short of touching Jane's belly. Something else catches his attention.

"And—you're holding hands." His voice sounds serene and sad. There's no judgment in his statement. Instinctively, I tighten my grip on her hand and close my eyes. I have to save her. Or at least *try*.

"There—there's still time," I say. "Let me save her."

The dark red blood puddle grows under us. Khof's head shakes almost imperceptibly, the diffuse illumination of the night highlighting the well-defined muscles on his chest. I swear he has a six-pack even through the ugly jersey. If he were a little bit less murderous, he'd be a better catch than me.

Khof grunts. "It's too late. There's nothing you can do."

Clearly, he doesn't know my abilities. But he may be right. It may be too late. The strength in her hand is gone, and I check on her one more time, wondering if she's still awake. She's paler than ever, her forehead covered in sweat, and her whole body shakes. Licking her lips, she glares at him.

He sneers. "I also had a crush like that. We're more alike than you think, Zeon. But like you and your girlfriend, Jean can't see the big picture. She's a fanatic. Jean never believes anything I tell her."

Jane and I lock eyes when warm blood pouring

from her belly reaches our clasped hands, gently tickling our fingers. Her body is losing too much blood, too quickly. After saving my life, she's going to die. This time, it's her hand clenching mine.

Khof kneels down closer to Jane, his face somber. "I just want you to know I get no joy from this. I'm sorry."

"Go... fuck... yourself!" she says with great difficulty.

Khof shoots to his feet, clearly affected by her insult. Even his eyes get watery. I don't know what he was expecting. If Jean was anything like Jane, her answer should've been obvious.

At that moment, Jane closes her eyes, and her pulse weakens. She's going unconscious. I close my eyes and grasp her hand as hard as I can, concentrating.

Soon after, her body disappears. It leaves only the riverbank in its place, darkened by her blood. I extend the palm of my now empty hand, and the warmth of the round pebbles hits me like a truck.

Jane died. The real Jane died. And once again, I killed her.

Even Khof seems shocked for a second, although this was the only expected outcome. Regardless of how it happened, her death jolts me with adrenaline, and my hand shudders as it clenches into a fist.

Ignoring the pain in my broken wrist, I use it as leverage and hurl a punch at Khof, but my fist never reaches his face. He unceremoniously shoots me point blank, and I'm soon back on the ground. A firestorm lights in my belly, taking my breath away, and a warm, dark red liquid pours from my stomach.

"*You* did this," I say, gagging and spitting blood. "Not the gods. You!"

Khof's arms begin to shake so badly that the

capacitor he's holding moves erratically. He lets the weapon fall on its strap and crosses his arms. His body still shakes despite his apparent attempts to hide it.

"I don't understand, Zeon. Why are you doing this?" He asks this as if I'm the bad guy. "You've been in my place. You know who the real enemy is. And I'm sorry, but Jane was dead the moment she was hit. No one could've saved her."

The wounded area in my belly goes numb, and my good hand touches it involuntarily, only to make me grimace in pain again.

"The only enemy I see here is you," I say.

He scoffs. "I'm just like you, Zeon. And Mark. Pawns of the messengers."

When I showed up in a hospital in Mike's body, Mike's daughter April had already been dead a long time. If Khof's version of events was in any way similar to mine, he woke up on Earth impersonating Mark. Mark's daughter Amy, however, was still alive when Khof was sent there. It boggles my mind to think he was so heartless that he killed her. But then again, he'd just let Jane die.

"You murdered Amy. A child. *Mark*'s child!"

A loud thud on my ribs makes me scream. Who would've thought I could still feel more pain? The human body is truly remarkable.

"You mother-tickler!" he yells. "I loved Amy. She was the child I never had. Whoever killed her is one of the dimwit angels, the messengers' minions. Jane must've been an angel just like Jean is!"

"You mean, just like Jean *was*," I reply. "You bastards killed her." Once again, I'm flabbergasted by the messengers and their layers of lies. Unless we see something with our own eyes, everything they say is dubious.

Another kick hits me in the chest, knocking the wind out of me. A few of my broken ribs act like knives and slash one of my lungs. This time, I barely manage to grunt. If I survive, I must disable all my pain sensors next time I go into battle.

Who am I kidding? There's no surviving these types of wounds.

"My people have specific orders to not kill her," Khof says. "Are you trying to make me mad?"

"She's dead, Khof. Shot through the head in front of me."

Khof takes a few steps back. "No. It can't be."

He drops to his knees and lets out a horrified sob. His arms hug his weapon with so much force it shakes wildly, and a low, guttural noise comes out of his mouth.

When Jean died, I assumed she was shot by the others. At the time, I didn't know they were Khof's people. However, I didn't see who actually killed her. It might've been anyone.

Khof weeps silently. It's clear he's trying to keep his composure by going tense, but he's failing miserably. Meanwhile, although the ringing in my ears is gone, the world swings around me. This would be the worst time to lose consciousness. I must focus. My work here is not done.

After what feels like minutes, he inhales deeply through his nose, and a long pause follows. When he finally exhales, he sounds like an old man.

"They're going to pay for this," he mumbles to himself, standing up. A stern look appears on his face.

Then he stares at me like he's seeing me for the first time.

"I'm not on anyone's side," he says slowly. "I just want the necromantes and the gods to fight each other. Make them weak. Then we take over whatever is left. *This* is how we win this." Khof is so calm now; it's as if he's explaining the menu in a restaurant. "Jane should've joined us."

"Go... fuck... yourself!" I mimic Jane's tone and timing. But unlike her, I have enough strength to give him two thumbs up. This was not a good idea. My chest and arms shiver in pain, and I begin spitting blood.

Khof hesitates for a moment, but then—maybe to take me out of my misery—he points his gun at my head and pulls the trigger.

Chapter 25

INJECTORS

LOCATION: JORA

When I open my eyes, I'm greeted by the high ceiling and sparse LED bulbs of Hangar Two. I gasp in pain and sweat breaks out on my forehead. A long time ago, Jane explained the dreadful sensations of waking up on Earth after dying in the hypersphere, back when it was still safe to die there. If anything, she was understating the awfulness.

On top of it all, my throat is sore, and every time I move, something scratches it from the inside. Oh no.

I swallow—or at least, I try to. A tube passes through my nose all the way down to my stomach. *This* is exactly why people don't like hospitals.

I gag. Adrenaline rushes through me, making my limbs tingle. When I glance at my arm to check how much it's shivering, the red button on the hospital bed winks at me. It takes several tries for my hand to press it. At this point, my thinking is reduced to basic instincts, and the only decision I must make is whether I'm going to sit to throw up or stay on my back and risk suffocating in my own vomit.

A few seconds later, I decide that not choking is, in fact, a brilliant idea, so I heave myself up into a sitting position, pull the tube out of my nose—as bad as it sounds—and discharge the scarce contents of my stomach.

These actions happen simultaneously, and I get my bed and everything in it soaked in vomit. Soon Jal appears with wide eyes, wrinkling his nose. He carries a submachine gun looking like a large pistol, with a long barrel and an extra grip on its back.

Kera runs in behind him. Unlike Jal, she's unfazed by my body fluids.

Red lines mark her face, as if her head has been stuck to something for a long time, and her hair's a tangled mess. She wears a purple tank top covered in penguins.

"<Saint Plehr!>" she says in surprise. "<You mother-tickler. You're back!>"

Interesting. For the first time, I hear her *Êndus* accent as she speaks Dïnisc. They tend to overemphasize the vowels. Thinking back to our earlier conversation, it boggles my mind to realize her English accent is somehow British.

Jal starts to pace around my bed, gripping his gun and watching the shadows of the dimly lit pavilion. He's in a one-piece, all-black army uniform with a bullet-proof vest and a round hat looking like a black Fez with no tassel.

Instead of talking to them, I try to keep my head stable as it quivers. A sharp pain from my arm reminds me it's still burnt. I'd forgotten.

I look up into Kera's eyes and smile. She puts her hands on her hips and smiles back at me. I suppose after all the deaths they've had here, having someone come back smiling and throwing up is better than the alternative, even if that someone is me.

But she has no idea why I'm really smiling. I'm alive, and Jane's probably safe as well.

The discovery that saved both Jane's life and mine happened when I learned that some people have auras, but others don't. While people that are "alive" in their planets have a small cluster of neurons where the aura converges, Primavera and Raj don't.

Now, you can say anything about me, and it's probably true, but the one thing I'm good at is remembering my own brain. I know without a doubt the tiny cluster isn't present when I'm on Jora. And, more importantly, Marie and Raj don't have that connection in their brains. Therefore, that specific bundle must be a switch that takes us to Pangea—at least for those of us with living bodies. And if we turn it off, we're sent back.

So, Jane *did* die in the Wheel—but I was the one who killed her, removing the layer of neurons that form the bridge to the hypersphere, allowing her to go back to Earth.

At least, I hope I did.

"<Is he hurt?>" Jal asks in a serious tone, narrowing his eyes at Kera as if he doesn't trust her. He hasn't smiled yet.

Kera observes the monitors. "<The temperature around his stomach, lungs, and liver is abnormally high.>" She puts on some goggles. "<I don't detect any bacterial or viral infection, though. The tissue in his arm is healing nicely.>"

Kera's eyes lose focus, and she starts to play with a silver pendant hanging around her neck. Her mind goes away for a few seconds, probably researching my odd symptoms on the net.

In the silence, I worry about Jane. When Khof shot me, I did the same thing to my own head. Since I'm alive on Jora, my crazy plan worked... but did it work for Jane as well?

"<I contacted Dooria,>" Kera states, coming back to the world of the living. "<She'll be here in half an hour.>"

"<Guys,>" I say, still grinning. "<I know how to send people to Pangea.>"

BEBE CAN'T STOP RUBBING against my legs as I connect to the net using a general entry port in my trailer. They let me come back here after I was debriefed on everything that happened while I was away. It's too bad the government hasn't yet reconnected me to the network, even though I'm not technically a prisoner. As a result, the only way I can browse the net is through open wireless hotspots like an illiterate garbage bot. Dooria explains they didn't get to it yet due to other priorities, and I was in the Wheel anyway.

"Sending people to Pangea isn't the problem, Zeon," Dooria says in English.

For the first time, I notice the wrinkles under her eyes and on her forehead. We haven't been in contact for years, and political ads—with their controlled lighting and their makeup—always show the best side of her.

But meeting her in the middle of the night without warning paints a different picture.

She sighs. "The problem is bringing them back safely."

I hold my own neuronal helmet as I program it. Actually, it's not mine. It's Harry's. And it's not the latest model, but it has the most important features I need—it automatically adapts to the user's brain—AI or human—and has a neural gun injector.

"No. The problem is you lied to me, Dooria. About Jane's message."

"It wasn't a lie. Jane was in danger."

Dooria always seems so sure of herself when talking to others, and her bleached blue skirt suit goes well with her blonde braided bun. But it contrasts with the gray roots of her hair and for the first time, I hear a tiredness in her voice.

I try to ignore the lump in my throat. "But she didn't send that message."

Dooria slowly paces the small trailer as if looking for a place to sit. The housing trailers here are smaller than the prison cabins, so I, Jal, Kera, Dooria, and Harry are cramped together. My workspace is near the north end of my trailer, where I use a portable computer to access the gun operating system. The neural injector gun itself is inside the helmet.

Eventually, Dooria sits across from my work area, watching me program the injector. "How would we know whether she sent it or not? The messengers asked us to tell you that, so we did."

Kera stands next to us, the pendant she was wearing earlier now lying on her hand. A quizzical expression crosses her face as she follows our discussion. Jal is on a couch beside Harry on the opposite side of the trailer.

I scoff at Dooria. "I thought no one was able to talk with the messengers."

Jal doesn't speak English, so instead he entertains Harry with magic tricks. Balls appear out of thin air and seem to teleport to his other hand. I doubt Jal's fooling Harry; the little robot's mind is fast.

"It happened before our people were drafted in droves," Dooria says. "Iris told us there would be a time we'd need your help, and she told us what to say to guarantee that."

I take a slow breath. Iris is the messenger in charge. Unlike most of the others, her body is red, and she doesn't know how to act like a human being. Perhaps I should give Dooria the benefit of the doubt.

Next to me, Kera studies the now open pendant, looking at the picture of a woman. Elquenna. One of the people who died in Pangea. The pendant abruptly closes when she notices us looking at it.

"You should've killed the mother-tickler," Kera says in a monotone voice. "Once again, Zeon, you dropped the ball." She leans back on a cabinet next to a small sink. There isn't anger in her eyes. Just defeat.

Dooria remains quiet, as if agreeing with her. I grit my teeth and close my eyes, trying to control my emotions. Perhaps I could've reached for Khof's arm and killed him instead. But we were surrounded, and I had already killed Jane, and I was injured. Any mistake and the outcome could've been worse. So, I shouldn't be ashamed. I did my best.

"How about the missile attack?" I finally ask, changing the subject. "Did you find out who fired at me when I was in prison?"

Dooria nods. "We did. It was Katon. He hacked the fake order sent to the unmanned submarine, to shoot the missile. We arrested him soon after you went to Pangea. He blames you for our failure last time. Calls you a traitor."

The last time I saw Katon, he and his friend Talaia were prisoners of Earth's protectors in Pangea. He didn't look like the murderous kind, but they spent more than a year as the Earthers' Pangea prisoners while their bodies were in deep sleep on Jora. I thought we were friends. We literally sang together. Well, most of the singing was mine.

"<Anyway,>" I continue in Dïnisc, so Jal can understand. "<To this day, the messengers control how and when we can go to Pangea. But we don't need them anymore to send people up.>" I smile, looking at Jal and watching Harry out of the corner of my eye.

Harry's sitting like a cat on his charger, staring at us. So far, he's keeping his promise to not engage with other humans anymore. They should never know how smart he is. The outburst he had when Dooria first met us will hopefully be forgotten in the midst of everything that happened that night.

Dooria eyes me with a concerned look. "<And you want to send more people there? On purpose?>"

"<We can send more soldiers, Dooria. Skeptics. World politicians. But more importantly, we'll send people that the messengers of the gods don't want there.>"

"<And who are these people?>"

"<We can start with the protectors that weren't summoned to help with the war. And to show them what Pangea is.>"

Jal raises his eyebrow at me, but I'm just following his suggestion. We should trust no one, so the more people that know about Pangea, the harder it's going to be to lie.

"<And what do we do about the—what do you call them again—necromantes?>" Jal asks.

I tilt my head at Dooria and Kera, who avoid my eyes. We discussed this earlier, out of earshot of Jal. They both knew the necromantes existed, and never told Jal. It's possible there's nothing we can do about it.

"<I don't know,>" I say. "<We must talk to the messengers.>"

Chapter 26

MISPLACED

LOCATION: JORA

ourteen hours after waking up in Hangar Two
with a bad death hangover, I'm back to the bed
that will cradle my body during deep sleep. In contrast
to the mess it was this morning, now it's in pristine
condition. I don't envy the job of the person who had
to clean it up. It's one of the many reasons I didn't
become a real doctor.

"<Jal, I have to be first,>" I say. "<It's my injector. My
idea. I don't want others to be at risk.>"

Jal's face is grim. He wanted to be the first person
sent to Pangea using the helmet, but I won't allow him
to do it. Instead, I'll be the guinea pig. Once I'm there,
I'll try to find a volunteer to be "killed" and sent back
to Jora to let them know the process is safe. As a result,
he's giving me the silent treatment.

The intensive care unit I'm in isn't as small as a
coffin, and it doesn't have a lid. Yet, it feels like I'm
attending my own funeral as Jal and Kera look down at
me. Since this is a long-term cocoon for unconscious

patients who can't complain, there's no such thing as a thick pillow or even a movable headrest.

"<Are you sure you want to do this, Zeon?>" Kera asks. "<It's dangerous.>"

I shift my back, trying to make myself comfortable. Changing the neurons with the injectors injures the brain. If I make a mistake, it may kill me.

"<It'll work.>"

Kera touches buttons on a monitor hanging near my head, preparing the injection. "<But how do you know you'll end up in the right hypersphere?>" she asks me. "<What do you call it, again? The Wheel?>"

"<I don't think we're powerless when we go to Pangea,>" I reply. "<There's a conscious or unconscious decision that happens every time. This is how I managed to go to Pangea so consistently—I always *wanted* to. And, if it fails, I can, uh, kill myself and try again.>"

She has a point, though. If the messengers know I'm projecting myself there with the injector, perhaps they can hijack my consciousness and reroute me somewhere else, maybe to my instant death.

On the other hand, messengers are not murderers. Supposedly.

Kera scoffs. "<No. If you kill yourself and come back to Jora, and if you're still alive—and these are big 'ifs'—you won't be able to try it again for a while. This is not Pangea magic. The brain needs time to heal.>"

And just like that, the bed feels even more uncomfortable. She's right. When I use this injector, I'll be damaging the area connecting me to Pangea's hyperspheres. If I ever come back to Jora, I'll have to wait a couple of weeks for my brain to heal before I can even *consider* going back.

"<It's a risk I'm willing to take,>" I tell her.

A few minutes later, we're ready. It's time to go back, but there are two problems. One, I can't use a hat if I'm connected to the injector. I wouldn't be able to use my old hat anyway, since we threw it away this morning. It was soaked in goo and beyond any help.

Also, although I have a respectable day-old beard, it's not big enough to disguise me in the hypersphere. For once, I'm upset they trim, shave, and overall take good care of the bodies in deep sleep. At least I can use my sunglasses.

"<I really hope it works,>" Kera says, clasping her silver pendant again. "<And if it does, *I'll* be next. Not Jal.>" She eyes Jal, maybe waiting for a reply, but he doesn't say anything.

When everything is ready, Kera raises her hand, all five fingers clearly showing. Five seconds. My plan is to keep my eyes open during the transition. She brings her thumb to her palm, leaving four fingers. Four seconds. As for the procedure, I'm only a bit worried. I'm pretty sure I'm going back to Pangea. Two seconds.

What's the worst that could happen?

When her palms become a fist, my body jolts in place. Kera approaches to take a better look, locking eyes with me, but I'm seeing double. The other image in my field of vision is the blue sky of a hypersphere, but not the one I was expecting. Maybe I should've been more specific.

"No!" I scream in both places, and Kera starts working on the bed interface. Jal shouts something at her, but there's nothing they can do. They fade from my vision, and despite the sunny day in my destination, the cold intensifies.

Goddamn it. Kera was right. This is not the Wheel.

Worse, I'm not dressed at all for this kind of climate.

I spring to my feet as my whole body shivers. So much for my hypothesis that hypersphere environments are always warm. As I fold my arms, I look around and find myself in the middle of a sparse evergreen forest covered by snow. There must be at least a foot of soft white powder, enough to make walking difficult.

For a moment, I think I'm on Earth, but when I shut my eyes, my mind is soon registering the ground, the snow, and the trees in a way that can only happen in Pangea. Everything is in focus, so this cannot be a dreamsphere.

This was not an accident. Someone must've redirected me here. But why?

Cupping my hands, I blow air into them to get some warmth. The steam of vapor escaping through my fingers distracts me. It twists in swirling shapes in front of my eyes, enhancing the contrast between the white snow, the pulsating trunks, and the hidden person moving behind the trees far ahead.

Uh oh.

I turn around and begin running in the opposite direction, also using the trees for cover. When I stop behind a sizeable one that can actually cover most of me, I shut my eyes and concentrate. Whoever it is has a bright aura like mine. Therefore, it's going to be easy to stay away from them. Well, except that my footprints are going to lead them directly to me.

When I think they're not looking, I walk backward awkwardly, hoping to trick my pursuer. My idea is to go around in a circle to take a better look at who's waiting for me here. Maybe it's a friend, but I can never be sure.

My plan doesn't work. In spite of their lumbering through the snow, it seems they can predict every move I make. They can't see me directly and yet they know where I am. After I reach another large tree, I stay behind it and wait. I have a good idea of who's coming now.

Tilting my head, I peek at her. What surprises me is not that she's wearing snow bibs with a pink jacket over them. It's the round sunglasses underneath the knit purple cap. They're the same type of glasses she wears on Earth because there, she's blind. But not here in Pangea, I think. Or I thought.

"Zeon? I know you're here."

Leaving my hiding place, I put my hands on my hips and frown at Louise. She walks a few steps closer, and I show her my hands, holding my palms forward. Before I can say anything, she stops. She can see me.

"Go ahead," Louise begins. "You can say what you want to say."

Ignoring the cold, I take a deep breath and look her in the eyes—uh, I mean her sunglasses. "Your eyes. They don't work in Pangea."

She nods but remains silent.

"You never needed eyes here." I choke. This is yet another betrayal. "You're like me," I continue. I was going to say, "an angel," but I don't feel like one. Plus, Jane's an angel, and she can't interfere with hyperspheres. "You can do stuff... here." I gesture around us. Whenever I'm stressed, my speech regresses, and I become the opposite of Shakespeare.

"The messengers call us archangels."

You've got to be kidding. They have a hierarchy of bullshit, and I was given some kind of manager position. I don't know what to say.

I take a few steps to my left. Louise doesn't move, but her head tilts in my general direction.

"How did you know?" she asks.

"John was right that the river stops flowing when the moons are aligned in the Wheel. But the energy barrier doesn't get weak. You must've opened it that day. Once I realized that, everything else started to make sense."

Two more steps to the right, and her head follows me. "Did you see my aura when we first met in the Wheel?" I ask, cringing. It's as if I'm talking to a fake psychic.

"Yes. I don't think my mental map goes as far as yours, but once you were close enough, I knew you weren't Khof. He doesn't have an aura." A sad smile appears on her face. "And Ravi's real best friend would never become a murderer."

Most people thought I'd killed Ravi. Louise avoided me after his death, and who could blame her? Even *I* thought I was involved, and I was there. I'm glad she knows I had nothing to do with it.

"You helped people to move to their apartments in the Wheel," I observe.

The units were all booby-trapped but someone like Louise could have helped them. Someone like me. Apparently, archangels make great realtors.

She crosses her arms. "I did."

It's not easy to process betrayal, and I'm glad she's patient with me. But there's an anger inside me, and I can't yet pinpoint why. It takes me a few seconds for the emotion to become words.

Taking a step closer, I point an accusatory finger at her. "You could've helped us!" People died in Pangea and she did nothing. "You could have helped *me*. I was *alone!*"

A deep frown appears on her face, and she holds her ground. "I'm sorry, Zeon. Like Jane, I trusted the messengers."

I close my eyes for a second, inhaling and exhaling, trying to calm down. Oh yes, why not throw Jane under the bus while you're at it? I snort. It's so obvious. They asked Louise not to interfere, and she remained a bystander while everything happened last time. While people were being killed.

No. Not just people. *Ravi.*

Tears roll down her face as she watches me go through the emotions.

"Can you fly and move boulders like Khof?" I ask her.

She shakes her head. "No, Zeon. I'm just like you."

It's obvious she changed sides after Ravi was killed. The question is, whose side is she on now? Slowly, I lean down and grab a two-inch-thick leafless branch the size of a baseball bat. I may have to do something drastic to defend myself.

Then, I ask the question that's been bothering me since Jane and I died. "Why did you warn Khof about our attack?"

She frowns. "What are you talking about? I didn't do anything like that, I swear!" She slams her fist into her other palm.

Okay. Maybe she's just like me. Either way, I press on with my questioning. "You hate the messengers. Just like Khof. And you helped him. How else would he know?" Besides me, she's the only one I know who can open the barrier. All of a sudden, someone creates a story about using the alignment of the moons to their advantage and brings us to be slaughtered. "You may have killed Jane!"

Louise takes a step back, shaking her head again.

"I'm telling you!" she insists. "I. Didn't. *Know*!" She sighs. "Can't you entertain the possibility there are more traitors among us? Think about Linda. And Bodan." She pauses, biting her fingernails. "Even Jane was one of them at some point. Who knows where the list ends?"

Louise has a point. For all we know, everyone is a double agent—or a triple agent, now that the necromantes are involved. My head hurts.

"You're right. How would I know? You're not exactly helping your case here." I'm glad I'm not paying that much attention to the fact I'm not dressed for this weather. Having a heated discussion with someone is a good way to distract from the cold.

"Oh, one more thing," I say. "You also put something in our wine. You're helping Khof *and* the necromantes."

"That wasn't me, Zeon." She tilts her head.

It's clear we're at an impasse. There's no way she'll convince me she's not a turncoat, especially now she brought me to a different hypersphere. We stay silent for several seconds as we both process the conversation. Louise looks down, and her head moves slightly side-to-side as she thinks. She absentmindedly scratches her chest.

"How did you bring me here?" I finally ask.

A moment later, she looks back at me, so to speak. A smile begins to form on her face.

"It wasn't me," she says, again.

Then something hard hits me on the back of my head. I jerk forward, slip, and fall face first in the snow.

Chapter 27

ERMEY

LOCATION: UNKNOWN HYPERSPHERE IN
PANGEA

A burst of contagious girly laughter is audible even through the dampening effect of the snow over my head. When I raise my head to look behind me, Primavera is there.

A huge smile appears on her face. "Gotcha!"

The phrase seems to be her calling card these days. Once the little girl helps me to my feet—also a common occurrence nowadays—another snowball immediately hits me harmlessly in the back. This time, Louise is the one laughing, because she's the one who threw it.

I dust the snow off my summer clothes. "Knock it off!"

Primavera laughs even harder. Like Louise, she's wearing heavyweight snow pants, but instead of a hat, she went for plushy pink earmuffs. Behind her, an armless one-eyed snowman stares at our group.

Louise walks up next to me and crouches, grabbing the tree branch I just dropped. With quick steps, she approaches the snowman and attaches the stick to it, like a thick arm.

She grins. "Sorry, Zeon. Primavera needed to talk to you. To us. She asked me to find you and bring you here."

I was so focused on Louise that I hadn't noticed the kid and her snowman—or snow-woman?—behind us. Primavera has no aura that I can see. I need to pay more attention to my surroundings.

My resolve falters, and I take a deep breath. Primavera and Louise know each other. "Can you explain what's going on?"

"Do you remember Dorothy?" Louise asks.

Narrowing my eyes in an exaggerated way—so she understands my suspicions—I say nothing. It's weird she's talking about a horse in this situation, no matter how cool she is. By that, I mean Dorothy, not Louise.

"How do you think Primavera got her to help Marie?" Louise asks. "Like you, I met Primavera the first time I was sent to the Wheel. So, when she asked me to get Dorothy to help save someone, I didn't think twice."

Louise finds another branch, and the snowperson finally has both arms. "I didn't like the idea of leaving Jane without her horse. But I couldn't give her Pierre."

Primavera frowns, pressing her hand to her chest. "Dorothy's *my* horse!" Her passion makes me chuckle. "Don't laugh. She's mine! I've had her for years!"

Trying to contain my amusement, I say, "So *you* brought me here, then. Why?"

The little girl grins. "Yes! I almost forgot. Wait here. I'm going to bring my house." With that, she darts into the forest.

There's nothing else to do except wait for her. Actually, there's one thing.

While Louise is studying a pile of small stones near an exposed gully, probably searching for the snowman's eyes, I make a snowball—and then, I finally have my revenge.

The sparse trees are a perfect spot for a snow fight, and we use the opportunity to blow off some steam. As she darts away, I follow her closely, throwing snowballs as quickly as I can make them. The exercise helps us warm up.

Puffing, Louise leans back on a trunk thicker than the others. "How did," she stops talking to catch her breath, "how did you... and Jane... escape from Khof?"

I stop running and somehow manage to stay on my feet. "I killed." I gasp for air. "I killed us."

Her head turns to me, and she frowns. "You did what?"

Since I still have a snowball in my hand, I use my other hand to steady myself by grabbing onto the trunk of a young tree. "I found the neurons that connect our brain to Pangea," I say, smiling thinly.

Louise takes one step toward me, already breathing normally. "Of course! And you must've removed them." Her eyes light up, and she raises her hand to touch the back of her head. We both still carry our snowballs. "I knew about the connection, but it never crossed my mind to try to change it."

Except her hand doesn't touch her head. It was a trick. Everything becomes white, when yet another snowball explodes all over my face.

"Ha!" Louise says, and runs away.

What a cheap shot. That's what happens when I lower my guard in Pangea. So, I follow her and crouch behind a small snow hill. "Does anybody else know about Primavera? Or about what you can do?" Maybe I should fight more and talk less.

"I don't think so," she says, and I can see her hands from behind a tree scooping another snowball. "Primavera begged me not to tell anyone. And I don't want anyone knowing about me."

My next projectile grazes her hat at the exact moment she peeks at me—I was waiting for her—and it falls off. Small victories.

Hiding behind a thin tree, I shout, "Why not?"

She grabs her purple hat and puts it back on her head in a single, elegant motion. "Because she's afraid of Iris. And because we don't know who we can trust."

Iris is an enigma. I don't think the red messenger likes us. Maybe she's behind all the planet killings Haides told us about.

A shower of wet and cold snow falls over my back and shoulders when a snowball explodes on the tree that was supposed to protect me.

Changing tactics, I sprint behind the snowman and try to hit Louise from behind. "How's Mike doing?"

She easily ducks out of the shot. "Missed again!" she calls out. For someone who's blind, she has good depth perception.

Before answering my question, though, she walks over, rubbing her gloved hands. A timely truce is implicitly called. I'm already completely out of breath, and my fingers are ice cold.

"Mike's doing great, actually," Louise tells me. "He's on Long Island leading the research to develop the portal. I moved there last year to help. It's the hottest research area on Earth. People are even talking about a Nobel prize."

The pause makes me shiver and I hug my arms around me. "So, you're not with CERN anymore?" CERN is the European agency with the largest particle collider on Earth.

She bows her head. "No. After what happened—you know, with Ravi—I decided if the messengers didn't want the portal, then building it was exactly what I wanted to do."

An unexpected gust from behind us makes Louise's long hair blow parallel to the ground. The strong wind and my now-chattering teeth suddenly remind me I'm only wearing a t-shirt. I turn around to find the trees behind us have changed into Primavera's unit. This time, her home is painted with large flowers. So, the pattern changes. I'm not even surprised.

Louise and I exchange a quick glance and shrug. We don't make the rules in this place.

When we walk inside, Primavera's waiting for us, wearing a white dress with a rose pattern, white shoes, and a pink jacket. The comfortable temperature is a relief to my icy-cold hands, and the warm air wraps around me like a blanket. I'm about to smile when I notice Primavera isn't alone.

"What the—" I say. Maybe the cold is making me delirious.

She's already filling up three cups of coffee in the living room. The third coffee is not for her. It's for the messenger who sits at the table that's covered with crisscrossed red stripes.

"Come in, guys!" Primavera says. Her skin seems way darker than I remembered. Maybe she's been spending more time outside. "Please take a seat next to Ermey and have some coffee."

I narrow my eyes in disgust. His thick and hairless eyebrows and his high forehead are unmistakable.

"Mercury," I seethe.

Louise remains silent by my side, her face stern but unconcerned. She seems too relaxed when a messenger of the goddamn gods is this close to us.

To my surprise, Mercury is wearing a gray flat cap, blue-sky shirt, beige pants, and honest-to-god black suspenders. Despite his weird clothing, the intertwined wickers on his white skin and the throbbing blue veins on his hands make it clear he's a messenger.

"You son of a—" I start, but I catch myself. Primavera is watching me with her wide brown eyes, playing with her braided blond hair.

"Oh no, son. I'm so sorry to tell you Mercury died," says the messenger. "I'm not him. I'm Hermes."

He raises his eyebrows, giving me the impression everything that happened was a big misunderstanding and that we're close friends. Somehow, he manages to pass all this information onto me just by the intonation of his voice and his welcoming open arms, and I almost believe him.

Meanwhile, my mouth drops. "But—but... you should be dead too!" I cry. "And she calls you *Ermey*!" I gesture at Primavera. Of all the messengers, I could never tell Hermes and Mercury apart. At the very least, he deserves a punch to the face. But I can't do that with Primavera right next to us. She's already looking uneasy.

"Ermey's not dead. He's right here!" She points at him.

Hermes grabs her tiny hand and looks at her with a captivating smile. "My dear, could you give us some privacy? There's a lot for Uncle Zeon, Aunt Louise, and me to discuss."

"Sure! I'll be outside playing." In a blink of an eye, she's back to the snow pants and earmuffs. I can't help but shiver for several reasons.

Once she's out of earshot and the door slides shut, Hermes and I look at each other, and I make a fist, wondering if I should punch him again.

Hermes gestures for me to take a seat, unaffected by my anger. "Like Khof, Mercury was a version of me from a parallel universe," he explains.

I wave my hand at his ugly outfit. "Why are you wearing clothes? And this ridiculous hat?"

He cracks up. "Not more ridiculous than a cowboy hat."

Louise snorts, and I catch myself laughing with Hermes, but my face goes slack once I realize he's manipulating me. His expression changes, and his tone sobers again. "I always dress like this for Primavera," he says. "I don't want to scare her."

After double-checking to make sure Primavera hasn't reappeared, I touch Louise's shoulder.

"Louise," I hiss. "He *killed* Ravi!"

She faces me but says nothing. And then I realize Hermes is right there with us. So, I walk dangerously close to the white messenger and point an accusatory finger at him.

"*You* killed Ravi!"

Clearly, Louise's reaction means she knew Hermes was alive. But not only is he responsible for killing Ravi —my best friend *and* Louise's boyfriend—I'm pretty sure he's the mastermind of everything that happened last time. Every death we had is on him.

"I didn't ask anyone to kill him," he says. "What happened was beyond my control."

I take a step backward and slowly release my breath. The messengers are always playing games.

"We all know what you're thinking," Louise says, which bothers me. Even I don't know what to make of this. "But please don't do anything before hearing the whole story."

Snorting, I wave my hand dismissively at them. I hate that—once again—things may not be what they seem.

Ignoring my gesture, Louise takes her seat and begins to furiously bite her nails.

"All right," I concede, and reluctantly take a seat and grab one of the mugs. Hermes has a lot of explaining to do and I need some coffee. But I need to be careful. His charm is off the charts. For all I know, I'll be apologizing in no time.

Nodding, he sits next to Louise and across from me at the cozy table. "When Primavera met me, she couldn't say my name. She always called me Ermey. It's so cute!"

A warm smile appears on his face, and my mouth twists into a grin for a second. He's right. It *is* cute.

Then I remember who he is, and I clench my fist. "You tried to destroy Earth and Jora. How can you possibly explain that?"

He raises his hand. "Please hear me out."

Everything around us transforms into what looks like the inside of a barely lit cave with a short, round ceiling, and I drop my coffee cup on the floor. I don't scream because I can't decide if I should yell "Help!" or a swear word. Only we, the circular table, and our drinks remain—or at least whatever wasn't spilled on the floor.

Louise touches my arm, and I flinch. "It's okay, Zeon. You don't have to be afraid."

A long and flat creature with possibly a hundred legs, four antennas, and no eyes slithers its way toward us. Its length is twice my height. The enormous brown millipede raises its head and front legs, opening its mouth to reveal dozens of ragged teeth.

"AHH!" I yell, jumping back. I manage to stay upright, but my chair falls to the floor.

"Don't worry," Hermes says in a soothing voice. "This is just a projection. What we're seeing happened exactly 389 Earth years ago. And the creature is not reacting to you, but what's behind you."

I turn and immediately yell again. At the back of the room, an even larger millipede raises its head in response. Its color is similar to the cave walls, made from some kind of dark red dirt.

"What are these *hideous* things?" For a change, my arms shake from the adrenaline and not from the cold.

"The smaller one is me. This is how I really look. It's my body. The other one is Iris. Our home planet has three times Earth's gravity and almost no atmosphere. We live inside it."

The walls projected around us are made from rock, but they're smooth, indicating they're man-made —*vermin*-made—and artificial. The messengers must also live on their own planets, and project their consciousness on Pangea. Unlike us, though, it seems they can change their appearances drastically in the hypersphere.

"*I am here to make you reconsider*," says Hermes' voice in my head. He's talking to Iris. Like the necromantes, the messengers are telepaths. It must be his millipede self that's talking this time.

"*Explain*," Iris replies. Her antennas rub together, and she licks them. Ew.

I watch the cave to avoid looking at these slimy creatures for too long. There are no lights there—the ambient brightness comes from nowhere. They don't have eyes, so perhaps Hermes added the illumination for my sake—and Louise's. Well, maybe not Louise's.

"*The population estimation was not correct,*" ugly Hermes says, his body snaking around the room. "*Most of our embryos matured.*"

Thinking about their embryos while watching Hermes dance like that makes me nauseous for a second. "*This is a problem, yes,*" he continues. "*But your resolution methods are misguided.*" He ends this thought with a loud hiss, before freezing in place.

Iris hisses back. "*We are following the gods' wishes. Are you criticizing the gods?*"

Vermin Hermes nods. So, he *does* have some guts.

"*They wanted population control of our embryos, but not murder.*" Ah, so he's spineless. I thought he was saying yes when he nodded. This is a common mistake I make. I always forget not to anthropomorphize arthropods.

The creature Hermes rises a little, while Iris' head lowers a bit, although she's still higher than he is. Their dance is so fascinating it surpasses my desire to squash them with a giant boot.

Suddenly, she moves alongside him, as if they're two monstrous combatants sizing each other up.

"*You didn't have a problem when we did that in the past. But now, your bias has worked against you.*" All Iris' antennas point at him. I never thought antennas could

be so judgmental. *"Now, you are attached to your...
child."*

I steal a glance at the real Hermes by my side, or at least his current hypersphere body, as I follow the creatures' dialogue. His human face is clouded by sadness.

"Please don't let her die," Hermes says. A wave of motion goes through all his legs, both sides in perfect synchrony. It would be pretty if it weren't nasty.

"Our decision is final. This is the end of this audience."

With that, the scene pauses and my mouth drops. Hermes' child was going to die because of overpopulation, and he wasn't able to stop it.

Or maybe... maybe Hermes *was* able to save her.

The cave and the creatures are finally gone, and we're back in Primavera's apartment. The distracting childish drawings on the walls seem to mock us.

I stare at Louise not knowing what to do with my hands. "Primavera's—*vermin!*"

I don't say "disgusting," but my contorted face implies it. Unfortunately, I don't notice Primavera's back in the room, watching us and ready to cry. Meanwhile, Hermes' mouth opens wide, and he stares at me with a hurt expression. I just offended him and his daughter.

"I am so, so sorry, Hermes!"

Chapter 28

EXPERIMENTS

LOCATION: PRIMAVERA'S HOUSE

"Why would you say that?" Primavera cries out and runs to her bedroom.

"I'm sorry!" I stand up to try to catch her, but it's too late. The door to her room slides shut, and a huge pink dinosaur painted on it looks back at me in disdain. I can almost hear Barney saying, "Tsk, tsk, tsk."

"I didn't mean it like that." I turn to Hermes again, who shakes his head. His reaction makes me feel even worse, as if I'm a disappointment. I don't even know why I care what he thinks of me. "I'm just... surprised, is all."

Louise clearly doesn't know what to do with her hands. Leave it to me to embarrass my friends. "No, Zeon. Primavera's not Hermes' daughter."

Hermes draws a deep breath. "I accept your apology. Primavera's like a daughter to me, but my biological daughter died hundreds of years ago."

Thrusting a hand through my hair, I think for a bit. "But Primavera told me you saved her."

He nods—this time, an actual human nod, since

he's not vermin here. "I did. Iris and I were grooming her to be one of Earth's best archangels, but she died. I couldn't possibly let her go."

I allow myself to sit again. Hermes was never this candid with me before. Maybe I can get some answers.

"But this doesn't make any sense," I say. "Why would you save Primavera but not your own daughter?"

For the first time since I met him, he looks away, avoiding my eyes. Louise just shakes her head.

"When my daughter died, Iris blocked me from coming to Pangea," Hermes says. "She guessed what I planned to do that time. But she had no idea I was going to save Primavera."

I swallow, trying to ignore the dryness of my mouth. Perhaps he shouldn't have pleaded for his daughter's life and just saved her instead, like he did with Primavera. The worst decisions to second-guess are those involving the loss of loved ones.

"Why are you telling me this?" I scoff. "Are you rebelling against the gods?"

He stares back at me with his brows furrowed. "Let me make this clear, Zeon. I cannot act against the gods. My species is genetically bred to obey them."

It makes some sense. They didn't want another race of necromantes.

"So, you can't do anything about it," I say.

Hermes hooks both his thumbs on his silly suspenders, and his white eyebrows add to the illusion that he's old and wise.

"Several years after my daughter's demise, I started an experiment. On some Earths, humans have more brain cells. It makes them smarter, albeit their thought processes are slower. On others, I created smaller brains with reduced capability, but with more connections, so they can think much faster than normal humans. Raj's and Khof's Earths, Yora and Terra, have the complex set of brains, while Jane's and yours, Earth and Jora, have the reduced sets. The remaining Earths I left untouched."

Well, I hope the kitchen has buckets, because I need one filled with coffee. Did I just hear him right?

"You're saying Jori have smaller brains?" I say, meandering across the kitchen. The counter pops from the wall and the telepathic user interface connects with my brain, giving me several choices of bean blends.

"In a way. And you have the fewest neurons of them all." He turns to face me again. He's not smiling, but Saint Plehr, that's a low blow. I tilt my head to stare at him with death in my eyes. "Unfortunately, my experiment is disrupting the gods' plan for the human race."

I smirk. "And what exactly is the gods' *plan* for us?" This is a question I never thought I'd be asking.

He shakes his head. "I can't tell you that. It'd be a betrayal."

"Does Iris know about this?"

If he's not working against the gods, why do the experiment? And why did he tell me about his daughter?

"Iris doesn't know who saved Primavera. I can lie to other messengers, but as I've already said, I cannot work against the gods."

Narrowing my eyes—because the options for coffee containers are on the way, projected into my mind—I stare at Hermes. There are no buckets available, but more importantly, I think Hermes is desperately trying to find a loophole where he can screw the gods. He can't do it by himself.

But humans can, as long as we have the right tools. It's as if he *wants* us to rebel, but his inbred loyalty fights against his desire.

"The results of the experiment are interesting," he continues. "Simpler brains with more neuronal connections allow people to see and change the microscopic constituents of Pangea. The small things."

My eyes widen with understanding. "And Khof's brain—larger, with fewer connections—allows him to throw boulders at people," I say.

Louise's face brightens underneath her glasses. "It makes sense. On Earth, computers have something similar. We have faster but dumber chips, and slower but complicated ones. Reduced versus complex. They're good for different applications."

Talking about engineering brightens her up. It must be difficult to stay here and hear Hermes talk with us after what happened to Ravi, even if Hermes is not directly at fault. Supposedly.

In front of me, a stream of life-saving black liquid starts filling a half-liter mug that came from nowhere, and a percentage icon in the form of an incomplete circle appears in my vision.

Hermes grins. "But more importantly, everyone from Khof's planet Yora can do it. And the same goes for Jori having *your* abilities. And Louise's Earth."

I finally take a sip of my humongous coffee mug. "But why can only a few of us change the hypersphere?"

"You're asking the wrong question, Zeon. The real question is why the others *can't.*"

I lick my lips for a second before saying anything. "And?"

"Because they don't know they can do it. It's a change of paradigm. You, Khof, and Louise learned it when you were kids."

Moving the mug below my nose, I take a deep breath to smell its contents, forgetting my problems for a while.

"Hermes, I was able to fly in Pangea, but I can't anymore. What happened?"

His all-white brow furrows. "Khof was becoming too strong for his own good. We had to curb his power, and this also affects you and Louise. If the restraints weren't in place, he'd be able to cause earthquakes, killing everyone. Even with his current powers, he can create a tear between hyperspheres and dreamspheres. The only things preventing that are the veils."

What he says makes me choke, and I cough, spraying coffee around me. More carefully, I take a smaller sip, tasting the sweet roasted flavor of the beverage. I know people like to say they want to die doing what they love but choking on coffee would never be my choice. If I had to pick, it would be something involving sex.

"How can I trust you now?" I ask. "You ordered Linda to kill April, her own daughter. Killing Amy made Khof even angrier."

He shrugs. "I did what I had to do. I owed Linda that much. Otherwise, Iris would have done it herself."

When I move away from the kitchen counter, it drops down as the user interface disconnects. Everything in the hypersphere, including this house with all its advanced pieces of alien technology, is controlled by the same kind of wireless communication we have on our planet.

"What about the necromantes?" I ask. We need more information about them. "Their sun is going to go supernova, and they're going to die. Why don't you let them back into Pangea?"

Hermes crosses his arms, his albino hands complementing the long bright blue sleeves of his shirt. "The last time they were here, they tried to destroy Entropia, and in the process killed millions of intelligent beings. Not just humans." He smiles, going back to his old self. "We're not the bad guys, Zeon. Believe me, we're not—"

I interrupt him. "Yeah, you're not murderers. Or so you keep saying." People that say "believe me" usually are not to be trusted.

He unfolds his arms and waves his right hand at me. "Anyway, we're not here for pleasantries. The necromantes are coming, and I have information for you and Louise. But later, you must apologize to Primavera.

Yes, I *will* have to fix that. Still, this is great timing. A crazy idea starts to form in my head, but I need Jal's help. And since Jal's on Jora, I must find someone here to contact him.

Chapter 29

TRUST

After that, Hermes briefs us on what's coming. It's bad, really bad. Once he's passed along what he knows, he vanishes—typical messenger—and I accompany Louise to the front door. We're both in a somber mood. The good news is the island and the mesa are visible through the transparent door and walls. Primavera's house is back to Earth's sector in the Wheel. I don't know how she does it.

When I'm sure we're out of earshot of Primavera, I look at Louise. "You said earlier that you hate the messengers. You're even helping Mike build the portal. So why are you siding with a messenger? And why Hermes, specifically?"

She sighs. "Don't be mad at me. It took me a year to forgive Hermes after Primavera re-introduced us. And it's not as though we're best friends now. But Hermes is trying to help us in his own way. We need all the help we can get."

The truth is Louise has nothing to apologize for. It must've been difficult just to be in the same *room* with

Hermes. So, instead of arguing, I just hug her, and she tears up.

"Wait for me to tell the... uh... news to John and the others," I say. "There's something here I have to do."

She gives me a faint smile. "Will do."

After Louise leaves the house, I go to Primavera's room for my apology tour. She and I end up playing a crossword game where we use tiles with letters to create words. It's one of the conditions of her forgiveness.

But it's not as easy as it sounds. We play on the only surface in her room that's not messy, and only because there's a table that slides out of the wall behind the window, facing the forest. Otherwise it would also be covered in stuff.

In the end, she beats me, but the game lasts for an hour and a half, and there's a lot of cheating.

"I didn't cheat!" she complains, folding her little arms.

"*Someone* cheated."

She scoffs. "*You* did. Several times! Ta-dah is not a word."

I wave both hands to make my point. "It is! Like abracadabra. Ta-dah!" Gosh, I wish I knew how to do a magic trick the way Jal does.

She narrows her eyes. "It's 'ta-da' with no 'h,' and even *that* word is not in the official dictionary."

"In my defense, I didn't know you had an official dictionary." If I did, I wouldn't have tried to cheat. "Anyway, I have to go. But first, I have one thing to ask you."

Excited, she jumps on the bed. "Awesome! I'm going to fight?"

Cringing inwardly, I guess what Jane would say

about my request. But Primavera is also at risk, and hopefully, I can keep her away from the main battle.

"Not exactly." I shake my head, emphatically, and cross my arms in what I hope is an authoritative gesture. "In fact, I'm forbidding you to fight."

Primavera's eyebrows furrow, and she sulks.

"True, I want you to help us defeat the necromantes," I continue. "And Khof. But you're not supposed to fight. And don't tell anyone else about this—not even Ernie!"

She sneers. "It's Ermey. I told you already." All of a sudden, she gasps. "You're saying Ernie on purpose!" Then she grins at me.

I smile too. She's too smart for me. I was just trying to push her buttons.

After a long discussion, she promises she'll do what I've asked. I don't even know why she trusts me, but I have enough confidence and apparently a good résumé.

Once we agree on the details of the plan, she walks out the bedroom door and into the hallway so I can exit the house. I follow her, trying not to step on anything. When we get to the front door, an incredible sight is waiting for us. Primavera's outer walls have been set to transparent, and we can see outside. Jane is there, waiting for me at the foot of the stoop, along with Dorothy.

My heart jumps a beat, and I even tear up a little. My plan worked. She's alive. Jane is back in Pangea after I killed her here. I steal a glance at Primavera, who seems oblivious to my reception committee.

Jane's black tank top has a print of a golden bird inside a circle, carrying an arrow, and she's also wearing a pair of jeans and boots. But why is Jane waiting for me? She can't possibly see the house if she hasn't been invited. I grimace at Primavera, but she's still not fazed.

"Good luck, Zeon." She opens her arms for a hug, and we embrace. "You're forgiven."

Without giving me a chance to ask her why she didn't tell me Jane was outside, Primavera dashes back to her room, and I'm greeted by Barney again.

So, after hesitating for a moment, I step outside the house, startling Jane. From her point of view, I must've appeared out of thin air. Despite the scare, she quickly recomposes herself and takes a few steps closer.

"I can explain," I say, trying to formulate a lie about what just happened. If she knows Hermes is alive, she'll freak out.

After a quick hug, she grabs both of my hands and pulls them up, staring at me with her beautiful black eyes. I smile, although I'm confused about the whole situation.

"Zeon, do you trust me?"

Here we go. I know exactly where this conversation is going. If I trust her, I must tell her what just happened. At least I'm not naked this time.

"No," I say.

It's easier to start a fight than to give up Primavera's secrets. Nonetheless, she doesn't react the way I expect. Her expression is calm and thoughtful.

"How about this, then?" She looks upward as she thinks. "You love me, but you don't like that I snort when I laugh." She twists her lips in a half-smirk. This is taking an odd turn. "You never had the courage to tell me you secretly believed the disastrous outcome of my relationship with Frederico was partially my fault—because of my childish romantic attraction to Italians that made me blind to his womanizing."

That's incredibly specific—and worst of all, true. How does she know that? Her eyes shift to the left, and she pauses as she apparently thinks of what else to say. As for me, I'm speechless.

Finally, she laughs but manages not to snort. "You cheat at board games. Oh, and you have a sexual fetish no one knows about."

"Okay, okay, stop! You got me."

I hope she won't say it out loud. I'm surprised she seems so cool about it. She shouldn't know any of this. "Who told you?" And why is she telling me now?

She grabs her ponytail for a moment. By this point, she knows I like the way she wears it, and I wonder if she's using it to manipulate me. But considering everything, perhaps I should give her some credit.

Then, she scratches her left earlobe and looks down. "You won't believe me. Pangea is more complex than what we perceive. Our minds joined for a second when you were busy killing me, saving us from Khof." Her eyes find mine again. "Zeon, I saw into your soul."

She's right. This is absurd. Maybe Khof told her, or maybe the messengers did. "And what else do you know?"

"I know there are some things I'm not supposed to know yet. But more importantly, after what happened, I know I can trust you. So, you don't have to lie about why you just popped into existence at the exact place Dorothy took me. You don't have to tell me at all."

I take a deep breath. She's probably being manipulated by the messengers of the gods somehow, but at the moment, there's nothing to gain by fighting with her.

"Okay, I trust you."

She snickers. "Liar. I told you, I know a lot about you now." Wrapping her arms around my waist, she pulls me closer. Apparently, we're back together—not that I'm complaining.

When our mouths are so close we could kiss, she says, "But you have to promise one day you'll do something for me, no questions asked. Can you do that?"

I bite my lip. "Yes."

To be honest, this is completely unfair. When she's this close, embracing me, she could ask me anything and I'd do it. I frown.

"Wait," I say. Perhaps I can still define some ground rules. "I won't insult John's mother." I shake my head. "Not again."

With the cutest grin, she jumps on top of Dorothy and helps me up. At first, I try to sit behind her, but she forces me into an undignified ride to their camp with me in front of her. But it feels great to have her this close.

"So, what's your fetish?" she asks, breaking the spell and chuckling. "That one wasn't true. I was just bluffing."

I turn back to give her an angry stare. On top of messing with my feelings, she has the nerve to start this type of conversation when I'm riding in front of her in a vulnerable position.

"We're barely back together and you want to know that? No way."

"Well, for someone from a planet so open about sex, you're kind of freaking me out now."

Dorothy nickers softly as we ride toward the village. As always, Jane doesn't actually have to guide the mare. Dorothy's a smart horse.

"Is it stockings? Clowns? Feet?" She snickers, in a better mood than I'd expect her to be. "Wait, I know you. It's butts." She nods vigorously, rubbing my back with her chin. "Or maybe buttocks..."

I roll my eyes at her, but she can't see me.

"Really, butts? How would butts be a fetish? It's part of the... *thing*! Fetishes are supposed to be weird." I gesture widely and lose my balance. With dexterity, Jane grabs my waist and saves me from falling off our high horse.

"What is it, then?" she prods. "You have to tell me."

I let out a long breath before answering. "It's tickling. Stop bothering me now." It's easy to say this out loud because Jane's from Earth, but it's still embarrassing. "And please don't tell anyone."

"Oh," she says with disappointment in her voice. "It doesn't seem that bad."

"It's a stigma on Jora. Despite all the sexual openness, tickling is taboo. It's because of a festival that happened a hundred years ago. Sorry, I'm not comfortable talking about it."

"I see. Does Nia know?"

"Stop it!"

She giggles, and we stay silent for a while.

"John's working on a plan," Jane says, finally changing the subject. "He wants to surprise Khof on his next attack."

The town is already visible from this small hill, and Dorothy slows down to better navigate around the roots as we descend the last slope.

"It won't work. I talked with Ermey—the messenger helping Primavera. I have new information."

"Which is?"

"I'll explain later."

When we get near the gazebo, we watch everyone running around doing chores. They're gathering food, water, energy ellipsoids, and other supplies for the upcoming battle. If we follow John's plan, this is going to be a long, bloody war.

It makes sense from his point of view, and if his assumptions are correct, Khof will definitely lose by attrition. This type of battle tends to wear down the army that's outnumbered ten to one, even if they have the technological upper hand.

Unfortunately, his assumptions prove to be wrong. The situation is worse than he thinks, and I'll have to set him straight.

When Dorothy stops, John shouts, "Wait! Don't get any closer."

I frown. John is treating us like the enemy. Well, maybe he's right. With parallel Earths and doppelgängers, we could be the enemy.

"Jane, what's the last thing I told you?" he continues. "Before you left today?"

Jane turns Dorothy around, maybe to face John better. She laughs before answering. "You were telling me a story—about the fourth point of contact!"

"Right." He grins at her. He approaches us with long, quick steps, extending his hand to help me down as Jane surreptitiously slides her fingers up my lower back below my t-shirt. I frown at her, and she just giggles while John watches us with wide eyes. Seriously, she can't be trusted with anything.

"You took a long time out there, Romeo and Juliet." He's back to simmering with anger, wearing his army-spec camouflaged uniform. It's great for guerrilla fighting, but it'll make him a target if we storm the island. "I shouldn't have let you guys leave earlier. We have a war to fight. There's no time for sex!"

Jane flushes and immediately steps in front of John, angry as a hen. I walk in between them.

"John, we need to talk."

PART III

Every battle is won before it's ever fought.

—Sun Tzu.

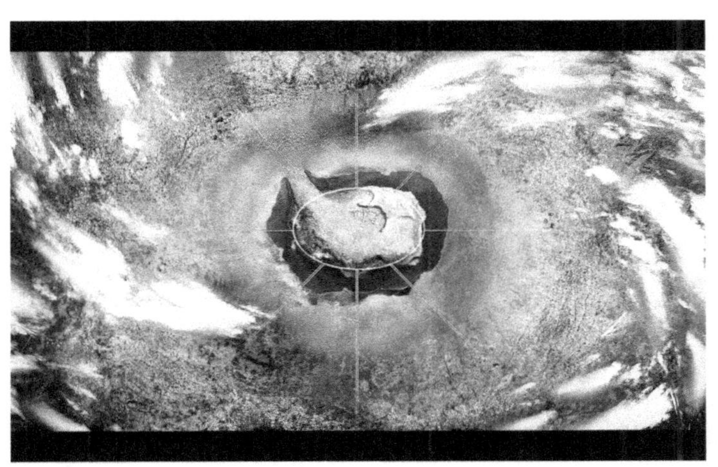

Chapter 30

MAP

Our party sits around a large mahogany table at John's apartment—it's their center of operations. Vladimir joins John as the military presence in the room. The rest of us—Louise, Raj, Jane and Paulo —are civilians.

While I drink my third coffee of the day, Raj sits next to me at the table, demonstrating his impressive knowledge of Hindi and English swear words.

"And that's why you're a selfish *backarchodu*." He pushes me as if inviting me to fight. I forgot how menacing his facial scar is. He looks like an Indian mobster, and the thought makes me smile.

Luckily, yelling and insults don't affect me anymore. Since this shitshow started, it's been happening to me nonstop. The only difference now is I actually know why he's mad at me.

"Why are you smiling, *bevakooph*? Marie must be beside herself. We have to go back and bring them here *now*!"

His rage is completely understandable. We left

Marie and the others in a hurry, and for all they know, Raj may already be dead. When we got to John's camp the first time, Raj was under the impression we would soon go back, but instead, I got killed, and he thought he was stuck here forever. He can't cross the veil by himself.

"He's right," John says from the head of the large mahogany table. "You have to go there and tell them."

I grasp Raj's shoulder in what I hope is a gesture of solidarity. "We're going back today, Raj. You have my word. But first I have to tell John something."

Raj's scowl deepens. "Make it fast. I'm going to gather my stuff, and you better be ready to go when I'm back."

Daylight briefly shines inside when the door opens and Raj leaves. The sun is never a problem for John's apartment because the outside walls face north, but today he has disabled the outside view and replaced it with a gray wall. The ceiling itself is bright, illuminating the room.

After briefly looking around the table at everyone, I turn to face John.

"Your plan relies on Khof not getting reinforcements," I begin. Based on John's intelligence, Khof has about two hundred trucks, tanks, mobile artillery, and armored troop carriers. And yet, he must have fewer than forty protectors fighting with him. "But this is going to change. According to my sources, Earth one is about to become Khof's ally, and they have more than a thousand people in the Wheel."

My source is, of course, Hermes, but they don't know it.

Jane and John look at each other in shock.

"Who told you?" Vladimir asks. He's the only one

not at the table. Instead, he leans against the wall in the corner, both hands in his pockets, watching us from a distance.

"A messenger called Ermey told me." Actually, he told me *and* Louise, but she's keeping quiet. She's also not wearing sunglasses anymore, so others will think she can see. "The humans from Earth one are mad at the messengers, and they were promised to be spared by the necromantes."

"He's lying. The messengers lie!" Paulo shouts. "*Mentirosos,*" he mumbles, showing his teeth. It's funny to see Paulo mad at something. He's always so easygoing.

"It doesn't matter," John says. "If this is the truth and we don't do anything, this war is lost."

As always, he understands the situation better than anyone else here. Truth or lie, the messengers are forcing our hand. Again.

Jane claps her hands together as if she's praying, and a 2D map of the Wheel is suddenly projected onto the top of the long table. Everyone in the room can see the exact same image—a top view of the island, surrounded by the impossible circular river and the unnamed sectors around it.

"I think we finally have the whole picture." She waves at the projection. "Earth five is Jora, six is Terra, seven is... Earth, I guess." The sectors flash on the map clockwise from the east and south and words in English are suddenly added to the scenery. With a concerned expression, she looks from side to side. "Interesting... it's a *smart* map. We have labels!" I don't think she's adding them. "Anyway, Earth eight is Yora. So, Earth one is between the west and northwest veils."

As soon as she mentions Earth one, the word

"Orbis" appears next to its label. Jane frowns, glances at me, and nods. "I see," Jane finally says. "Orbis must be how they call their planet."

Paulo approaches the table and gestures at the unlabeled northern part of the map. "What about those Earths?"

"Hmm." Jane flips her hand horizontally and the map magically follows her arm, focusing on the sectors next to Orbis. "Haides said the necromantes killed three planets. If true, that means there should be no humans alive in sectors two, three, or four."

Someone gasps—it might be me—when a skull and crossbones icon appears above octants two, three, and four. The room goes quiet. The realization that three planets are dead—actually five, if we count Yora and Terra—is not something to take lightly.

"Ahem." I clear my throat to pull their attention away from the heartless, all-knowing map. The bad news is just starting. "Ermey also gave me another piece of information that may help us. There's a land passage between Earth one's sector—or, I guess, Orbis' sector—and the island."

"Passage?" Jane says. "Louise, do you know anything about this?"

"Well, I've never felt it before." I stare at Louise in disbelief. She's accidentally outing herself. "I mean, I've never seen it."

I look around the room, but no one seems to have noticed her *faux pas*. She's right. It wasn't there the first time I visualized it in my mind map.

"It's there," I say. "It's slowly appearing."

John starts interacting with the map just like Jane did, by extending his arms and joining his hands. But unlike Jane, he pushes his hands apart as if he's swimming. The floating map responds by zooming in to the riverbank in front of sector one. "There's nothing there."

"The map is lying." I wave at the projected image. "If you send someone to the shore, I bet it's already visible."

John turns to Vladimir, who's already on the move and out the door before anyone says anything else. No one calls me crazy or a liar. By this point, they must know better.

"I don't understand," Paulo says, clenching his fists. His accent and mannerisms remind me of Alfredo. "Their vehicles float over the river."

"But horses don't," Jane says. "The passage must be there for the humans that aren't on the island."

I nod. "The Wheel was designed as a battle game by Iris to test all the Earths. And the passage, the veils, were all part of it." These boneheaded messengers of the gods keep doing these tests on us to see if we're worthy, but this time, Khof took them by surprise.

There's much more to tell Jane and the others, but I've already made the decision to not discuss anything here in Pangea. If Hermes is telling the truth, I don't want to expose his brain experiments to Iris, at least not yet. She may be listening. Primavera's house—or Primavera herself—is somehow off limits to their surveillance.

The door makes a swooshing sound, and Vladimir runs toward us. He tries to catch his breath before speaking. "Didn't go far. It's like a long dirt road over the river. It's visible from here." No one is surprised when the manipulative map finally shows the image of a semi-transparent pathway connecting Earth one and the island.

John inhales and exhales, his good mood apparently forgotten. "Well, at least the veils are going to slow them down."

I sigh, look down, and slowly shake my head.

The major abruptly stands up. "Oh, no. No, no, no." He moves in toward me, his hands formed into fists. "Don't you say what I think you're going to say—"

Now it's John's time to forget I don't make the rules. And he's about to shoot the messenger.

"Uh... th—the veils," I stutter. There's no easy way to say this. "The veils are getting weaker every day. It was part of Iris' original design. They're going away. Soon. And once they're gone..."

Instead of hitting me, John slumps his shoulders and walks away from the table, sighing. I've never seen him look so down.

"With the force fields gone, Khof will slaughter everyone," he says. His gaze is distant, away from us. "We'll need to fight inland, hidden..." His voice trails off. The war is not looking good for us.

Sinking into my chair, I glare at the back of his head. There's more. There's much, much more. The protectors look at me and back at John, probably guessing I'm not done. No one warns him.

John turns around, surveying the silent room. Everybody immediately looks away. When our eyes finally meet, his frown deepens. "What else? Spill it, damn it!"

I gulp. "It's worse than that. When the force fields disappear, Khof will use his powers to tear this hypersphere so the necromantes can invade Pangea."

The whole place goes into a complete uproar. Everyone tries to talk over each other.

"*Meu Deus!*" Paulo says. "We're doomed!" He speaks

so loudly we can actually hear him. Louise only purses her lips.

"Quiet!" John shouts, hitting his fist hard on the table. Because of the loud noise, the room goes silent. It's almost funny. He was looking defeated just a few seconds ago, but now that the situation has become literally impossible, he's back to his old self.

"Panicking isn't going to help us," John says calmly. "So—does anyone have any ideas?"

Paulo clears his throat. "This is going to sound crazy, but what if we do what Khof's asking?" he says, and we all look at him as if he just said he hates little kittens. The tall Brazilian never contributes much to the discussion, and certainly not for major subjects like these. "Join him and the necromantes?" he elaborates.

A rush of air comes from the entrance when the door opens again, and Raj enters. He looks at us perplexed. The mood has drastically changed since he left.

Moving quietly—as if he just caught us in the middle of mass—he sits next to me.

The long silence says a lot about how uncertain our situation is, but I think the decision is obvious. Still, no one dares to add anything. Everyone in the room seems to wait for Jane's or John's view on Paulo's outrageous suggestion. The fact they're taking this long to answer is not a good sign.

"No," Jane finally says. "Allying with Khof is genocide. We may not like the messengers, but at least we're still alive."

With the exception of Raj, who seems oblivious, we collectively breathe a sigh of relief. There's no easy decision here, but it's better to maintain the status quo and fight Khof, the necromantes, and anyone else on our own terms. I'm glad Jane said that. I didn't want to go rogue again.

But this is not going to be easy. I know exactly what's going to happen. Jora, Terra, and Earth will have to fight against humans from Yora and Orbis—and against necromantes. It's going to be a massacre. Worse, if Orbis has even a couple of armored vehicles when we get there, everything is going to be lost.

"Very well," John says. "We must go to Orbis right now."

I stare at John in defiance. "No. I'm going to gather Raj's people first."

John shakes his head. "There is no time. Every hour we waste here may result in them getting another tank or piece of artillery from Khof, and you're the only one who can help us travel through the barriers. We can't let you go."

He's right, to a point. Louise also can do that, but he doesn't know.

"Let him go," Jane interjects, and we all look at her as if she just badmouthed the Second Amendment. There's no reason at all for her to be on my side. She doesn't even know what I'm planning to do.

"Why?" John and I ask together.

Jane's eyes shift from me to the major as if she's wondering how to answer the question. Eventually, her focus settles on John. "We're not ready yet, and Zeon can easily pick the Terrans up tonight. We'll get to Orbis in the next day or so."

John narrows his eyes at her and then looks at me, thinking. Thirty or so extra people may not make a difference at this point, but they couldn't hurt, especially a few battle-hardened soldiers.

With his hands behind his back, the large, muscular major begins walking around the table. "Okay." When he's behind me, he stops and lowers his head, making me nervous. Once he's low enough that he must have the same point of view from the battlefield projection that I have, he extends his arm.

"You're going here." He points at the floating six, Terra's sector. "But this is off-limits." He moves his finger above five, Jora's sector. "I don't trust those scumbags."

As if mocking me, Jora's octant on the floating holographic image blinks red with the words "Off-limits for Zeon." It makes sense. Earth and Jora fought against each other for years, and there's a lot of bad blood between them.

"I'd never do that, John," I tell him. "You have my word."

Not even an idiot would go there after giving his word to John. Too bad I'm not a regular idiot. Hell, based on what Hermes said about the brain experiments, I must be the dumbest of them all.

Chapter 31

MIRRORS

It's about two hours after midnight, and the three musketeers are getting ready to gather the troops. Raj will ride with me to find his people, and Louise insisted on coming too. She convinced me if she and I worked together, we could open a larger passage and move the people more quickly. Therefore, Louise and her moody horse Pierre are accompanying us.

Paulo's in charge of the horses, and he brings me one that's smaller than Pierre and overall, not that impressive. Just a brown stallion that looks exactly like any plastic horse you'd find in a toy store.

He tries to cheer me up when I complain about it. "Oh, no. Don't worry. Whiskerey's a thoroughbred." Paulo sometimes adds nonexistent vowels to the end of words. "True, he's a small animal even for his breed, but Jane asked me to give you a fast one instead of a battle horse. Jane said, and I quote, 'Zeon can't handle a battle horse.'" He wags his index finger on every word that Jane supposedly said. The nerve.

"Whiskerey?" I caress his crest. It takes me a long

time to get into the saddle, but now I'm here, I won't get down unless absolutely necessary.

"He's fun," Paulo says, smiling broadly and showing all his teeth.

"After Whiskey?" I ask. I guess Daiquiri and Margarita were already taken.

"No. Because he has whiskers. Like a cat."

He twists his index finger and thumb on his face for emphasis while tapping on the horse's neck with his other hand. Whiskerey promptly nods.

"Earth has some weird-ass cats," I joke, and Paulo laughs, walking over to help Raj get saddled.

Raj's mare is the ugliest of the bunch. She's about the same size as Pierre, but sturdier, and it's as if her front part is one breed, making her a brown horse, while her back end looks like a Dalmatian. Paulo explains that the mare is an Appaloosa, one of his favorite breeds. Since she's still nameless, he lets Raj choose her name—Antonia.

"What's up with the bright red jersey anyway?" Raj asks me once we're ready to go. "You couldn't find one with a target on it?"

I look down at my red soccer jersey, which sports the logo of a Brazilian soccer club.

I gesture at it. "I needed one with this exact color."

Paulo scoffs at me. "But why *Inter*?" He looks at the logo on my shirt and shakes his head. "*Flamengo* from Rio de Janeiro is much better." Clearly, he knows more about Brazilian soccer than I do. I prefer American football.

Nearby, Raj throws up his hands and interrupts us. "And why didn't you pick Chesnea's jersey? Or one from Leyrpole? They're also red."

Paulo eyes me with an amused expression and

shakes his head. "Your friend's nuts!" He's not used to the names people have on Terra. He's probably talking about Chelsea and Liverpool.

"No. This is the exact shade of red that I need."

An hour later, we are at the cliff where Raj and I first walked into this sector, standing at the border between Earth and Terra. The last time I was here, I'd been running for my life. This was the place where I'd melted his blade after he tackled me. He's since found a new knife, but it doesn't have a curved blade. He's still upset about it.

The moons give us enough light to move about without tripping. We have flashlights in case we need them, but it's better to stay in the dark. Man-made lights and sound go through the walls. Meanwhile, John's deploying about a hundred protectors to surround the area, trying to be discreet.

Although there are more clouds in the sky than I've seen before—sometimes they hide one of the moons—it's not raining. The cliff we're on gives us a gloomy view of the dark valley below, and Fortress' island looms on the horizon.

After we dismount, I tell Raj to remain close as I touch the wall with my left hand.

Closing my eyes, I begin to explore beyond the veil. As Hermes told us, the wall is weaker than the first time I interacted with it.

There are two sentries on guard on the other side. One is up in the trees, sleeping, while the other is next to a campfire behind a tree, apparently having a snack. Like Raj, they don't have bright auras, but I can still perceive them as different from their surroundings, especially when they move.

The threads of the veil hum with energy, reacting

to my hand. Opening a diamond hole like I did last time would illuminate the whole valley, eventually alerting everyone in the Wheel that we're here.

Instead, I replicate Louise's subtle method of unlacing and parting the threads like a curtain, starting with a five-centimeter-wide opening that runs from my hand down to the ground.

Opening my eyes, I wave my free hand, and Raj kneels next to the opening. We're ready.

Then, he cups his hands around his mouth and calls out, "Hello? It's Raj!"

The man behind the tree drops his snack into the fire and peeks at us. Scrambling to his feet, he blows a whistle. I'm pretty sure it's Alfredo, who must be seeing Raj's face through the opening by now. Up above, some of their soldiers do a military crawl over wooden platforms to get a better look. A few seconds later, about a dozen other protectors are running toward us.

"Alfredo, is that you?" Raj asks.

"Raj?" Alfredo's voice comes from the other side of the trunk. "Are you alive?" He finally shows his face and smiles. "Marie's going to be so happy!"

"Alfredo, stop!" Jonathan shouts from nearby. "We don't know who these people really are."

"It's me, Jonathan. Raj!"

Jonathan crouches behind a tree, gesturing for his troops to surround the area. After he whispers something to Alfredo, he runs around the trees, positioning himself along the barrier to the north of us. Despite the darkness, I can sense everything he and his small army are doing, so there's no way he'll catch us by surprise.

Once Jonathan gives him the thumbs-up, Alfredo lingers near us. He's visibly shaking, but in spite of his discomfort, he's still way more courageous than Frederico. Frederico would be running for the hills the moment he heard a voice calling out of the veil.

"What's up, Freddy?" Raj asks through the gap, grinning. That's an interesting development. I used to call Frederico "Freddy" in a derogatory way. It seems here they use it as a nickname.

"Raj? Oh, my God, Raj!" Marie shouts, suddenly appearing from the tree line and running toward the veil's opening. Alfredo grabs her and holds her in place. Raj jerks his head toward me, but before he says anything, I enlarge the crack, making a three-meter-high by two-meter-wide hole that opens just like a curtain, creating a strong tear that will stay open by itself for a while.

It's too dark for them to see my face, but I tiptoe north to remain hidden, just in case. No reason to let them think Khof is around.

Once the gap is wide open, Raj runs to Marie, who in turn pushes Alfredo away to hug her partner. Meanwhile, Jonathan jumps through to our side, gun raised. Soon, he's right next to me, holding his double-barreled capacitor to my head. "Khof! You *motherfucker!*"

Time slows down to a crawl as I instinctively engage my fast mode. Perhaps I'm the dumbest of this world, but I'm also the fastest, and I can dodge them, letting John's army take over. However, I decide to do nothing and instead see how this will play out. Before Jonathan can pull the trigger, John jumps from a tree just behind us and points his gun at Jonathan.

"Drop the weapon, Jonathan," John says in a calm voice. "You're surrounded by hundreds of us."

Jonathan's eyes narrow at John. Maybe he'll pull the trigger out of spite.

Meanwhile, Alfredo appears from the hole in the wall, hands trembling, his own capacitor pointing at John. "I can't believe you're helping this murderer."

"He's not Khof," John says. "He's Zeon. And we need him to fight Khof."

This is the point where I could plead for my life—remind Jonathan I saved Marie and healed him. If I were Khof, what would be the point of helping them? Also, Raj would never put Marie in danger. He'd probably kill himself before he led Khof back here.

So, I say nothing. Jonathan's a smart guy. He can figure this out himself.

"How do I know Raj is actually Raj?" Jonathan asks.

As always, he has a great point. Before we're able to answer, Raj shouts from the other side of the veil, "the night Jean was killed, and Marie disappeared." He instinctively bows his head to cross the passage to our side, even though it's high enough for him to stand up. "You went into town by yourself, and I found you on a park bench. You were crying."

Jonathan shakes his head. "You're mistaken. I just had something in my eye."

After a long pause, Jonathan finally lowers his weapon, looking thoughtful. Alfredo follows suit, watching the pair of them. Then, Jonathan turns to John with a big smile.

"So, who's this handsome son of a bitch?"

John lowers his own weapon and grabs Jonathan's hand firmly, shaking it with a grin of his own. "I'm John. You sure are a sight for sore eyes!"

Jonathan's smile broadens. "I guess beggars can't be choosers."

I shake my head in disapproval and try to change the subject. "Where's Ivan?" He's one of Jonathan's best soldiers and yet he's not here.

The major shrugs. "He's AWOL. We haven't seen him since you left."

Looking around, I rapidly wiggle my eyebrows and try to make eye contact with anyone who's thinking what I'm thinking, but no one acknowledges me. Everyone else seems oblivious.

Jonathan snorts. "Are you having a stroke?"

"It's Ivan," I say. "We can't trust him. I think he tried to kill us."

Then I explain my suspicions to the group. Ivan must've crossed the barriers and added something to our wine, pretending to be Vladimir. Maybe we need to create some kind of code with the real Vladimir.

Jonathan sighs. "I hate that I'm agreeing with you of all people, but it makes sense."

Just when I think the awkwardness is gone, I catch Raj and Marie looking at Louise. My heart sinks to my feet. While Marie is fascinated by Louise's face, a mirror of her own, Louise tilts her head toward Marie's belly. The archangel knows.

"Louise," Marie says, a shy smile on her face. "It's so nice to meet you."

Marie doesn't have the same mannerisms as Louise, like avoiding eye contact or not looking straight at objects. Unlike Louise, Marie isn't—or wasn't—blind on her planet. This must be another blow to Louise. Marie's life could be hers.

It takes a long time for Louise to smile, even after a hug from Marie.

"Thanks for helping Raj," Marie says. "Oh, do you have a Raj of your own, on your side?"

Louise's grin, which was probably fake anyway, disappears.

Before I can do anything to help Louise, Raj takes Marie's hand and pulls her out of the hug. "His name was Ravi."

Marie's brows furrow, her cheeks turn red, and she steps back. "I'm so sorry."

Raj remains silent. I can relate.

"Raj, Jonathan." An interruption from John saves us from this train wreck of a conversation. "We should gather your people and bring them to our side. There's a lot for us to discuss, and we don't have much time. Do you think you can have everyone here early in the morning?"

Morning is only a couple of hours from now, but Jonathan nods. "Yes, we can make it."

As everyone starts walking into Terra's sector through the opening, Louise remains motionless, looking down. I take her arm, pulling her away. It seems like she's holding back tears.

"You could've told me," she whispers, almost crying. "I have no right to be upset, but..."

I understand what she's feeling. Marie and Raj are not responsible for what happened with Ravi, and the fact Marie's pregnant shouldn't affect her. But it does. She's human, after all.

"If it makes you feel any better," I whisper back to her, "they're all dead."

Louise looks at me with horror in her eyes. "What the hell is wrong with you?"

Chapter 32

SECRET AGENT

Dawn in the Wheel takes my breath away. Besides the palette of morning colors, the moons are still in the sky, and the valley below the ridge makes for an impressive scene. The forest of trees with purple trunks gives it even more color, and I wish I had a camera with me.

Meanwhile, Louise makes this scene look like a painting, although in a sad way. She's seated with her legs folded, watching the sunrise. With her long, messy hair, the dirty purple riding pants, a long-sleeved black blouse, and a cigarette in her hand, her slim, defeated figure seems to give purpose to the landscape.

Raj's people are gathering the last of their belongings as we wait for them next to the force field. On John's side, horses graze nearby, waiting for the thirty or so survivors of a whole planet.

I swallow a lump in my throat. Only thirty... Still, they seem happy today. Jonathan is even forcing John to eat some of the rodent meat.

"We never talked about children," Louise says,

staring at the consumed cigarette butt. It's her fourth since I started counting. "Ravi and I, you know?" She gives me a sad chuckle and grabs another cigarette. "*C'est des conneries!*"

Uh-oh. She's going to talk to me about feelings, and I won't know what to say. Perhaps I should tell her they were together only for a short period of time. It'd be weird to discuss kids that early. I could say she has her whole life in front of her, and that Ravi wouldn't want her to become bitter and unhappy, but she knows all that.

"I know." I lean against one of the pulsating purple trunks. "It sucks." I wish Jane were here with us, helping Louise through this. And I'll have to dump Louise really soon, making things even worse. It's time to go back, but I won't be joining her. Not right now, anyway.

To complicate things, Whiskerey's on the other side of the veil. John's not letting any horse through in case I try to go to sector five. This means I'll have to walk for several hours, assuming I don't get caught.

"After Ravi died, I didn't want to get over him," she sobs. "I thought it would be disrespectful to his memory." She's now weeping openly. "And now we meet Raj, and everything comes back to me. Including the guilt."

I nod. It's tough. I like to think our loved ones would want us to be happy again. But it's easier said than done.

Jane appears from the shadows. "Great! You guys are here."

"I thought you'd stay to organize the *résistance,*" I say.

She smiles at me, but her expression changes when she gets a better look at Louise. For a moment, she looks at me and frowns, but soon her eyes snap wide open. It's amazing how much can be communicated even without words. She doesn't know about Marie's baby, but she must've seen Marie and Raj already.

Jane crouches next to our blonde friend. "Are you okay, Louise?"

"Yes." Louise smiles, but the sadness in her eyes doesn't change. "I just need some time."

Jane reaches for Louise's hand and stares at her. "Let me know if you need anything. I just need to talk to Zeon for a second."

"Sure. I'll keep an eye on the *wall*." Louise winks at me.

Jane and I hurry north, following the trail next to the Earth-Terra veil on Terra's side, the same path Ivan, Alfredo, and I took the first time I saw Khof. The barrier opening will stay as is for at least half an hour, and Louise can always discreetly keep it open if necessary. Of course, Jane doesn't know that.

"What was that wink about?" Jane asks. "Are you hiding something?"

Before I can answer, she laughs. Jane's not insecure, and she knows how much I abhor cheating. Except at word games.

"I am. But it's not my secret to tell." I'm a terrible liar, and we have other things to worry about. "Besides, I thought you knew everything about me."

She tilts her head at me. "Well, clearly not *everything.*"

Although we've already been out of earshot for a long time, Jane keeps walking, and I start to get worried. We've been on the move for at least five minutes, and John's goons are going to be after us soon. Maybe Jane *is* one of his goons?

The trees grow sparse as we draw near the shore of the river, but we're still fairly far away. There's a lot of empty terrain between the riverside and the tree line. If we were walking to the river, it would take another thirty or forty minutes to reach it.

Still looking ahead, Jane raises her hand, gently touching my chest in the process, and we finally stop. The flats are still far away, and the island looms in the distance. Turning to face her, I lean down to kiss her, but instead she gives me a backpack. I was so distracted by Louise's situation that I didn't even notice she was carrying it.

"Uh... what?"

The backpack feels heavy in my hand. Jane's already carrying one of her own. Maybe it's the supplies we'll need for the upcoming battle, although there's no reason to bring them here.

She walks to the force field. "Paulo's going to start a distraction soon. If I counted my steps correctly, Whiskerey and Dorothy are just across the veil." She tilts her head at the wall. "You just have to open a passage, and they'll gallop over here—and we'll be on our way."

Removing the rubber band from her ponytail, she readjusts her hair as she waits for an answer.

"Uh... what?"

She chuckles. "You're not James Bond, you know? Everybody knows exactly what you're planning, so John asked me to keep an eye on you."

How awkward. So they all figured I'm going to Jora's sector, even though John forbade me. Sometimes, I can be so predictable.

"Why is Dorothy there? You're not going with me."

She bursts out laughing as if I just told her a joke,

and I smile back unintentionally. Then, Jane leans closer and wraps her arms around my waist. "This is non-negotiable, *darling*. We'll do this together. As a couple."

As soon as she kisses me, the darkness of the early dawn is interrupted by a flash of light. It comes from the forest behind us, around the place where I created an entrance to Terra's sector. The sound of fireworks soon follows, and even from here, we can hear people yelling.

"Wow, that was a good kiss," I say, snickering.

Jane turns her head to look at the flashing lights, a big smile on her face. "It's time," Jane says. "Let's go!"

Stepping past her, I slap my hands to the veil and concentrate. We can't see the horses through it, and there's no time to use my mental map. But lo and behold, when I create a curtain-like opening in the barrier, Dorothy and Whiskerey casually walk through it as if they were expecting us.

As for me, I don't know what to feel. Jane's acting so weird today, and too willing to help me. But, as Jonathan would say, I shouldn't look a gift horse in the mouth. Two horses, in this case.

In silence, Jane helps me up into my saddle.

"Whiskerey's a fast horse," I tell Jane. "You told Paulo that Dorothy wouldn't work for me because she's not as fast."

She's already on her own saddle doing her pre-flight checklist, or whatever horse riders do to get ready to go.

"She wouldn't work for *you*." An unsettling smile forms on her face. "But *I* can handle her."

Jane squeezes her legs together and Dorothy snorts, jumping ahead. Without warning, Whiskerey follows, almost dumping me. The next thing I know, we're galloping down the trail toward the beach. I wish people would warn me about sudden equine departures.

The path we're taking—strung between the trees and the desert—makes sense. Like it or not, it's the shortest way to the other veil, the one between Terra's and Jora's sectors. However, it takes all of my strength and concentration to stay in the saddle, and I must confess I'm not in control of my horse. I can't see anything, and my only hope is that Whiskerey is actually following Dorothy and Jane. Under this stress, I can't use my mental map for anything, and Jane's the only one guiding us.

While we ride, I consider our situation. People from Jora, Earth five, must not be happy with Khof. A lot of our protectors must've been killed by Khof at some point; they're the bodies stored in black bags in Dooria's compound. It would be hard to convince them to ally with him. I bet they'd shoot him on sight.

Which brings me to another problem. I look exactly like Khof. Hopefully, my red jersey should help clear the confusion. This is not a stupid plan at all.

Much later, the horses slow down, and I'm finally able to look up. I'm far behind Jane, who brought us closer to the tree line. The terrain here is uneven from all the purple roots, dust, and low bushes, and it would be impossible to keep the same pace. I take this chance to check our surroundings, and I confirm no one is following us—at least, no one with an aura.

"How did you convince Paulo to help you?" I ask, once Whiskerey's able to catch up with Jane.

"He didn't know," she replies. "I asked him to

deliver a large locked chest to Jonathan." A mischievous smirk appears on her face.

My eyes snap wide. "Jonathan's going to kill us!" More precisely, he's going to kill *me*. There's no way he'll believe I wasn't involved in it.

"It's just a harmless prank. Mostly..."

Above us, the orange and red clouds fade into a partially cloudy day with a few breaks of blue. Jane takes us south, away from the shore and through the beginnings of the forest. It's nice to have a bunch of trees to hide in if we need them. It keeps our options open.

An hour after we fled, we're finally getting close to the other axle of the energy wheel. When Dorothy's about ten meters away from it, she stops. Whiskerey stops next to her, and we all study the land on the other side.

Just as with all the other veils, we can't see people or animals through it, so most of what's happening there will be hidden from our sight unless I concentrate and study my mental map. However, as it stands, that's not necessary.

Jane stares at the sandbanks near the shore in Jora's sector. "Oh *fuck*," she exclaims. "We're too late. But I thought..." She turns to look at me, clenching her teeth. Her face shows a mixture of fear and accusation, as if I'm responsible for this.

Two tanks and three armored personnel carriers are parked near the shore. Four trucks with turrets are moving about the land, sporadically shooting inland. Only Khof has vehicles in this hypersphere. Therefore, Jora's sector is under attack by his forces.

Chapter 33

LICENSE TO SOFT KILL

"I thought—I thought you had everything under control," Jane whimpers, unshed tears accumulating in her eyes. "I thought you had a plan!"

I dismount Whiskerey, considering the situation. Good luck with that. If she really knew me, she'd have realized that my plans never work out.

"I do have a plan," I tell her. Several plans, in fact. I try to remain calm. "But I didn't expect that." I gesture at the vehicles. "Khof wasn't supposed to be here."

Looking nowhere in particular, she gets off Dorothy and she shakes her head. "We have to go back. It's too late for your people."

"This looks bad, I get it. But no. I need to find someone first."

"THEY! CAN'T! HELP! US!" she shouts. Dorothy's ears fold back, and the mare turns to me, stomping her hooves menacingly, forcing me to step back. Whiskerey turns around as if pretending he doesn't know me. Even the horses are against me.

"It's okay, Jane." I try to calm her and the judgmental livestock. "You can wait here. I'll be back as soon as possible."

Holding onto Dorothy, Jane closes her eyes and inhales. Dorothy's ears move forward again and the horse nods, snorting. Then, Jane folds her arms across her chest and looks at me intently.

"Tell me your plan, Zeon."

Watching Dorothy carefully—the mare is overprotective sometimes—I take a step toward Jane, but don't touch her. She's still mad at me.

"I'll tell you part of it, but not everything. The messengers... they must be listening."

Jane pulls her ponytail forward and brushes it with her fingers. Instinctively, I look around before saying anything further, as if that would prevent them from eavesdropping.

"It's true the Jori could help us in the upcoming battle, but John's right. We can't trust them. Even if they agree to help us, we might be bringing a Trojan horse into our camp."

A flash of confusion crosses her face as she hears me. "We're not here to draft them." I guess what she was about to ask me. "I only need to find Nia. And I can't tell you why."

Jane's eyes move rapidly from side to side as she processes this conflicting information. Her puzzlement is understandable. How would talking to one person —*any* person—help us in any way? And especially Nia, my former fiancée? It's too bad I can't give her more details.

Leaning closer to Dorothy, Jane touches her face on the horse's neck before wrapping her arms around it.

"Okay, Zeon. Let's find Nia."

We spend the next half hour going southeast,

following the wall. The vehicles on the shore keep firing, clearly indicating some kind of resistance. The large trucks can't go through the forest, so they must either do an all-out assault with ground troops—if they have enough people—or just fire missiles at them from afar.

Due to the terrain, this battle could be over soon if the number of protectors helping Khof is large enough. But I doubt it. I expect most Jori are fighting against him, using the guerrilla warfare John predicted.

The trail follows the terrain up a hill and then down again, and we stop at the edge of a small ridge not too different from the one the next sector over. Using my mental map, I find the auras of several dozen protectors in the forest about a kilometer away from the nearby veil. This is it. It's all or nothing.

"Let me go alone," Jane asks before I open a passage. "You look exactly like Khof. And you really miscalculated when you picked this bright red jersey."

I glance at my red outfit. She wouldn't understand. "No. I won't let you go. You'll wait here. This is my plan, after all."

Jane tries to pull rank on me. She argues she's the civilian in charge of John's forces. In response, I tell her I'm not technically *from* the Earth's forces and she doesn't know half of the story.

"I was hoping you'd finally trust me for a change," I say, angry at her.

She sneers. "Trust? Look who's talking. You never tell me anything. I feel like I'm on probation every time I'm around you."

During our argument, someone says the words "bossy" and "overbearing." It might have been me. As a result, a few minutes later, we're *both* on Jora's side of the veil, mad at each other.

"On the plus side," I say, trying to make amends, "they won't catch us by surprise. I can see them in my mental map."

As if to prove me wrong, this is the moment the bombardment starts.

The first clue something's off is when the ground below us trembles like a mini earthquake. Immediately, all the monster bees in the trees fly away, making a noise sounding like dozens of branches scratching their leaves on the ground.

I grab Jane's arm to stop her from moving, but she's already frozen in place. The hits are still far away, but they're pushing the people I noticed earlier toward us. They'll be here in five minutes or so.

"We have to run!" I tell Jane, pulling her back toward the veil. But she doesn't let me go. Instead, she wants us to go in the opposite direction, toward the Jori. She's insane.

"That's the wrong way!" I'm hesitant to run into people that may or may not be friends.

"You don't understand!" she says. "The next missiles are coming here!"

"What are you talking about?" I yell over the explosions. She doesn't have any powers here—how does she know that?

"It's a common artillery tactic. You trap your enemy—"

The next thing I know, an artillery shell explodes next to the barrier, exactly where we would be if Jane had followed me. It's still close enough to throw us to the ground, and I'm knocked unconscious an instant later.

~

A RINGING NOISE in my head is intermittently interrupted by soft slaps across my face.

"<Zeon?>" a familiar male voice calls in Dïnisc.

Whoever he is, he should know not to slap someone who may have a concussion. When I open my eyes, I'm surprised to see a familiar tattooed face and single-piece black uniform. Pain is shooting all throughout my body, restraining my movements.

"<Jal?>"

For a second, I think I'm back on Jora, but my brain is connected to my surroundings. I'm still in the Wheel.

He laughs, helping me sit up. "<You tough bastard!>"

"<Where's Jane?>"

His face doesn't change when I ask him, so I know Jane's alive before he even answers. "<Her forehead is bleeding, but she's okay. Nia's helping her nearby. Khof's army is busy elsewhere, running after our main force to the East.">

That explains why the explosions sound far away now. We're surrounded by trees, and while I hear people around, no one can see us. I'm so happy to see Jal here. It means I don't need to ask Nia anything. All I needed was Jal. A sense of relief washes over me.

"<You're lucky you're wearing this hideous red jersey.>" He's teasing me because he's a Blue Warrior, a fan of my rival soccer team, and I'd think less of him if he didn't mock me about it. "<I was *this* close to shooting you when I saw you unconscious. But Khof would never wear red.">

This is the advantage of knowing your enemy.

Khof's exactly like me—a soccer fanatic—and he wouldn't be caught dead or unconscious wearing the colors of a rival. The only difference is that red and blue are swapped on our planets.

Also, it doesn't even matter that the jersey I'm wearing is, technically, from a different team. I picked it because it has the exact same shade of red as our team, so the Jori would know it was me and not Khof. By this point, everyone has seen him out and about with his flying colors.

"<I always told you blue is evil.>" I smile.

We keep insulting each other's teams as we hug like good friends do. Jal says although the color is right, he could immediately tell it wasn't the right jersey. We have a special radar to identify our rival's logo from a distance.

"<What are you doing here?>" I eventually ask him after our usual bantering.

"<Funny, I have the exact same question for you!>"

After I take some time to tell him as much as I can about what's happening, including the fact the veils are getting weaker, Jal tells me they were tired of waiting and decided to try my prototype helmet anyway. Everyone there wants to fight Khof. More importantly, he knows he didn't die on Jora because others are coming here after him, and they all say the bodies on the planet are fine, including mine. They just weren't sure if they would end up in the right hypersphere, but Hermes didn't redirect the Jori like he did me.

An explosion far away breaks up our conversation.

"<About a hundred protectors from our planet have joined Khof,>" Jal says, addressing the other elephant in the room. "<They took us by surprise,

keeping us at bay as Khof moved his vehicles onto shore. It was a blood bath.>"

"<Let me guess.>" I draw a long breath before asking, "<Bodan's leading them?>"

"<No. Bodan's on our side. Talaia is leading Khof's forces. She's a Ringer. She hates the messengers more than you do because of what they tried to do with the Ring.>" He gives me a sad chuckle. "<And she's a fan of you, you know. You were the only one who stood up to them before Khof.>"

Ringers are radical followers of the Church of the Ring, the asteroid belt that surrounds Jora that used to be the moon.

"<Jal, I need your help.>"

It's funny how things are working out. I spent this whole time looking for Nia because I had an enormous favor to ask that involved killing her. But I don't need her anymore. Her whole mission would be to contact Jal. But he's right here, in front of me.

He grins. "<Ask me anything. I trust you.>"

His face quickly changes from cheerfulness to misery as I tell him exactly what I want. Unfortunately, I can't use certain words out of fear the messengers are listening, but after a lot of back and forth, pantomimic gestures, and non-sexual innuendo, he finally understands what I want him to do. It doesn't make him any happier, though. He'll have to go back to Jora. And there's only one way to send him there.

"<I know you're suffering here under Khof's attack,>" I say. "<But the thing I told you about can only happen when the veils go down.>"

In truth, I'm not sure if it's going to work. I hate to do stuff without testing it first, but it is what it is. And I don't have to bother Jal with my doubts, especially considering the burden he'll have to carry.

"<It's okay.>" His face is somber. "<I have an idea how to end this fight.>" He looks at the smoke plumes behind us.

There's a scolding tone in his voice, and it takes me a while to guess his thought process. He's going back to where all the Jori bodies lie in deep sleep, including the ones rebelling against us.

I rest my hand on his slumped shoulder. "<Please don't kill Talaia or the others. It wouldn't work. And there's a better way.>"

Time's running out, so we go through the plan once more to be sure we're on the same page, including how to deal with Talaia and the defectors. Fortunately, he agrees with me. There's no need to kill when there's a perfectly good alternative.

Luckily, Jal's braver than anyone I've ever met. It's one thing to go through what I asked of him when there's no other option. It's a completely different thing to do it out of faith in your friend. It's when the going gets tough that you learn who you can really trust.

Jal sits next to me, and sweat starts dripping from his forehead. "<I'm ready, Zeon. Let's do this.>"

"<Thank you. You're a great friend.>"

And then, just like that, I shut my eyes and kill him. It happens quickly, which means I'm getting better at this. At this exact moment, Nia and Jane show up. Nia has her arm under Jane's shoulder, and Jane barely manages to stand up.

"<Zeon?>" Nia shouts in Dïnisc, as his body disappears. "<You *asshole!*>"

Chapter 34

CHARISMA

Nia lets go of Jane, who leans against the trunk of a sequoia-sized tree, holding a roll of compressed white rags against her head. Then, Nia grabs her capacitor off the strap at her belly and points it at me. If there's ever a bingo chart for Pangea, "Points a weapon at Zeon" should be at the center.

I raise my hands, still sitting on the ground. "<Wait!>" I reply in Dïnisc. "<It's not what you're thinking!>"

It's been years since I last saw Nia. She's always been beautiful, and this younger version of her is no different, but her youth is a disadvantage for her. She looks too girlish. Or maybe I'm just getting old.

She cautiously moves around me to keep both me and Jane in her field of view. "<What the hell do you mean? You killed Jal!>" Her hand brushes her hair from her face, displaying her sparkling fractal jewelry on her left temple.

The black diamonds reflect the light with multiple colors, somehow perfectly matching her stunning brown hair. The fractal begins above her eye and delineates her face, reaching the top of her cheek. It symbolizes the twilight sun flickering on the rocks of the Ring, a phenomenon called the Ring Flames.

"<I did.>" I keep my hands up, trying to calm her down. "<But he agreed to it.>"

Instead of wearing a skin-tight *cêlçê*, her go-to outfit for anything on Jora, in hyperspheres she prefers a *bämbêchê du prundê*. It's a better garment for combat while still making her look great.

Jane limps toward us, but Nia keeps us both in check with her weapon.

"<What did you do, Zeon?>" Jane asks. Because she's an angel, she also knows how to speak Dïnisc. "<You were looking for Nia, not Jal.>"

Jane stops a few steps away, and both she and Nia wait for my answer. I have to be careful about what to tell them.

"<I *was* looking for Nia, but not anymore.>"

Nia's long hair is beautiful. For several years after we broke up, she tried wearing it short. I always wondered if she cut it short because she knew I preferred it long. But perhaps I'm giving myself too much credit. It's always easier to move on when you start with the basics.

"<What?>" Nia says. "<Did you want to kill me as well?>"

Technically, yes, but perhaps I shouldn't say this until I explain the situation better.

"<Technically, yes,>" I blurt out. I'm still not thinking straight.

Nia tightens her grip on her weapon. "<What?>"

The next words tumble out of me. "<I sent Jal back

to our planet. Alive. It's a *soft* hypersphere killing, as a manner of saying. It hurts the same, though.>"

In truth, I'm not that concerned about the pain. It'll go away. My worry is that Jal's mind may have blended with mine like Jane's did, and maybe he now knows too much about me. At least he won't be able to come back soon to tease me about my tickling fetish, because he'll need to heal from using the helmet injector. This is why I didn't go myself.

As Nia watches us, Jane—still furious about me killing Jal, I guess—walks up to me and extends her hand. She helps me slowly rise to my feet. The next night we spend together, we'll have one of those talks. Relationship talks.

"<And why did you want me to go?>" Nia asks, scratching her temple jewelry with her free hand. The other hand has the capacitor that still points at us.

"<I thought Jal was still on Jora,>" I explain. "<The whole point was for you to go back, find Jal there and give him some instructions to help us in our fight here. Come on, Nia, you know I wouldn't actually kill him.>"

"<Nia? Jal? Are you okay?>" a female voice booms from behind Nia.

Oh well. I guess it's tourist season in the Wheel. Wearing long beige pants and a white shirt stained all over with blood, Kera approaches our group. Like Jal, she must've been sent using my injector. When she sees us, her brow wrinkles, and she stops in her tracks.

"<Zeon?>" Her face takes on an offended look when she notices Jane next to me. "<And *you!*>" Her surgical gloves are blemished with dark red spots.

"<Nice to see you again, *Kera,*>" Jane replies. I don't know how many times these two have met each other, but at least once I had to intervene to stop Kera from killing Jane.

"<Zeon just sent Jal... back,>" Nia says, finally dropping her weapon.

"<You *killed* him?>" Kera blurts, taking her gloves off. They're too dirty, and she has a box of clean ones attached to her waist. I'm always amazed by the health-care professionals who spend their times seeing so much gore and death but still keep their cool and a morbid sense of humor.

"<I sent him on, uh,>" I hesitate, "<a mission.>"

We all look at Kera for a moment, waiting for her real reaction. Either she's going to get mad and try to kill me, or...

"<Of course!>" Kera cries, her hands outstretched for emphasis. "<Send me back too, Zeon. I want to kill those *ticklers!*>"

My eyes dart from Nia to Jane, who both immediately look away. Nia actually blushes. I roll my eyes.

"<No,>" I tell Kera. "<Killing people on our planet while they're here still leaves their bodies alive in the hypersphere.>" This is exactly what happened to Raj. "<You need to stay in the Wheel, helping the injured.>" I wave at her dirty clothes as I take a step toward Nia, but Nia recoils, moving closer to Kera. This is what happens when you kill people, even when they're willing. "<Nia, you should warn whoever's in charge here about what's coming.>"

"<You can tell me now,>" Bodan says from beside us, taking us by surprise. A huge rocket launcher rests on his right shoulder, as if he's in a parade.

His boyish looks, alongside his weatherproof dark green pants, remind me of our years as best friends. Even his silly black muscle shirt, the only socially acceptable excuse for bullying people, looks good on him. It makes me nostalgic.

Nia takes a step back. "<How did you know we were here?>"

The corner of his mouth twists into a devilish grin. "<Nia, you and Jal are special to me. I always keep an eye on you. And it paid off.>" He turns to me before continuing. "<And how are you doing, old friend?>"

"<You tried to kill me!>" I shout, waving my hand at him. I'll never forget his betrayal.

He gestures around. "<So did everyone else here. And yet, you're singling me out.>"

Instinctively, I look around, doing the math in my head just to prove him wrong. He's right, this is just like one of those tacky shows where everyone sleeps with each other, only instead of sex, it's attempted murder. My gaze stops on Nia, who quickly looks down, not saying anything. True, she's never tried to kill me, but she cheated on me with Bodan.

Damn. This is *exactly* like those sleazy shows. We just have to figure out who slept with Kera. Maybe it was Nia too. Who am I kidding? It must've been Bodan.

While I wallow in self-pity, Nia changes the subject. "<Bodan, shouldn't you be leading the retreat?>"

He gestures at the trees. "<The main tanks can't get in here. But they're sending the smaller ones with accompanying infantry to the town. We're moving to the flanks and hiding, so we can take them down later. That's why I'm here.>"

Up above, the clouds of smoke caused by the artillery are actually helping the Jori, hiding their movements. Khof's forces didn't think this through.

"<Anyway, I don't care if we're not friends anymore, Zeon.>" Bodan walks around us, kicking dust off the forest trail. "<But we're at war and I don't have time for this. You said you wanted to warn me.>"

Rubbing my forearm to sweep away dust he "accidentally" sent in my direction, I take a last look at Jane before opening my mouth.

At that moment, a tall, overweight man interrupts me.

"<Bodan!>" he shouts, barely able to breathe. "<They—the enemy—they abandoned the truck!>" But when the newcomer sees me, he jerks his head, moving his curly hair away from his eyes.

"<Khof!>" he exclaims with horror, but his expression quickly changes to confusion as he looks me up and down. "<And he's wearing... red?>"

"<Get your shit together, Animon,>" Bodan says, walking toward Animon and resting his hand on his chest to calm him down. Despite his insult, his body language must be putting Animon at ease. "<He's Zeon, not Khof. What's going on?>"

Animon takes a last look at me, frowning, and faces Bodan again.

"<Arlo was driving the truck, and Peeri was manning the gun, firing at us. But they disappeared into thin air! The ones following the truck are now retreating. I think they're afraid of getting into the truck and disappearing as well.>"

Bodan shoots me a glance and smiles. "<Animon, tell everyone to take control of the vehicles.>"

"<But... what if we vanish?>"

"<Trust me, you *mother-tickler*! Check if the tanks and the mobile artillery have stopped and attack them too. I'll be there soon!>"

"<Yes, sir!>" Animon runs away after nodding at

our odd group. Once he disappears into the forest, everyone looks at me.

"<What did you do?>" Bodan asks with a broad smile.

I smile back for a change. "<Jal's sending people back from here to our planet. The ones fighting for Khof.>"

Then I explain what I did. Jal's using my helmet injector to cut their connection with Pangea, basically doing the opposite of what he and Kera did to come here.

The injector works to send people here and back. This will technically kill them here, and they'll react just like I did when they wake up there. But they're still alive. What happens when they get there is Jal's problem now.

"<I didn't know we could do that,>" Kera says with a cryptic smile.

I'd taught Jal the procedure just before I left, in case they needed to bring someone back from Pangea. No one else knows about the extra capabilities of the neural injector. Nia was supposed to go back to tell him this, among other things, but Jal's presence here made everything easier.

"<I see,>" Bodan says. "<Good work, Zeon!>" He talks like a leader giving praise to a naïve subordinate just for following orders. "<And what will *we* do after that?>"

Clenching my hands at my side, I fake a smile. There's no "we" here.

"<Well, Jane and I are going back to fight the main battle against Khof and the necromantes.>"

Bodan moves the rocket launcher to his other

shoulder. The thing must weigh a ton, and he carries it like it's just a fishing pole.

"<You mean when the veils disappear.>" He somehow knows what's going to happen. "<Let us help. If you wait a day, we can probably go with you.>"

I wonder who keeps him in the loop. He didn't bat an eyelid at seeing me here, and he seems to know we can go through the barriers. Or, at the least, he wasn't surprised to see Jane with me here.

"<There's no time to wait, Bodan,>" I reply. "<And you have your own battle to fight here.>"

Chapter 35

PREPARATIONS

Jane and I don't wait for Bodan's counterattack; we leave before the rest of Talaia's group disappears. Nia and Kera stay behind to help with their defenses. I feel a bit guilty I can't stay there to help the injured, and I hope Nia doesn't get hurt. However, we have bigger fish to fry.

It's mid-afternoon, there are twenty-something kilometers to go, and John must be pissed at us. How fast do horses travel? I don't know.

"Mother-tickler?" Jane asks in English, smiling.

Dark and gloomy gray skies accompany us as we ride through Terra's sector. The last time I crossed the barrier between Jora's and Terra's sectors, I had to break the veil to go through it, and my sudden apparition on this side resulted in Jean's death.

"It's a common swear term on Jora." I cringe, trying not to think about it. The expression sounds weird in English. It's one of those that don't translate well.

"So, I take it Nia knows about it, huh?"

A single bolt of lightning illuminates the sky, and

we both wait, counting the seconds. But we never hear the thunder. It's too far away.

"Can we please stop talking about it?"

"On one condition."

As Dorothy goes over a rough patch on the road, Jane holds onto the saddle horn, and I can't help but appreciate her hips moving up and down. She's riding to my left and a bit ahead of me. Her denim pants and brown boots make her legs stand out, but this is not what attracts me.

Jane guessed right earlier. Butts are one of my fetishes. I wonder if it's inappropriate to stare at her, considering we're in a relationship—at least I think we are, but at this point, I'm too afraid to ask. On Jora, it'd be fine. In fact, I'd be in trouble if I didn't do it.

I almost fall from Whiskerey, barely having time to grab my own horn. I got distracted by Jane and didn't realize Whiskerey was going through the same unsteady terrain.

Focus, Zeon.

"Try me," I say.

Jane looks back and catches me staring at her behind. I hold my breath for what feels like minutes until a smile shows on her face. Only then do I exhale. Phew.

"Tell me what Jal's real mission is," she finally says.

"I already told you."

Jane cocks her head. I'm a bad liar.

"Khof's people weren't supposed to be there," she says. "You were as surprised as I was."

If I say anything, I'll probably let the cat out of the bag and spoil everything. The fact is, the cat's not ready to be let out yet, so I remain silent. A moment later,

Jane maneuvers Dorothy around and stops in front of Whiskerey, glaring at me.

"Whatever you planned for Nia to ask Jal, removing people like Talaia from the Wheel couldn't be it. How are we going to fight Khof? God, how are we going to fight the *necromantes*?"

The sudden stop highlights how sore my buttocks are, and I wince. Whoever romanticizes horse riding should be put in front of a firing squad.

"You're right. Stopping the mini-revolution going on in Jora's sector is a bonus, but it's not part of my original plan."

We both look at the clouds growing larger on the horizon. A beautiful country landscape is now the stage of a war. I guess even in Heaven, humans can't have nice things. None of us are soldiers back on our Earths, but in a war of annihilation, there are no civilians.

"I have to be honest with you," Jane begins. "I went through a dark time after we went back to our planets. It was so bad that John and Louise somehow managed to get me committed for a few nights. Worse, they took my guns while I was at the hospital." She scoffs. "All of them. I didn't even know they could legally do that in the United States."

She chuckles and her eyes fill with tears. Her contradictory feelings are understandable. Guns are one of her favorite hobbies—she loves the Second Amendment—but her friends love her too. Since her horse is so close to mine, I extend my arm and she lets me take her hand.

Sniffing, she looks away. "Coming back to Pangea to fight for something made me feel alive again, but the shock of seeing you killing people was too much for me."

I frown and shake my head, and she holds her hand up. "It was Khof—I know that now, but didn't at the time. The problem is that I had this idea that at least *someone* in this universe was not willing to kill people... and then seeing you—or what I thought was you—doing the opposite destroyed me."

I smile at her. "It wasn't me. I'm awesome."

She looks away and frowns. "Of course, you're far from perfect. You're selfish, inappropriate, goofy, and always ready to embarrass me. And now there's the tickle thing..." She laughs.

"I love you too. Geez!"

Our eyes meet again, and we both grin.

"It's not like that," she says. "My point is I trust you. I trust your plan, whatever it is. And I understand you can't tell me because others can hear us. I get it. But will it interfere with our fight here?"

Far away, a swirl of darker clouds surrounds the island, making the landscape look eerie. There's a constant uncomfortable breeze following the cloud pattern, giving me the sensation a storm is coming. Even the horses are quieter than normal.

I let her hand go. "If it works, it'll help. If it doesn't, nothing changes. And it's a long shot, anyway. Don't expect a Hail Mary."

In reality, I'm not expecting just one Hail Mary. I'm hoping for two.

～

JOHN'S A BORN KILLER, an army major, and there's more muscle mass on one of his arms than on my whole body. And do you know what's worse than him yelling at you like a drill sergeant? It's when there are two of them, taking turns. Even Jane's in trouble this time.

It's late at night, and we're back at John's apartment in Earth's sector. Unlike the previous time we were here, today it's so crowded that there's a fifty-percent chance of finding two people who share a birthday.

John's top lieutenants and several of Raj's people watch Jane and me getting dressed down by the rage twins. I'm pretty sure the Johns are waiting for an excuse to kick my ass.

"While these fopdoodles were out there shitting rainbows," John rants, "the rest of us, in charge of protecting, let me check—" He stops and fake counts on his fingers. "I don't know, *all* of humanity, were waiting here, ready to be slaughtered."

Despite Jane's smaller size, she's not to be underestimated. If I were to stop and compare girlfriends, something our significant others *always* encourage us to do, I would say Nia is the girlish type, and Jane's more like a scorpion.

So, while I cower behind her saying, "Sorry, sirs," and "It's not going to happen again, sirs," she stands her ground. Her face is red hot, both of her fists are clenched, ready to strike, and I think she even makes Jonathan flinch a bit when she talks.

"I'm sorry, MOM!" she shouts back. "But we're here, and there's plenty of time. We had a mission to do, and it's done, and now we're back. I suggest we put this matter to rest, Majors." She then mouths the word "assholes" silently for everyone to see.

Jonathan makes a vulgar gesture with his hands. "And what was Harold and Susan's mission about?" Paulo and I have to grab Jane by her waist to stop her from hitting him. It's uncanny how similar John and Jonathan are.

"Harold and Susan?" Louise asks, watching us from across the room, mostly uninterested in the actual discussion. Raj stands between her and Marie, all three of them leaning against the wall.

"Yes," Raj replies. "From *When Harold Met Susan*? The movie?" He holds his elbow with his right hand and draws a small circle in the air with his finger. You know what? I hate his version of Earth. I hope I never learn what they call my favorite science fiction shows from Earth there. I bet they're "Star Journey" and "Star Battles."

"*Hvatit!* Stop it!" Vladimir says. He's the only one actually sitting at the table, waiting for us to go back to planning. "Forget it. They're here. *Blyat!*"

After a long pause where Jane and the Johns avoid looking at each other, people in the room start to calm down. Jane shoots me a "you'll pay dearly for this sometime later" look, takes a deep breath, and addresses the crowd. I suppress a smile. She looks great when she's angry.

"Zeon had to talk to his people," Jane says, "so they'll be ready when the time comes."

John sighs. "Okay. We need to get ready to leave in the next few hours. We have to be in Orbis' sector just before sunrise, so we must leave at midnight to get there in time."

Crossing her arms, Jane stares at everyone in the room. "Let's do this," she says.

An hour later, I'm back in my apartment getting ready for the raid. The red jersey did its job, but it won't work for our next brawl. The new color must match *Khof's* team exactly, just like the red one did for me earlier today.

One would think it would be easy to find, considering how many jerseys are here, but it baffles me how many clubs' jerseys have the pajama-like stripes instead of a beautiful solid color. There's even one that's red *and* blue with the word "Messi" on its back. Messy indeed. What were the designers thinking?

"Why don't you pick a jersey that won't stand out?" Raj asks, watching me go through the large selection. He has no idea how much people are obsessed with soccer on Jora.

I give him a side look. "What are you doing here again?" Raj and Marie were assigned their own apartment, and they should also be getting ready for the upcoming battle.

He sneers. "The girls told me to watch you. You're a troublemaker!"

It's funny he calls them girls. Marie and Louise are in their thirties, and Jane's almost there.

"What are they afraid of? That I'll abandon you guys and go off on a dumb errand that'll make everything worse?"

A look of concern crosses his face for a second. "You can read minds now?"

"I wish." I grab a jersey that may work for my plan and show it to him. "What do you think of this one? It even has the Sword constellation on it. I dare say it's not that ugly."

He looks at it intently.

"You mean the Southern Cross." He observes it for a moment. "You know this one's blue, right? Based on what I've heard, it's not going to be easy for you to wear it."

"You have no idea." Of all the things the messengers and the gods have made me do, this is the worst one of them all. Someone will pay for this one day.

Raj takes a few steps back and avoids looking at me for a moment. It's probably not because of my bare chest as I switch shirts—far from it. It must be because of the humiliation of what I'm about to do. Taking three long breaths, I put the damn thing on and try not to look at myself in the closet mirror.

"But tell me, Raj." I change the subject as quickly as I can. "What's the real reason you're here?"

Raj folds his arms as he watches my new outfit. Then, he raises his head and stares at me.

"It's about Marie. I asked her not to go, but she'll hear none of it."

If Marie is anything like Louise, she's a fighter. I don't blame her. Even if she survives and we beat Khof and the others, if someone ends the Wheel by finding the flashing disk we all know must be here somewhere, she'll die. Worse, unlike all the battles we had in Pangea before, only the winning team will go back to their planets.

And if either Yora's or Terra's people get to it—the people who are dead—then no one will survive at all. I'm guessing this is the only reason Khof hasn't captured the flag, as a manner of speaking.

"And I know you have these... special powers here," Raj goes on. "Please don't let her get hurt."

"Raj." I look him directly in the eyes and touch his shoulder. "You have my word."

In truth, there isn't much I can do if things go wrong, and I bet he knows that. But I'll do whatever I can.

Chapter 36

DECEPTION

LOCATION: WHEEL – YORA'S SECTOR

The sight of thirteen-hundred people riding horses is mind-boggling. What we see in movies doesn't do justice to reality. Instead of a homogenous mass of riders, the distribution is much more organic, making the pack look more like a wool knitting pattern with large holes in the middle. As a result, it takes two hours to shepherd everyone across the force field and into Earth eight's sector—Yora's.

This is Khof's original sector, and we must be extra careful. But the landscape is eerily empty. If there was anyone here, they're long gone. There's plenty of wildlife, but no humans left. Khof's people moved to Fortress just before the barriers went up and, with all the transports and tanks they have, they don't need the local horses.

Boulders the size of houses lie next to the energy walls, both inland and near the shore. According to John, Khof tried to break into the veil from this side to flank John's forces, but it didn't work. The veils dividing the sectors are stronger than the hub's wall around the island. This was probably by design.

Around four o'clock in the morning, we stop at the final veil of our journey, the border of Yora and their new allies from Orbis. As we always do in this situation, we stay near the forest line, roughly five kilometers back from the shore.

The wind has picked up, and a warm rain is starting to fall. Raj mentioned it rains once a month here, but according to him, there's never been a storm this big.

Unlike Bodan's sector, which split its forces into groups for and against Khof, it's clear Earth one is united. My mind map tells me there are six stationary tanks and artillery trucks parked along the shoreline. They either joined Khof willingly or were conquered by him.

It doesn't seem like that many vehicles, though. If we count all the vehicles in Bodan's sector plus the ones here, Khof has deployed less than ten percent of his fleet off the island. He probably doesn't trust anyone yet.

Before we cross into enemy territory, I call John and Jonathan to discuss the terrain, and Jane, Louise, and Raj also join us. They can't see much past the wall, especially at night and in the rain, so they rely on my inner sense to learn what our enemy is doing.

It turns out the habitants from Orbis are still "alive." Like Jane's and my people, I can sense their auras. But something is horribly wrong.

"About ten or fifteen people are guarding the vehicles on the shore," I tell them. "The rest are in the town, and most of them are asleep. But there's one problem." I swallow hard. "There can't be more than three hundred souls there."

John locks eyes with Jonathan before replying. "So, either they never had a large force here..." John starts.

"Or they killed the ones who disagreed." Jonathan finishes John's sentence.

To no one's surprise, John and Jonathan have a plan for this exact situation. We're going to split the group into two forces. The larger one will attack the town, and a small suicidal team will take on the armored vehicles. Guess who was unwillingly drafted into the suicide squad? This guy.

John's in charge of the main group that'll go to the town, while Jonathan will lead the attack on the vehicles on the shore. Jonathan's force is mostly made of his own people because they have no auras. It gives us a better chance of sneaking past if they happen to have someone like me.

"Wait," I say. "What about the necromantes?"

"It depends," Johnathan replies. "If it's only a few of them, we'll fight. Otherwise, everyone should run for the forests in the back."

Honestly, I think if they show up, and my plan doesn't work, we'll be dead. Johnathan didn't see what Jane and I saw. But no need to say anything—he probably knows.

With nothing else to discuss, we start our two-pronged attack led by the Johns.

First, I open several passages through the veil, and our most dangerous border crossing begins. If we're seen at any point now, the armored trucks will quickly destroy us, even from afar.

Jonathan and his team walk through the force field

first. He's leading thirty people from Terra, as well as me. Unfortunately, we can't take our horses to attack the armored vehicles at the shore. It'd increase the chances of someone noticing us. Raj is part of our special force, and he's happy I asked Marie to go with Jane and the cavalry.

Next, John starts his own operation of getting at least three hundred riders on this side. The plan is to move them to the town as soon as possible. Anyone crossing the veil after that will follow them.

But the special-ops team doesn't have time to wait. It'll take an hour for us to get near the vehicles on foot, and the earlier we start, the better.

Just before I leave, Jane approaches me with Dorothy faithfully following her. Droplets of rain mark her t-shirt, and water rolls down her smooth face. When she gets close enough that our lips almost touch, we kiss.

Despite the situation we're in, the battle we're about to fight, she looks happy.

Looking at me, she says, "Don't screw this up!"

Then, she laughs and hops back on Dorothy so fast that she puts my riding skills to shame. Despite everything, she's always the optimist.

"Do I ever?" I say as she rides into the night, her wet ponytail jumping against her back.

"We need to hurry," Jonathan whispers. "It'll be dawn in an hour or so."

He strides toward the river, and we follow him. Lightning flashes, and for a quick second, it exposes our group. The thunder that comes after makes me nervous, and just like that, the little courage I have disappears. In the past, I could do a lot of things in Pangea that would help me survive, but I don't have most of those powers anymore. The messengers have turned them off. So there's a chance I'll not live through this.

The thing is, I don't have Jonathan's muscles, military training, or anything, really. My only card is that I look like our enemy's leader. The whole idea seemed so perfect when we were in John's climate-controlled apartment. But now I'm second-guessing myself.

Forty-five minutes later, it's pouring rain, and we stop about half a kilometer away from the vehicles. They're parked near the land bridge that goes over the river and reaches the island—a dry passage that wasn't there a week ago. It's made of sedimentary layers—the same type of rock that makes up Fortress.

Meanwhile, John must be ready to start the attack on the town. If we don't time it correctly, we may end up trapped between the apartments and the tanks.

"Spread out!" Jonathan says in a low voice. Rainwater drips from his serene face. "Except you, Zeon."

My body trembles slightly, and not because I'm all wet.

The sheets of rain almost hide the six vehicles parked near the shore. They're neatly arranged at an angle, facing away from the river.

The middle four are your run-of-the-mill three-person trucks. They have a large energy turret on top with a barrel as thick as a person, and they carry a huge vertical ellipsoid in the back to power it. I know them well from our previous excursions in Pangea.

The other two are just armored personnel carriers, each with their own gun turret, and although those turrets are bigger than anything we're carrying, they're barely larger than Bodan's rocket launcher. The purpose of these vehicles is, after all, to carry people.

Most of the enemy troops are inside the carriers,

but four are outside on guard duty in the rain, probably feeling miserable in this weather.

Despite the humidity, my mouth feels dry as I draw closer and my arms shake even more, and I try to keep them close to my body to hide my emotions. I was told Khof rarely has a gun on him since he can move mountains—literally—so I don't have one either.

Clearly, the people outside weren't planning for this storm. Not one of them has a raincoat. It's too dark for me to make out details, but an Asian woman keeps swiping her hand across her face, wearing a completely soaked pair of black pants and a dark blouse.

A red-haired man next to her keeps brushing his long hair back as if trying to get the moisture out. They both carry large double-ellipsoid capacitors, a good choice for keeping a mob at bay, but bad for close-quarters combat.

When I'm so close I could throw a rock at them, I realize a problem with our plan. Who knows if they speak English or Dïnisc on Orbis? Maybe it's a completely new language. Shit. If I don't announce myself soon, they may shoot first and ask questions later. To make matters worse, I don't recognize any one of them, so I can't even guess.

"Khof!" I shout, startling the guards. Names are the only words that work in all languages. In visible shock, the man steps back, slips in the mud, and falls.

The woman is steadier on her feet, managing to point her weapon at me. "Khof?" She frowns, not helping me at all in the language department. Well, confidence is everything, so I take another step toward her.

I nod. "Khof." I glare at her as if saying your own name over and over is normal.

The man pulls himself up and watches me, confused, while the woman lowers her weapon slightly.

"<What are you doing here?>" he finally asks in Dïnisc, and I mentally breathe a sigh of relief. Not only do I know what language to speak, Khof's not here. It would be really hard to explain if he were. Soap opera hard.

"<Call everybody here,>" I tell him. "<I want to explain our new plan.>"

She drops her weapon. "<What do you mean? You told us to just wait here through the night.>"

"<I did. But we have a small problem. Quickly! We don't have much time!>"

The man starts to run and slips again, but manages to use the truck to steady himself. The Asian woman rolls her eyes at him.

"<Everybody! Khof's here!>" He runs behind the closest armored carrier.

I take this time to turn around and walk several steps southwest, toward the town, as if I'm looking in that direction. The farther away they are from the vehicles, the better, so Jonathan's people can get to them first.

Then, I turn back to face the small crowd gathering as they pour out of the protection of the carriers.

"<Damn this rain,>" a male voice complains. It seems my plan is working. They seem more concerned about the weather than my sudden appearance.

As they gather around in a semi-circle, I watch their faces to see if I recognize anyone, but no luck. It's true I'm bad at remembering faces or names, but I was expecting to see at least one familiar face. And if Khof's not stupid, he'd leave a trusty friend from his troops in charge.

Then, someone comes from behind the group wearing a cheap black raincoat. His face is hidden by the hood. Unlike the others, he walks toward me with his head up, moving people out of the way. It doesn't take long for me to recognize Jal's face and his fascinating tattoo.

Except that, for the same reason I'm not Khof, he's not Jal. He just looks like him.

"<Khof? Did something happen?>" He looks me up and down, but his eyes quickly settle on my chest. No, not on my muscles. His eyebrows furrow as he studies the patch on my blue jersey. Yes, the color's right, but the team's logo is completely different. Someone who doesn't follow soccer wouldn't notice, but a fanatic like Jal must know the difference.

I point at my face. "<My eyes are up here.>"

With narrowed eyes and mouth twisted in anger, he draws his weapon.

Chapter 37

SACRIFICES

He's close, so I take a step forward and pull his weapon down before he can point it at me, pushing the barrel against his stomach. I do it quickly, taking advantage of my fast mode. At least I have that here.

"<It's over,>" I tell him.

Jal's doppelgänger can easily push me and regain control of his weapon. After all, it's still hanging around his neck on a strap. And yet, he doesn't do anything.

"<Drop your weapons!>" I shout, looking at the others. "<You're surrounded by hundreds of us,>" I lie.

Shadows move around the vehicles, taking up firing position. A commotion starts, and a few of the enemies raise their weapons, searching for a target, but most look either confused or scared. There's nothing they can do now. Jonathan's people, at this point, must have all of their weapons sighted on them.

"<Sal?>" the Asian woman asks the one who looks like Jal, her voice cracking.

Jonathan steps beside me with his own weapon hanging down, extending his arms to Sal as if asking for something. They don't speak the same language, but the intent is obvious. These two have been battling for so long, and it's finally over.

And no, Jonathan doesn't appear to be gloating. His whole gesture seems to give Sal some dignity, like when a Samurai soldier is asked to give his sword away.

"<You're fighting for the wrong side, Zeon,"> Sal tells me, ignoring Jonathan's gesture. His voice is so calm it creeps me out. "<Khof hacked the nuclear missiles on Terra, yes. But he wasn't the one who pulled the trigger.>" He moves his head in a circle, looking down. "<He didn't kill Raj's body on Terra, despite what the others are saying. Someone else shot Raj. Khof was there, trying to save him, but he was too late.>" Then, he stares into my eyes with a look of sorrow, or maybe pity. "<You could've been him.>"

Is he right? Maybe the reason I didn't become him was because Mike and I managed to meet early. Or perhaps it was the luck of the draw, and one of us had to be the bad guy.

Sal gazes at Jonathan, thinking, but there's nothing to consider. He lost. My guess is their job was to protect the vehicles from falling into the wrong hands, and they failed. Dying will accomplish nothing.

Finally, he turns to face the woman next to him, for once showing some emotion, his eyes filling with tears. He grabs her shaky hand firmly, as though they're a couple ready to walk out on us, but he doesn't look her straight into her eyes.

Instead, he clasps her wrist. "<I'm sorry.>" There, he finds a bracelet I hadn't noticed before, which has a single discreet button on top. Then, like a magician, he takes advantage of the misdirection and drops an oval object from his other hand.

A normal person wouldn't have noticed it, but I do, and I re-enter my fast mode. There are two immediate threats, and I must identify which one is the most dangerous. The falling object's an ellipsoid grenade, and if it goes off, everyone around us will be killed. Whatever the button does is unknown.

When the grenade is knee-high, I crouch and grab it mid-fall with my right hand, concentrating. Unfortunately, my move leaves me vulnerable to Sal. His eyes go wide when he sees what I'm doing, and his right leg begins a movement that can only be described as a punter ready to kick a field goal—except my head is the ball.

It's too late to stop the button on the woman's band—Sal's pressed it already. And no matter how fast I am, I don't have time to avoid Sal's strike and deactivate the explosive device at the same time. As such, Sal's foot connects with my head at the exact moment I disable the grenade. Weapons discharge around me and I fall backward.

As I hit the ground, mud splashes outward, and my clothes are instantly soaked. The unpleasant smell of burnt flesh fills my nose, and super-hot water lashes my skin.

Most of Sal's soldiers are quickly shredded by the capacitors discharging around us, but before I can do anything else, someone throws a second grenade. Jonathan jumps on top of me. After a bright flash, a crackling sound is the last thing I hear.

The absence of sound confuses me for a second, but I quickly realize Jonathan's body on top of me is not moving. In a panic, I shove him off and try to sit up. Doing that in complete silence is surreal.

When I'm finally able to kneel before him, the person that's me but doesn't feel like me punches his chest over and over. I can't even hear myself yelling his name.

It's too late. Jonathan vanishes.

~

OUR ARMY IS REUNITED under a sea of tents. The gray one I'm in wobbles in the wind, but does its job, protecting the people inside it from the rain.

I didn't even know we were carrying tents, but we must have, since I'm inside one, lying on a warm, soft pad. The tent is large enough to hold eight patients on makeshift cots. That's what happens when you're not part of the team organizing stuff. You're kept out of the loop.

Even though it's been about four hours since our encounter with Sal, my body's still numb. Trying to help Jonathan as he was dying was a mistake, and I could easily have been killed. Fortunately, the showdown with Sal's people ended quickly, albeit with casualties.

I was really lucky. My left eye is heavily bruised, my head is dizzy, and there are superficial wounds all over my body, but I'm alive—and so are Alfredo and Raj, who share this side of the hofset. Four others lie on cots near the tent's entrance, but I can't see who they are from here. For the moment, I don't even care. Louise forced me to come inside to treat my injuries after I spent more than an hour trying to save people.

After laying me down on one of the cots, she

reaches for some bandages and kneels beside me, touching my forehead and my left eye with the soft fabric. Her lips move, but I still can't hear anything. Then, she touches my face and closes her eyes. I didn't know she could heal like I do, but I shouldn't be surprised.

Jane enters the tent at the exact moment a loud ring shrieks in my left ear, and when the unbearable noise reaches the right one, I scream in pain. The grenade shockwave must've ruptured my eardrums. It didn't even register with me.

The ring soon dwindles, and the noise of the heavy rain battering against the side of the tent becomes louder by the minute, as does the thunder.

Jane sits beside me, watching Louise with a wrinkled nose. When her eyes meet Louise's, the tiny blonde quickly jerks her hand away from my face. Jane then glances at me with the same inquiring look.

"Jonathan's dead," Louise says, as if I didn't know it.

A whirl of emotion hits me as I remember what happened. If I had been faster, perhaps I could've stopped them. But I wasn't, and people died. At least Raj survived. Adrenaline makes me sit up, and now it's Jane that touches my face, worried.

"How much time do you think we have?" I ask, my heart beating fast. I feel a bit nauseous.

"I've been measuring the brightness of the veils," Jane says. "If it matches their power, we must have less than half an hour until the veils disappear." She shakes her head. "By the way, taking the town was easy. You guys had the most casualties. And we even arrested Ivan there. It seems someone helped him cross the veils."

Then I remember something. Having my hearing back must have helped to clear my mind.

"We have to find John!" I say, touching Jane's hand with my own. "They can't move the tanks and the carriers!" If Khof's watching and sees them moving, he may figure out something's wrong.

Louise looks down. "The vehicles are useless. The brains controlling them are just black goo now."

That must be what Sal was doing when he pressed that button. He didn't want the vehicles to end up in the wrong hands. He achieved his objective, but at a high cost. Many people from his party were killed in the fight.

"Zeon, we're getting ready for the battle," Jane says. "But you can stay here." Her eyes close for a moment as she fidgets. "You were right, by the way. People from Orbis told us that Khof killed most of their people." Then, she looks me up and down as if sizing me up. "But you're not fit for combat."

"No." I ignore the lingering pain in the left of my head. My mental map is not working well anymore. The pain makes it harder for me to concentrate. But I'll not sit back and watch as my friends die. "I won't back down, Jane. Not now."

Thankfully, Jane doesn't press the issue. She probably said that just to give me an out. This is a do-or-die kind of a situation. The more of us helping, the better chance we have. So, I get off the bed and go outside.

John's in a nearby tent getting his gear ready. The tents are a mistake. Dozens of them are spread across the terrain. Khof must've spotted them already.

"John!" I shout when I finally get to his quarters. Only Jane follows me. Water drips from our clothes, and I carry a lot of mud inside. "The tents! They must know we're here!"

He looks at me with indifference, as if figuring out who I am again.

"They're camouflaged and behind the hill," Jane answers instead, giving me a double-barrel capacitor. "And Khof's forces are not doing anything unusual. We're okay."

With the exception of the major, each one of them grabs a single weapon. Jane argues that carrying more will just make us slower, and for our strategy to work, we need speed, a huge element of surprise, and boat-loads of luck.

When we step outside again, the water leaking into my injured eye makes me wince. Gusts of wind push us back.

"Is it wise to fight in this weather?" I shout at Jane, who helps me on to Whiskerey. The noise of the storm is too loud, and it's not like I have perfect hearing now.

She guides Dorothy forward. "We don't have a choice!" she shouts back.

Our force slowly positions itself near and around the unnatural pathway now connecting this land with the island. The occasional flash of lightning illumi-nates the battleground, and the hairs of my neck try to stiffen with the static electricity in the air, but they're too damp for that.

As usual, we can't see anything except buildings and vehicles through the wall, and Khof's armored units at the bottom of Fortress haven't moved since yesterday. This is good news. They must not know we took over Orbis' sector. They can't see a thousand protectors on horses, ready to fight.

Whiskerey slowly positions himself and me to the

right of Jane, who's about two meters away from the land bridge, facing the island with gloom in her eyes. Interesting. She was so positive earlier, but the upcoming battle must be getting to her. She keeps brushing her forehead to take the excess water away, and her ponytail's heavy with water, sticking to her back like it's glued there.

Louise and Pierre stand to Jane's left, while Raj and Marie ride next to me. John, Vladimir, and the other soldiers finally maneuver their horses ahead of us, answering my unasked question of who'll be the suicidal heroes. Whoever's leading the attack is probably not going to survive.

John's horse, larger than Dorothy, marches with confidence ahead of us. John flashes both hands open with his fingers spread out. Ten minutes. We do the same signal for the ones around and behind us.

On second thought, why aren't *we* behind us? We're too close to the front. Here I am again, afraid of battle.

A few minutes later, Jane slides across her saddle to touch my arm, gathering my attention. Her slender body has to stretch all the way over here, and if I had to move in the same way she does now, I'd be on the ground already.

Once I'm looking at her, she gestures toward the southern part of the island, and our plan shatters in front of our eyes. To our horror, a large number of Khof's units begin to drive in our direction. The downpour makes it hard to see it well, but the movement is evident.

Time to close my eyes to get a better sense of the battlefield, especially since I'm feeling a bit better. About five hover tanks and ten armored personnel carriers approach the river on the east side of the passage, and a similar configuration of vehicles is coming from the south, totaling twenty carriers and ten tanks.

Six artillery trucks powered by enormous vertical capacitors maneuver to block the passage, and several missile launchers position themselves on top of Fortress.

Most shocking are the troop carriers. Khof cannot possibly have that many people manning those vehicles. They come from behind the mesa, and once they are out in the open, the auras of the people inside shine like eighteen-wheeler high beams.

The people captured from Orbis were lying. The rest of them are coming at us. If the personnel carriers are at capacity, more than four hundred of them in heavy armored units are coming to fight our horseback army. If I didn't have a concussion, I'd have been able to detect them before the battle started even when they're that far. It's too late now.

"Everyone! Retreat!" John yells, galloping sideways. They must've figured this out just by the sheer number of vehicles coming. Khof doesn't have that many people to ride them. They have help.

I still don't understand why Khof started his plan this early, since the veils are still up. As if answering my question, a single missile is launched from the top of the mesa toward us while his vehicles continue to move toward the still-functioning veil.

Everyone freezes in place, watching the projectile. What they're doing makes no sense; no one's weakening the energy walls, and there are still a few minutes to go. Why would they attack us now?

Against all our expectations, the missile comes through the veil as if it's not even there, hitting the middle of the river and making its own rumbling sound. It looks like they were just testing it. As soon as this happens, the trucks, carriers, and tanks also cross the island's veil unabashed and begin the crossing, floating above the river. They're accompanied by dozens of new missiles launched from Fortress. This time, they're aimed at us.

They didn't have to wait after all. The veil is already weak enough.

Chapter 38

HAIL MARY

Khof himself crosses the island's veil soon afterward. He's flying fast, and only Vladimir and John have the state of mind to fire at him, though they miss. Before we know it, Khof is behind our lines, causing havoc. Our troops are trapped between him and his main force. The first wave of missiles strikes the ground, hitting our troops in a few places.

What comes next should be expected, but still catches me by surprise. Lightning strikes the main veil around the island, making all the energy walls flash white, blinding us with their brightness. It takes a few seconds for me to be able to see again, and when I do, the veils are gone.

The landscape is free of its cages, and the Wheel a free-for-all once again.

And then, our worst fears are realized. An extremely loud popping noise is followed by a swoosh of wind that almost throws us off our horses. I can feel the electricity in the air. The battlefield becomes inexplicably quiet, and everyone from both armies freezes in place, watching the impossible unfold.

In front of us, above the bridge, a skyscraper-sized diamond-shaped tear opens like a portal to another reality. An alien sky shines visibly through the opening, creating a glaring contrast between their azure sky and our stormy weather. There, only a single fluffy cloud is visible.

Louise pulls up next to me, riding Pierre. "That cloud—it's moving!"

I gulp and pull the reins tight to keep Whiskerey in place. "It's not a cloud."

"Necromantes!" Janes mumbles.

No new missiles are launched. With the exception of some nickering and snorting from the horses, the wind is the only sound. I glance at the people on both sides. Khof's forces have stopped, and on our side, no one is following John's original orders to retreat. This would be the time to run, but instead, we just stay in the same place like deer caught in the headlights.

I squeeze my eyes, trying to better see the other side of the colossal hole in the sky. Maybe I need glasses. There are a few mountains in the distance through the tear, but they're too hazy unless I really focus on them. Parts of the cloud sometimes become clear moving dots, but most of the time, they're just faint little blurs.

Near the bottom of the lacerated reality, a single necromantis appears. He pushes the fabric of the hypersphere to the side with his outstretched hand. Most gasp at his appearance, but not Jane or I. We know him.

"Is time." Haides projects his thought to—based on the shocked expressions around me—everyone.

"Underworld army. Reinstated." His vocabulary pales in comparison to the actual message he sends telepathically to us. They're going to kill us, unless we obey him.

Haides opens his forelimbs wide and floats up, watching us from right above the border between our worlds. The dark skin forming his wings appears below his arms. If my assumptions are correct, their world has two-thirds of Earth's gravity, just like this hypersphere, so he should be able to fly here. But in Pangea, he doesn't need his wings.

A lightning strike illuminates the battlefield again, and Haides' torso reflects and amplifies the light as though a sun is flashing at us. Behind him, every single necromantis also brightens like a cloud of out-of-focus fireflies.

"Humans. Benevolent. Join us." Haides is making a last-minute plea for us to avoid the bloodshed. But even if he spares us, a lot of other people and intelligent beings are still going to die. I'm not a fan of the gods or the messengers, but the alternative is worse. We have to at least *try* to stop this.

I pull Whiskerey forward, wink at Jane—so she doesn't screw this up again—and address the giant creature. "Haides!" I shout, hoping he hears me. Against my expectations, everyone in the battlefield hears me. Haides did something to project my voice back telepathically just like he did with his own. "We accept. We'll join you."

"What?" John shouts from afar. He doesn't realize I'm just trying to buy time. I put my index finger on my lips, shushing him Earth-style.

"Zeon!" Jane says. "What are you doing? They're telepaths! They know you're—"

As if on cue, Haides' voice booms again in our heads, interrupting her sentence. "Dishonesty. Intolerant. Attack."

Behind him, his flying army changes to a spherical formation. At the same time, he broadcasts to our brains the gruesome deaths of other humans that opposed them. I flinch.

While Jane and I have seen this before, this time Haides projects on our minds the fear and hopelessness those people felt when they were slaughtered years ago. A bone-deep chill goes through my spine.

"We have to run!" Jane shouts, and we almost obey her. Before we do, however, another fantastical event catches our attention. A ghostly red blur appears behind Haides, approaching him from above in an arc. His tiny face turns around to see the unidentified object, but before we can process what's happening, his backpack is separated from his body.

Except, as Jane and I already know, it's not a backpack. Someone just cut Haides' brains off. The backpack-shaped brain and Haides' body fall down for a few seconds until, eventually, both disappear, still high in their alien sky. I hear gasps and smile.

The ghostly shape that killed Haides stops exactly where he had been hovering. Floating in the air, still inside the other reality, Primavera waves at us. She grins, glowing red this time. Besides her long double-edged sword, she now wears a braided ponytail, along with a purple shirt, pants, and sneakers. And it's not the red cape flapping behind her that makes me smirk. It's her honest-to-God purple mask.

Pain pulses through my left arm. I look around and find Jane, who somehow just punched me all the way from Dorothy's saddle.

"What did you do?" she asks in horror. "She's just a kid!"

Rubbing my arm, I avoid Jane's eyes. "She's fine. Everything's going to be—"

"They're going to kill her!" Jane interrupts me, pointing at the portal.

My mouth opens. The swarm behind Primavera changes into a cone aimed right at her. Events are unfolding too fast for me to reply to Jane.

Primavera doesn't seem to be fazed. Still giggling, she turns around and jumps higher, pointing her sword sideways. The bugs start moving toward her, quickly gaining speed. There are thousands and thousands of them. She can't fight that many.

By the time the first necromantis reaches the girl, she points her sword down and drops like a bullet. Her glow intensifies and she becomes a vertical red blur. The cone of necromantes changes direction, pursuing her as she flies down, but she hits the ground first.

And then, just like when they appeared, there's a loud pop followed by a gust of wind—but this time, from the back. The portal in front of us sucks the air from around us and collapses. The tear in reality is gone, and the Wheel is whole again. The adjacent hypersphere, which was actually a dreamsphere, vanished before our eyes when Primavera popped the it with her sword while all the necromantes were still inside.

We breathe a collective sigh of relief.

The only problem is that this solution is temporary. We've just bought some time. If Khof gains control of the Wheel, he'll open Pangea again for the necromantes, and they'll use another dreamsphere. Primavera won't be able to close them all.

Worse, the war is far from over, and we're still outgunned and outmatched even with the grasshoppers temporarily out.

A scream breaks the confusion that follows. "NOOO!" Khof yells. "You're going to pay for this!"

Large boulders rise into the air over our army, and the bombardment resumes, the enemy missiles already hitting home. The shots and the shower of rocks take several of our riders with them. Khof is behind us again, killing people.

Despite the necromantes' setback, we're still losing this battle. If it were only Khof fighting us, it'd take just a sniper shot to his head to end it. As it stands, with so many transports filled with enemies from Orbis, and all the artillery they have, we're losing badly.

I gulp. If Jal did what I asked, the attack should've stopped already. But Khof's forces are still on their way, which means he may have failed. There are so many things that could've gone wrong, and I'm starting to think the plan didn't work. Like a real Hail Mary, the odds of it working were really low anyway.

"Fall back!" Jane yells, extending her arm and making a circle in the air with her index finger. Instinctively, I shorten the reins and lower my center of gravity as I fall into a gallop, and soon our small group is following her as we ride east toward the town. Part of our force remains there, keeping the others prisoner.

Our luck runs out when one of the shells hits our group nearby, throwing people and horses to the ground. It takes me some time to understand what's happening, since one moment I'm dashing through the rain, leaning down and grasping Whiskerey's mane, and the next, the sky becomes the ground and I'm sweeping the mud with my head and shoulders.

Even before I stop sliding, I close my eyes and concentrate. The adrenaline is paradoxically helping me concentrate, and perhaps I can still do something. The situation is dire. Whiskerey's guts are gone and he dies quickly, and poor Pierre has lost his rear legs.

Dorothy's the only one who seems unscathed, but she's down, and so is Jane. Meanwhile, Raj is seriously hurt with an unnerving crack on his head. Saint Plehr, he's going to die. Louise lies next to him, and her left leg is a mess. If we don't do anything, she's going to bleed out in seconds.

And yet, it's far from over. Hundreds of missiles are coming, the enemy vehicles are already midway across the river and passage, and Khof's throwing large rocks at our retreating forces. It's a carnage. The only thing I can do is run to Raj and Louise and try to help them. If I can.

But then it happens.

A series of explosions illuminates the dark and stormy day. Every single airborne missile transforms into a bright, conical shape, leaving a faint, harmless heatwave in its place. For a moment, it looks like we're watching Saint Plehr's festivities.

Unlike fireworks, though, the spectacle doesn't last long. The sky darkens to gray, and the battlefield goes eerily quiet. Even the wind dies down, and the rain turns to drizzle. There are no more missiles flying, and all the tanks and carriers stop moving. Khof's assault force is motionless on the battlefield, and most of his army is stuck inside the stationary transports.

Dorothy takes this time to stand, grunt her good-bye, and run for the hills, followed by several of the now riderless horses. Jane's unconscious, but still breathing, with no signs of other trauma.

I take a quick look back toward the impressive Fortress Mesa, and the sight of motionless vehicles everywhere almost makes me smile. Their troop carriers are now completely useless, floating above the raging river, and the artillery trucks and tanks are stranded on the land passage and beach. In a split second, Khof lost most of his advantage, albeit still with heavy losses on our side.

We're finally winning, but it's too late for many.

John's already circling back, bringing the riders still standing to advance and take the island. I see him watching me from afar, but he doesn't approach us. It's not over, and this is not the time to ask questions about how the hell the whole mechanized enemy force just stopped in their tracks.

I avoid looking at poor Whiskerey, and I don't have time to deal with Jane.

Louise is grabbing Raj's hand, crying, and Marie half-swims through a mix of mud and horse remains to reach him. Marie's rain-soaked blue dress is already an odd choice for horseriding, but it's definitely not well-suited for traversing muddy terrain.

"His head, Zeon. His head!" Louise weeps, ignoring her own missing leg. It seems she stopped her own bleeding for now, but it's not going to last.

Marie's face goes white when she sees how badly Raj is hurt. She lies on the ground next to him, putting her hand on his chest.

"No. No. No!" she yells, sits up, and grabs his now straight knife from his belt, ignoring the ongoing battle around us. Cutting through his clothes with her wobbling hands, she exposes his wounded chest and kneels down on top of Raj to stop his bleeding.

But his chest is the least of our worries. The back of

his head is way worse, with some gray matter exposed. This is Ravi's death all over again, but this time, I have company.

"Our baby," Raj mumbles, coughing blood and almost losing consciousness. "Take care..." He licks his lips, not able to continue.

His skull is fractured, and his brain is quickly swelling. I can't cut his connection with Pangea and send him back because there's no body for him to go back to. And I can't heal his injuries either. Not like this. Marie and Louise both turn to me, staring in despair. But I just shake my head.

To make matters worse, Louise's leg begins to bleed again, and she manages to look even paler than before, so I slither next to her. At least I can do something with the leg. However, she pushes me away with her free hand and grabs Marie's arm. The sudden movement makes Louise whimper in pain, and she winces, though her hold on Raj's hand and Marie's wrist doesn't falter.

"It's a *girl*," Louise says, ending her sentence in a high-pitched voice, broadcasting her pain. Raj opens his eyes for a second and smiles weakly.

And then, both Raj and Louise die.

Chapter 39

RED TEST

Deaths in hyperspheres are different than on Earth, where the body remains. The empty vessel that once held our family member or friend gives us a sense of closure, even if the person we knew isn't there anymore—even if your best friend was just shot in front of you.

In a hypersphere, however, the result is more shocking. The body just disappears in front of you as if its presence is an insult to the living and must be erased. It's even worse when more than one person dies at the same time.

Louise and Raj disappear simultaneously, and Marie nearly falls over, splashing in the pool of bloody mud as she catches herself with her hands. Unfortunately, Louise pushed me away just before she died, so, unlike what happened with Jane and Jal, it wasn't me who did the killing. Granted, Raj was beyond my help, but I could've soft killed Louise and sent her back to Earth—but I didn't know she was that badly injured.

For a long, excruciating moment, Marie feels

around the ground as if looking for Raj. But reality settles in as she leans over the mud, standing above the dirty pool with her hands still dipped in it, as if she is doing a half push-up.

Meanwhile, Jane rolls over and coughs. She raises her head to watch us, shell-shocked.

I walk over to Marie and crouch, touching her back, pretending I'm stronger than I am right now. Flashbacks of what happened to Ravi are pushed down for the moment as I try to comfort her.

Marie turns her head to face me, her lips shaking. Despite all the fake strength I'm trying to pass on to her, I just can't look straight into her eyes, so I avoid her gaze, not saying anything. In the process, I accidentally stare at Jane, but she doesn't look back at me. Instead, she sits up abruptly and leans to her side, trying to grab her capacitor.

Her effort is fruitless, though. The long rifle moves by itself, flying away in an arc as if an invisible hand's throwing it. All the weapons nearby soon follow, leaving us with nothing to defend ourselves.

"You did this," a male voice booms. About twelve feet above us, Khof hovers in place like a god disappointed with his subjects. He's wearing his battered blue shirt and the same shorts I saw him in last time. My own blue shirt is unrecognizable due to the rain and the mud. "You and the messengers."

I search nearby for help, but all the uninjured soldiers from our army, including John and the other veterans, are already on the island. Most of Khof's troops are trapped inside the carriers that stand still, hovering mid-river. As such, it's only us here, and we're completely defenseless.

"The gods are brainwashing you," Khof declares.

"It's a cult. But they're evil, Zeon. They're no different than the necromantes." He gives us a sad chuckle. "All of them are enemies of humanity."

Perhaps if I pick up a rock or something, I can throw it at him. It's so frustrating. He's too much like me, so stubborn. His mind is already made up.

"But it doesn't matter anymore," he continues. "We're all dead anyway. I'm going to finish this game." He turns his hands into fists and looks up. We all follow his gaze. Up in the sky, an impossibly large circle appears below the clouds, flashing red. The end-of-the-game disk.

Oh no. This is so unfair. You can only get there if you can fly. And if he gets to it, *everyone's* going to die, even his people. And there's nothing we can do to avoid it.

"You're a fucking *murderer!*" Marie yells, tightening her grip around the useless knife as she runs for him. The thought of throwing the knife crosses my mind, but it's not like we've trained for it, and even if we hit him, he'd probably still survive. It would take a long stabbing session to take him down.

While Marie swears at Khof, a rock the size of an apple bounces off his arm. He seems shocked for a moment but soon laughs, rubbing his arm. I don't think Marie saw that because she clenches her teeth so hard I'm afraid she's going to break them. From her point of view, it's as if he's laughing at her pain.

A second rock misses him by an inch, and he spins in place to have a better look at Jane, still chuckling in amusement. Throwing rocks is even less effective than throwing knives.

Jane doesn't care, though. Her face is contorted in

fury, and she keeps bending down and picking up all kinds of objects from the ground and throwing them at him, ignoring the futility of her efforts. I look at her with a knot in my stomach. We're out of Hail Marys.

He shakes his head, staring at Jane. "I don't want you to die, and I don't care about the others." Khof snickers, but I don't think he actually finds this funny. "I'm not a monster, Jane." He waves his hand in my direction. "Zeon can still save you like he did once before, and I'll let him."

I hold my breath. He means I'm allowed to soft kill her. This show of mercy is unexpected. Perhaps we can still change his mind.

He shoots a quick glance of disdain at me, then back to Jane. "Out of everyone I've met here, you're the only one with the guts—"

Khof's speech is interrupted by the horrible sound of gurgling. His body twists, and he starts to fall.

Attached to his back like a spider that just caught its prey, Marie keeps stabbing him over and over, screaming. Jane and I look at each other for a second, confused. Neither one of us knew she could fly.

Their descent accelerates, but Khof is strong, and he throws Marie away before they crash. She falls onto a group of low bushes, producing a quieter thud than I expected. Khof hits the ground next, splashing mud. He's bleeding badly, but still alive.

Jane rushes to where Marie now lies face down, sobbing uncontrollably on a pile of crushed brush and leaves. Her arm and face are scratched, but she's probably not crying because of her injuries. Meanwhile, Khof stands up and coughs blood, stumbling on the slippery ground.

The Earther girl who I fell in love with years ago wraps her left arm around Marie, helping her stand up. They both look at Khof, who has death in his eyes.

"I didn't want you to die too, Jane," Khof says. "I'm sorry for what I'm about to do."

Khof slips again and kneels, using his right hand to stay half upright. I extend my arm to help him, and he takes it, perhaps instinctively. He's stronger than anyone in the Wheel, but clearly, he forgot what I can do here. Or maybe he just doesn't understand it.

He realizes his mistake too late, trying to pull his arm away. But I'm too fast. Since I was thrown into the mess that the messengers and gods created, I never killed anyone. Sure, I soft killed people, but never really had blood on my hands. Everyone else—all the other protectors and angels—have had their share of killings. But not me.

The thing is, I never accepted the fact this is a real war, and that if I don't fight, or don't kill, even more people are going to die. It's choosing the lesser of two evils. But it's easier said than done, and not surprising I still hesitate to pull the trigger, metaphorically speaking. But this time, I have no other choice. At least, that's what I'm telling myself.

A large rock is abruptly plucked from the ground. It probably has my name on it. But regardless of what Khof can do here, I'm still faster than he is. And to be honest, I was waiting for this. A reason to do what I have to do. Killing doesn't come easy.

Sure, there's the threat of ending the game, but it feels so distant. Abstract. Now, a boulder being thrown at you is real. The truth is no one likes to kill an unarmed person. I needed an animalistic reason to fight back.

In my fast mode, I have the time to take a final look at Jane, dreading what she's going to think of what I'm about to do. Still embracing Marie, she nods, and this simple motion makes me tear up.

"No," I tell Khof in a monotone voice. "This stops now."

Time slows down when I shut my eyes, and in a split second, I do to Khof what I've already done to Jane, to Jal, and to myself. My mind crawls inside Khof's brain, and I disconnect it from Pangea. Maybe our minds are joining at this point. Perhaps he'll learn more about who I am. I don't know. And I don't care. I have to do this.

So, just like that, his brain cluster winks out of existence. For all intents and purposes, Khof is finally dead. To an outsider, it must look like I blink and Khof disappears. But it feels a lot longer for me.

Unlike all the others I soft killed, Khof's original body has been dead for years. This means he's not going back to Terra. Instead, his mind will be sent to another place in Pangea—Entropia. There, Khof's mind will quickly vanish. It's where every one of us goes to die, permanently.

With my eyes still closed, I think about what I just did. The fact that Khof is gone doesn't make me happier. In a way, he was right; the gods are the ones that started all of this. They'll have to pay for it.

The sounds of distant shooting and one-off explosions indicate the battle continues, but it's dying down. With Khof dead, the messengers will be able to take control of the Wheel again, and the necromantes won't be able to use him to take over Pangea anymore.

I open my tear-filled eyes to see Marie and Jane kneeling on the mud, hugging and sobbing. Now I understand how Marie saved us. Hermes said everyone can do what we do in Pangea, but it took despair for her to be able to fly.

Chapter 40

KITTY

We spend the rest of the day going from tent to tent, helping treat the injured. I've lost count of how many I've soft killed so far to send them back to their planets. "Soft" is a misnomer, though. It feels like a real death.

Still, depending on the injury, it's better to end their lives this way—by waking up puking on their Earths—instead of risking real death by working directly on their brains, as I did with Marie. My healing process is not exactly FDA-approved. The people watching our bodies on our planets must be having a field day as they greet a mass migration of protectors awakening and throwing up.

Worse still, all the people I send back may be gaining unwanted information from me—from my mind. I was okay with Jane and even Jal learning my inner secrets, but when I'm doing this to strangers—and, worse, to Khof—I feel my privacy is being violated. And yet, I have no other option.

The ones that take most of my time and energy are

Khof's and Jonathan's people. There's no place for them to go back to, so I have to rely on my ad-hoc brain-surgery methods to heal them. It's mostly been a success, but I lost two from Khof's army who didn't trust me and couldn't stop moving.

Despite all that were saved, the ones I lost bother me more than I like to admit. On top of that, Raj's and Louise's deaths are slowly taking over my thoughts as the day goes by.

Hours later, Bodan's troops arrive at a battle that's already ended. To their credit, they've been helping us with the wounded. Meanwhile, Jane's in charge of integrating everyone. There's a lot of bad blood going around, and we're not exactly sure who we can trust.

When all the seriously injured are taken care of, I walk outside the tents to breathe some fresh air. The sky's blue again, since the clouds are long gone, and the sun is setting.

A wave of tiredness rushes through me as I lean against a thick purple trunk, finally thinking about Louise. She'd be here next to me, smoking and teasing me about something, probably calling me a useless bystander who did nothing to save her. A nobody who watched her, Ravi, Jonathan, and Raj die.

During our final confrontation with Khof, Jane was throwing rocks, refusing to accept her fate, while Marie spectacularly knifed Khof down. Even the event that stopped Khof's attack wasn't actually done by me, although I initiated it. At least I did my part, killing Khof in the end. But in hindsight, I keep thinking there was something I missed—some other way to save my friends.

And on top of it all, I was forced to murder someone. Worse, I did it in front of Jane. I don't second-guess the decision, but my stomach strongly disagrees. Every time I think about it, the bitter taste of metal overwhelms me.

After a while, I decide to walk up to the cliff to have a better view of the valley below, along with the unusual circular river with the motionless vehicles floating there. The Orbi that were inside them are now on top of the carriers, waving at us, but there's nothing we can do. The river's too violent for any kind of swimming, and Marie was not able to fly again. We got lucky when she took down Khof.

Walking by myself helps me think. I have to consider what's next. Once everybody is back to their homes, it'll be a long time until I see Jane again. Even if I'm free on Jora, our planets are going to be our own prison. On the other hand, I'm told Mike's working on the portal that'll connect our planets. So, like my previous prison, this one may be temporary.

When I reach the top of the cliff, I'm not even surprised to see Primavera's ridiculous house there, waiting for me. Primavera herself is outside, petting an unusually large black cat. It makes me smile.

Her yellow dress and shoes and her light blue cropped jacket are actually a good match for her odd apartment. For once, all seems to fit in place. This is her place, her turf. Primavera's cute amber eyes light up when she sees me, and her small black pigtails shake when she smiles.

I gaze at her in confusion. "Amber eyes?"

"I think they're pretty." Her eyes flicker and the girlish smile vanishes. "You don't like them?"

"Oh, no. They're beautiful, but I thought they were brown." Or black. Actually, maybe they were blue, and wasn't she blonde one time? I don't know—I'm bad with faces, but this doesn't look right.

Primavera smiles again, and just seeing that brightens my spirit. For once, I try not to think of how many times her innocence is going to be crushed in the future by these stupid messengers.

"Oh." She giggles. "I change them all the time. Harry liked them!" She crouches to pet the cat, who's so large he's nearly her size, and I swear I hear him purring.

Who'd have thought that in Pangea, Harry would look like a giant black Maine Coon? I knew his brain was based on a feline, but I'd never in a million years guess he could actually purr. At least he has a tail here. He looks so much better with it.

I grin. "How did you even meet?"

She grins back at me, still petting Harry. "I found him in the river. I had never seen an animal with a bright aura like that."

I give her a hug. "Thanks, girl. You saved us all."

The thing is, we didn't know exactly how the underworld army would appear in the Wheel. But Haides said the necromantes were only allowed in dreamspheres, so I guessed they needed to be in a dreamsphere before entering a hypersphere—and Primavera had already demonstrated she could close dreamspheres.

Which reminds me of something.

Folding my arms, I say, "I told you not to fight with the necromantes. You could've been hurt. You were supposed to just pop the dreamsphere."

She scoffs. "I knew what I was doing. And it worked! As soon as I saw the dreamsphere, they lost."

"That was a very public performance, Primavera.

People weren't supposed to know about you, remember?"

She folds her arms, her mood souring. "I always hide my aura outside. And I wore a mask, remember?"

I make a mistake by laughing at her sudden bad mood, and she gets even madder. She goes from happiness to anger faster than even Jane does. I didn't know this was possible. The little one doesn't have a short fuse—she has *no* fuse.

"Aura?" I ask, trying to defuse the situation. "I never noticed." I quickly close my eyes to detect it, but there's nothing there.

She grins as if she wasn't angry at me a second ago. "It's there. Everyone has it. But auras from people connected to planets are different and brighter. You just need to practice to see mine." She grins.

I kneel down to pet Harry. "And thank you, Harry." But the gesture feels—I don't know—wrong. This is one of my friends, after all, even if I made him.

"Did you hear him?" Primavera asks. "He said the machines in Pangea speak the same language as Ethae." She looks at Harry, confused at her own words. Then, she gasps. "She was a *missile*?" Primavera asks.

"Oh, you can talk to him?" I ask. "How?"

"Harry's a telepath."

His brain is based on a feline, and when he was sent to Pangea, he must've assumed a cat's form. Cats don't have the right vocal strings, so it makes sense he can't talk. But I *am* surprised at how quickly he learned telepathy. Even I'm not able to do it.

Primavera crosses her arms. "The helmet injector worked." She voices Harry's thoughts and frowns, shaking her head. "Helmet? He's speaking gibberish now."

I laugh. Harry was my second Hail Mary. The reason missiles and military vehicles can't cross the veils is because they have brains. Once I realized all the machine brains in Pangea behaved exactly like the ones on Jora despite how advanced their armament was, I thought the little robot would be able to stop them the same way he'd saved us from the submarine's missile on my prison island.

And I was right. Jal's real mission was to go back to Jora and bring Harry here using the helmet injector.

Primavera leans in closer to me, covering her mouth with her hand and glancing at the cat. "He's *really* chatty." She nods emphatically. I know exactly what she's talking about. "And he keeps calling me April for some reason."

I blink blankly and stand up. Harry starts to rub himself against my legs, oblivious to my shock. My mouth is dry when I ask, "Why?"

Primavera shrugs. "I dunno. It's like a nickname." She smiles. "I like it!"

I tap on Harry's head as he nuzzles me, trying to organize my thoughts. If Harry's calling her April...

"Harry, can you stop with the rubbing for a second?"

Unaware of my introspection, the little girl slaps her hands on her hips. "But you always liked it when Bebe did it to you." She looks offended, again speaking for Harry. "Who's Bebe, by the way?" she adds.

For a moment, I toy with the idea of saying Bebe's the next-door neighbor who has a crush on me, but I'm not yet ready to joke about anything.

"Bebe's my cat. And I hate when she does that. I always trip on her."

Maybe I should tell her my hypothesis—but first, I

have to be certain. Primavera's a bit old to be April, but Hermes once told me time in Pangea is not linear. I need to have another talk with him, and perhaps even send a message to Mike. For now, it's better if I don't say anything.

After we catch up on the events of the day, Primavera invites me inside her house. I can tell she regrets it as soon as I take my shoes and socks off. They're caked with mud, and my clothes are filthy. Even Harry has to clean his paws thoroughly before Primavera lets him enter.

When we get to the living room, Marie's waiting for us, holding a pair of round sunglasses. I gasp. How many people know about Primavera?

But something's odd. The way she looks at me, not exactly in a straight line, biting her fingers nervously.

It's not Marie.

Chapter 41

ENTROPIA

Louise is in the living room, alive, her eyes misted with tears. I don't ask questions at first. Instead, I just embrace her, and we hug like old friends despite my dirty clothes. I may have some tears of my own.

Her body is back to normal, her legs intact. She was hit below the knee, and the previously injured limb is now bare, the pants rippled where it happened, but at least it's intact. Despite the fact she's acting a bit unfocused, she looks fine. Before I have time to ask her how she did it, she grabs my hand and pulls me inside one of Primavera's bedrooms.

Tears appear on Louise's face. "He's back, Zeon."

The bedroom we're in is not Primavera's main one, but like the rest of the house, it follows the same type of decoration. Clouds, dogs, horses, and cats are painted on the walls and ceiling on top of an underlying layer of sky blue.

The king-sized bed is no exception, and the pillows and blankets are blue with puppy stamps. There we find Raj sleeping, his dirty clothes staining Primavera's linens, although she doesn't seem to mind.

The blood drains from my face and I lean on the wall, struggling to stay upright. "You saved him?" I smile, looking at Louise. "How?"

She points at the young girl standing next to us. "It was all thanks to Primavera."

I tilt my head at the little girl. "I take it Primavera told you that Hermes saved her when she was a child?"

"Not only that," Louise says, "she taught me how to *do it.*" She then gives Primavera a side hug, and the girl smiles back at her.

"How did you do it—you know, save her?"

Leaning forward, she folds her arms. "When you die, your consciousness goes to Entropia. It's a dark place, still in Pangea, but outside the hyperspheres and dreamspheres." She waves her hand around. "There, your mind quickly vanishes. It's where the gods live, and even *they* are not immortal. Their minds expand for thousands of years until they also eventually disperse." She places her hand on Primavera's head, who, in turn, smiles. "Beings with *caged* brains like us need strict boundaries. But there's no structure in Entropia—no cranium of any type—so our minds only last seconds there."

Louise takes a moment, as if trying to organize her thoughts, and rubs her neck with her hand. "However," she continues, "you can bring someone back if you have an anchor in the hypersphere, although they'll have severe memory loss. When Primavera died, Hermes attached himself to Mercury so he could catch her just in time."

Interesting. The gods are mortals, and their brains

can grow. A million questions come to my mind. Louise seems to know too much.

I press my lips together. "Wait. You said you needed someone—an anchor in the hypersphere—to do that," I say, walking over to Raj to touch his forehead. His temperature's normal and there's no sign of his previous injuries. He's just sleeping. Pangea is indeed a magical place.

"And I had one. Marie. Raj died and was ejected from the hypersphere, but I followed him, dying as well. But just before that, I connected with Marie and formed a link between us. A link not unlike the connection that binds our bodies on Earth to Pangea. It created a bridge allowing us to come back."

I've got to hand it to her. Perhaps to be able to save someone from death, you need not be a soulmate but a similar soul—and there's no one else here that would be more compatible.

"Is that what Hermes did when he saved Primavera?" I ask. "Connecting with Mercury?"

"It's more complicated than that. We can't come back directly to a hypersphere. It has to be someplace special. Someplace like Primavera's house."

I smile in spite of myself. By saving Raj, Louise has redeemed herself. She didn't do much last time, and Ravi ended up dying, but today she literally killed herself to save someone. And not just someone—Ravi's soon-to-be-a-father doppelgänger.

Either way, despite the miraculous event she's describing, Louise isn't in a good mood. There's something wrong.

"Louise, what's really going on? Is there something you're not telling me?"

Her chin trembles a bit, and she glares at me while

I wait patiently for her answer. Finally, she nods. "It's bad, Zeon. I couldn't bring Raj back as he was. No one can. The Raj we knew—the Raj that Marie knew—is gone. He'll have severe memory loss. He may not even remember his time in Pangea."

My heart skips a bit and I look at Raj, who's still sleeping. My healing powers in Pangea can't detect memory loss, but I still can check him for concussions, traumas and the like. But he's as healthy as he can be.

After I'm satisfied with his condition, I finally ask, "Does Marie know? About him?" I wave at Raj as if Louise doesn't know what I'm talking about.

Whoever talks with Raj when he wakes up will have a tough time. The Raj who fell in love with Marie is gone. Yes, Louise saved him, but forgetting a major part of your life still feels like a type of death. Considering they're stuck here in Pangea forever, I guess they'll get back together eventually, but they'll have to start from scratch.

She shakes her head, staring at Raj. "Not yet. Primavera went outside to look for her earlier but found you instead." Louise glances at Harry, who hasn't left Primavera's side. "And, apparently, a cat."

"His name's Harry," Primavera says. She walks in front of Louise and takes her hand, gently. If anyone's an angel or an archangel, it isn't me or Louise. "Don't worry, we'll find Marie." She smiles.

After that, faster than I can react, she sprints outside with Harry following her. I wonder if I'll ever have Harry back. Perhaps Harry wasn't meant for me.

Once they're out of sight, a flicker of sadness appears in Louise's eyes as we both watch Raj sleeping. He snores exactly like Ravi did, and maybe she's having the same memories. When you love someone, you miss even the things that bother you.

She puts on her sunglasses, but probably not to look cool. "I have something to ask you." She holds back a sob. "I can't take it anymore. The dark place... tore me apart." She lets out a single cry, pausing a bit before continuing. I shiver. Out of all of us, Louise is the one who was closest to real death.

"I'm tired," she continues. "Tired of dealing with Pangea and the messengers. Pierre was the only thing keeping me alive here, and now he's gone. I hate it here. Please, let me go home and start a new life. I don't want to be an archangel anymore."

This place brings her so much pain that she prefers to go back to a sightless life without superpowers than playing the messengers' games.

"Most people should be going home soon, anyway," I say first. "The battle is over. Why do you need my help?"

She sighs. "Because if *you* do it, the messengers won't be able to draft me back at will." She looks into my eyes. "I'll be really free."

"Jane managed to come back," I point out.

Her right palm touches my cheek, and I feel her in my mind. "Jane isn't an archangel. Our connections are more complex than anyone else's."

The ghostly foreign presence inside my head is like a bright yellow light. At the moment, it highlights the part of our brains that connects to Pangea. We're not blood related, but I can't help but feel that Louise— and, to an extent, Primavera—are like sisters to me. We're all archangels, after all. In fact, based on Louise's soothing flare inside my consciousness, she's as strong as Primavera. But perhaps she doesn't have the training yet.

Suddenly, I realize how dry my mouth is, and I lick my lips, worried. So far, I've been sending people back due to their physical injuries, but emotional pain can be just as bad. It feels wrong to do this, though—to kill her after all she's done.

More importantly, it won't actually do her any good. She can't flee from herself. Wherever she goes, her pain will be there with her. But who am I to judge her? It's her call, and after saving Raj, she deserves it. Even if it goes against my instincts. Even if, in the end, it won't save her from herself.

She frowns and crosses her arms. "You don't have to actually do it." Maybe she's noticing my hesitation. "Just teach me."

I wave her away in a dismissive manner. "No. I'll do it." It's too dangerous to let her try.

She slides her arms around my neck, hugging me as a goodbye gesture. Then, she gives me a kiss on my cheek.

"And don't feel bad about killing Khof," she says out of the blue. "I know words won't help you now, but it'll get better with time. Don't worry about what Jane thinks of you. She understands. You did the right thing. Trust me."

"How..." I say, flabbergasted. How does she know about my deep, unsettling feelings of killing him?

"*Adieu, mon ami,*" she says, ignoring my question.

I think about it a bit, but let it go. Clearly, she learned a lot during her trip to Entropia. Maybe one day she can tell me about it. For now, I'll send her back to Earth.

"It'll hurt." I already regret what I have to do. "A lot."

"I know." She wipes away her tears. "Perhaps it'll make me feel alive."

~

AFTER LOUISE'S BODY DISAPPEARS, I leave Raj asleep at Primavera's house and go check on the others. My shoes get even dirtier as I navigate my way back around puddles and muddy paths. The clothes I'm wearing will have to go into the trash, and I badly need a shower.

Either way, I can't help but smile as I go down the cliff, watching John and his army deal with the carriers finally arriving at the riverbank. Khof's people are on top of them with their arms up, surrendering. Harry must've told the vehicles to go ashore so the people on them wouldn't die of starvation. Sometimes I think I don't deserve him as a friend, and I feel bad for all the times I insulted him.

The sun has already set below the horizon, but the sky is still surprisingly bright. The light refracting from the atmosphere bathes the hypersphere with a gradient of colors, and the double moons help illuminate the rest.

At night, after a long bath, I join an impromptu celebration around the gazebo. It's a weird party. The protectors both mourn our fallen comrades and commemorate our victory.

There are several small campfires everywhere, and a large and dangerous bonfire on the main road. It's made from fallen trees and wood boards that are fantastically lit from hot flashes coming from small, cylindrical batteries that used to power tanks.

Besides the risk of someone getting burned by these incredibly unstable and flammable cells, my complaints about lung cancer and such fall on deaf ears. It's okay for those going back, but Terrans and Yori actually live here now. Or so I hope. I have no idea what's going to happen to the Wheel.

Paulo is back to wearing his sheriff's clothes. He eyes the bonfire while drinking mulled wine, of all things. I sit next to him on the lawn, drinking a glass of Chardonnay, the only white wine I could find. Like this party, it's dry and bitter. And yet, it's also a bit fun, because of the alcohol.

"This is a sad, very sad *São João*," he says, whatever that means. No explanation is given.

Oddly enough, some people are not around, including Jane and Bodan. The thought of betrayal crosses my mind—but more likely, she's off processing the fact I'm a killer now. But I decide to just ignore these feelings. I'm going to be a grown man and trust her for a change.

When my glass of wine is empty, Vladimir shows up with another bottle of Chardonnay. He raises and lowers his eyebrows and refills my glass. "*Ypa!*"

In response, I look him in the eyes and take a long sip, fearlessly. He smirks at me and drinks a shot of his own drink. Vodka, I think. And I thought he would never forgive me for accusing him of drugging our wine.

The rest of the night is a blur, and the last thing I remember before falling asleep is Paulo complaining about women for some reason.

The next thing I know, Jane's voice wakes me up. "Zeon?"

I smile for a second but quickly frown. It's daytime now, and I'm lying on the grass and awkwardly hugging Paulo. He also wakes up, and we both jump backward, shooting to our feet. This is not the only thing that surprises me. I assumed the messengers would send us back, like they did the other times, and I'd be back to Jora by now. But I'm glad I'm still here, where I can say goodbye to Jane.

"Big party yesterday?" Jane asks.

My smile widens when I see her smirking. Jane's coal-black hair is loose over her shoulders, and a jolt of hormones goes through my young body. Perhaps we can be happy, at least for the time being. And there's so much I have to tell her.

But Paulo's having none of it. His face twists into a grimace and he walks dangerously close to her.

"Oh, *Ms. Engel.*" He looks her up and down. Mostly down. "Finally! How dare you?" When he's mad, his accent sounds Russian. "Zeon spent the night miserable, saying how you were probably kissing Bodan somewhere. Or worse!"

I laugh nervously. "Shut up, Paulo. Let me talk to her—uh, I mean to *them.*"

Jane's not alone. Beside her, a young woman with short blonde hair looks intently at me. She wears a knee-high summer dress common on Jora, and the winged lions on her temple indicate she's in Bodan's family. Maybe she's a distant cousin.

Paulo grunts at Jane, showing his teeth, and leaves us alone. "*Sem vergonha!*"

"Paulo's just joking," I say. Who knows what I told him last night? That's why I shouldn't drink when I'm upset about something, especially not right next to a tattletale.

Jane's hair is loose for a change, partially covering her small denim cropped jacket—what's up with these half-jackets lately?—and white blouse. When I try to kiss her, she blushes and shows me her cheek instead. I chuckle. Jane's always the prude, but there's no reason to act awkwardly in front of—wait a minute.

The blonde smiles. "Jane, my dear. You can kiss Zaén. I don't mind."

I frown. "Dooria? How long have you been here?" She looks so different. I forgot people return to their younger years when they show up here.

"I arrived yesterday with Bodan's army," she explains. "And your injector got me to Pangea." She wraps her arms around me, and I reluctantly hug her back. "I'm so proud of you," she says. "I knew you'd help the gods."

Breaking the embrace, I step back. "Well, I just wanted to stop the bloodshed. And we weren't alone. We had a lot of help."

This is not the time to have an argument about the gods. And, anyway, Jane has some explaining to do. Paulo does have a point. I narrow my eyes at her. "Where were you last night?"

Jane and Dooria exchange glances. "We were speaking with the messengers. They're already sending people back to their Earths," Jane says.

"I hope everything's okay," I say.

Slumping her shoulders, Jane looks down. "For the moment."

Her body language definitely doesn't give me confidence. "Wait. What's going to happen to the people that can't go back?"

Dooria smiles. "They'll be fine. The messengers deactivated the end-of-the-game mechanism."

Jane pulls her long hair to the side, as if self-conscious about it being loose. Her eyes meet mine again. "And the Wheel will stay here forever, Zeon. Raj, Marie, and the others will have a place to live."

Dooria places her hand on Jane's shoulder. "I'll leave you lovebirds here." Clearly, she's leaving Jane here to explain something. "Zaén, take your time. I'll be waiting for you on Jora."

Chapter 42

BENCH

When Dooria's out of earshot, I ask Jane, "Okay, what the hell is going on?"

There's no one around—or, I should say, no one awake. There are plenty of people sleeping on any surface they can find. It's early, and most went to sleep late last night. I've never seen this place so calm. So quiet.

Jane motions me to follow her. "Not here." But I don't move. My heart is not ready for a twist at this point of our story—hers and mine. I just wish we could spend some time together. But maybe I crossed the line when I killed Khof.

Perhaps realizing my hesitation, she clutches my arm and pulls me forward in a hurry. The gesture takes me out of my stupor, and I follow her, wondering what she has on her mind.

We stride past a few units in silence, observing the aftermath of the battle and the celebration. There's no easy way to know if the black smudges and distorted metal are from the melee or just campfires.

A few minutes later, we find none other than Dorothy, who calmly grazes on some of the bushes that have managed to grow through the pavement. I didn't know horses could eat that. Dorothy raises her head and nods when we approach her.

Jane caresses the mare's crest, smiling thinly. "Zaén? Ladybug?"

"Oh, shut up!"

She snickers. In my defense, men are the ones who wear colorful dotted skirts on Jora. But that won't help my case.

"Dooria is a great person," Jane says. "She negotiated with the messengers as if she was their equal. You should be proud of her."

No wonder she's called the Whisperer back home. Before I'm able to reply, Jane bends down on one knee, but instead of proposing marriage, she clasps her fingers together to help me climb on the saddle.

I pause for a moment, but eventually, I step on her hands and she pushes me up.

Once I'm on top of Dorothy, Jane jumps up behind me. "Anyway, I'm sorry I didn't tell you everything."

Her arms wrap around my waist as she grabs the reins, and we race ahead. We can't talk much during the trip because of how fast we're going, and I lean down on Dorothy, so I don't fall over. The ride reminds me of Whiskerey. I miss him.

The Orbis' town is similar to others in the Wheel. We ride past large empty silos just outside town—no stables here—and Jane silently takes me to a place high on a hill with a single familiar bench overlooking Fortress and the river.

After we dismount—technically, I fall arms first—I hold Jane's hands, looking into her gorgeous eyes.

"This bench," she says. "It's our moon bench."

If you grow up with a moon in the sky all the time, you take it for granted. But since I come from a planet that doesn't have one, the experience of seeing it never ceases to amaze me. One uncharacteristically warm November night, Jane caught me open-mouthed, watching the full moon on a bench at the Rochester National Laboratory. At the time, I told her, jokingly, that it was my "moon bench," and it became an inside joke.

I smile. "It looks exactly like it."

"I found it yesterday. It's odd to have one here, but the messengers do have a sense of humor sometimes. Or maybe it was foreshadowing."

She sits on the bench first, crossing her legs, emphasizing her poorly fitted jeans. "I think it's time for us to be completely honest with each other. Can you do that?"

I sit next to her. "Yes, but..." I measure my words. "But there are still some secrets that are not mine to tell."

"Fair enough." She uncrosses her legs. "I'll start. We're passing the messengers' tests."

Wow, I did not see that coming at all. What the heck is she talking about?

"Uh... tests?"

She touches my arm. "Yes. Years ago, we actually passed when we didn't destroy our own Earths. This time, we passed again for the same reason. We're not bloodthirsty jerks like the necromantes. Most of us, anyway."

I contort my face to show my contempt. "No. Iris specifically said we *didn't* pass it. So, all you're saying is conjecture. Speculation is not the same as a secret."

She pulls her hand off me. "This isn't speculation." She stays silent for a while. "The secret is that Hermes is alive."

I watch her eyes in anticipation, waiting for more, but I forget to act surprised. I wasn't supposed to know that.

She folds her arms. "You knew?"

"Uh... yes. I met him in Pangea. I didn't tell you yet because... because I was worried about you. Did he tell you about his daughter?"

Jane nods. We stay quiet for a while, the noise of the river suddenly reminding me where I am. The cold cast iron bench arms and the hardwood tricked me, and for a second, I was foolishly searching for the moon—Earth's moon—in the sky.

"Hermes told me about the tests." She breaks the silence. "We passed. It was all a ruse. Even the Wheel was a test, although they did lose control of it."

Perhaps she's right, but the messengers cannot be trusted. And on top of that, I don't like being tested by anyone, and certainly not by those two-faced bastards. I shrug.

"Maybe Hermes was lying," she continues, as if guessing my thoughts. "And the tests are not fair to us. Even Hermes dislikes them, but Iris outranks him." She shakes her head. "It doesn't matter. We're now involved in the war between the gods and the necromantes regardless of what we think. And the messengers are not all on the same side."

I scoff. "Did Hermes tell you that?"

I swear I see something flickering in front of us, but it's just a small breeze throwing leaves around. It makes me see things.

"Yes. Like humans, the gods are not a single entity.

Some are siding with Hermes, others with Iris. Some helped Khof. A small number of them are working with the necromantes. There are even double agents. It's a mess. We now know Ivan worked for Khof, but Hermes said he also killed Jean. We're pretty sure a messenger asked him to do that, but we don't know which one. Maybe it's someone we haven't even met yet."

I scoff. "So why are you still siding with the messengers, after what happened last time?"

Her sudden angry stare makes me chuckle and her frown intensifies. "I'm not that naïve person you met years ago. The gods don't have that power over me anymore. But we can't stay here idle. We must protect Earth. And the best way to do that is to be right there with them."

In the distance, Fortress Mesa starts to get blurry. I blink, and it's normal again. Perhaps I shouldn't have had that many glasses of wine. "Keep your enemies close."

"Exactly."

"What else?"

"No." She chuckles. "It's your turn."

I tell her everything about Hermes and Primavera, except the April part. I'm still not sure about that. I explain how Louise knew about Primavera, though I don't mention Louise is an archangel. She's suffered too much already.

Jane clasps her hands, studying them as if admiring her smooth fingers. Sighing, she stays quiet, deep in thought.

"Louise," she finally says. And then, she mumbles something almost inaudible that sounds like "she likes you."

I stare at Jane in disbelief. "Wait, what? Louise is like a sister to me."

Jane laughs so hard she snorts, and I can't help but laugh with her. "I said *she's like you*, you doofus. Special." When she recomposes herself, she wipes a single tear from her eyes. "I'm not stupid, Zeon. And don't worry. I won't talk to her about it."

Jane chuckles when she sees my mouth hanging open. Perhaps I went too far and said too much, at least enough for Jane to figure it out. Story of my life. She waves dismissively at me. "It's obvious now," she says. "Louise must've been the one who gave me the weapon that killed Mercury years ago."

I scratch my head and try to change the subject. "Your turn."

She sighs. "Okay. When you killed me, there was no mind meld. I didn't read your thoughts. I'm sorry I lied to you."

Here we go again. I draw a breathless sigh and blink, trying to decide what to say. This means all those people I soft killed—including Jal, Louise, and Khof—didn't get into my head. That's a relief.

"So how do you know so much about me?" I ask.

"I also have some secrets I can't tell. This is one of them. But the other thing I learned is that something big is going to happen, and we'll be directly involved in it."

I sit on the edge of the bench and lean toward her. "Is this about the necromantes?"

She ignores my question. "Nothing is happening at the moment," she says. "But it's the calm before the storm. The war in Pangea will escalate. And we'll be at the center of it."

I hunch my shoulders. Despite my hate for the

messengers and their games, she's right. We must prepare for whatever they throw at us. Worse, knowing Jane, she probably has a list of things to do—probably a *list* of lists.

"And what do we do now?" I ask her.

Her face looks grim. "Mike will try to open the portal between our Earths earlier than we thought. It'll be during Saint Plehr's 1,000-year festivities at Fire Woods Park. You should tell your scientists. Do you know what that means?"

"Yes, I know the date."

It's not enough to have the technology to open the portals. We need an exact place and time to connect our Earths with a portal. Jane just gave me that information.

"No." She gazes at me. "It means we won't see each other for another year."

We had previously agreed on a date about three years from now, but apparently technology has advanced faster than we thought. One year is better than three, but it's still far in the future. A knot rises in my throat for several different reasons.

"And what about—what about what I did with Khof?"

She rubs her neck. "Well, are you happy about it?"

I take a long breath and shake my head, studying her eyes. "No. I feel miserable. I thought the feeling would go away, but it seems to get worse every time I think about it."

"Exactly." She smiles broadly. "*This* is why I like you."

We're interrupted by a flicker of light in the grass in front of us. The brightness increases, forming a circular shape, and soon it's replaced by a floating and dim closed hatch. It looks like a holographic projection; its presence seems to disagree with the environment.

Jane is not affected at all by this strange apparition. Instead, she stands, grabs my left hand and pulls me up. With her other hand, she brushes back the strands of hair that spill over her face. This is one of the reasons she prefers ponytails.

"The messengers must now have full control of Pangea," she says, not letting go of my hand. "Do you trust me?"

She pulls me toward the door. The hatch opens by itself, but the scenario on the other side doesn't give me that many clues. Another blue sky is waiting for us there.

I gulp. There's nothing else that can surprise me, right? And worst-case scenario, I can just soft kill myself and go back to Jora. "Sure, why not?" I give her a weak grin.

She grins back, and we walk through the door.

Once we cross it, our now scantily clothed bodies are greeted with a blanket of warm air, and the sand touching my bare feet tickles my toes. My sneakers are gone. A few beach chairs are arranged in front of a mid-sized hut, and the noise of crashing waves is like music to my ears.

That's when I notice Jane has a ponytail again. She's wearing a red bikini, and I only have on a pair of beach shorts. Our previous clothes—and hairstyles, apparently—are gone. And then it hits me. "I remember this place. This tropical beach. Isn't here where you—" I stop myself just in time.

A thin smile appears on her face. "Punched you? Yes, great memory."

We look at each other briefly before embracing. My heart beats faster as her hair partially covers my face, and her arms firmly wrap around my waist. When we break our embrace, she holds my hands tenderly for a second. Her watery eyes and trembling lips worry me at first, but her attempt at a smile puts me at ease.

"I asked the messengers for this," she finally says. "A little time off, just for us. We have a week, and then..." She trails off, her eyes distant, looking at the ocean. "Then... I don't know."

I gently pull her face back so she can look at me. "Jane, we'll always have Pangea."

A broad smile appears on her face. "Yes! And we can do anything here, right?" As usual, she misunderstands my movie joke. Instead, she's probably remembering the time we made magical love in Pangea. Not that I'm complaining. She gives me a sly grin. "And no consequences."

My mind flashes to Marie and her pregnancy, and I frown. "Uh... about that..."

Thanks for reading Enemy of the Gods. If you liked this book, please review it. Reviews help authors to write more books and to improve their writing.

Author's website: https://www.hofsetz.com

Also by C. Hofsetz

**Challenges of The Gods by C. Hofsetz, Book 1
Sometimes, Heaven is Overrated.**

People shift uncomfortably and the rustle of murmuring skitters around the room. They are… shocked? No matter what the "messengers" show us, it's only fabricated. I mean, what are they going to do, destroy Earth in front of us?

Then I watch as they destroy Earth in front of us.

It starts to disintegrate inward, slowly at first. My left brain is thinking about how complicated—but still plausible—it'd be to simulate this, while my right brain floods with the emotion of billions of people dying. I realize with a sinking feeling of nauseous clarity this is not just a visual presentation.

Somehow, I can sense their screams, their distress, their hopelessness. Whole families, whole cities, whole countries are disappearing. All lives fading in a couple of seconds.

This is real. This is really happening. My eyes fill with tears. People are crying around me; Jane and the man hug. Others cluster around the couple, trembling.

Who do these creatures think they are? Why do they have this power?

Acknowledgments

Writing a second book is a lot like having another child. It's not your first, so most people aren't that excited about it, and many say they'll only read it after it's published. In other words, people don't care anymore. Well, I really hope you're happy about this book. And I mean it.

Thanks to my wife, Berenice Hofsetz, who gave me invaluable feedback. She hates battle scenes in any book, and mine is no exception, but she plowed through them to help me improve.

Thanks to the beta readers that quickly figured out the weakness of my first draft. But I didn't do what they suggested at first. Instead, I sent it to my editors, who not only noticed the same problem, but explained it in more technical terms. The original version had too many twists, and that took the reader away from the story. So, I fixed that. Or so I hope.

Finally, thanks to all the editors who, in the end, did the heavy work with me to finalize this story: Kisa Whipkey, Elizabeth Buege, Mica S. Kole, and Annie Jenkinson. If you liked it, thank the editors. If you didn't like it, also thank the editors. Trust me—it was way worse before they did their passes. In fact, I have a secret fear I make my editors second-guess their careers.

About the Author

Originally from Brazil, Christian Hofsetz has a Ph.D. and an M.Sc. in Computer Science. After working for several years as a professor in Brazil, he moved to the United States and changed careers. Currently, he is a Software Engineer Manager at Microsoft by day, and a writer by night.

Software engineering and computers have been his passion since he was a teenager, but he's been reading novels for longer than writing code. One day, he couldn't help it anymore. He wrote the first chapter of a book. How bad could it be? But things escalated quickly. Next thing he knew, he was writing yet another chapter, and then the next. He tried to hide it, but his family knew he was up to something. When they figured out what he was doing, it was too late—he accidentally had started a whole series.

The result of this journey is Challenges of The Gods, a series about a fantastic world of gods meddling with humans.

For more info, check the links below:
https://hofsetz.com
https://twitter.com/hofsetzdotcom
https://www.facebook.com/hofsetzdotcom
https://instagram.com/c.hofsetz/